ARMAGEDDON

Edited by
DAVID DRAKE
&
BILLIE SUE MOSIMAN

BAEN

ARMAGEDDON

Copyright © 1998 by David Drake, Billie Sue Mosiman & Martin Harry Greenberg. All material is original to this volume and is copyright © 1998 by the individual authors.

A Baen Books Original

Baen Publishing Enterprises
P.O. Box 1403
Riverdale, NY 10471

ISBN: 0-671-87876-X

Cover art by David Mattingly

First printing, May 1998

Distributed by Simon & Schuster
1230 Avenue of the Americas
New York, NY 10020

Printed in the United States of America

CONTENTS

The Last Battle, Elizabeth Moon 1

Ils Ne Passeront Pas, Harry Turtledove 9

The Call, Joel Rosenberg 42

Leeward of Broken Jerusalem,
Carla Montgomery 47

*O'er the Land of the Freaks and the Home of
the Braves*, Gregory Nicoll 67

Riding Shotgun to Armageddon,
S.M. Stirling 79

Dead Men Talk A Lot, William C. Dietz...... 103

A Watery Silence, Billie Sue Mosiman 123

Basic Training, Mark L. Van Name 146

Mrs. Lurie and the Rapture,
Esther Friesner 167

With the Sword He Must Be Slain,
David Drake 215

Twelve Gates to the City, Margaret Ball 239

The Last Battle
Elizabeth Moon

I was brought up on the Bible stories, like most kids I knew. Joshua and Jericho. David and Goliath. Tyler Sims used to blow on a paper towel roll, pretending he was Joshua and we was all supposed to fall down, not that we was the wall, but that's how the game went. We was all David, one time and another, in our own heads, but nobody wanted to be Goliath.

We knew who Goliath was. Goliath was somebody else, from somewheres else, that took Daddy's job or Mama's parking place, that didn't speaka-da-Eengleesh too good. Them guys on the talk shows, they knew who Goliath was. The feds, sure, always interfering with people's rights, and godless humanists killing babies, and manhating feminists destroying the American family, and woollyminded treehuggers destroying American industry. All them was Goliath, one time or another. And the guy on the talk show, yelling into the mike so loud you could hear his spit sizzle, he was always David, or on the side of David and God, that's what he said.

But I never saw a giant, not a real giant, until now, and I surely don't feel like no David.

And I don't think there's a slingshot in this world's gonna take this one down.

The way it's easy for me to talk, the way I grew up talking, you'd think I was just like any other guy you'd see out

1

here with his neck burnt so's he's a natural redneck, which was no shame where I come from, with a longneck in hand and a gun I wasn't gonna let no fat-assed law officer take away from me slung across the back of my pickup where a gun's supposed to be. And I woulda been, if it hadn't been for Ethel Marie Serriere and her interpretation of the no-pass/no-play rule.

Which is neither here nor there, except that I got just enough education to know that I should be writing something that will live forever . . . only it won't, because I can't, because of who I am and what I am and the damn-fool things we did that got us in this mess in the first place.

This mess where there's a giant up there, big as life and not natural at all, and none of the stuff that we've thrown at it has so much as made it shiver.

The politicians were still arguing over why, the last time there was power to run a television. Moral decay, one side said, and all due to homosexuals and transsexuals . . . you'd think they never heard that there was queers and such thousands of years ago, so if all it took to end the human race was a few people of the same sex fucking each other, it sure took a long time for the bad magic to work. Then the other side said it was moral decay, all right, but due to not caring for one another in a gentle and generous way, and starting wars and fighting, which is something else humans have been doing for thousands of years without any apparent effect on the world as a whole. Certainly no giants, even if you believe in angels, which to be honest, I don't.

And if you think I sound more educated now, well, I am, when I think about it. It's hard to think about it with a hostile giant over there about ten miles away—its feet, I mean—throwing buckets of blood and slimy guts at every patch of what used to be clean water. Fuller's Creek, which until a couple of days ago, even with the climate change, was full of sunfish and even a channel cat or two—now it's stinking red goo that won't even dry in the sun.

Somebody said that part's in the Bible, but I never did like Revelations, all that about seven horns and cloven feet and women that are symbols of something else rather than just women. Eyes and wings, thrones and all that. So there's a lot I don't know about Revelations, or what the End Days are supposed to be like. The preachers I heard always said fire and brimstone and the wrath of God like a mighty wind, and the City of God rising up or coming down or anyway being there in the sky with the glory on it.

I always figured it was some drunk looking up at a thundercloud at sunset, which if you've ever been out in the country, and seen one towering over the land, can be just like a golden city floating in the air.

The only thing I ever heard about heaven which sounded right to me, was something I heard on a bus one night, when this one old lady was telling another one about a dream she had. But that was years ago, and she's probably dead already and if she's in heaven I'll never know it.

I figure I'll be dead soon, and I just can't fix my mind on heaven, not with the creeks running red goo and that giant looming over everything. Brother Sims, he used to say that if you put your mind on Jesus, no wiles of the Devil could keep you from reaching heaven. We was all supposed to sit there putting our minds on Jesus, but I never could. My mind would always run off into how the Cowboys had fucked up yet again, stealing another defeat from the jaws of victory (nobody in my family cared how many Super Bowls they won, it always seemed like they lost the games we watched on TV). Or maybe it would wander down the path to the creek, where Luanne skinny-dipped sometimes when she was sure no one could see her, only I had. Thoughts like that would never get me to heaven, I knew that, and I also knew the Devil had nothing to do with me thinking them.

But at least I know the name for what's going on here, and it's Armageddon, the Last Battle, the Final War. God's gonna win, in the end, but most people will die first, in one miserable way or another. Starvation, war, plagues of disease, that's nothing new. People been dying of those since before whenever. But giants poisoning the water and the winds, that's new. It's not rumors of war anymore, not rumors . . . but real.

So here I sit, one not-so-good ol' Texas boy, had a pickup and lost it when I couldn't make the payments. Had a rifle but never was that good a shot. Had a little education, thanks to Ethel Marie Serriere, though I didn't thank her at the time for knocking me off the football team in the last half of the season, just because I cheated on an exam and she caught me. Had a lot of opinions I was sure were one hundred percent right, about how the world was, and how it worked, and how I was born to be on top of the heap, being a sure-enough white man born in America and even better than that, in Texas.

Had a wife once, but she left. Had the cutest baby girl you ever saw, but I guess she died with Shirley when the bombs hit Houston. I told her the city would kill her . . . but I didn't know. I never thought bombs would fall on Houston. Nobody did. New York City, maybe, which would've served them Yankees right, but not Houston. Course it wasn't just Houston.

There's really not a lot to say about Armageddon when you're in it. I read a lot of stories that come out better than you'd think partway through. Something comes along and saves the hero, something changes. But I got this feeling, that awful smell in the creeks and that giant on the horizon . . . that's not going to change. That's not going away. There's no rescue coming for good ol' boys like me; I'm not in line for any white robe and golden crown, or no harp. It's too late for the apologies, for turning over a new leaf (which I never could stick with, which is why Shirley left). God's just flat run out of patience, like Ethel Marie Serriere with the football team, only He's got a hell of a lot—I mean a whole lot—more clout.

You might wonder why I'm still here. Any sensible man woulda left awhile back, that's perfectly true. Any sensible man, that is, who didn't have about half the U.S. Army, or what's left of it, settin' over there between Burnet and Lampasas, and as far west and east as you care to go, not about to let a living soul, if there is one, get out to the north, because they think one of us might be related to that thing, that giant they can't kill.

You might wonder why, with the world coming to an end, I'm bothering to talk about it. Why not just shut up and die, like old Tyler Sims told me to do a few hours ago, when he went wild and started smashing the last cans of peaches with the little hatchet his uncle Jay used to keep in the broom closet. I said stop, and what you doin' Tyler, and don't be stupid Tyler, and he turned on me like a wildcat, that hatchet cocked back over his shoulder, and said jes' shut up and DIE, Cody, and then he curled into himself like a tobacco worm when you put a hot cigarette on it, and choked.

I walked away. Maybe it wasn't the right thing to do, but it was that or kick his head in; I'd been kind of anticipating them peaches, the last sweet thing we had, and plenty of sugary juice, and Tyler'd already smashed them into the dirt, all that juice soaked up by ground as dry as Texas drought can make it. So I walked off, under the slatty shadow of the dead live oak that almost seems hotter than the sun, remembering when it made a cool shade so dense you couldn't see into it.

The preachers always said we'd fuck it up, though of course they didn't say it that way. That's what they meant, though. They always said it, but nothing ever happened, really, nothing you couldn't explain away on the basis of the federal government or the company or the welfare mothers or them immigrants. I looked over the fields at

the ugly redbrown thing that went up in the sky too far
to see, and really could not think of any sin big enough
to bring that on. A few drunks, that time with the gal out
behind the bar, and the $57.62 I never reported to the
IRS and God sends down a giant that turns the rivers to
blood?

I'm more inclined to think about what Ethel Marie
Serriere said; it made more sense to me even then. Trouble
is, I can't remember more'n half of it, because it gave
me a very bad feeling at the time and I did my best to
put it out of mind. A man can't be thinking of every little
thing when he's got a family to care for, not that I did a
terribly good job of that.

So far though, Armageddon is a battle I've stayed out
of, not being a soldier myself and not having any weapon
to fight with. Who'd I fight? That giant? I've seen
helicopters bounce off its sides, tanks bump into the feet
and go nowhere. Those big old shells they fire don't do it
any harm, might as well throw sand at a barn.

The preachers said it was gonna be a battle of good
against evil, the armies of the righteous against the powers
of Satan, but . . . I don't see no righteous, and if that's
Satan I'm sure not going over there and stomp on his
toes. All I want—all I ever wanted—was just to live my
own life my own way, kick back with a little beer and fun
Saturday nights, love a good woman and have her love
me, raise my kids, same as my daddy did.

Not that I never fought—of course I did, got in some
good ones, too. We drove them homos out of town, beat
'em up proper, let 'em know that only real men was
welcome here. Shirley wasn't too happy with me, when I
come back that night with a few bruises (and not from
them fruitcakes, but from that idiot Tyler, who never did
learn to look before he hit the guy in front of him). She
thought we'd get in trouble, I guess, but nobody ever said
nothing much. Deputy came out, walked into the cafe,
and said, "I guess you fellas don't know anyone who'd do

something real stupid like beat up a buncha fags in front of witnesses who might tattle."

"Reckon not," Tyler said, grinning through a swollen lip.

"Be smart enough to do it someplace nobody'd see, if anyone up here did anything like that," the deputy said. He was from another precinct, but I'd worked for his dad one summer, hauling rock. He didn't meet my eyes.

"Reckon so," Tyler said. Trey knocked his coffee over, trying to shut Tyler up, and the deputy just looked at us and walked out.

But I wasn't a brawler, really, not like some. Tyler, now, he got into something just about every Saturday night; if it was too quiet at the bar in town, he'd drive halfway across the county to find someplace lively, as he said. Comes of being a preacher's son; either they turn preacher, or they turn mean. I guess I haven't had even fifty good fights in my whole life, even counting school, and Tyler Sims drug me into at least half of them.

Besides the whack in the ribs he gave me the night we beat up them queers, it's on account of Tyler Sims that I broke my hand on some dumb Polack's jaw after a football game on that side of the county, and got a knife in the back the time we ventured into South Austin and he decided to use his little bit of dirty Spanish on a tableful of Mexicans. By the luck of history, at the time I grew to manhood, there wasn't no draft, and I never did hanker after the Army or nothing, my uncles having told me enough about Nam.

So all my scars are, as Shirley put it that last week before she walked out, just pure meanness and stupidity.

And here I am at the Last Battle of all with no weapons and no more idea than a treestump what I'm supposed to do, besides just die, which doesn't look any more appealing now than it did a year ago before all this started. Like I said, I ain't David, even if that giant was Goliath, which it's not.

❖　　❖　　❖

I sure wish I had a drink. That canned-peach juice would've gone down nice, sweet anyways if it wasn't cool. I could just about kill Tyler for wasting it. The shape he's in, bet I could take him now.

When I look back, there he is, holding up a can of peaches he'd hid somewheres, holding it up and grinning at me . . . and the bastard has a can opener. Well, he ain't no Goliath neither . . .

Coda:

Rev. 18:14 "And the fruits that thy soul lusted after are departed from thee, and all things which were dainty and goodly are departed from thee, and thou shalt find them no more at all."

Ils Ne Passeront Pas
Harry Turtledove

As the sun rose from the direction of Germany, Sergeant Pierre Barrès rolled out from under his filthy, lousy blanket. His *horizon bleu* uniform was equally lousy, which he loathed, and equally filthy, which he minded not at all, for it made him a harder target for the *Boche*.

He yawned, rubbed his eyes, scratched his chin. Whiskers rasped under his fingers. When had he last shaved? Two days before? Three? He couldn't remember. It didn't much matter.

Under the blanket next to his in the muddy trench, his loader, Corporal Jacques Fonsagrive, was also stirring. "*Bonjour, mon vieux*," Barrès said. "Another lovely morning, *n'est-ce pas?*"

Fonsagrive gave his opinion in one word: "*Merde.*" He always woke up surly—and stayed that way till he fell asleep again.

"Any morning I wake up and I am still breathing is a lovely morning," Barrès said. He pulled his water bottle off his belt and shook it. Half full, he judged: maybe a liter in there. He pulled out the cork and drank. *Pinard* ran down his throat. The rough red wine got his heart beating better than coffee had ever dreamt of doing.

"Well, then, odds are there won't be many more lovely mornings left in the world," Fonsagrive said. "Fucking miracle we've had this many." He scratched himself, then

9

stuck a *Gitane* between his lips. His cheeks hollowed as he sucked in smoke. He coughed. "Christ on His cross, that's worse than the chlorine the *Boche* shoots at us. What's for breakfast?"

"Ham and eggs and champagne would be nice, especially if an eighteen-year-old blonde with big jugs brought it to me," Barrès answered. Fonsagrive swore at him. Unperturbed, he went on, "What I've got is *singe*. How about you?"

"*Singe* here, too, and damn all else," Fonsagrive said. "I was hoping you had something better."

"Don't I wish," Barrès said fervently. The company field kitchen—like about half the company field kitchens in the French Army—was unserviceable. Some capitalist well back of the line had made a profit. If the troops who tried to use the worthless stoves went hungry . . . well, *c'est la guerre*.

Glumly, the two men opened tins of *singe* and stared down at the greasy, stringy beef. "Goddamn monkey meat," Fonsagrive said. He started shoveling it into his face as fast as he could, as if he wanted to fuel his boiler while enduring as little of the taste as he could. Barrès followed suit. Even washed down with more swigs of *pinard*, the stuff was vile.

He flung the empty tin out of the trench, almost as if it were a grenade. It didn't clank when it came down, which probably meant it landed on a corpse. There were more corpses around than anything else, he often thought. The stench was all-pervasive, unbelievable, inescapable— a testament to what all flesh inevitably became. He wanted to delay the inevitable as long as he could.

And how likely was that? He spat. He knew the answer too well. "Verdun," he muttered under his breath. "World's largest open-air cemetery."

Jacques Fonsagrive grunted. "Visitors always welcome," he said, taking up where Barrès had left off. "Come on in yourself and see how you'd make out as a stiff." He sounded like an advertising circular filled with a particular sort of repellent good humor.

"Heh," Barrès said—more in acknowledgment that the words were supposed to be funny than an actual laugh.

Cautiously, he reached up and plucked the cork from the muzzle of the Hotchkiss machine gun he and his partner served, then pulled away the oily rag that covered the machine gun's cocking handle. He and Fonsagrive could get soaked and maintain their efficiency. The machine gun was more temperamental—and, in the grand scheme of things, more important to the French Army.

Even more cautiously, he peered over the edge of the parapet. Ahead and over to the north lay what had been the Bois des Fosses. It was a wood no more, but a collection of matchsticks, toothpicks, and bits of kindling. Like gray ants in the distance, Germans moved there now.

Sharp cracks behind him announced that the crews of a battery of 75s were awake, too. Shells screamed overhead. They slammed down in the middle of the wood, scattering the gray ants and sifting the remains of the timber one more step down toward sawdust.

"Nice to see the artillery hitting the other side for a change," Fonsagrive remarked. Like any infantryman who'd ever been under fire from his own guns, he had an ingrained disdain for cannons and the men who served them.

Barrès said, "Those 75s are too close to bring their shells down on our heads."

"*Merde*," Fonsagrive said again. "With those bastards, you never say they're too close to do anything."

The sun rose higher. The day was going to be fine and mild, even warm. Barrès faced the prospect with something less than joy. Heat would make the stench worse. And it would bring out the flies, too. Already they were stirring, bluebottles and greenbottles and horseflies not too finicky to feast on human flesh as well.

Thunder in the east made Barrès turn his head in that

direction. Dominating the terrain there, Fort Douaumont was one of the keys to Verdun—and a key now in the hands of the *Boche*. Barrès neither knew nor cared how the fort had been lost. That it had been lost, though, mattered very much, for with its loss the Germans held the high ground along this whole stretch of front.

French artillery was doing its best to make sure the *Boche* did not rest easy on the heights. A gray haze continually hung about Fort Douaumont. Black shellbursts from a battery of 155s punctuated the haze. Below and around the fort, nothing at all grew. The ground was bare and brown and cratered, like astronomical photographs of the moon.

More thunder boomed, this closer. German 77s and 105s were replying to the French guns harassing the *Boche* in the Bois des Fosses. The French field pieces defiantly barked back.

Some of the German shells fell short, a few falling only a couple of hundred meters beyond the trench in which Barrès stood. He did not deign to look back at them, but remarked, "Back when the war was new, misses that close would have put my wind up."

"Back when the war was new, you were stupid," Fonsagrive answered. "And if you'd got any smarter since, you wouldn't be here."

That held too much truth to be comfortable. Sighing, Barrès said, "When the battalion has taken seventy-five percent casualties, they'll pull us out of the line. That's the rule."

"When the battalion has taken seventy-five percent casualties, odds are three to one you'll be one of them," his loader said. Fonsagrive punctuated the words with a perfect Gallic shrug. "Odds are three to one I'll be another."

Barrès nodded. No one had shot him yet, though not for lack of effort. He didn't know why not. His belief in luck had grown tenuous—had, to be honest, disappeared—from seeing so many comrades wounded and slain around him. He had no reason to believe he was in any way different from them. Yes, he'd lasted a little longer, but what did that mean? Not much.

He said, "The one good thing about fighting is that then you don't think about all the things that can happen to you. You just fight, and that's all. It's before and after that you think."

"There is no good thing about fighting." Fonsagrive spoke with authority a general might have envied. "There are some that are bad, and some that are worse. If I kill the *Boche*, it is bad. If the *Boche* kills me, that, I assure you, is worse. And so I kill the *Boche*."

For the *Boche*, of course, the pans of that scale were reversed. The German trenches lay only a couple of hundred meters away. They had been French trenches till the field-gray tide lapped over them. The field-gray tide had briefly lapped over the trench in which Barrès and Fonsagrive stood, too, but a French counterattack had cleared it again. Some of the rotting corpses and chunks of corpses between the lines wore field gray, others *horizon bleu*. In death, they all smelled the same.

Behind their rusting barbed wire, the Germans were awake now, too. Here and there along the trench, riflemen started shooting up the slope toward the French position. *Poilus* returned the fire. Their rhythm was slightly slower than that of the *Boche*; they had to reload rounds one by one into the tubular magazines of their Lebels, where the Germans just slapped fresh five-round boxes onto the Mausers they used.

Sighing, Barrès said, "There are quiet sections of the front, where for days at a time the two sides hardly shoot at each other."

"Not at Verdun," Fonsagrive said. "No, not at Verdun."

"*Tu as raison, malheureusement*," Barrès said. A moment later, he added, not unkindly, "*Cochon*."

And Fonsagrive was indeed right, however unfortunate that might have been. In front of Verdun, France and

Germany were locked in an embrace with death—a *Totentanz*, a German word the French had come to understand full well. The town itself, the white walls and red-tiled roofs four or five kilometers back of the line, had almost ceased to matter. In the bit more than a month since the Germans swarmed out of their trenches on 21 February, the battle had taken on a life of its own. It was about itself, not about the town at all: about which side would have to admit the other was the stronger. And it was about how many lives forcing such an admission would cost.

As if to underscore that point, a German Maxim gun snarled to life. The *Boche* was a good combat engineer; a concrete emplacement protected the machine gun from anything short of a direct hit from artillery. Sandbags protected Barrès' Hotchkiss. He envied his counterparts in field gray their snug nest.

But, regardless of his envy, he had a job to do. "If they are feeling frisky, we had better pay them back in kind," he said to Jacques Fonsagrive.

The loader already had one of the Hotchkiss gun's thirty-round metal strips of ammunition in his hands. He inserted it in the left side of the weapon. Barrès used the cocking handle to chamber the first round, then squeezed the trigger and traversed the machine gun to spray bullets along the German trenches like a man watering grass with a hose.

As soon as the strip had gone all the way through the gun, Fonsagrive fed in another one. Barrès chambered the first round manually; the Hotchkiss gun, again, did the rest. It didn't have quite the rate of fire of the German Maxim with its long, long belts of ammunition, but it was more than adequate for all ordinary purposes of slaughter, as a good many of the German dead could have attested.

Barrès had no idea whether any individual bullet he fired hit any individual *Boche*. He didn't much care. If he fired enough bullets, some of them would pierce

German flesh, just as, if he played roulette long enough, the ball would sometimes land on zero, missing both red and black.

Unfortunately, the same applied to that Maxim down the slope. A *poilu* perhaps fifty meters from Barrès let out an unearthly shriek and fell writhing to the bottom of the trench, clutching at his shoulder.

Fonsagrive spat. "In most factories, it is an accident when someone is hurt—an accident that causes work to stop. What we make in this factory is death, and when someone is hurt it is but a death imperfectly manufactured. I hope the *Boche* who fired that round gets a reprimand for falling down on the job."

One more casualty, Barrès thought as a couple of men helped the wounded soldier up a zigzagging communications trench toward a medical station. *One more casualty that is neither Jacques nor I. One casualty closer to the three quarters who have to be shot or blown up before they take this battalion out of the line.* That was a revoltingly cold-blooded way to look at a man's agony and probable mutilation. He knew as much. Being able to help it was something else again.

He did his best to return the disfavor to the *Boche*. Methodical as any factory worker, Fonsagrive fed strip after strip of bullets into the Hotchkiss gun. Barrès knew from long experience just how hard to tap the weapon to make the muzzle swing four or five centimeters on its arc of death. Had the Germans come out of their trench, they would not have lived to reach his.

Presently, the doughnut-shaped iron radiating fins at the base of the barrel began to glow a dull red. Over in the trench the *Boche* held, the mirror image of his own, the water in the cooling jacket surrounding the Maxim gun's barrel would be boiling. The Germans could brew coffee or tea with the hot water. All Barrès could do was remember not to touch those iron fins.

After a while, the German machine gun fell silent, though

rifles kept on barking. Barrès turned to Fonsagrive and asked, "Have we got any of that newspaper left?"

"I think so," the loader answered. His words seemed to come from far away; Barrès' hearing took a while to return to even a semblance of its former self after a spell of firing. Fonsagrive rummaged. "No newspaper, but we've got this." He held out a copy of *L'Illustration*.

"It will do," Barrès said. Taking the magazine, he scrambled up out of the trench and into a shell hole right behind it. A couple of bullets whipped past him, but neither came very near; he'd had much closer calls. He unbuttoned his fly to piss, then yanked down his pants and squatted in a spot that wasn't noticeably more noisome than any other. In some stretches of the line, trenches had latrine areas soldiers were supposed to use. The trenches around Verdun had been shelled and countershelled, taken and retaken, so many times, they were hard to tell from the shell holes in front of and behind them.

As Barrès did his business, he glanced at an article about the fighting in which he was engaged. He needed only a couple of sentences to be sure the writer had never come within a hundred kilometers of Verdun or, very likely, any other part of the front. "Confident hope rings a carillon of bells in our hearts," the fellow declared.

"I know what hope would ring a carillon of bells in my heart, *salaud*," Barrès muttered: "the hope of trading places with you."

Slowly and deliberately, he tore that page from the copy of *L'Illustration* and used it for the purpose for which he had requested the magazine of Fonsagrive. Then he used another page, too; like a lot of the men on both sides here, he had a touch of dysentery. A lot of men had more than a touch.

He set his pants to rights and then, clutching the magazine, dove back into the trench. He drew more fire this time, as he'd known he would. "The *Boche* would sooner assassinate a man answering a call of nature than do battle when both sides have weapons to hand," he said.

"So would I," Fonsagrive replied. "The pigdogs"—he liked the feel of the German *Schweinhund*—"are just as dead that way, and they can't shoot back at me."

Barrès thought it over. "It could be that you have reason," he said at last.

"And it could be that all the world has gone mad, and that reason is as dead as all the other corpses in front of us in no-man's-land," Fonsagrive said. "That, I think, is more likely. If there were a God, these would be the last days."

"I was, once, a good Catholic," Barrès said. "I went to Mass. I took communion. I confessed my sins." He scratched his head. Something popped wetly under his fingernail. "I wonder where the man who did those things has gone. The man I am now . . . all that man wants to do is to kill the *Boche* and to keep the *Boche* from killing him."

"All I used to want to do was get drunk and fuck," Fonsagrive said. "I still want to do those things. Like you, I also want to keep the *Boche* from killing me, especially when I have my pants down around my ankles. What do you say that you feed our friends down there another couple of strips, to show them you were not taken up to heaven while answering nature's call?"

"And why not?" Barrès peered over at the German trenches. He was very careful not to lift his head above the parapet in the same spot twice in a row. *Boche* snipers knew their business. The Germans would not have been where they were, would not have been doing what they were doing, had their soldiers not known their business.

His eyes slid past motion out in no-man's-land, then snapped sharply back. Any motion out there was dangerous. But this was not a *Boche*, sneaking from shell hole to shell hole to lob bombs into the French trench. It was a couple of rats, fat and sleek and sassy and almost the size of cats, on promenade from one favorite dining spot in field gray or *horizon bleu* to the next. Rats thrived at Verdun—and why not? Where else did men feed them so extravagantly?

Barrès was tempted to knock them kicking with a burst from the Hotchkiss. In the end, he didn't. There would only be more tomorrow, eating of their obscene meat. And these were as likely to go down and torment the Germans as they were to come up and molest his comrades and him.

Then Barrès spotted motion *in* the trenches of the *Boche*. A man so incompetent as to give away his position to a machine gunner did not deserve to live. Barrès squeezed the Hotchkiss' trigger. The German crumpled. "I got one," Barrès told his loader. "I saw him fall."

"One who won't get us," Fonsagrive replied.

The Germans promptly replied, too. Their riflemen picked up their pace of fire. The Maxim gun came back to life, flame spurting from its muzzle as if from the mouth of a dragon. And, a few minutes later, the *Boche* artillery began delivering presents to the French trenches. Barrès scuttled into the little cave he had scraped out of the front wall of the trench. The Germans—and, he understood, the English, too—forbade their soldiers from digging such private shelters. If a shell landed squarely on one, it would entomb the soldier huddling there. But a man in his own little cave enjoyed far better protection from splinters than one simply cowering at the bottom of the trench.

Some of the rounds—77s, 105s, and 150s—exploded with a peculiar muffled burst. Even before *poilus* started banging on empty shell casings—carillons of dread, not hope—Barrès yanked his gas helmet out of its case and pulled it down over his head. He got a quick whiff of chlorine, enough to make his throat scratchy and bring tears to his eyes, before he could secure the helmet.

He took several anxious breaths after that, fearing the pain would get worse. But he'd protected himself fast enough; it eased to a bearable discomfort. He stared out at the world through round windows, filthy as the portholes of a cabin in steerage. Wearing the helmet, he had to move more slowly and carefully, for he wasn't getting enough air to do anything else. A man who exerted himself too strenuously in a gas helmet was liable to burst his heart.

But, when the *Boche* used gas, he was liable to send assault troops as soon as the barrage ended. And so, regardless of the high-explosive shells still coming down with the ones carrying chlorine, Barrès got out of his shelter and took his place at the Hotchkiss gun again. Better the risk of a shell fragment piercing him than the certainty of a bayonet or a bullet if the *Boche* got into his trench.

He spied no special stirring in the German trenches. Jacques Fonsagrive peered over the parapet with him. "Nothing," Barrès said. "Nothing at all, not this time."

"Not quite." When Fonsagrive spoke, his voice, heard through two thicknesses of varnished cloth, sounded as if it came from the bottom of the sea. The laugh that followed seemed even worse, almost demonic. "Look at the vermin."

Out between the lines, several rats kicked and frothed as chlorine seared their lungs. They were enough like men to sneak about. They were enough like men to steal. They were enough like men to prey on the dying and the dead. But they were not quite enough like men to invent such ingenious ways of murdering one another, or to come up with defenses against that deadly ingenuity.

"I don't miss them a bit," Barrès said.

"Nor I," the loader agreed. "As when you shot that German earlier today, I merely think, there are a couple who will not gnaw my bones."

"Even so," Barrès said. The gas shells were still raining down. "I hope we do not have to wear these cursed helmets too much longer."

"Ah, to hell with a mealy-mouthed hope like that," Fonsagrive said. "What I hope is that the wind will shift and blow the gas back on the pigdogs"—yes, he was enamored of that word—"who sent it to us. They deserve it. They are welcome to it. Hope for something worth having."

"That is a better hope," Barrès said after due reflection. "It is also a hope that could come true without much difficulty." The German trenches lay downhill from the one in which he stood, and chlorine was heavier than air. Even a little breeze would give the *Boche* a taste of his own medicine.

"Do you want to feed them a few strips?" Fonsagrive asked. "Let them know they have not put paid to us?"

"I had in my mind that thought," Barrès said, "but then I thought again, and I decided I would rather not. If they know they have not gassed us, they are likely to drop more ordinary shells on our heads, are they not?"

Behind the gas helmet, Fonsagrive's expression was as hard to read as the unchanging countenance of a praying mantis. After a little while, though, he nodded. "That is a good notion. We can give them a nasty surprise if they come at us, and by then their men will be too close for them to shell us."

"I wish they would give it up soon," Barrès said. "I would like another swig of *pinard*. Even a tin of monkey meat might not taste bad right now."

"My poor fellow!" Fonsagrive exclaimed. "You must have inhaled more of the gas than you think, for your wits have left you altogether."

"It could be," Barrès admitted. "Yes, it could be. Did I truly say I wanted to eat *singe*? No one in his right mind— no one who is not starving, at any rate—would be so foolish."

"I wonder if we will be starving before too long," Fonsagrive said. "The *cuistots* will have a hellish time bringing supplies to the line through this."

"That is a duty for which I would not care," Barrès said— no small statement, coming as it did from a machine gunner at the front. The *cuistots* walked, or more often crawled, to the front festooned with loaves of bread as if with bandoliers, and with bottles of *pinard*. They paid the butcher's bill no less than anyone else—more than many—and had not even the luxury of shooting back.

And, if the bread arrived covered with mud and loathsome slime, if some of the wine bottles got to the front broken . . . why, then the weary, hungry, thirsty, filthy *poilus* cursed the *cuistots*, of course. And if the bread and wine did not arrive at all, the *poilus* still cursed the *cuistots*, though in that case the bearers were more often than not in no condition to take note of curses.

"Bread and wine," Barrès muttered. "The communion of the damned." He'd had that thought before, as no doubt many Catholics at the front had done, but it struck him with particular force today.

"What is it you say?" Fonsagrive asked. The gas helmet muffled voices and hearing both. Barrès repeated himself, louder this time. Fonsagrive gestured contemptuously. "You and your God, *mon vieux*. How important you think you are—how important you think we are—to merit damnation. I tell you again: if there is a God, which I doubt, as what man of sense could not, then we are not damned. We are merely forgotten, or beneath His notice."

"You so relieve my mind," Barrès said. Through the gas helmet, Fonsagrive's chuckle sounded like the grunting of a boar. Barrès cocked his head to one side, listening not to the loader but to the German bombardment. "It is easing off." He might have been speaking of the rain. Indeed, he had so spoken of the rain many times; in the trenches, rain could be almost as great a nuisance as gas, and lasted far longer.

After another hour or so, Jacques Fonsagrive cautiously lifted his gas helmet from his head. He did not immediately clap it back on. Neither did he topple to the ground clutching at his throat with froth on his lips. He had done that once for a joke while Barrès was taking off his own helmet, and had laughed himself sick when his partner on the machine gun pulled it back down in a spasm of panic. Barrès had not known he could curse so inventively.

Now he pulled off the gas helmet with a sigh of relief. The air still stank, but the air around Verdun always stank. If anything, the chlorine that remained added an antiseptic tang to the ever-present reek of decay. Behind him, the sun was sinking toward the battered horizon. "Another day at the shop," he remarked.

"But of course," Fonsagrive said. "Now we go home to our pipes and slippers." They both laughed. They might even sleep a little tonight, as they had the night before, if the *Boche* proved to be in a forgiving mood. On the other hand, they might stay awake three, four, five days in a row—if they stayed alive through the end of that time. Barrès had done it before.

Fonsagrive did light a pipe, a stubby little one filled with tobacco that smelled as if it were half dried horse dung. All French tobacco smelled that way these days. For lack of anything better—the only reason a man with a tongue in his head would do such a thing—he and Barrès opened tins of *singe* and supped as they had breakfasted. Even in the twilight, the preserved beef was unnaturally red.

"Poor old monkey," Barrès said. "A pity he got no last rites before he died." He took another bite and chewed meditatively. "He tastes so bad. . . . Maybe he was a suicide, and they found his body two or three days later and stuffed it in a tin then. That would account for the flavor, to be sure, and for his getting no rites. Yes," he went on, pleased with his own conceit, "that would account for a great many things."

"Would it account for your being an idiot?" Jacques Fonsagrive inquired. Barrès chuckled to himself. *He is jealous*, Barrès thought. *Usually, such foolishness falls from his lips, and I am the one who has to endure it*. But then Fonsagrive continued, "We are all suicides here, and none of us shall receive the last rites. It is true, is it not? Of course it is true. We are suicides, and the *Boche*, he is a suicide, and the whole cursed world, it is a suicide, too, throwing itself onto the fire as a moth will hurl itself into the flame of a gas lamp."

Pierre Barrès dug into the tin of *singe* and ate without another word till it was empty. It was not that he disagreed with his loader. On the contrary: he felt exactly as did Fonsagrive. But some things, no matter how true they were—indeed, because of how true they were—were better left unsaid.

Fonsagrive seemed to sense the same thing, for when he spoke again, after flinging his own empty tin out of the trench, what he said was, "Perhaps the two of us will succeed in botching our own suicides. We have botched so many things since this *tragédie bouffe* began, what is one more?"

"Maybe we will," Barrès said, glad for any excuse not to contemplate what was far more likely to happen to him.

And then, from down the trench, voices were raised in simultaneous greeting and anger. That could mean only one thing. "The *cuistots* have got here at last," Fonsagrive said, spelling out that one thing, "and the bread is even filthier than usual. Either that, or they have no wine at all."

"Fuck you and fuck all your mothers, too, the ugly old bawds," a *cuistot* was saying furiously in a voice that broke every fourth word: he couldn't have been above seventeen. "I suppose you stand up and wave when the *Boche* drops shells on *your* heads. If you think my job is so easy, come do it."

"If you think fighting up here while you're starving is so easy, *you* come do it," one of the *poilus* retorted. But his voice held less outrage than those of the front-line troops had before; the *cuistot's* answering fury had quelled theirs, as counterbattery fire reduced the damage gun crews could do. None of the soldiers cared for the notion of becoming a *cuistot* himself: no, not even a little.

Eventually, Barrès and Fonsagrive got bread and wine

for themselves. Barrès' share of the wine did not quite
fill his water bottle, and he had to use his belt knife to
cut away several muddy, filthy spots from the chunk of
bread. Even after he'd done that, it still stank of corruption
and death. Or perhaps it was only his imagination, for
the whole battlefield stank of corruption and death.

Fonsagrive gave the bread such praise as he could: "Lord
knows it's better than *singe*." He drank some of the *pinard*
the *cuistot* had brought forward. "And this is better than
horse piss, but not much."

With his belly full, Barrès was inclined to take a
somewhat more charitable view of the world. "Let it be
as it is, Jacques," he said. "All the grousing in the world
won't make it any better."

"To hell with the world," the loader replied. "If I grouse,
I feel better." His eyes glittered in the gathering darkness.

Barrès decided not to push it any further. What the
devil was the use? What the devil, for that matter, was
the use of anything up here at the front line? Survival
was the most he could hope for, and his odds even of
that weren't good. "Let me have a cigarette, *mon vieux*,
will you?" he said. "Either that or some tobacco for my
pipe. I'm just about all out."

"Here." Fonsagrive handed him a leather pouch. "Help
yourself." Tobacco got to the front even less reliably than
pinard and bread. A few days before, he'd been the one
who was low, and Barrès had kept him smoking.

A brimstone reek, as of a fumigation or an exorcism,
rose from the match Barrès struck. He got his pipe going
and sucked smoke into his mouth. It was vile smoke, but
less vile than everything else around him. He leaned back
against the wall of the trench, savoring the pipe. The *Boche*
must have been at his supper, too, for there was silence
in the trenches about the space of half an hour.

He looked up. The stars were coming out, as if all the
world beneath them were at peace. He always marveled
at that. The stars did not care. Maybe it was just as well.

From high above, cold and thin in the distance, came the sound—Barrès dug a finger in his ear, for his mind at first would not credit what he heard—of a brazen trumpet blowing a long blast. "That is not a call of ours," he said, repose dropping from him like a hastily donned cloak. "That is surely some thing of the *Boche*."

"Bugger the *Boche*," Fonsagrive said, but he too scrambled to his feet. Barrès set his finger on the trigger of the Hotchkiss gun. If the Germans wanted to pay a call on his stretch of trench by night, as they had been known to do, he would give them a warm reception. Fonsagrive went on, "I think they mean to bombard us from above: that horn must surely be coming from an *avion*."

"So it must." Barrès shrugged and sighed. "If only our own *avions* were worth something more than an arse-wipe article from *L'Illustration*."

"If only, if only, if only," the loader mocked him. "If only you did not say 'If only' so much. The *Boche* has more artillery, he has more men, and he has more *avions* as well. Such is life. We shall go on killing him anyway, until we are killed ourselves."

Down in the German trenches a couple of hundred meters away, men were shouting and stirring, as the French soldiers were to either side of Barrès' machine gun. Barrès thought he saw movement, and started firing. The German Maxim gun answered instantly, and riflemen on both sides also opened up. Muzzle flashes stabbed the night.

Then the aerial bombardment Fonsagrive had feared began. It was like no bombing raid Barrès had ever known: hail and fire rained out of the sky together. "Mother of God!" Barrès shouted, diving for shelter. "The *Boche* has learned how to take his cursed flamethrowers up into *avions*."

"So he has," Fonsagrive answered. "What he has not learned to do, the stinking pigdog, is to aim his flying fire. Listen to them howl down the slope, roasted in their own ovens!" He chuckled in high good humor.

"Might as well be our artillery," Barrès said, laughing, too. The Germans *were* howling when hail smote or fire burned, and the bombardment seemed to be falling on them and the French almost impartially. Barrès cocked his head to one side. "Truly their pilots are great cowards, for they are flying so high, one cannot even hear the sound of their engines."

"As you say, might as well be our own artillery." Fonsagrive got to his feet. "And this bombardment is not so much of a much, either. Shells or bombs would do far worse than these drippy wisps of fire." A hailstone clattered off his helmet.

Barrès did not think the *Boche* could come out of his trenches and attack, not when he was being bombarded, too. Nonetheless, the Frenchman peered toward the enemy's line. The rain of fire had started blazes in the wrecked and battered woods, although, thanks to the hail, they weren't spreading very fast.

Fonsagrive stuck up his head, too. He shrugged. "One part in three of the forest on fire, more or less," he said. "I had not thought the Germans to be such a slovenly people. If they have this weapon that burns, they would do better to bring it all down on *our* heads, not scatter it about as a running man with dysentery scatters turds." He sounded rather like a critic explaining why a dramatist had ended up with a play worse than it might have been.

After a while, the rain of hail and fire eased, both ending at about the same time. Never once had Barrès heard the buzz of an *avion's* motor. The woods and such dry grass as remained on the ground burned fitfully. They would, Barrès judged, burn themselves out before long: so many of those trees had already burned, not much was left on which flames could support themselves.

He said, "With any luck at all, the next time the *Boche* trots out his fire, he will use it against the English farther north."

"It could be," Fonsagrive said. "He honored them with

poison gas before he gave us our first taste of it, but now he shares it with them and us alike. He is a generous fellow, the *Boche*, is he not?"

"To a fault," Barrès said. "I wonder when he will do us another favor of this sort. Not soon, I hope."

In that hope he was disappointed, as he discovered within minutes. He had been disappointed a great many times since the war began, and was hardly surprised to have it happen again. As if proud of their ingenuity, the Germans heralded the new onslaught with another of those trumpetlike blasts that seemed to come from everywhere and nowhere at the same time.

"Look up in the sky!" Fonsagrive exclaimed. "One of their *avions* must have walked into a shell, for it is burning, burning."

"That is a very huge bastard of an *avion*, to be sure," Barrès replied. "I wonder—I wonder most exceedingly— how such a machine could even so much as hope to get off the ground. Look at it, Jacques. Does it not seem like a great mountain burning with fire?"

"So it does," Fonsagrive said. "And may all the Germans inside it burn with fire, too. There it goes, by God! It will crash in the river."

Crash in the Meuse it did, behind the French lines and to the west of the trench in which Barrès and Fonsagrive huddled. The ground shook under Barrès' boots. "Good!" he said savagely. "All the bombs and all the fire the *salauds* still had with them have gone up. Now there can be no doubt they are dead."

"They are dead, yes, and probably one fish in three in the Meuse with them," Fonsagrive said. "That was a formidable explosion."

"A pity the *avion* did not crash into the trenches the *Boche* holds," Barrès said. "It would have been sweet, having him hoist by his own petard."

"So it would," Fonsagrive said. "It would also be sweet if, having made a nuisance of himself in the first part of the evening, the *Boche* would roll up in his covers and go to sleep for the rest of the night. As you said, another favor like the falling fire we do not need."

But the respite the two Frenchmen got did not last long. For the third time that evening, the horn sounded not behind the German line but, as best Barrès could tell, above it. "What *is* the *Boche* playing at?" he demanded in a cross voice. "When he does strange things, I grow nervous, for then I do not know what he is likely to try next."

Even as he spoke, a great searing white light sprang into being above him. "Parachute flare!" The cry rose from up and down the line. Barrès ducked down below the lip of the parapet. In that pitiless glare, the Germans would have had an easy time picking him off.

He waited for the Maxim gun in the trench down the slope to take advantage of the flare and start potting *poilus* less cautious than he. But the enemy's machine gun stayed quiet, as did his own Hotchkiss. He wondered why. When he said so aloud, Fonsagrive answered, "Could it be that no one told the *Boche* machine gunners the flare was going up? Could it be they think it is ours, and wait for us to shoot at them?"

"It could be, I suppose," Barrès said dubiously, "but it sounds like something our own officers are more likely to do than those of the Germans." He had a healthy, indeed almost a fearful, respect for the men who wore field gray and coal-scuttle helmets, and for their commanders. They had come too close to killing him too many times for him to feel anything but respect for them.

Slowly, slowly, the parachute flare sank. It was an extraordinarily fine one. It scarcely flickered or dimmed as it came down, staying so bright, Barrès could not even make out the 'chute supporting it in the air.

It lit in a muddy puddle—a water-filled shell hole, no doubt—off to the right, in the direction of Fort Douaumont. Even after it sank into the puddle, its light still shone for a moment. The *Boche* remained in his trenches. "Whatever he was supposed to do, he has buggered it up," Fonsagrive said.

"So it would seem," Barrès agreed. "Who would have thought it of him?"

From that muddy puddle, and perhaps from all the other sodden shell holes nearby, of which there were a great many, rose a bitter odor penetrating even through the horrid stench of the battlefield of Verdun. "What the devil is that?" Fonsagrive said. "Some new German gas?" He grabbed for his gas helmet.

But Barrès held up a hand. "No, that's not a gas," he said. "Don't you recognize it? That's the smell of wormwood."

"Wormwood?" The loader frowned. "The stuff that goes into absinthe?"

"The very same," Barrès replied.

Fonsagrive snorted. "And what do you know of wormwood, of absinthe, eh, *mon vieux*? I suppose you are going to tell me you were one of those Paris dandies who knocked back the stuff by the beaker before they made it against the law because it drove some of those dandies mad?" As Barrès' eyes readjusted to the night, he saw Fonsagrive gesture airily, as he guessed a Parisian dandy might do. Whatever effect the gesture might have had from a Paris dandy, it altogether failed of its purpose when coming from a filthy, unshaven corporal.

"Oh, yes, I used to guzzle absinthe by the tumblerful," Barrès said.

His loader snorted again, louder and more rudely this time. "The truth, if you please. Do you know what the truth is?"

"Better than Pontius Pilate. Better than you, too," Barrès retorted. But then he sighed. "Oh, very well. The truth. Back when the war was new, my company commander used to drink the stuff. Every day, at noon and in the evening, he would pour some absinthe into the bottom of a glass, hold a perforated spoon filled with sugar above it, and drip a little water through the sugar and into the absinthe. Then he'd drink it down. I don't know where he got the stuff, but he had plenty."

"What sort of officer was he?" Fonsagrive asked, interest in his voice. "Did the absinthe make him crazier than those who don't drink it?"

"Not so you'd notice," Barrès answered. "He was just a soldier, like any other. He's dead now, I heard."

"As who is not, these days?" Fonsagrive said. "It's almost a fucking dishonor to stay alive, if you know what I mean."

"Only too well, *mon ami*—only too well." Sadly, Barrès shook his head. After he'd done it, he wished he hadn't. "Those cursed fumes of wormwood are giving me a hangover, and I didn't even get to enjoy the drunk."

"Life is full of tragedies," Fonsagrive said. "Shall I weep for you?"

"If you would be so kind," Barrès answered. His loader rolled his eyes. Both men laughed. After a little while, Fonsagrive began to complain that his head hurt, too. "Ah, *quelle dommage*," Barrès said, his voice full of lachrymose, even treacly, sympathy. "How I grieve that you suffer!"

"How I grieve that you lay it on with a trowel," Fonsagrive remarked. The two soldiers laughed again.

Barrès said, "The *Boche* has been trying all sorts of strange and curious things tonight. I wonder whether he is finished, or whether he will show us something else new and interesting."

That made Jacques Fonsagrive stop laughing. But then, after some thought, the loader said, "The *Boche* has shown us strange and curious things tonight, *oui*, but I cannot see that he has hurt us very badly with them. His fire did him as much harm as it did us, and if he somehow turned water into absinthe—well, so what? Jesus Christ turned water into wine, and look what happened to *Him*."

"If a priest heard you say that, he would swell up and turn purple, like a man stung by many hornets," Barrès said. "But, since it is my ears you assail . . ." As Fonsagrive had earlier in the day, he shrugged a fine French shrug.

A fourth trumpet blast sounded, above and beyond the battlefield. Barrès tensed, but not so much as he had done when that strange horn call first sounded. These German attacks were strange and curious, true, but, as his loader had said, they were less dangerous than most of the things the Germans had done before.

For some time, he wondered if this trumpet blast were merely sound and fury, signifying nothing. But then Jacques Fonsagrive asked, "Where has the moon gone?" By his tone, he suggested that Barrès was hiding it in one of the pockets of his uniform tunic.

Looking east, Barrès saw that the waning crescent moon which had crawled up above the German-held land in that direction—without his noticing, the hour had got well past midnight—was now vanished. He spied no cloud behind which it could have disappeared . . . and, for that matter, the stars in that part of the sky also seemed to have gone.

"Absinthe fumes," he said again. "What else could it be? They poach your wits like the eggs in eggs Benedict."

"Hmm." Fonsagrive pondered the phrase as if he'd seen it in some new essay from Anatole France. "Not bad," he said at last. "Soon the sun will be up. If you see strange things in the light of day, you will know your wits are not poached, but as addled as the eggs a Picard peasant sells you for fresh."

A good many of the infantrymen in the trench with them were Picard peasants. If they heard, if they thought the comment a slander on their habits, they gave no sign. *Probably laughing up their sleeves*, Barrès thought.

And the sun gave no sign of coming up. When a waning crescent moon rises, the sun cannot be far behind. So a lifetime of experience had taught Barrès. But, even though the sun did not rise and did not rise, he refused to let it fret him. After all, among all the other stenches, the stench of wormwood remained strong in the air. "A few minutes seem like an hour," Barrès remarked after some time had passed.

"True: time marches on hands and knees," Fonsagrive said, adding, "It could be that we should put on our gas helmets, to clear these fumes from our heads. The sun should have risen long ago."

"To the devil with that," Barrès said. He waved out across no-man's-land. "The *Boche* is in the same state we are. The *Boche* must be in the same state we are, or he would have come over here and done us a mischief." He leaned against the wall of the trench and closed his eyes. "I am going to sleep for a bit, while I have the chance."

"Not the worst idea in the world," Fonsagrive agreed, and he stretched out, too. They knew they could be up and firing in a couple of seconds if the Germans had been rendered less nearly insensible than seemed to be the case.

When Barrès opened his eyes, he was prepared to swear on a stack of Bibles two meters high that he had dozed only a few minutes. But the sun, that suddenly treacherous beast, stood high in the sky, having somehow traveled a third part of its journey across the heavens while he lay snoring.

Ever so cautiously, he sniffed. Yes, the odor of absinthe lingered. If it had thrown him into such a stupor, maybe he should have thrust the gas helmet over his head in the darkness. But, while it might save his life, he hated it, just as he hated donning a rubber that might save him from disease.

Fonsagrive woke up a couple of minutes later. "What's going on?" he demanded, pointing toward the sun. "Where'd that little bugger sneak out from while we weren't looking?"

"Damned if I know," Barrès answered. "But there he is, and we just have to make the best of it."

They weren't the only ones who'd taken advantage of what still felt like unnaturally extended darkness. All up and down the line, *poilus* who'd just awakened were exclaiming in wonder at how the sun had come out of nowhere. Barrès spoke no German past "*Hände hoch!*"— which he mispronounced abominably—but he knew surprise when he heard it. By the noises the *Boche* was making down in his trenches, he was as surprised as his French foes.

Before Barrès had a chance to marvel at that, the aerial trumpet sounded again: the fifth time overall, the first in daylight. Fonsagrive made a disgusted noise, then said, "Ahh, I thought we were done with that weird crap."

Then, together, he and Barrès exclaimed not in disgust but in fright. A shell—it had to be a shell, though it glowed like a star even in broad daylight—was falling from the sky, seemingly straight toward them. Barrès had seen plenty of German 420s and flying mines: half the terror of those things was that you *could* see them as they fell. The same held true here. This was no parachute flare, like the one that had somehow brought with it the reek of absinthe. This one plunged to earth unimaginably faster than any stooping hawk.

Barrès barely had time to dive into his cave before the starlike shell burst in no-man's-land. By the way the ground shook beneath him, it had landed not far in front of his Hotchkiss gun. Dirt and gobbets of decayed man's-flesh rained down on the trench, as they did after any near miss from a big shell. He gritted his teeth, bracing himself for the storm of steel sure to follow that first shot.

But the storm of steel did not come. When it didn't come, Barrès scrambled to his feet and seized his machine gun's trigger instead of sheltering in the hole he'd scraped for himself in the front wall of the trench. Maybe something had gone wrong with the *Boche's* artillery signals, and footsoldiers in field gray were about to swarm out of their trenches and up the slope toward him.

He saw no swarming footsoldiers, for which he heartily thanked God. He did see the enormous hole the shell had dug, about halfway between his line and the forwardmost German positions. From that hole, a great smoke rose: perhaps the star shell had been of armor-piercing make, and had penetrated deep enough into the soft earth to ignite a stock of cooking oil or motor oil merely buried by all the other thousands of rounds that had slammed into the slope. The smoke spread quickly, all but blotting out the light of the sun that had so mysteriously reappeared in the sky.

Something stirred, there at the edge of the hole. Barrès' finger tightened on the trigger of the Hotchkiss gun. But then, frantically, he jerked his hands away from the weapon, snatched the gas helmet off his belt, and stuffed it down over his head. "Holy Virgin Mary Mother of God," he gasped, almost as if the phrase were but a single word. "The absinthe fumes were ever so much worse than I thought."

Beside him, Fonsagrive was also putting on his gas helmet with desperate haste. "Tell me what you see," the loader begged.

"I will not," Barrès said firmly. "In no way will I do that. You would think I was mad. I would think I am mad, did I put into words what my fuddled brain makes of what my eyes see."

Locusts the size of horses? Locusts the size of horses with the tails of scorpions and the faces of men? Locusts the size of horses with iron breastplates, with wings that rumbled as they shook them out? Locusts with women's hair streaming out from under golden crowns, with the fierce teeth of lions huge in their jaws?

Though Barrès breathed clean air now, the absinthe fumes had already fuddled him, and the hallucinations— for such they had to be—did not resume their proper form, which could be nothing but men in field gray with coal-scuttle helmets on their heads.

"I do not care what they look like to me," he declared as the impossible things began to advance on the trench.

He was lying. He knew he was lying, but saying the words helped him control his fear, even if he could not banish it. And what he said next was surely true: "If I can see them at all, I can kill them."

He squeezed the machine gun's trigger and sent a strip of ammunition into the Germans who did not to his mind look like Germans. Mechanical as if powered by steam, Jacques Fonsagrive fed the Hotchkiss another thirty-round strip, and another, and another. All along the trench, *poilus*, some wearing gas helmets, some not, emptied their rifles at the advancing enemy as fast as they could.

The slaughter was gruesome. The *Boche* had to be throwing in raw recruits, for they knew nothing—less than nothing—about taking cover. Barrès had heard that the Germans were trying out armor like that which knights of old had worn. Maybe the breastplates he thought he saw on the giant locusts were in fact breastplates on Germans. If they were, they weren't proof against machine-gun bullets.

And then Barrès laughed out loud, a huge, delighted laugh. Some—perhaps even half—of the Germans in no-man's-land, unable to stand up against the withering French fire, started back toward their own line. And the Germans in that line, as fuddled from wormwood fumes as Barrès was himself, opened fire on their comrades as if they were Frenchmen. The Maxim and Mausers worked an execution as ghastly as the Hotchkiss and Lebels.

A few got into the trenches on either side. None lasted long, not against bullets and bayonets and grenades. Then one more rose out of the pit. Maybe the fumes were fading from Barrès' head, for this one looked like a man. But *what* man he looked like kept changing from moment to moment. Now he had lank, dark hair, a small mustache, and wore what looked something like a German uniform, save with a red armband bearing some kind of symbol on his left arm. Then again, he might have been a short, pockmarked fellow with iron-gray hair and a large mustache, wearing a suit halfway between military and civilian cut, with a gold star hanging from his left breast pocket. Or—

Barrès waited to see no more. He fired at the man who shifted shape. So did the German Maxim gunner. They both started shooting at essentially the same instant. They both scored hits, too, a great many hits. The man—a German officer?—went down and stayed down. He didn't look now like one man, now like another, not any longer. He just looked dead.

"Is that the end of it?" Barrès asked.

"Am I God, that I should know such things?" Fonsagrive returned. "I will tell you what I think, though. What I think is, it will never be over for us, not until we are killed. In the meanwhile, we are obliged to make ourselves as difficult for the *Boche* as we can."

Since Barrès thought the same thing, he did not argue with his loader. Down the trench, someone was screaming, "It burns! Aiee, it burns! The sting, the horrible sting!" Barrès wondered what the absinthe fumes had made that poor *poilu* imagine he was fighting.

And then, clearly audible even through the varnished cloth of his gas helmet, Barrès heard that trumpet sound for a sixth time. "*Merde alors!*" he exclaimed angrily. "Has the *Boche* not yet realized that, whatever his wormwood-filled gas shell may have done to us, it has done likewise to his own men?"

"If our generals are fools, why should the *Boche*'s generals not be fools as well?" Fonsagrive said.

Whatever the wormwood-filled gas shell had done to Barrès, its effects had not left him. Nor, as he'd thought, had they diminished. Rushing hard toward him came a host of cavalry straight from the imagination of a madman. The horses wore breastplates of fire and brimstone; their heads looked like those of lions. Instead of tails, snakes grew from the end of their spines, snakes with great poisonous fangs. The lion heads breathed out flames and smoke. Some of the riders had wings.

"Gas!" Fonsagrive shouted. "Horsemen with poison gas!" Barrès nodded. His gas helmet kept him safe. And he had before him a target of which machine gunners could commonly but dream. He fired and fired and fired, till the cooling fins on the Hotchkiss gun glowed red. Fonsagrive fed him strip after strip of ammunition.

"The *Boche* is mad, to attack us with cavalry," Barrès said. "But however mad he is, they shall not pass!"

That he too was mad, to see the German *Uhlans* as he did, went without saying. But a man who had spent so long breathing absinthe fumes could hardly be expected to remain in his right mind. And anyone on the front lines at Verdun was apt to be mad anyhow. He was sane enough to keep the machine gun pointed in the right direction, and that was the only thing that really mattered.

Some of the improbable-looking cavalry charged back toward the German lines, as had some of the footsoldiers who'd looked to him like giant locusts. The Germans shot them down as cheerfully as Barrès did. He laughed. They were making his work easier for him.

He did not think any of the horsemen got into either set of trenches. Both the Empire and the Central Powers kept cavalry divisions behind their lines, awaiting breakthroughs that never came. Cavalry, in any case, melted under machine-gun fire like frost melting under hot sunshine. To anyone who'd spent time in the trenches, that was obvious. Generals on both sides, though, had a way of staying back at nice, comfortable headquarters. What was obvious to the soldiers who did the fighting and dying must not have seemed so plain ten or twenty kilometers behind the line.

At last, Barrès stopped shooting. "Have we got a jam?" Fonsagrive asked anxiously.

"Not at all," Barrès replied. "The gun performs splendidly. But I see nothing more alive in front of me. Why, then, should I waste cartridges I shall need to try to beat back the next German attack?"

Rain mixed with sleet—Verdun surely had the most

abominable climate in all of France, and yesterday's warmth was forgotten—began pelting down. A great clap of thunder sounded, and another, and another, until there were seven in all. Jacques Fonsagrive laughed. "Do you know, *mon ami*," he said, "that I used to be frightened of thunder, and would hide under my bed during a storm?"

"Artillery fire will cure one of that, *n'est-ce pas?*" Barrès said. "I would like to hide under my bed when the *Boche* shells us. I would like to have a bed under which to hide when the *Boche* shells us."

"An iron bed, by choice," Fonsagrive said. "But yes, after artillery, how is one to lose one's nerve over thunder?" He shook his fist at the sky. "If there is a God up there, which, as I have said, I do not believe, how could He do worse to us than what the Germans and our own officers have visited upon us here? Such a thing would not be possible."

Barrès scratched himself. "It could be that you are right. But it could be that you are wrong, too. After all, when the *Boche* shelled us with poison gas yesterday, he did kill a great many rats, as we both noted."

"I beg your pardon." Fonsagrive's nod was full of exquisite, understated irony. "If God is as all-powerful as most fools say, no doubt He could give us rats and poison gas at the very same time. Or He might simply give the rats gas helmets, which would save Him a miracle."

"Very good. Oh, very good indeed." Barrès clapped his hands. "I wish we had a chaplain here, to listen to these brilliant blasphemies."

"Chaplains are no fools," Fonsagrive said. "Nothing requires that they come to the front line, and so they do not. If nothing required me to come to the front line, I would not either, I assure you."

"Nor I," Pierre Barrès answered. He shrugged. "But the nations are angry. It is the time of the dead. And so we are here: the dead, but not quite yet." The ground shook under his feet. "Is that an earthquake?"

"What a fool you are," Fonsagrive said. "That's someone's ammunition dump going up. I hope very much it is an ammunition dump of the *Boche* going up." He cocked his head to one side, to hear from which direction the roar of the explosion would come.

So did Barrès. He heard no explosion, though, only the endless patter of the rain. And then, though the rain, high and thin, came a seventh trumpet blast. He glanced over to Jacques Fonsagrive. The loader nodded: he had heard it, too. They both braced themselves for whatever the Germans might throw at them next.

"We are not dead yet," Barrès repeated. "We have heard six of these horn calls, and endured them. What is one more?"

"Perhaps one too many," Fonsagrive said. "But then again, perhaps not, also."

The ground shook again. There were lightnings and thunderings. The sleet turned to hail. After shell fragments, hail was at worst a minor nuisance. But, little by little, the foul weather eased. The sun came out once more—not by stealth, as it had before, but simply because the wind blew away the clouds.

Barrès and Fonsagrive both nodded. "It is done," they said together.

They looked at each other. Somehow, it should not have been their voices saying those words, but Another's. They both shrugged. Who had time to think of Another, here in the man-made hell of Verdun? And, as Jacques Fonsagrive had said, what even from the last of days could be worse than that which soldiers endured here?

Barrès took off his gas helmet. A last few raindrops fell, though the sky seemed clear. They tasted of salt, almost as if they were tears.

A buzzing in the air swiftly swelled to a mechanical roar. With a grunt of fright, Barrès threw himself into the hole he'd scraped in the trench. Bullets from the machine guns of several low-flying *avions* decked with black crosses chewed up the French entrenchments. Men screamed as they were wounded.

As soon as the *avions* had passed, Barrès emerged and sent what ammunition was left in his machine gun after them. He did not think he scored any hits. A man on the ground with a Hotchkiss gun knocked down an *avion* only by luck. He knew it. He accepted it. But if a man on the ground did not bet, how could he hope to win?

Maybe his puny act of defiance angered the Germans. Whatever the reason, their artillery opened up on the position his regiment occupied. A man on the ground with a Hotchkiss gun could no nothing whatever against artillery. Barrès knew that, too. He had trouble accepting it. That was one of the reasons he hated gunners so much.

Slow as usually, the French artillery eventually got around to responding to the *Boche* bombardment. That tardiness was another reason why Barrès hated gunners, even gunners in *horizon bleu*. Also as usual, all too many of the French shells fell short and landed on the same trenches the Germans were pounding. That gave Barrès— and every other *poilu*—a most excellent reason for hating his own gunners.

By the time the two rival sets of artillerymen (so Barrès supposed they were, even if they sometimes seemed joined in a malign alliance against the French infantry) had finished plowing up the trenches and the ground between them, no one could have told from what manner of creature the chunks of flesh out there had come. Germans? Very likely. Horses? Very likely. Giant locusts with scorpion stings? No one could not have proved otherwise.

Little by little, the shelling slowed. Barrès came out of his hole, wondering if the *Boche* intended rushing up the slope at him. But the men in field gray seemed content for the time being to stay where they were. He took out a tin of *singe*, opened it, and stared resignedly at the red, red meat inside.

Jacques Fonsagrive was opening some tinned beef, too.

"I wonder if the *cuistots* will be able to get more bread up here any time soon," he said.

"Whether they do or not, we'll get by," Barrès answered. "We still have monkey meat and we still have *pinard*. We can go on a while longer."

"You have reason, *mon vieux*," Fonsagrive said. "And the fighting's been a little quieter the last couple of days, eh?"

"Yes, I think so." Barrès nodded, then shrugged. "Who knows? I would not care to bet on it, but we might even live. You have any more tobacco?" Fonsagrive passed him a *Gitane*. He lit it and took a long drag. "Ahh. Thanks. That's good, by God."

The Call
Joel Rosenberg

°ring° °ring° °ring°
Hello. Joel here.
Joel, it's God.
Carl? You sound kind of funn—
No, not Carl. God. God.
I must be hearing you wrong—could you spell that?
God. Capital G. O. D. God.
I *don't* need this. °click°

°ring° °ring°
Yes?
Joel, it's God.
This is an unlisted number.
I know.
I mean—
I know what you mean. Really.
—as I was *saying*, I don't know how you got it, but there's
a reason why I keep it unlisted. I've got a book that's
overdue, two kids, and a wife, and a dog, and not a lot of
time for phone pranks—
This isn't a prank. It's God.
You keep saying that, and—
I want you to listen to—
—interrupting me. Well, I hope you've enjoyed your
little prank; I have to get to work now. Have a nice—

Ouch! Shit, that hurt.

I know. And—

I mean, this is ridiculous, I'm just sitting here, and I get a pain in the right nut that feels like somebody put it in a vise, and—

Testicle. The proper term is testicle. Here's another, just a bit worse.

Yeow! Okay, okay, what's the joke? How did you do that?

Joel, I'm God. Really.

Well . . .

Yes, yes, I know. It's usually like this. I've been through this before. Several times, in fact. It doesn't get a lot easier. But never mind . . .

I mean, damn, that hurt. I don't know—

It was meant to get your attention. Do I have your attention, or do you need another jolt?

But what's really—*yeeeow!* I can't *believe* how much that hurt.

Believe it. But take it easy; we're done with pain. I knew it would distract you, but if I hadn't tried it, you would have taken another ten minutes to take Me seriously. I've got all the time in the world, but I don't necessarily want to spend more of it on the phone with you.

How did—?

I know these things. Let's try another one: Take your right hand out of your pocket and look at it.

What the—

Looks like snow, all over it. No?

Yes, it—

It's called leprosy. You don't see a lot of it around, not these days. okay, now stick your hand back in your pocket, then pull it out again.

Why—

Because I said so. Just *do* it.

Okay. Hey—

It looks normal now. It *is* normal now. You want me to do it again?

N-no. But this is kind of confusing. I—

Well, yes it is confusing—for you—but if you concentrate on what I'm saying, it'll all go quicker.

Okay. So you really are God. Umm, well, er, I mean, like, uh, it wasn't really my fault that—

Oh, relax. I didn't call you up on the phone to talk to you about that. Or that, or that, or even *that*, although you really ought to have known better. And as for the blasphemy you're worrying about now, tell Me something: would you go to a lot of trouble to punish an amoeba who gave you the finger?

Well, no, I wouldn't, I guess.

You sure?

I'm pretty sure. I mean—

I know what you mean. So don't sweat it. We can talk about that some other time, maybe. Now, pay attention: I'm God. I called you up because I want you to do something for Me.

Now, wait a minute. You're calling me on the phone. You're *God*, and you're calling me on the *phone*.

You know, there are times I really wish I'd done a better job with this free will stuff. Yes, I'm calling you on the phone. Would you have preferred a burning bush?

Actually, I would—

I knew that. But that's a rhetorical question. Forget it: you don't get the burning bush. You are going to get an entirely undeserved swelled head that I called you in the first place; I don't want to add to that, and it's My call, not yours. You don't get the burning bush, you don't get parting-the-waters, you don't get the voice out of the storm—and trust Me, you really *don't* want the voice out of the storm—you don't even get Jonah's gourd. Understood?

I guess so. But—

But how can you be sure it's really Me? If the leprosy wasn't enough, what *would* be enough to prove it to you?

Well—

That was another rhetorical question. And the answer is no. I'm God, not Robin Williams. I'm not going to give you any wishes, and even if I did give you some, you wouldn't get that one, anyways. Not that it's any of your business, but Valerie Bertinelli is happily married, and she has free will, too.

But—

No. Not even water into wine.

I—

Oh, very well: one quick one. See that glass of water on the desk?

Sure. I poured it just before the phone rang. Trying to cut down on coffee, and—

Yes, I know. Pick it up. Take a sip.

Waitaminute. I know I poured myself water, but that's—

Freshly squeezed orange juice. From Byerly's. Pretty good; just the right amount of pulp. You listen closely; I play nice. Understand?

Yes, er, my lor—er, well, what *do* I call you?

God will be fine. Or you can call Me anything, really; it's not a big deal. For Me.

Well, I mean, like—

I know, I know. There's that tetragrammaton, and the whole elohim thing, and the My Lord stuff, and all of that. But, don't worry about it. Call Me anything you want. I don't mind.

You mean, like, Fred?

Sure. Would it be easier if you just called Me Fred?

Well, yeah, it would. That's strange, how did You . . . never mind. Another one of those rhetorical questions, eh?

Yes.

Takes a bit of getting used to, doesn't it?

Well, not for Me.

I see your point. Okay, er, Fred. What can I do for You?

Start by sitting back down in front of your computer, please. Good. Now, bring up Automap—don't panic: you left the disk under that copy of *Playboy*, yes, right next to that stack of bills.

Got it. Hang on a sec . . . okay, it's coming up.

Good. Now, there's this little town in Pennsylvania called Nineveh . . .

Leeward of Broken Jerusalem
Carla Montgomery

He was lost.

A branch clawed his face as he tripped again in the dark and the sting spread across his cheek in a razor-thin line. Black tree trunks. Dripping water. Around him, the sound of urgent prayers rose out of the forest and hung in the air with the mist. There were no fires.

It was almost dawn. He had to find him before it started.

He slipped and went down on his hands and knees in cold mud. Before him, a figure separated itself from the murk and stalked away into the woods.

He got to his feet and stumbled after it, shouting for him, for all of them, to stop.

Harry woke with the sharp realization he had just been elbowed in the ribs.

"You're yelling again," the woman lying next to him answered before he could ask. She mumbled something and turned over, pulling his half of the sheets with her.

He sat up and tried to remember something about the dream while his fingers rubbed the sore spot on his side. It was gone. There was nothing left of it but the same sense of dread and barely-controlled panic he had woken with every morning for the past seven years.

Why him?

Harry stood up and crossed the bedroom of the bungalow

to the window, keeping one eye out for the scorpions that scuttled around the tiles at night. A breeze smelling of oleander and the sea drifted in through the open louvers. The sounds of the surf rose fifty yards away. It would be a clear day, good for flying. With any luck, the supply planes would be in by noon.

Involuntarily, his gaze followed the still-darkened horizon to the northwest, to the sullen glow spreading out from the continent like a cancerous cloud. Tokyo. Sao Paulo. New York. Again, he watched the immolated cities, choked with the dead and dying, collapse in charred husks as the chaos began. Moscow. Washington. Beijing. Casualties of the war. Los Angeles. Baghdad. Hong Kong. Incinerated to prevent the Judgment Plague from spreading. Mexico City. Bombay. His own lost London transformed into a place out of hell—Auschwitz and the Blitz and Poe's Red Death combined.

He saw again the transmissions of the skeletal hordes pouring out of the Tubes at night to prowl its wasted streets. The old woman on the stairs trying to beat off a pack of dogs. A child caught gnawing a human finger. His own father, blindfolded and bloody, fighting to remain on his feet as the mob pelted him with rubble from the ruins of the Tower. And, in the last dim flickers, the jumbled stuff of nightmares and ancient myth, somehow alive and moving, before the blue screens mercifully went dead.

Whatever it was, it was growing, getting closer each day. It was only a matter of time before it would be on top of them. They all knew it. Someone had to do something.

Harry glared at the dull redness smeared across the sky, a laughing, blood-caked mouth.

"Right." He sneered at it. "Me and what army?"

The rooster he had tried to shoot twice crowed in the yard. It was getting close to dawn. He began to dress, watching the sleeping woman's bare chest rise and fall, noticing again the way the white sheets made her skin look dark as molasses and soft as satin. Martinique, named after her mother's island. She was the owner of Falstaff's, the only decent pub left in the Virgin Islands. Her father, she said, had been a British cricket player.

She stirred when he kissed her. He left before she could open her eyes.

The sun rose out of the Atlantic and masked the eerie glow in the north as Harry walked the two-mile stretch of cracked asphalt to the airstrip at Taylors Bay. Cars were outlawed on the islands. All the fuel they managed to get their hands on was hoarded for the planes and supply boats that kept the fragile network of the West Indies going.

"Good morning, Your Highliness," a deep, Jamaican voice rolled out from under a grove of palm trees beside the road.

It was Clarence "Juju" Leonards, leader of the island bush pilots and Harry's closest advisor. Harry hated it when he called him that.

"Morning, Juju," said Harry.

The tall man stepped out of the shade to Harry's side with a fluid grace. They walked together for a while in silence.

Behind the easy smile and the dreadlocks, Leonards had one intense passion. Flying. His lime-and-fuschia twin engine was famous in the Caribbean and he worked hard to keep the stories growing. But he was a hero who had little tolerance for the mundane aspects of maintaining island life, a man who preferred to simply go his own road. Nothing could keep him earthbound for long.

They understood each other. Both of them knew the only reason half the islanders followed Harry was because Juju followed him.

"You look like you want to walk all the way to Trinidad this mornin', Harry," Leonards said, laughing softly. "Rough night?"

Harry ignored the jab. There were sounds of yelling coming from down the street.

"What's going on over there?" he asked.

"Maybe I shouldn't tell you," said Juju. "Don't know if you're in the mood for Nimley and Poole. I passed them on my way here."

"They're at it again?" Harry glanced at the man beside him. "What's it this time?"

"A goat. Nimley says Poole stole his best milker. Poole's got it locked up in his attic."

Juju tossed his dreadlocks impatiently and stared down the street. The muscles of his jaw clenched, released.

"The poor beast's got its head stuck out the window, bleating to wake the devil, and the old coots look ready to kill each other this time," he said. "The whole neighborhood's out cheering for them to hurry up and do it. Want me to handle it?"

Harry sighed. After three years of dealing with the feud, Leonards would probably settle things by slamming their heads together.

"No. I'll take care of them," he said. "You go on ahead. There's a flight due in at 0900 from Kingston. Meds, I hope."

"And I hope we don't have to waste them on those two fools," said Juju.

Harry watched him saunter around the corner, then headed toward the noise at the end of the street.

It took awhile to break up the jeering crowd and send them on their daily business. Then Harry sat down on the canary yellow steps of Poole's front porch and listened to the embellished grievances of the old men while the goat stamped and carried on overhead. At last, they wound down to a few sputters. Harry fined them one prize milkgoat for disturbing the peace and told them to keep out of sight of each other for at least a week.

It was nearly noon and the sun was high in the tropical sky. Harry borrowed a bike from the fruit seller across the street, handed him the goat, and pedaled the rest of the way to Taylors Bay.

He was hungry and hot when he finally reached the landing strip. The others, a group of about fifteen men and women, were gathered around a table in the shade of the single hangar. They looked worried.

"Sandoval's got some news for us," said Leonards. "It's no good."

Harry's stomach turned. He asked one of the crew to pass him the water pitcher. He poured a glass and sat down.

"Tell me."

"I was in Kingston two nights ago," the young pilot said. He paused, shook his head as if to wake himself.

"Cuba's gone."

"Gone?"

The pilot ran one hand through his short, dark hair.

"I was supposed to fly into Guantanamo for equipment in the morning," he said. "We were having a couple of beers that night in the hangar. You know, working on the planes. And we started picking up this mayday on the shortwave. It was weird. Crazy sounding. They said they'd lost Havana the night before, that people were killing each other. They kept begging us to come get 'em out. We didn't know what to do. Then there was this sound like a hurricane coming in, fast, and all of a sudden they start yelling this stuff about a red wall and diablos and shit."

Sandoval looked up at Harry with strangely lit eyes.

"Then, there was something else there. I heard it."

He glanced around the group.

"I got in my plane and flew like hell."

Harry sat back in his chair. The water glass shook slightly in his hand and he quickly set it on the table.

"There's something else," a woman's voice broke the tense silence. It was Yorke. "I just flew in from Santo Domingo. Every boat in the Caribbean's making for us."

In some ways, it made sense, Harry thought. Theirs was the most remote, inhabited island in the West Indies, just leeward of a deserted blip known as Broken Jerusalem.

It was the easternmost point of the curve before the archipelago swept down again to South America. The refugees were fleeing as far away from the thing bearing down on them as could get. But what did they think they'd find when they got there? There was barely enough to feed the existing population of stragglers that had gathered there over the last seven years. Fresh water was even scarcer. What would he do with them all?

Harry cursed under his breath. Damn it. Why wasn't his brother here to deal with this?

The next two hours were spent arguing over various strategies. Harry sent a message to Martinique to call a town council meeting later that afternoon. Someone brought him a couple of biscuits smeared with goat cheese and a mug of coffee. He took one and bit into it. It tasted like a buttered scouring pad.

"What's the word on the *San Juan*?" he asked.

"Invited themselves to a party on St. Croix last week and made the usual mess," said Juju, quietly. "No one's heard from them since."

One of the formerly American bush pilots pounded the table with his fist and stood.

"Geez, it's like they think they're on some sort of cruise or something."

A few of the others around the table looked uncomfortably at each other. The crew of the *San Juan* had earned a reputation early on as having more in common with a band of pirates than a military vessel. When the U.S. Navy had finally unraveled, they had opted to stick together on their own terms. Now, they drifted around the Caribbean, taking what they could get away with and keeping their allegiance to themselves. It rubbed a lot of the islanders, especially their former countrymen, the wrong way.

Harry stared into his coffee mug for a moment. The crew of the *San Juan* was young, too young for this, but he needed them. He only hoped he could keep them entertained long enough to make use of their ship.

"They'll think differently when that thing gets here, won't they?" he said, forcing a brief smile at the angry pilot. There were a few nervous laughs. He looked at Leonards.

"Juju, I want you to take a team out and find that ship. I don't care what you promise 'em. Just get them here."

Leonards nodded, began signaling some of the pilots around the table.

"Jamy, Yorke, Sandoval, Greene," Harry said to the others. "I want you to stay here for now. Contact Bitter End and tell them what to expect up there. If anything else comes in, find me and let me know."

He paused.

"No one besides you touches equipment or fuel. I want the weapons ready, but locked up safe, right?"

"Right." They replied together.

"The rest of you are coming into town with me," he said. "We've got to get the docks ready before dark."

The group started to break up. Harry crammed half a biscuit in his mouth and washed it down with a gulp of the weak brew. He stood and tossed what was left of the liquid into the gravel outside the hanger. How long had it been since he had tasted a real cup of tea?

Plane engines sputtered, then roared. He eyed his silver single engine, wishing he were going with them, then led the way back to Spanish Town.

Harry sat in his usual dark corner outside Falstaff's. It was the one place where, even if they saw through the baseball cap and sunglasses, they left him alone.

He nursed his third drink and listened to the sounds of steel drums and pool drift out the open door of the bar. He could hear one of his crew inside loudly retelling Sandoval's story amid shouts from the other patrons to shut up while a faltering chorus belted a drinking song that died off into laughter. Martinique was doing a good business tonight. Harry swirled the dark liquid in his glass and took another drink. He was looking forward to closing time.

After the initial panic, the council meeting had settled into a sort of stunned acceptance. Harry had outlined the situation and offered his tentative plan. Martinique helped convince the other council members to adopt it. The marketplace just off the docks would become a temporary refugee camp until the newcomers could be relocated to some of the larger, uninhabited islands nearby. Food and water rations would be tightened. The locals would be asked to donate what they could spare.

The *San Juan* had been spotted late that afternoon, just off of Jost Van Dyke. They wanted two nights in Spanish Town and twice the usual rum to help transport refugees and supplies. In the end, they settled for a day and night in Long Bay, three miles up the beach, and a triple load of rum once the job was finished.

Harry filled his glass again.

They could have the booze for all he cared. It was the one thing he had in endless supply. But he wasn't about to let them into town afterward. Not that crew. He wondered how long the alcohol would hold them.

Someone began to whistle nearby. Harry looked up past the low, bamboo fence of the courtyard to the street. Two cows, tied to a rusted parking meter, chewed blankly. Beyond them, a man walked down the center of the deserted road, his white slacks and T-shirt glowing slightly in the last of the twilight. Something about the way he moved made Harry lean forward. The man paused across the street from him, took out a cigarette, and struck a match. Yellow light bounced up and off of his face.

Harry started and blinked. When he looked again, the man was gone. A faint whiff of tobacco drifted to him on the air.

"What's wrong, Harry? You don't like the fish tonight?"

Martinique slid into the chair across from him. She was wearing a dress the color of ripe mango. He wanted to kiss her.

"No, Mar, the food's fine, as always," he said. "I just saw

someone. Some guy with a cigarette. For a second, he looked like Will."

"You still miss him, don't you."

She reached across the table and picked up his glass. Harry watched her raise it to her mouth.

Miss him? That was part of it. The two brothers had been spearfishing off Anegada, when it happened seven years ago. One minute, William had been next to him aiming at a prize snapper and the next, he had disappeared in a vortex of bubbles and noise. The fishing party had thought it was a freak shark attack. They had searched the area until darkness forced them to give up. It wasn't until they got back to Bitter End that they found out what had happened. Millions of people, everywhere, gone without a trace.

Sure, he missed him. And sometimes, he hated him.

Prince William, always the good son. Always so ready to step up and fulfill his destiny. He was gone before the real shit even began. Damn him! He hadn't had to watch it, hadn't even had to die like their father, just disappeared and left him king by default. Only there weren't any Britains anymore, just a ruptured, poisoned world of the desperate and the dying. He was Harry the Ninth of Nothing. He hadn't even felt a tug.

"There's a lot of things I miss," he said, holding his hand out for the glass. Martinique hesitated, then gave it back to him. She shrugged.

"Sure, Harry, we all do," she said, and stood again. "But some of us have bars to run."

She started to walk away. A loud crash and raised voices inside the building stopped her before she got halfway across the candlelit courtyard. Harry was on his feet in an instant. He reached her just as a man holding a bottle lurched out of the open door, tripped on the top stair and sprawled, howling, to the ground in front of them.

He was wearing a tattered navy dinner jacket with a gold anchor unraveling on the breast pocket—a member

of the stranded yacht club set. His salt-and-pepper beard
was trimmed short. He teetered to his feet and spun,
shaking the bottle he still clenched in one hand at the
crowd gathered in the doorway behind him.

"It's the winepress of God, I tell you!" he screamed.
He staggered backwards and waved the bottle wildly in
the direction of the red glow that pulsed like a malignant
borealis in the northwestern sky. It was brighter tonight.

One of the bartenders started down the stairs. The drunk
sidestepped and turned back toward Harry and Martinique.
His gaze, blue and unfocused, fell on her.

"Don't you see?" he hissed, staggering forward. "We're
dead already. Rotten. Pulp under His feet."

Harry stepped in front of Martinique.

Quick as a striking snake, the bottle flashed toward his
head. He ducked, taking her down with him. The bottle
smashed into the fence behind them.

"Drowning! Drowning in a river of blood!" the drunk
screeched. He shook his fists at the sky, then ran out into
the street.

The crowd stood silent until the man's screams faded
into the island night.

Harry held Martinique tight against him as they walked
to her place. They made love like cornered animals until
exhausted, they slept.

*Horses were screaming, crumpling around him with
sharpened stakes protruding from their chests and sides.
Floundering men in mail hacked at each other with swords
and maces. Others stabbed wildly around them with pikes
and clumsy knives until they fell and were trampled
underfoot. Red puddles formed and spread in the churned-
up mire. The air rang with the shouts of the wounded
and the whine of arrows.*

*Then he saw him, circled by a wall of men with shields,
his armor smeared with grime and blood. The golden circlet
around his helmet was bent on one side.*

Harry pushed his way forward through the chaos. A man with a sword rushed at him, then fell at his feet screaming in French, an arrow embedded in his cheek.

The circle of knights had broken and disappeared. He looked around frantically, slid deeper into the mud of Agincourt.

Then he was in shadow. A rearing black horse, the edges of its eyes white with terror, loomed over him. Foam flew from its mouth as it tossed its great head. The rider, all in black armor, tilted its horned helmet toward him. It seemed to shake with laughter. Harry couldn't move. The rider raised its sword as the horse reared high again and, with a sudden motion, drew the weapon across the animal's muscled neck. Black hooves raked the air as a crimson fountain burst from the horse's throat, spraying Harry in blood. Its death scream went on forever as it toppled like a falling tower toward him.

Harry was halfway down the hall before he was fully awake. Another dream. This time, he knew he had been yelling. He closed his eyes and leaned against the wall for long minutes until his heart stopped slamming against his ribs. Martinique wasn't in the house, had probably gone out on her morning swim. Her orange dress lay glowing in a sunbeam where she had tossed it the night before.

It was still early. He needed to get out.

He found her in her usual spot.

For a while, they swam together. She pointed out the parrotfish and sea urchins that still managed to survive in the shallows of Devil's Bay. He found an octopus eating a shellfish. The tentacled creature pulled the shell after it as it slipped into a hiding place in the reef and watched them in turn with intelligent eyes. When they tired, they climbed out to warm their bodies on the golden sand and stare across the waters of Sir Francis Drake's Channel.

A dozen other islands jutted up out of the sea around

them. The Dogs. Ginger Island. Tortola. Each with a story to tell. Salt Island. Where the rocks were half crystal and looked like rock candy but tasted like tears. Once, New World adventurers had anchored offshore and used the pulverized stones to preserve the fish in their holds, laying it in until their ships sank low in the water and they were ready to roam and plunder again. There was Dead Chest, where Blackbeard left fifteen mutinous men to die with nothing but a chest full of rum, and Money Bay that had inspired Robert Louis Stevenson to write *Treasure Island*.

He looked southward to an ugly tumble of boulders and stunted manchineel trees that dripped acid when it rained. Broken Jerusalem. Its half-sunken twin, Fallen Jerusalem, lay just beyond.

Nothing lived on them anymore. Now, the pilots used them for target practice, flying low in their jury-rigged airplanes, dropping homemade bombs out the windows, dipping and careening like angry gulls. Their histories melted away bit by bit, tiny pieces of civilization blown into the sky and swallowed into the sea with a steamy hiss.

Perhaps that was as it should be, thought Harry. It was all sinking back where it came from now.

The wind shifted. Clouds like wind-filled sails appeared in the northwest. Harry searched for signs of the first refugee boats on the horizon. They were coming.

"Do you ever remember when you were a kid?" Martinique asked. "Anything was possible then, you know?"

She turned to face him, eyes hidden behind mirrored glasses.

"I mean, I was always planning out what I would be, who I'd marry, if I'd have kids."

She put a brown hand on his arm.

"Harry," she said. "I don't think about any of that anymore."

The boats started arriving that afternoon. Sailboats. Ferries. Rusty fishing boats. Dilapidated yachts. Even the

old glassbottom tour boat from St. John. All of them ready
to sink under the weight of the people and animals and
jumbled belongings piled on board. Far too few of them
carried food or water.

They worked solidly until long after dark. Juju's group
secured the boats to the docks and tried to keep family
members together until the mostly useless things they
had brought with them were unloaded and sorted out.
Harry and his team did what they could to rig flimsy
shelters up in the marketplace stalls and settle disputes
over space. Martinique got her cooks started on a food
line, then organized volunteers from the town to turn the
General Store into a supply warehouse. Even the doctor
from Bitter End showed up to treat dehydration and minor
injuries.

All of them listened to the terrified stories of flight again
and again.

By midnight, the harbor looked like a floating trailer
park and the marketplace of Spanish Town had been
transformed into a tangled warren of people too tired and
afraid to do anything but stare at each other in the
torchlight. More were still arriving, but they would have
to wait offshore until morning.

Harry picked his way across the square, trying not to
step on any of the sprawling forms. The wind had picked
up during the day and the water was getting choppy. A
baby cried somewhere like an abandoned bird. He needed
to rest.

"You're him, aren't you?"

The thin voice came from a cot as he passed. Harry
stopped and looked at the occupant. It was an elderly
woman, frail-looking, wrapped in a worn shawl for a
blanket. Her accent brought back memories of small town
pubs and rolling pastures.

"I'm sorry, I didn't hear you," Harry said, stepping closer.

"You're King Henry," she whispered, motioning him
nearer. "Poor Charles' boy."

She held out her hand to him weakly. Harry hesitated, then took it. It felt light as a child's.

"My husband and I came here to find you," she said, smiling up at him. She closed her eyes.

"We knew you'd know what to do."

Early the next morning, the *San Juan* churned in across the channel and pulled in. The gray bulk of the nuclear-powered cruiser nearly blocked the entrance to the harbor. They wasted no time calling in.

"What the hell is going on?" the current captain, a pit bull of a man by the name of Hoffman, demanded over the spare radio Harry had set up inside the doctor's tent. "We had to dodge that fleet of idiots the whole way!"

"You guys should really pay more attention," said Harry. He explained the situation, reminded them of their agreement.

"You'll start loading supplies for Cooper Island immediately," he said. "Passengers this afternoon. You read?"

There was a long pause before the sneered reply.

"Yes . . . sir."

The weather worsened. Strange, yellow clouds sped across the sky from the north and west. A dry wind topped the swells with white and turned the sea from turquoise to jade to dirty gray. It clouded over and rained briefly, splattering the barrels and pans set out to catch the precious water with a rust-colored liquid that reeked of sulphur.

The refugees kept coming, clinging to anything that would float until the harbor was choked. Then they swarmed the beaches, delirious and confused. Some shrieked about alien war machines and bat-winged demons swooping out of the sky, while Harry and the others tried to calm them down. The later ones only clutched the arms that held them in silent terror or rocked back and forth with worm-eaten stares. Slowly, they began to fall into fever and unconsciousness.

The doctor said it was something she had never seen

before. Harry wanted to think it was some sort of neuro-logical weapon. He knew it was something else.

The day grew darker and oppressively hot. Some of the weaker rafts began to fall apart in the harbor and sink as the rising wind drove the waves higher. The crowd in the marketplace grew more and more restless. Rumors flew. Jamaica and Haiti were gone. Puerto Rico was under attack. Harry noticed the townspeople glancing nervously at each other and begin to drift away.

Some of the island members of the First Church of the Redemption arrived in the afternoon, marching through the town in a loud procession and into the middle of the camp. They had been at it for hours now, shouting the Word into a bullhorn and singing against the wind about atonement and Judgment Day. Harry was ready to arrest the entire lot.

"Harry?" Leonards poked his head inside the doorway of the doctor's tent where Harry had been trying to contact the *San Juan*. They weren't receiving.

"What is it?"

"We've got a problem with that first group of evacuees," he said. "They won't leave."

The crowd closed in behind the two men as they made their way to the group at the entrance of the square. The evacuees sat calmly in a circle, their hair whipping in the wind. The boats waiting to ferry them to the warship bucked wildly in the surf. Spray flew in the air with each wave that crashed into the docks and heavy, misshapen clouds crept low over the water.

"You can't make us go back out there," a Hispanic man with lopsided glasses shouted over the wind.

"But you can't stay, there isn't enough water," Harry tried to explain. "There's a spring on Cooper Island."

"How do we know you won't just leave us there and take our stuff?" said a teen clutching a smashed cardboard box on her lap. Something inside of it whined. A murmur rose from the crowd behind him.

Harry raised his hands for silence.

"It's the only way," he said. "We'll be back next month with more animals and supplies," said Henry.

"No you won't," another voice shouted over the crowd. It was one of the First Churchers, a large woman standing on a table holding the bullhorn. She pointed it upwards.

"There isn't gonna be a next month."

Above them, the sun went out behind a bank of eerily lit clouds. A ripple ran through the crowd as twilight spilled over the refugee camp. Then, a flash of light shot up over the harbor into the premature night. A flare from the warship. It hung in the air, casting strange shadows across the crowded square, then plunged downward. Someone screamed. Darkness and bedlam descended as the light fell into the water and went out.

Harry and Juju shoved their way through the milling chaos back to the hospital tent. They found Martinique at the radio.

"It's the *San Juan*," she said. "You better listen."

"I repeat," said a shaking voice Harry didn't recognize. "St. Croix just disappeared. No longer responding. We're getting out."

"Who is this? That you, Hoffman?"

There was a long pause.

"Hoffman isn't here. This is the new captain."

"You can't leave. We need more time."

"No such thing," said the voice. "We might still outrun it in the open if we leave now."

"Damn it! There are people here, stranded," shouted Harry. "Take some of them with you."

The radio crackled with static.

"Good luck," it said. "Over."

Martinique and Juju followed Harry back out into the square. The crazed mob was beginning to boil out into the streets of the town. A green flash of lightning flickered on the hull of the *San Juan* as it pulled away from the harbor. The slow roar of thunder followed in the distance, like a hungry beast pacing the northwestern sky. A wall of shifting, reddish cloud was descending on the horizon.

"It's closing on us," said Harry.

Suddenly, above the din, distant shots echoed from the direction of the airstrip.

"The guns!" shouted Leonards. "They're breaking into the hangar!"

He began pushing his way through the frenzy.

Harry grabbed Martinique.

"Get to Falstaff's," he said.

She shook her head, opened her mouth to speak. Someone sprawled into them. Harry was knocked to the ground and she was yanked away from him into the thrashing sea of people. He was kicked hard in the back and someone drew blood down his forearm with their fingernails. A heavy foot ground his hand into the dirt. Harry clawed his way to his feet again, oblivious to the pain. He was carried out of the marketplace by the press and tossed into a narrow alleyway. Martinique was gone.

Lightning struck again over the channel. Then closer. Harry felt the hair on the back of his neck rise. Overhead, the sky throbbed with red light. He started to walk, then run. Something in the wind began to hiss beside him, the sound of ancient languages whispered in dark places. A voice like a serpent's hovered near his ear.

"But if the cause be not good, the king himself hath a heavy reckoning to make . . ."

He stopped, whirled. There was no one there. The wind gibbered and rattled the fronds of a bent palm tree. A dog barked. He heard a brittle crack, turned to see a web of lines spread outward on the window of the building next to him. The window bulged outward, then exploded in a shower of glass.

Harry ran madly through burning streets where shadowy figures looted and fought. The voices in the storm laughed and roared while devils in human skin leapt in the firelight and danced under a blazing, wine-colored sky.

✧   ✧   ✧

Harry's arms burned. He looked down at his own gloved hands, shaking with exhaustion on the hilt of a sword. The knights pressing around him panted in the heat. Around them, the dead lay twisted in gory heaps. Soldiers circled across the battlefield, pulling together again into tight formations.

"Our archers are spent, sire," said one of them in Leonards' voice.

Only Leonards was dead now. He'd seen him fall out of the sky in a thousand glowing pieces, his plane crumpled and batted by a cloud like a giant clawed hand.

"They are preparing to charge," said another. Sandoval? Yorke?

No. Both of them dead, too. He'd found them. Sandoval, shot just outside the burning hangar. Yorke, stretched out in the gravel by her plane.

A short man—was it Jamy? Greene?—burst forward and grabbed at his arm.

"They're attacking the baggage train! We're surrounded!"

Desperate shouts and the ring of metal rose from the trees behind him.

They were trapped. They would all die here. The knights stared at him expectantly.

"Kill the prisoners," he said.

"Please, don't shoot me."

Slowly, the red mist cleared away from Harry's eyes. A man was kneeling in the ashes before him, face frantic with fear. Behind him, the blackened walls of Falstaff's sent thick coils of smoke to join the pall that hung over the town.

In his hands, Harry held the muzzle of a revolver pressed to the pleading man's forehead. Slowly, he pulled them back. The man scrambled to his feet in the dust, backed away to the edge of the street, and bolted.

Frayed images buzzed and melted in Harry's mind.

Nimley, crying, rocking Poole's broken body on canary yellow stairs. The man in white half-buried in sand, the gash on his forehead a drying, crimson crown. Juju dying in a fountain of flames. An old woman's voice calling, faintly, "Where is the king?"

The gun thudded to the ground.

Harry walked through the empty, smoldering streets of Spanish Town. He realized, numbly, that the voices in the wind were gone and the air was still, expectant. All the red had spilled out of the sky and drained away to gray.

He found Martinique on her beach, watching a few boats with tattered sails pull away from the shoreline.

"They burned my bar," she said. "They burned everything."

He looked at her. Her face and arms were bruised and smudged with soot. Her clothes were singed.

"It's not too late to try and leave," he said, softly.

"Leave? And go where? There's no place left to go."

She picked up a broken shell, threw it hard into the waves.

"Listen, Harry," she said. "We fought, I fought, to keep it going here, but it's over. This is it, the end, and I'm not going anywhere."

The gray above them was stirring. She took one of his hands in hers. It was still wet from the shell.

"This is my home," she said. "I'll wait for it here."

"I can't do that," he said.

She kissed him.

"I know."

He left her standing with her feet in the sea.

In the east, a pale, muddy light was growing behind tattered ribbons of cloud. The sky was turning from gray to lavender. Dawn. The last dawn of the world.

Harry circled the ruins of the island once in his plane, then dove and flew close to the water, a silver pelican, taking one last look at Long Bay and Savannah Beach.

He spotted the tiny figure of Martinique sitting on a boulder at the southern tip of the island and dipped a wing in salute. She waved.

He was over Broken Jerusalem now, desolate and lonely. His radio chirped. He picked it up. Heard nothing.

Martinique was right. It was over. All the monuments, the empires and the cities swept away. How many had died for the causes of kings? How many for governments? Beliefs? It was all gone now, an ephemeral dream. Gone with the universities and strip malls, the churches and homes.

There were no Jerusalems, only the fallen, the broken. Without them, there could be no kings.

The east turned rose and gold. Harry angled his plane into the glare of the rising sun and the roar of the engines swelled in him, the sound of wing beats and music.

Below him, the ocean flashed and danced like mercury as the last king of the west disappeared into the crystal sky.

O'er the Land of the Freaks and the Home of the Braves

Gregory Nicoll

Rett and Steve generally agreed that the three things they'd missed the most since The Day The Bomb Dropped were toilet paper, Hershey bars, and pussy—though not necessarily in that order. There were times, however, when either boy would have traded his left nut and dozen .44-caliber hollowpoints for something as basic as a big bucket full of springwater and coupla inches of hose bandage.

This was one of those times.

They both knew that a man could survive out here in newly invaded Braves territory with a sore ass, a sweet tooth, and stiff cock; but without a fast and reliable ride back home to Shelter, he was as good as scalped and sodomized already.

Steve ran a greasy hand through the rough, sweaty tangles of his long brown hair, keenly aware of its worth to their enemies. "Got any ideas, Rett?" he asked quietly.

Rett felt a chill pass over him and zipped his jacket up more tightly. It was getting cold much earlier these days, and the warmth of their little armored truck's disabled diesel engine wouldn't last long. He couldn't hazard a guess as to how its radiator hose had been punctured, and he was completely mystified as to how far they were right now from the nearest mountain stream; but with darkness falling rapidly they needed to prepare for the unpleasant prospect of late-night raiders.

"Okay, first let's move her off the road a piece," he said.

Steve pushed from the rear gate while Rett applied his weight against the doorframe on the driver's side, steering as he shoved. The metal was cold to the touch of their bare hands but the truck's engine was still warm, its exhaust pipe smelling powerfully of the cooking grease and animal fat it used as fuel. The little vehicle rolled slowly at first, weighted down by its cargo of dark glass-bottled homebrew, but it picked up speed as it left the paved road and rumbled down the embankment. Then the tall grasses and thick shrubs caught it and, bending slowly under their unexpected burden, eased it to a stop.

Rett wiped a droplet of perspiration from his forehead and nodded at the truck where it lay askew in its resting place. "Good enough," he said.

"Hey, it looks like we cleared the runway just in time," observed Steve.

Rett's brow furrowed. "Runway?"

Steve smiled. "Yeah. Air Traffic Control's routed a 747 our way."

Rett couldn't remember the last time he'd seen an airplane. Five, maybe six years ago? A helluva lot longer if you were talking anything resembling a commercial passenger jet. He was about to point this out when the distinct clip-clop of metal horseshoes on Georgia blacktop caught his attention. Following the other boy's intent stare, he spun in place and looked back up the road.

Although it was clearly traveling on the ground, the bizarre conveyance heading straight toward them did look vaguely like an airplane at first glance. But only at first.

It was, foremost, a stagecoach. Looking like a prop from a John Wayne western, it was pulled by a team of six lathered brown horses and rumbled noisily forward on huge spoked wooden wheels. A tiny human figure wearing a buckskin jacket and an incongruous white motorcycle helmet flicked the reins, urging the team onward. But the most startling aspect of this bizarre sight was the vehicle's wings—huge, wide brown wings which protruded out for several yards on either side through the open doors of the coach. If President Abraham Lincoln had had his own Air Force One, it probably would have looked a lot like this.

Rett and Steve stood motionless and dumbfounded as the winged coach approached. Its driver, whose face was concealed by the dark sunglass shield on the front of his helmet, apparently noticed them and reined the horses back hard. The coach rolled to a stop with a dramatic groaning of wood and creaking of bullhide straps, punctuated by the six big animals' frightful whickering and clatter of hooves.

Steve smiled. "Is that Little Debbie I see up there?"

Rett's mind raced to make sense of everything he saw. Now that the coach was up close he could tell that its "wings" were actually the ends of an enormous roll of carpet. He also saw that the coach had a small trailer in tow behind it, on which rested something resembling a medieval catapult. And the little coachman, whose jacket bore the stitched pink insignia of a radical lesbian survivalist sect called the Militia Ethridge, was in fact a coachwoman.

With a hearty knock of oak against birchwood, the driver set the coach's handbrake and then tilted up the faceplate of her helmet. "Howdy there, Steve," she said, her voice an earthy rasp, "and good to see you too, Red." She pulled the helmet off and passed a leather gloved hand over her smooth, almost hairless head. Tiny gold rings rattled in her multiply pierced ears, nostrils and eyebrows.

"Rett," he corrected her. "But that's okay. It's been a while."

In fact it's been nearly two years, he thought, since Shelter negotiated our truce with the Militia Ethridge.

Sure, there'd been some minor contact with some of them since then, but this was the first time since the peace talks that they'd run across Little Debbie.

Rett's gaze moved up and down her form. He was relieved to see that, unlike many of her sect, she chose not to wear a decorative necklace made of severed male genitalia. However, he noted the wooden handle of what looked like a Smith & Wesson Scofield protruding from a shoulder holster only partially concealed beneath her jacket. Although he was quite aware that she was a ceremonially tattooed and pierced lifelong member of the Militia—and it was certainly no secret where and how often the Militia pierced their initiates—Little Debbie was the immediate focus of his more-than-just-professional interest. She wasn't much to look at—sort of a Danny DeVito with tits—but she was, undeniably, a woman. And it had been way too long since he'd been around one.

Damn shame about those piercings, though, he thought. *I bet if you marched her through one of those old-fashioned metal detectors, it'd probably make a sound like Devo playing the William Tell Overture.*

"Oh, yeah—Rett," she said. "Sorry." She nodded at their truck. "Outa fuel?"

Rett shook his head. "No. Busted radiator hose. I don't suppose you got any duct tape with you . . . and a barrel of water?"

Little Debbie snapped her head back in the direction of the coach's rear boot. Her earrings rattled. "There's at least four rolls of tape in my toolkit. But aside from two jugs of Klon's homebrew, the only liquid refreshment I've got is what's left in my canteen." She smiled and raised her eyebrows. "If you boys wanna hitch a ride with me, though, you're welcome. Grab your guns and climb up here. Two more miles up the road there's a good clean stream that runs right offa the Chattooga. I was gonna stop there anyway, on account of these horses bein' thirsty.

You got a can you can use to bring some water back with ya?"

Steve frowned. "No, we don't. When we stopped at Klon's, we filled up every container we had with his new pine beer."

"Well," said Little Debbie, grinning broadly, "then I'll just have to help you empty one of 'em, won't I? Call it cab fare."

The coach rumbled down the road, picking up speed as the six horses slowly got back into rhythm. Little Debbie slapped the reins across their backs and then took another long, generous swallow of the dark brown beer. When she finished with it, Steve hefted the big jug carefully from her gloved hands and slurped a hearty draw from it for himself before passing it back to Rett.

Rett lifted the big, wobbly plastic jug up and pointed its opening at his mouth, but beneath him the coach lurched on its leather thoroughbraces and the beer sloshed down the front of his jacket. He tried again and this time got a generous mouthful of the rich, earthgrain flavor.

Drinkin' it sure beats wearin' it, he thought.

"Hey, Debbie," he shouted, "since when was the Militia in the stagecoach business?"

She laughed. "In the last year or so, we've phased out almost all our motor fleet. Easier just to feed the corn straight to these hungry horses than to keep refinin' it into all that fuel."

"But a stagecoach?"

"Why not? By the way, this isn't just any ole stagecoach. It's the Deadwood Stage. Right now you boys got your asses parked where Buffalo Bill Cody and Sitting Bull blew their farts."

Rett and Steve glanced at each other.

Little Debbie laughed again. "Hard to believe, huh? Yeah, the coach was outa the museum and away on a tour with some kinda traveling exhibit when the Big One Dropped. The Militia traded for it with some Mennonites about six months ago. Still in perfect working order, too."

"And did all this carpet come in the deal?" asked Rett, trying hard to keep from making a rather obvious joke about "rug-munchers." He took another long swallow of the pine beer.

"Naw, I picked that up at Klon's Place," she answered. "He got it from some Daltonians. It's quality carpet. I swapped him a Winchester with a broken lever for it. Damn .32-caliber was too small to be much good against Blueboys and Braves, anyway. Besides, lately Cheryl and Molly been keepin' me awake half the night complainin' about how damn cold our barracks floor's been. I reckon with this much carpet we can cover the floors at Kelly and Fran's place too."

Steve reached up and got the beer jug away from Rett. He glanced over his shoulder at the trailer rattling along behind the coach. "And what's the story on this catapult back here? You planning to storm the Bastille or something?"

Little Debbie shook her head. "Klon threw that in with the deal. A buncha poots from some RenFest cult laid siege to his trading post using a whole buncha that total retro Monty Python gear—catapults, longbows and wooden shields. Didn't work. You ever see what the bullets from an AK-47 will do to a piece of wood?"

Rett burped. "I saw one cut down a pine tree. . . ."

"Yeah," said Debbie, "the way Klon described it, it was kinda hard to separate the bodies from all the splinters, once the shooting finally stopped."

"So what do you want with this thing then, anyway?" asked Steve.

Debbie shrugged. "It might be more useful as a defensive weapon to my Militia than it was as an offensive one to those Knights Who Said Knee. I tested it at Klon's. The dang thing can throw a 150-pound crate clear over his wall and halfway to the Clayton Crossing."

"You ladies plannin' to take up jousting, too?"

"No," she said, drawing her Smith & Wesson and rolling it expertly on her finger. "There's still no substitute for gunpowder."

"Well, why the catapult then?" asked Rett.

"Because," she answered, smoothly dropping the revolver back in her holster and reaching for the beer jug, "we haven't got any AK-47's."

When the coach reached the edge of the stream, Debbie motioned for the two boys to go on ahead and fill the now empty beer jug while she unhitched the horses. Steve carried both his own Remington pump shotgun and Rett's .44 carbine while the older boy eased himself down the embankment and waded barefoot out into the center of the stream. The water was dark and very cold, smelling strongly of green moss. It lapped hungrily around his knees as he lowered the jug and filled the vessel once just to rinse it. When it was completely full he turned it upside down and poured all the water out slowly, making sure to wash the last sticky vestiges of pine beer from it. Almost finished, he was startled by a spray of gravel splashing into the water. Rett looked up and saw Steve, his face a contorted mask of oh-shit-we're-in-trouble-now alarm. Steve was half running, half sliding down the embankment, flailing his arms in panic and waving both guns in crazy circles.

Rett knew better than to shout out any questions. From the look on Steve's face, it was clear that they'd better keep damn quiet. Steve hit the bottom of the embankment, caught his breath, and then whispered a single word that spoke volumes.

"Braves," he gasped, nodding upward.

The sun was almost completely gone as Rett brought the binoculars up to his eyes, but with the aid of the lenses he could see clearly what they were up against. The Braves had stripped Little Debbie and tied her across a pair of sawhorses. He was mildly amazed to see the extent of her tattooing, clearly revealed in the light of the roaring bonfire. Whatever the Braves had in mind to do with her—and it sure didn't take a Jeopardy finalist to figure out what that was—they hadn't started yet. Some sort of argument had broken out in their ranks. Rett watched with fascination as the Braves, all of them burly men costumed in the helmets, jackets, and uniforms of their long-defunct Atlanta baseball team namesake, enacted a shouting match more akin to an old-time hockey game. They shook their bats in the air as they roared at each other.

Rett had always disliked sports, but never more so than right now.

He scanned the periphery of the camp and noted that only a few sentries guarded its perimeter. The Braves had set up their tepees in a circle down by the riverbank, at the end of a steeply sloping trail. They had also erected some small portable fencing on either side, primarily as a hitching post for their horses, but had left the trail into their camp unblocked. Only two sleepy-looking guards, both wearing catcher's masks and carrying AK-47's, stood watch at the entrance.

"Do we really think we should try to get her back?" asked Steve. "I mean, just the two of us?"

Rett lowered the binoculars and nodded. "Yeah. It's in the terms of the treaty that Shelter signed with the Militia. Besides, if she doesn't make it back, the Militia may well think we took her. They obviously didn't know any Braves had moved this far north yet, or else they never woulda sent her out on her own."

"Good point," Steve agreed. "Okay, then. So what are we gonna do now, General? Call in an air strike?"

Rett grinned. "Sort of. Tell me, exactly how much do you weigh?"

"This seems really dumb," Steve muttered as he climbed into the launch cup of the catapult. He tightened the strap of Debbie's motorcycle helmet under his chin.

"We're just damn lucky that all the Braves took was Debbie and the horses," said Rett, "and, uh, that your head was small enough to fit that helmet. Now be sure to wait till I'm at least halfway down the trail before you go triggering that thing, okay?"

Steve nodded and looked glumly at the taut rope they'd rigged to the launch lever. All he had to do was cut it with his Bowie knife and he'd be racking up frequent flier miles over the Land of the Freaks and the Home of the Braves.

Leather and wood creaked slightly as Rett stepped up into the stagecoach and closed the door. He yanked the strap he'd fastened to the handbrake, freeing it up, and the coach began to roll—slowly, softly and almost silently—on its big carpet-wrapped wheels. Steering with harnesses affixed to the front axle assembly, he moved the coach in a gradual right turn and then pointed it straight down the trail, into the Braves' encampment. It creaked and rattled, but the mighty trademark rumbling of its wheels was sufficiently softened by their new carpet jackets. The guards at the camp entrance didn't even notice until it was only a few dozen yards away, and then they lost precious seconds staring in bewilderment as the horseless—and apparently driverless—vehicle rolled closer.

Rett picked off the Brave guard on the left with a single well-aimed shot from his .44, and he ducked low as the second man opened fire with an AK set for full-auto. Bullets buzzed by, nipping and chipping at the coach's hardwood frame like the blows of tiny hatchets. Somewhere in the midst of the gunfire he heard Steve whoosh through the air overhead like the Greatest American Hero, screaming something as he passed.

It sounded like, "Gerrronimo!"

To say that hell broke loose right then would be like describing ground zero at Hiroshima as "hot." As the boiling mass of Braves abandoned whatever they were

doing with Little Debbie to charge toward the stagecoach,
Steve's airborne, carpet-cocooned body struck the side
of the largest tepee in the rear of the camp and he slid
softly and swiftly to the ground, shrugging off the rug
and firing the Remington as he fell. The air exploded with
the bright orange of muzzle flashes and the stink of spent
powder. The first blast of Steve's heavy buckshot slammed
three men chin-first into the dirt, with chunks of skulls
and pieces of necks and shoulders following behind like
croutons and stewed tomatoes tossed atop an endive salad.
A few random pistol shots pointed in Steve's general
direction went wild and a several baseball bats swooped
near his head, but with two more .16-gauge blasts—fired
rapidly from the hip—he stopped all further commentary
from the dugout.

Back in the coach, Rett waited until the second guard's
cartridge clip ran dry, then yanked the brake strap hard
and leaned from the stage's open door, thrusting the muzzle
of his Marlin carbine into the man's masked face. When
he jerked the trigger, the Brave's head blew back like a
Pez dispenser spilling cherry-tinted innards.

"You okay, Rett?" asked Steve as the smoke cleared.

"Yeah. It looks like this is one ballgame that's not gonna
run into overtime," Rett observed, surveying the corpse-
strewn campground. "Is Debbie all right?"

They found her—quite all right—back by the saw horses.
A few strokes from Steve's knife and she was freed of the
ropes, her face beaming in the firelight like a fresh-polished
cartridge casing.

"What was that big argument back here about, anyway?"
asked Rett. "Were they fighting over who'd take you first?"

Still naked, and with her full-body tattoos displayed
dramatically in the glow of the campfire, Debbie laughed
and shook her head. "No, they were squabbling over
whether they oughta take out all my beads and rings 'fore
they got started."

Steve raised his eyebrows and shrugged. "It wouldn't

matter either way to me." He smiled. "So listen, Deb, is there any chance you feel like rewarding one of your heroic liberators, with or without your beads and rings?"

She grinned. "Oh, all right—but only if you don't mind keeping your trousers on until after I've had a chance to go around and collect a few fresh trophies offa my captors."

"Uh, never mind," Steve grumbled quietly, looking away. "Suddenly, I'm just not in the mood any more."

Debbie knocked a fist proudly against the side of the coach. "The ole wagon here held up pretty good against those AKs. Go figure."

"Amazing," Steve muttered sarcastically.

"The secret's ash," said Rett.

"Ashes?"

"No, ash. It's a kinda wood they made the frames of Concord stagecoaches from. Really tough stuff," he said. "I once saw Pete Townshend at a Who concert, trying to smash a Fender guitar made of ash. Split his amp in half, and there wasn't even a crack on the Fender."

Debbie ran her hand down the weathered side of the coach. "Yeah, and lest we forget, this crate here is the Deadwood Stage, too." She paused thoughtfully. "I reckon if this thing could survive over a hundred years of outlaws, buffalo hunters, and wild Indians in the Black Hills of Wyoming, what harm could a nuke and a few Russian machine guns do to it?"

Rett nodded. "My thoughts exactly."

Debbie walked off into the darkness, returning a few minutes later dressed in a bloodied Braves jacket smiling an I'm-smarter-than-you-idiots-are smile. "So, are you boys interested in a good used catapult, yours free and clear, to take back to Shelter tomorrow?"

Rett's jaw fell. "But I thought—"

Debbie proudly hoisted up two prizes she'd just claimed as spoils of war. "Well," she said, "seein' as now I've got these AK-47's . . ."

"Aw, geez," muttered Steve. "When you said you were gonna take trophies, we thought—"

"Yeah," she asked, her earrings rattling, "just what did you think?"

"Never mind, Debbie," said Rett. "Just never mind." He pulled himself up close to the campfire, drawing a heavy wool Braves blanket over his shoulders.

And carefully, purposefully, crossing his legs.

Riding Shotgun To Armageddon
S.M. Stirling

The cannon were keeping up well with the chariots; Pharaoh would be pleased.

Djehuty, Commander of the Brigade of Seth, was a little uncomfortable on horseback even after months of practice with the new saddle with stirrups. Still, there was no denying it was convenient. He turned his horse and rode back down along the track beside his units, with the standard-bearer, scribes, aides and messengers behind him. The rutted track was deep in sand, like most of the coastal plain of Canaan . . . where it wasn't swamp mud or rocks. The infantry in their banded-linen corselets plodded along, their brown faces darker yet with dust and streaked with sweat under their striped headdresses of thick canvas. Big round-topped rectangular shields were slung over their shoulders, bronze spearblades glinted in the bright sun. After them came a company of Nubians, Medjay mercenaries from far up the Nile. Djehuty frowned; the black men were slouching along in their usual style, in no order at all . . . although anyone who'd seen one of their screaming charges could forgive them that.

Then came one of the New Regiments, with their muskets over their shoulders and short iron swords at their sides. They wore only kilts and pleated loin-guards, but there were leather bandoliers of papyrus cartridges at their right hips. Djehuty scowled slightly at the sight of them, despite the brave show they made with their feet moving in unison and the golden fan standard carried before them on a long pole.

Their weapons are good, he acknowledged. "But will they stand in battle?" he murmured to himself. They were peasants, not *iw'yt,* not real soldiers whose trade was fighting, raised from childhood in the barracks.

After them came the cannon themselves, wrought with endless difficulty and expense. Djehuty's thick-muscled chest swelled with pride under his iron-scale armor at the number Pharaoh had entrusted to him—a full dozen of the *twelve-pounders,* as they were called in the barbaric tongue of their inventors. Each was a bronze tube of a length equal to a very tall man's height, with little bronze cylinders cast on either side so that the guns could ride in their chariotlike mounts. Very much like a chariot, save that the pole rested on another two-wheeled cart, the *limber,* and that was hauled by six horses with the new collar harness that bore on their shoulders rather than their necks.

Better for the horses, he admitted grudgingly, passing on to the chariots. Those had changed in the last few years as well. Besides a compound bow and quiver on one side, there was a scabbard on the other for two double-barreled shotguns, and the crew was now three, like a Hittite war cart—one being a loader for the warrior who captained the vehicle.

He reined in and took a swig from the goatskin water bottle at his saddle. It cut gratefully through the dust and thick phlegm in his mouth; he spat to the side and drank again, since there were good springs nearby and no need to conserve every drop. Years of work, to make the Brigade of Seth the finest in Pharaoh's service, and then to integrate the new weapons. Something his father had told him . . . yes: *To be good commanders, we must love our army and our soldiers. But to win victories, we must be ready to kill the thing we love. When you attack, strike like a hammer and hold nothing back.*

"Stationed in Damnationville with no supplies," he said, quoting a soldier's saying as old as the wars against the Hyskos.

"But sir, there are plenty of supplies," his son said.

Djehuty nodded. "There are now, boy," he said. "But imagine being stuck here on garrison duty for ten years."

The young man looked around. To their left was the sea, brighter somehow than that off the Delta. The road ran just inland of the coastal sand dunes; off to the right a line of hills made the horizon rise up in heights of blue and purple. Thickets of oak dotted the plain, and stretches of tall grass, dry now in midsummer. Dust smoked off a few patches of cultivation, here and there a vineyard or olive grove, but the land was thinly settled—had been since the long wars Pharaoh had waged early in his reign, nearly thirty Nile floods ago.

And those did not go well, he remembered uneasily— he'd been a stripling then, but nobody who'd been at Kadesh was going to believe it the great Egyptian victory that the temple walls proclaimed.

A village of dun-colored mud brick huts with flat roofs stood in the middle distance, dim through the greater dust plume of the Egyptian host passing north. The dwellers and their stock were long gone; sensible peasants ran when armies passed by.

By the standards of the vile Asiatics, of the hairy dwellers in Amurru, this was flat and fertile land. To an Egyptian, it was hard to tell the difference between this and the sterile red desert that lay east of the Nile.

"War and glory are only found in foreign lands," the younger man said stoutly.

"Well spoken, son," the commander said. He looked left; the Ark of Ra was sinking towards the waves. "Time to camp soon. And Pharaoh will summon the commanders to conference in the morning."

Pharaoh was a tall man, still lean and active in the thirty-sixth year of his reign despite the deep furrows in his

hawklike face and the plentiful gray in his dark-auburn
hair. He stood as erect as a granite monolith, wearing the
military kilt and the drum-shaped red crown of war with
the golden cobra rearing at his brows, waiting as still as
the statue of a god. The officers knelt and bowed their
heads to the carpet before him in the shade of the great
striped canvas pavillion. There was a silence broken only
by the clank of armor scales and creak of leather. Then
the eunuch herald's voice rang like silver in the cool air
of dawn:

"*He is The Horus, Strong Bull, Beloved of* Ma'at; *He of
the Two Goddesses, Protector of Khem who Subdues the
Foreign Lands; The Golden Horus, Rich in Years, Great
in Victories; He is King of Upper and Lower Egypt, Strong
in Right; He is* User-Ma'at-Ra, *Son of Ra; Ramses, Beloved
of Amun.*"

The officers bowed again to the living god, and Pharaoh
made a quick gesture with one hand. The officers bowed
once more and rose.

Djehuty came to his feet with the rest. Servants pulled
a cover off a long table. It was covered by a shallow-sided
box, and within the box was a model made of sand mixed
with Nubian gum, smelling like a temple on a festival day.
Its maker stood waiting.

There is the outland dog, he thought. Mek-andrus the
foreigner, the one who'd risen so high in Pharaoh's service.
He wore Egyptian headdress and military kilt but foreign
armor—a long tunic of linked iron rings. *Foreign dog.
Disturber of custom.*

"The servants of Pharaoh will listen to this man, now
Chief of Chariots," Ramses said. "So let it be written. So
let it be done."

Djehuty bowed his head again. *If Pharaoh commands
that I obey a baboon with a purple arse, I will obey,* he
thought. Mek-andrus was obviously part Nubian, too, with
skin the color of a barley loaf and a flat nose. *The will of
Pharaoh is as the decrees of fate.*

The foreigner moved to the sand table and picked up a wooden pointer. "This is the ground on which we must fight," he said. His Egyptian was fluent, but it had a sharp nasal accent like nothing any of the Khemites had ever heard before. "As seen from far above."

All the officers had had the concept explained to them. Some were still looking blank-eyed; Djehuty nodded and looked down with comprehension. There was the straight north-south reach of the coast of Canaan, with the coastal plain narrowing to nothing where the inland hills ran almost to water's edge; a bay north of that, where a river ran into the sea. The river marked a long trough, between the hills and the mountains of Galilee to the north, and it was the easiest way from the sea inland to the big lake and the Jordan valley.

"The Hittites, the men of Kar-Duniash, the *Mariyannu* of the Asiatic cities, the Aramenaean tribes, and their allies are approaching from the northeast, thirty-five thousand strong not counting their auxiliaries and camp followers, according to the latest reports."

The pointer traced a line down through Damascus, over the heights, along the shores of the Sea of Galilee, then northwest from Bet Shean.

"Of those, at least five thousand are infantry equipped with fire weapons, with thirty cannon, and four thousand chariots."

None of the Egyptian commanders stirred; there was a low mutter of sound as the Sherdana mercenary commander translated for his monoglot subordinates, their odd-looking helmets with the circle of feathers all round bending together.

"Favored of the Son of Ra," Djehuty said. "If we are here"—he pointed to a place half a day's march before the point where the coastal plain pinched out—"can they reach the sea and hold the passes over Carmel against us?"

Mek-andrus nodded; he no longer smiled with such

boorish frequency as he had when he first came to Egypt. "That is the question. They were here"—he tapped the place where the Jordan emerged from Galilee—"yesterday at sunset."

Another rustling. That was a longer distance than they had to travel, but it was over flat land with supplies to hand; in time of peace the harvest of the Jezreel went to Pharaoh's storehouses. The Egyptian force must cross mountains.

"Thutmose did it," Mek-andrus said. "If we take this pass"—his finger tapped—"as the Great One's predecessor did, we can be *here* and deployed to meet them before they expect us."

Thutmose . . ., Djehuty thought. Then: *Ah.* One of the great Pharaohs of the previous dynasty, the one that had petered out after the Accursed of Amun tried to throw down the worship of the gods. His eyes narrowed as he watched Mek-andrus. How did the outland dog know so much of Khem? Djehuty *knew* the barbarian didn't read the Egyptian script, so he couldn't have simply read the story off a temple wall the way a literate, civilized man might. The fire weapons themselves weren't sorcery, just a recipe, like cooking—plain saltpeter and sulfur and charcoal, whatever the peasants might think. But there was something not quite canny about Mek-andrus himself.

Yet the gods have sent him to us. Without Mek-andrus, the Hittites and Achaeans and other demon-begotten foreigners who knew not the Black Land or the Red would have had the new weapons all to their own. That would have been as bad as the time long ago when the Hyksos came with their chariots, before any Egyptian had seen a horse, and it had taken a long night of subjection and war to expel *them.*

"Who should take the vanguard?" Pharaoh asked.

Mek-andrus bowed. "Let Pharaoh choose the commander who has both wisdom and bravery . . . and many cannon, so that they can hold off the enemy host until the whole army of Pharaoh is deployed."

Remote as jackal-headed Anubis deciding the fate of a soul in the afterworld, Pharaoh's eyes scanned his generals.

Djehuty fell on his face as the flail pointed to him. "Djehuty of the Brigade of Seth. The vanguard shall be yours. Prepare to move as soon as you may. You shall cross the pass and hold the ground for the rest of our armies. So let it be written! So let it be done!"

It was a great honor . . . and possibly the death sentence for the Brigade of Seth.

Djehuty slid gracelessly down off the horse, keeping a tight grip on the reins as it whinnied and shied sideways. Its iron shoes struck sparks from the rocks beside the trail. The column was winding its way upwards, through rocky hills covered in resin-scented pine forest, towards the saddle between two peaks. He tossed the reins to a groom and walked back down the narrow twisting passage—it would be boastful to give it the name of road—as the sweating files of infantry and charioteers made their way upwards. The chariots were no problem; even the heavier new models could still be lifted easily by two strong men when the going became very rough. The cannon, though . . .

A wheel lurched over a rock and came down with a slamming *bang* that made him wince as if his testicles were being drawn back up into his gut. He let out a sigh of relief as the wheel stayed in one piece and the tough Nubian ebony of the axle *didn't* crack.

"Halt!" he called. "You, Senefer—get a company of infantry up here, a hundred men, and ropes." They could repeat the process with each gun from this point to the saddle of the pass, changing the infantry companies as needed.

He ran a hand along the sweating neck of the lead horse in the gun team, murmuring soothingly when it blew out its lips in weary protest.

"Peace, brother of the field of war," he said. "So, so, my pretty. Soon you may rest."

An officer must be thrifty with Pharaoh's goods. There was no sense in killing valuable horses with overwork when peasants were available.

"I do not like the thought of cowering in a hole," Djehuty said.

The valley stretched out before him, land flat and marshy in spots, in others fertile enough even by an Egyptian's standards. Stubble stood sere on that half of the plowland that made this year's harvested fields, blond-white and knee high; the fallow was densely grown with weeds. Olive trees grew thick on the hills that rose on either side of the southeastward trend of the lowlands; orchards of fig and pomegranate stood around hamlets of dark mud brick, and green leafy vineyards that would produce the famed Wine of the North. These lands were well-peopled, a personal estate of Pharaoh and on a route that carried much trade from the north in times of peace.

"All the courage in the world won't stop a bullet," Mekandrus said. "A man in a hole—a *rifle pit*—can load and fire more easily, and still be protected from the enemy's bullets. They must stand and walk forward to attack; and the Divine Son of Ra has ordered us to defend."

Djehuty made a gesture of respect at the Pharaoh's name. "So he has," he said. *You purple-arsed baboon,* he thought to himself. Pharaoh was a living god, but a commander in the field was not always bound by his sovereign's orders—it was the objective that counted. And occasionally Egyptians had committed deicide . . . *No.* He thrust the thought from him. That was a counsel of desperation, and Ramses had been a good Pharaoh, strong and just.

"How do you advise that we deploy, then?" Djehuty said.

He looked back. The land fell rapidly from the saddle,

and most of the Brigade of Seth were out, forming up in solid blocks.

"Let us keep the pass to our backs," the foreigner said.

"So—half of a circle?" Djehuty said, making a curving gesture.

"No, not today. That would disperse the fire of our guns. Instead—"

Mek-andrus began to draw in the dirt with a bronze-tipped stick he carried. "Two *redoubts*, little square earth forts, on either end of a half circle whose side curves away from the enemy. That way they can give *enfilading fire*."

"Please, O Favored of the Divine Horus, speak Egyptian; I plead my ignorance."

Mek-andrus looked up sharply. Djehuty gave him a bland smile; let him see how a civilized man controlled his emotions.

The foreigner nodded. He held both hands out, fingers splayed, then crossed those fingers to make a checkerboard. "*Enfilading fire* means that the paths of the balls or grapeshot from the cannon cross each other so," he said. "Instead of one path of destruction, they overlap and create a whole field where nothing can live."

The Egyptian's eyes went wide. He struggled within his head, imagining . . . and he had seen what cannon could do. *Those Nubians who tried to raid the fort,* he thought. A great wedge had been cut through their mass, as if sliced by the knife of a god. Within that triangle only shattered bone and spattered flesh had remained. Some of it still twitching and screaming. In his mind's eye he overlapped that broad path of death with thirty more, and put Hittite charioteers in place of naked blacks with horn-tipped spears. His hand went of itself to the outlander's shoulder.

"I see your word!" he exclaimed, smiling broadly. "Your word is a thing of beauty. And how shall we place the musketeers?"

Djehuty's son listened closely, waiting in silence until Mek-andrus strode away. "Father and lord," he said hesitantly. "Is it possible that . . . some among us have been mistaken concerning the outlander."

His father shook his head. "He knows much," he said. "But it is still a violation of *ma'at*, of the order of things, that an outlander should stand so close to the Great One. And to be granted a Royal woman as his wife! Not even the Great King of the Hittites was given such honor, when we were allied with them and at peace. No," he went on, dropping his voice. "The day will come when the foreign dog who knows not the Red Land or the Black will have taught us all he knows. On that day . . ."

Father and son smiled, their expressions like a wolf peering into a mirror. Then Djehuty raised his voice: "Officers of Five Hundred, of a Hundred. Attend me!"

"They come," the Medjay scout wheezed, pointing behind himself with his spear. His body was naked save for a gourd penis sheath and his skin shone like polished onyx with sweat. His tongue lolled, his smell rose rank, compounded of seldom washing and the cow tallow mixed with ochre smeared on his hair. "Their scouts chased me, but I lost them in rough ground."

Djehuty nodded; the Nubian mercenaries in Pharaoh's host were recruited from desert nomads south of the great bend of the Nile—hunters, herders and bandits. They could outrun horses, given time, loping along at their tireless long-legged trot. And they could track a ghost over naked rock, or hide in their own shadows. Djehuty knew it too well. His first command had been patrols along the southern frontier. You didn't forget waking up and finding a sentry with his throat cut and his genitals stuffed into his mouth, and nobody in camp any the wiser until the Ark of Ra lifted over the horizon. That was Medjay humor . . . but they were useful, no doubt of that, and true to their salt.

"Many?" he said.

"Many," the barbarian confirmed, opening and closing

his hands rapidly. "As a Real Man runs"—that was their heathen name for themselves—"an hour's distance."

"Fetch my war harness," he said to his son. To a runner: "A message to the captains that the enemy approaches."

His chariot came up, the plumes on the team's heads nodding, and the Egyptian commander ducked into the leather shirt of iron scales. Sweat soaked the linen backing almost immediately; he lowered the helmet over his head and buckled the strap below his chin. The sunlight was painful on the bronze and gold that decked the light wicker and bentwood of the car, and the iron tires shrunk onto the wooden wheels. He climbed aboard, his son after him; the boy made a production of checking the priming on shotguns and pistols, but he was a good lad, conscientious. More eager than was sensible, but this would be his first real battle.

"Keep your head," his father warned, his voice gruff. "It's the cool-blooded man lives long on the threshing ground of battle."

"I'm not afraid, father!" Sennedjem said. His voice started low but broke in a humiliating squeak halfway through. He flushed angrily; his mother had been Djehuty's first woman, a fair-skinned Libyan captive, and the boy's olive tan was a little lighter than most men of Lower Egypt.

"That's the problem, lad," Djehuty grinned. "You *should* be frightened." He turned his attention to the work of the day.

The signal fire on top of the bare-sloped hill to the southeast went out. "Soon now," Djehuty said.

Dust gave the chariots away. The Egyptian squinted; his vision had grown better for distant things in the last few years, worse for close work. *Chariot screen*, he thought. Thrown forward to keep the Egyptians from getting a close look at their enemy's force before they deployed for battle. Whoever commanded the enemy host was no fool. Now he must do the same. Without a close description of his position, the enemy commander would be handicapped.

"Forward!" he barked.

Well-drilled, the squadrons fanned out before him. The driver clucked to his charges, touched their backs gently with the reins, and the willing beasts went forward. Walk, canter, trot; the dry hard ground hammered at his feet below the wicker floor of the war cart. He compensated with an instinctive flexing of knees and balance, learned since childhood. The enemy grew closer swiftly with the combined speed of both chariot fleets, and he could feel his lips draw back in a grin of carnivore anticipation.

Syrians, he thought, as details became plain—spiked bronze helmets, horsehair plumes, long coats of brass scales rippling like the skins of serpents, curled black beards and harsh beak-nosed faces. *Mariyannu* warriors of the northern cities, some rebellious vassals of Pharaoh, some from the Hittite domains or the ungoverned borderlands.

They came in straggling clumps and bands, by ones and twos, fighting as ever by town and by clan. He could see the drivers leaning forward, shouting to the horses in their uncouth gutturals, the fighters reaching for arrows to set to their bows.

"We'll show them our fire," he said.

A feather fan mounted on a yard-long handle stood in a holder at his side. He snatched it out and waved to left and right. The Egyptian formation curled smoothly forward on either hand. *Fast as ever*, he thought—the new harness let a team pull the heavier chariots without losing speed or agility. A drumming of hooves filled the air with thunder, a choking white dust curled up like the sandstorms of Sinai. The horses rocked into a gallop, nostrils flared and red, foam flecking their necks. The first arrows arched out, the bright sun winking off their points. Djehuty sneered: much too far for effective archery. Dust boiled up into the unmerciful sky, thick and acrid on his tongue. Soon . . .

"Amun! Amun! The Divine Horus!" the Egyptians roared. Savage war cries echoed back from the enemy.

"Gun!" he barked, holding out a hand. Check-patterned acacia wood slapped into it as Sennedjem put the weapon in his hand.

Thumping sounds smashed through the roar of hooves and thunder of wheels. Syrian chariots went over, and the high womanish screaming of wounded horses was added to the uproar. Djehuty crouched, raking back the hammers with his left palm and then levelling the weapon.

Now. An enemy chariot dashing in out of the dust in a dangerously tight curve, one wheel off the ground. Close enough to see the wild-eyed glare of the *Mariyannu* poised with a javelin in one hand. Bring the wedge at the front of the paired barrels to the notch at the back. It wasn't so different from using a bow, the body adjusting like a machine of balanced springs; but easier, easier, no effort of holding the draw. Squeeze the trigger, nothing jerky about the motion . . .

Whump. The metal-shod butt of the shotgun punished his shoulder. Flame and sulfur-stinking smoke vomited from the barrels, along with thirty lead balls. Those were invisible—strange to think of something moving too fast to see—but he shouted in exultation as he saw them strike home. The horses reared and screamed and tripped as the lead raked them, the driver went over backward.

"Gun!" Djehuty roared, and Sennedjem snatched away the empty one and slapped the next into his father's grasp, then went to work biting open cartridges, hands swift on ramrod and priming horn. Djehuty fired again. "Gun!" Sennedjem put a charged weapon in his grip. "Gun!"

They plunged through the dust cloud and out into the open; the surviving Syrian chariots were in full retreat. Others lay broken, some with upturned wheels still spinning. One right at his own horse's feet, and the driver pulled their team around. A wounded *Mariyannu* stumbled forward with a long spear held in both hands; Djehuty shot him at ten paces distance, and the bearded face splashed away from its understructure of bone. Some of the shot carved grooves of brightness through the green-coated bronze of the man's helmet. Out of the corner of his eye he was conscious of Sennedjem reloading the spent shotgun, priming the pans and waiting poised.

"Pull up," Djehuty rasped. "Sound *rally*."

The driver brought the team to a halt. Sennedjem sheathed the shotgun and brought out a slender brass horn. Its call sounded shrill and urgent through the dull diminishing roar of the skirmish. Man after man heard it; the Captains of a Hundred brought their commands back into formation. Djehuty took the signal fan from its holder and waved it.

Meanwhile he looked to the northeast. More dust there, a low sullen cloud of it that caught the bright sunlight. He waited, and a rippling sparkle came from it, filling vision from side to side of the world ahead of them like stars on a night-bound sea.

"Father, what's *that*?" Sennedjem blurted; he was looking pale, but his eyes and mouth were steady. Djehuty clipped him across the side of the head for speaking without leave, but lightly.

"Light on spearpoints, lad," he said grimly. "Now it begins."

The redoubt was a five-sided figure of earth berms; there were notches cut in the walls for the muzzles of the cannon, and obstacles made of wooden bars set with sharp iron blades in the ditches before it. Djehuty waited atop the rampart for the enemy heralds; they carried a green branch for peace, and a white cloth on a pole as well—evidently the same thing, by somebody else's customs. And flags, one with white stars on a blue ground and red-and-white stripes. His eyes widened a little. He had heard of that flag. Another beside it had similar symbols, and cryptic glyphs, thus: U.S. COAST GUARD. He shivered a little, inwardly. What wizardry was woven into that cloth? A touch at his amulet stiffened him. Gilded eagles topped the staffs, not the double-headed version of the Hittites, but sculpted as if alive with their wings thrust behind them and their claws clutching arrows and olive branches.

So that is why the strangers from the far west are called the Eagle People, he thought. It must be their protector-god. He nodded; whatever else you could say about them, they must be wise in the ways of war.

"I am Djehuty, Commander of the Brigade of Seth in the army of Pharaoh, *User-Ma'at-Ra,* son of Ra, Ramses of the line of Ramses, the ruler of Upper and Lower Egypt," he barked. "Speak."

"Commodore Marian Alston," the figure in black-enameled steel armor said. He lifted off his helm. *No, she, by the Gods—the rumors speak truth. Odd, but we had a woman as Pharaoh once, and she led armies.* Djehuty's eyes went wider. The enemy commander was a Nubian; not part-blood like Mek-andrus, but black as polished ebony. His eyes flicked to the others sitting their horses beside her. One was a woman too, yellow-haired like some Achaeans; another was a man of no race he knew, with skin the color of amber and eyes slanted at the outer ends; the other two looked like Sherden from the north shore of the Middle Sea as far as their coloring went, although their hair was cropped close. A *Sudunu* stood uneasily by the foreign woman's stirrup; he stepped forward and bowed with one hand to his flowerpot hat to keep it from falling off.

"I shall interpret, noble Djehuty," he said uneasily; the Egyptian was fluent, but with the throaty accent of his people. Djehuty glared for a second. Byblos, Sidon and the other coastal cities of Canaan were vassals of Pharaoh; what was this treacherous dog doing aiding his enemies? Then he nodded curtly. *Sudunu* would do anything for wealth.

"Tell this woman that no foreigner goes armed in

Pharaoh's dominions without his leave, on pain of death. If she and her rabble leave at once, I may be merciful."

The *Sudunu* began to speak in Akkadian, the Babylonian tongue. Djehuty could follow it a little; it was the tongue kings used to write to each other, and not impossibly different from the language of the western Semites, which he did speak after a fashion. The interpreter was shading the meaning. That often happened, since such a man was eager to avoid offending anyone.

"Tell her exactly, as I told you—don't drip honey on it," he broke in.

The swarthy, scrawny man in the embroidered robe swallowed and began again. The black woman gave a slight, bleak smile.

"Lord Djehuty," the interpreter began. "Commodore— that is a rank, lord—Alston says that she is empowered by her . . . lord, the word means Ruler, I think—Ruler of an island across the River Ocean—and the Great King of the Hittites, and the Great King of Kar-Duniash, and their other allies, to demand the return of *George McAndrews*, a renegade of her people. If you will give us this man, the allied forces will return past the border of Pharaoh Ramses' dominions, and peace may return."

Djehuty puzzled over the words for a moment before he realized that the name was Mek-andrus, the outland favorite of Ramses. "Barbarians make no demands of Pharaoh," he snapped. *Although I would send him to you dragged by the ankles behind my chariot, if the choice were mine.* "They beg for his favor, or feel the flail of his wrath. Go, or die."

The coal-black face gave a slight nod. *No, not a Medjay,* Djehuty thought with an inner chill. *Except in color and cast of feature.* They were like fierce children, their *ka* plain on their faces. This one had discipline; doubly remarkable in a woman. And she showed no sign of fear, under the muzzles of his guns. *She must know what they can do. Mek-andrus is of her people.*

If the stranger was a renegade from the service of his King, much was explained. He schooled his own face.

"Pharaoh commands; as it is written, so shall it be done," he replied. "This parley is over. Depart his soil, at once."

BAAAAMMMM.

The twelve-pounder leapt back, up the sloping ramp of dirt the gunners had shovelled behind it, then back down again into battery. Stripped to their loincloths, the crew threw themselves into action. One man shoved a pole with a wet sponge down the muzzle, twisting and withdrawing it, and the hot metal hissed. The powder came forward in a dusty-looking linen cylinder, to be rammed down with a wad of hemp and then the leather sack of lead balls. Stinking smoke drifted about them, and the confused roaring noise of battle, but the men labored on, wet with sweat, their faces blackened by powder fumes until their eyes stared out like white flecks in a black mask, burns on their limbs where they had brushed against the scorching bronze of the cannon.

These are men, Djehuty thought, slightly surprised. *More than that, they are men worthy to be called iw'yt, real soldiers.*

He wasn't sure about the warriors surging about his line, but whatever they were, they didn't discourage easily. He squinted through the thick smoke that stung his eyes, ignoring the dryness of his tongue—they were short of water, and he meant to make what he had last. This band of the foe looked a little like Hittites, stocky and hairy and big-nosed, but taller and fairer, and their gear was different. They didn't shave the front of their heads, either.

Here they came again, over ground covered with their dead. Swarms of them, sending a shower of javelins before them as they came closer.

BAAAAMMMM. BAAAAMMM. The guns were firing more slowly now, conserving their ammunition. Grapeshot cut bloody swathes through the attackers, but they kept on. Dead men dropped improvised ladders of logs and sticks; others picked them up and came forward. Their cries grew into a deep bellowing; the first ranks dropped into the ditch around the redoubt, where the spiked barricades were covered with bodies. Others climbed up, standing on their shoulders to scramble up the sloping dirt or setting up their scaling ladders. Some of them knew enough to cringe at the sound that came through shouts and cannonade. The sound of thumbs cocking back the hammers of their muskets.

"Now!" Djehuty shouted, swinging his fan downwards.

All along the parapet, hundreds of musketeers stood up from their crouch and levelled their pieces downward into the press of attackers.

"Fire!"

A noise that thudded into chest and gut, like one long shot that went on for a full second. A fresh fogbank of smoke drifted away, showing the ruin below—the muskets had been loaded with what Mek-andrus called *buck and ball*, a musket ball and several smaller projectiles. The ditch was filled with shapes that heaved and moaned and screamed, and the smell was like an opened tomb that had drained a sewer. Djehuty winced, very slightly; he was a hardy man and bred to war, but it was one thing to see men fall pierced with arrows, or gashed with the sword, but this . . . this was something else. Not even the actions in the south had prepared him for it; the barbarians there were too undisciplined to keep charging into certain death as these men had.

"They run away, Father!" Sennedjem said.

"Down!" Djehuty barked.

Everyone in the little earth fort took cover. Away in the gathering dusk, lights blinked like angry red eyes. A long whistling screech came from overhead, and then the first explosion. The enemy cannon were better than the ones Mek-andrus had made in Khem; instead of firing just solid roundshot or grape, they could throw shells that exploded themselves—and throw them further. He dug his fingers into the earth, conscious mainly of the humiliation of it. He, Commander of the Brigade of Seth, whose ancestors had been nobles since the years when the Theban Pharaohs expelled the Hyskos, cowering in the dirt like a peasant! But the fire-weapons were no respectors of rank or person. *And they will shred my Brigade of Seth like meat beneath the cook's cleaver.* So Pharaoh had ordered . . . and it might be worth it, if it turned the course of the battle to come.

Earth shuddered under his belly and loins. He had a moment to think, and it froze him with his fingers crooked into the shifting clay. *Why only cannon?* he thought. From the reports and rumors, the newcomers had taught their allies to make muskets too, and better ones than the Egyptians had—something to do with twisting grooves inside the barrels. Yet all the infantry and chariots his Brigade had met here were armed with the old weapons; some of them fashioned of iron rather than bronze, but still spear, sword, bow, javelin.

The barrage let up. He turned his head, and felt his liver freeze with fear. Sennedjem was lying limp and pale, his back covered in blood. Djehuty scrambled to him, ran hands across the blood-wet skin. Breath of life and pulse of blood, faint but still there. He prayed to the gods of healing and clamped down; there, something within the wound. A spike of metal, still painfully hot to the touch. He took it between thumb and forefinger, heedless of the sharp pain in his own flesh, and pulled. His other hand pressed across the wound while he roared for healers, bandages, wine and resin to wash out the hurt. When they came he rose, forcing himself to look away and think as his son was borne to the rear.

"I don't like the smell of this," he muttered, and called for a runner. "Go to the commander of the northernmost brigade of Pharaoh's army," he said. "Find why they delay, and return quickly. Say that we are hard-pressed."

❖   ❖   ❖

"Back!" Djehuty snarled.

He smashed the pommel of the sword into the fleeing spearman's face, feeling bone crunch. The witless howl of panic stopped as the man dropped boneless. Behind Djehuty, the men of his personal guard levelled their double-barreled shotguns, and the madness faded out of the faces of the soldiers who'd panicked. Those who still held their spears lowered them, and in the uncertain light of dawn he could see them shuffle their feet and drop their eyes.

"If you run from death, it follows you—and death runs fast," Djehuty said, his voice firm but not angry. "Remember that it is ruin to run from a fight, for you cannot fight and flee, but the pursuer can still strike at your naked back as he chases *you*. Return to your positions."

"Sir—" one said, desperate. "Lord, the thunderbolts strike us and we cannot strike back!"

"I know," Djehuty said. The bandage on one forearm reminded them that he ran the same dangers. "But they cannot take our position unless they send men forward to claim it, and those men you *can* strike." *Those of you still alive.* "Return to your companies! Strike the foe!"

He turned, stalking through rows of wounded men groaning on the rocky dirt, through shattered carts and dead horses—someone was skinning them for cooking, at least, and he must find who'd thought to organize parties to fill waterskins—and looked up the pass. Nobody, nobody but his reserves, and they were few enough.

If Pharaoh does not come, we will die here, he thought. Unless he withdrew now, leaving a rearguard . . . *No. We have lost too many of our draught beasts. I cannot save the cannon or the chariots.* A grim satisfaction: *I have done my part, and my men as well. If the plan fails, it is not our doing.* Pharaoh's doing . . . he thrust the thought from him.

Then there *was* something in the pass: a messenger. A *mounted* messenger, plunging recklessly down the steep

rocky way, leaning back with feet braced in the stirrups
as his horse slid the final dozen yards almost in a sitting
position. It hung its lathered head as the messenger
drummed heels on its ribs and came over to him, wheezing
as its flanks heaved like a bronzesmith's bellows.

The man looked nearly as done-in as his horse, his face
a mask of dust. "Here," Djehuty said, passing over his
waterskin.

The man sucked at it eagerly; the water was cut with
one-fifth part of sour wine.

"Lord," he gasped after a moment. "From Pharaoh."

He offered a scroll of papyrus; Djehuty touched it to
his forehead in the gesture of respect and broke the seal
to read eagerly, his eyes skipping easily over the cursive
demotic script, so different from the formal hieroglyphs
of sculpture and temple.

*Enemy ships with many guns at the Gateway of the
North,* he read, and grunted as if shot in the belly. That
was the fortress of Gaza, the anchor of the Royal Road
up the coast. Only if it was securely held could even a
single man return to Khem across the deserts of Sinai.
*Troops armed with fire-weapons are landing and investing
the fortress. Pharaoh marches to meet them. Hold your
position at all hazards; you are the rear guard.*

Djehuty grunted again, as a man might when he had
just been condemned to death. That was where the cream
of the enemy forces had gone, right enough.

"Sir!" Another messenger, one of his own men, and on
foot. "Sir, the enemy attack!"

The steel *kopesh* was lead-heavy in Djehuty's hand as
he retreated another step; the ring of Egyptians grew
smaller as they stood shoulder-to-shoulder around the
standard. *For Khem*, he thought, and slashed backhand.
The edge thudded into the rim of an Aramanaean's shield,
and the leather-covered wicker squeezed shut on the blade.
The nomad shrieked glee and wrenched, trying to tear

the weapon from the Egyptian's hand. Djehuty's lips bared dry teeth as he smashed the boss of his own into the man's face, then braced a foot on his body to wrench the sickle-sword free. *For Sennedjem!* he thought, swinging it down. Distracted, he did not see the spearhead that punched into his side just below the short ribs. Bent over, wheezing, he saw the spearman staring incredulously at the way the bronze point had bent over double against the iron scales of his armor, then scream frustration and club the spear to use the shaft as a bludgeon. Exhaustion weighed down his limbs as he struggled to turn, to bring up shield and blade. Something struck him again, he couldn't tell where, and the world went gray. His last thought was that the earth tasted of salt with blood.

Bits of the formulae for addressing the Judge of the Dead flitted through Djehuty's head along with blinding pain as his eyelids fluttered open. But it was not jackal-headed Anubis who bent over him, but a foreigner with a cup of water. The Egyptian sucked it down gratefully before he thought to wonder at it.

Prisoner, he thought. *I must be a prisoner.* But he was not bound, and beneath him lay a folding cot with a canvas bead, not the hard ground. He turned his head carefully. He was under a great awning, amid rows of others. Sennedjem! His son lay not far away. Djehuty gasped relief to see his chest rising under a mummy's swath of bandages. But what was held in the clear glass bottle that was connected to his arm by a flexible tube?

Djehuty's eyes went wide when he realized that the same piece of sorceror's apparatus drained into his *own* arm. Gradually the fear died, and the pain in his head became less. When the foreigner's black commander came, he was able to stare back with something approaching dignity as she sat on a folding stool beside his cot.

She spoke, and the *Sudunu* interpreter relayed the words:

"You and your men fought very well."

Djehuty blinked, then nodded. Nevertheless, the scales had swung against him. "You deceived us very well. Ransom?" he went on without much hope.

She shook her head. "When the war is over, we will release all our prisoners."

Djehuty blinked again, this time in surprise, caught between relief and doubt. It would take a strong commander to deny victorious troops the plunder of victory, and the sale of prisoners was an important part of that. Even Pharaoh, the living God, might have difficulties. With an effort, he fought down bitterness against Ramses; what the Pharaoh decreed, must be done . . . even if it destroyed the Brigade of Seth at the word of the foreigner Mek-andrus.

"Your king must be a ruler of great power," he said.

"We have no king," she said, and smiled slightly at his bafflement. "We come from . . . very far away," she said. "In distance and years. You might call us exiles."

"Your whole nation?" he said in bafflement, as the explanation went on. *Powerful sorcery.*

"No," she went on. "Just one small island of us, and a ship. So we were stranded here and now."

"Ah," Djehuty said bitterly. "And with arts of war like none we know, you seek to carve out a great empire."

Long black fingers knotted into a fist on a trousered knee. "No. *Some* of us saw that they might become kings here, with what they knew. The rest of us . . . must fight to enforce our law upon them."

"No king . . ." Djehuty frowned. "I find that hard to believe. Only a powerful king can make a people strong in war."

She shook her head. "That is not so, Djehuty of the Brigade of Seth. We have arts that your people do not, is that not so?" He nodded, reluctantly. "Well," she went on, "not all those arts are arts of war. We have found that one man's wisdom is not enough to steer a great nation, and how to . . . to melt together the wisdom of many."

"I do not understand."

"Let me tell you," she said, "of a thing we call a *Constitution*, which is a government of laws and not of men . . ."

When she rose with a promise to return and speak more, his head was whirling as badly as it had when the spearshaft clubbed him. He heard words in the foreign commander's language:

"And that'll cause a lot more trouble than gunpowder, in the long run."

"Wait," he said. "One thing—what name will this battle be given? Surely it is a greater one than Kadesh, even." Let the chronicles remember it, and with it the name of Djehuty. Chronicles that did not lie, like the ones that called Kadesh a victory for Ramses.

She turned, smiling wryly. "We will name it from the hill that overlooks the battlefield," she said. "Har-Megiddo. Armaggedon, in our tongue."

Dead Men Talk A Lot
William C. Dietz

I'm waiting to die. Well, not die exactly, since there's no such thing but I won't be alive either. Not like I used to be, up walking around, checking things out. Not hardly. Not after the padre comes, not after the doctor does his shit, not after the lethal injection.

It's confusing. That's why I'm writing this down, to keep my thoughts straight, and to tell my side of the story.

I mean Larry's been dead for more than a year now, and he's been on everything from *Sixty Minutes* to the *Oprah Winfrey* show. The miserable bastard. It's all part of what some regard as the end of the world—and others see as the beginning.

It all started when this little-known researcher at Lucent Technologies married some sort of artificial intelligence thingamajig to a voice synthesizer, and hooked the whole thing to the telephone network.

All of a sudden the poor bastard's talking to dead people! He didn't believe it himself until his mother got on the line and chewed him out for skipping breakfast.

Well, everyone said he was crazy, or a fraud, or both, but it wasn't long before the geeks at MIT, UCLA, and any number of telephone companies duplicated his results.

Wow! You wanna talk about chaos!

Religions took it the hardest, which is kinda funny, since

they're the ones who used to work overtime trying to convince everybody that life continues after death.

Well, they were right. There is life after death, but not the kind they envisioned. No streets of gold, no angelic choirs, no celestial virgins, just a place where things are what you make them and people are all jumbled together. And that's where the problem comes in . . .

I mean with no paradise to look forward to, why load your car with explosives, and ram an embassy? Why eradicate people who call god by some other name? Or build their temples in funny shapes? Or dress differently?

The conservative Christian, Jewish and Muslim groups were hardest hit, but others suffered too, especially when it turned out that relics, holy books, prayer wheels and crystals don't mean much. They're symbols—ritual elements—and aids to concentration. It's what you actually *do* that counts.

The New Agers fared a little better, since their theories about karma and reincarnation turned out to be true, but hundreds of disappointed women sued their channelers when it turned out that the real Cleopatra had incarnated into a male body and was driving a bus in the Bronx.

In any case talking to dead people is no big deal anymore. No medium, no trumpets, no ectoplasm. So everyone yacked it up, burning ether between this world and the next. And the implications were enormous . . .

Sorrow caused by the death of a loved one became a thing of the past, old people smiled a lot, funeral homes went out of business, send-off parties became all the rage, historical figures phoned historians in an attempt to tell *their* side of the story, new religions popped up all over the place, politicians both living and dead discussed the possibility of "two-dimensional democracies," and the IRS began to file tax cases against "disincarnate citizens."

And it was right in the middle of all this that Larry and I decided to rob a bank. Not just any bank, but Seattle Trust, a nice little establishment conveniently located across

from our apartment on Capitol Hill. Stupid, huh? But
that's what bank robbers tend to be. Stupid.

You could see the bank through the window of our cheap
studio apartment. A low-slung building on the other side
of funky, funky Broadway. A dry cleaners once, and
specialty store after that, all dressed up in brick with no
place to go. Like most of our really stupid ideas this one
originated with Larry. He was dressed in his usual uniform
of Grateful Dead T-shirt, ripped blue jeans, and filthy
Reeboks. He had long blonde hair, beady little eyes, and
the biggest honker you ever saw. He strode back and forth
across our twelve-foot-wide living room and gestured
towards the bank.

"Hey dude, it's just sittin' there, waiting for us to come
on down. You've been in there, you know there's nothin'
but a couple of ugly lookin' chicks, and a geez with glasses.
Shit, the old fart ain't even got a gun!"

At this point Larry pulled out the chrome-plated .38
he'd stolen from his father—and waved it under my nose.
I'm no coke head, but I do drop a little LSD once in a
while, and the barrel of Larry's gun looked like the inside
of a railway tunnel.

"Woooo woooo!" I said in my best imitation of a steam
locomotive. Larry ignored me. He resumed pacing back
and forth. "I don't know about you, dude, but I'm tired
of flippin' burgers, and takin' shit from management
trainees. So we walk in the bank, introduce the clerks to
Mr. Smith and Wesson here, grab the money and haul
ass. Ain't nothin' to it."

"Yeah," I said brightly, "ain't nothin' to it."

Right," Larry agreed, lighting a Camel. "So let's go."
He stuck the pistol in the back of his pants, threw me a
black baseball hat with RIDE TO LIVE, LIVE TO RIDE inscribed
across the front, and headed for the door. Like a fool I
followed.

The trip down the rickety back stairs, up the side of
the building to Broadway, and across the street passed in

slow motion. I remember getting lost in the traffic and feeling a tug on my sleeve. "Come on, dude, it's green."

The bank sensed our presence and opened its door. The old man in the blue uniform looked up from his *Field and Stream*, nodded, and went back to reading.

The counters were straight ahead but the chandelier caught my eye. It had tulip-shaped fixtures that seemed to pulsate in and out. It meant something but I wasn't sure what.

I heard someone yell, felt Larry grab my arm, and found myself running out the door.

Outside there was the usual mix of street people, old ladies, and business types on their way to lunch.

I bumped into someone, Larry's hand disappeared, a bus pulled up and I stumbled on. It jerked into motion and I fell forward. Hands helped me up. There was the babble of voices as someone asked me for money and someone else said I was "wasted." Doors hissed open, and I half walked, half fell onto the street.

I don't remember much after that, except the afternoon passed slowly, and I spent a lot of it in a park. Along about dusk I made my way back to our building, climbed the stairs, and entered our apartment. I called for Larry but there was no reply.

Collapsing on a beat-up futon I turned on the tube. Oprah interrupted one last guest, made way for a block of commercials, and they segued into the news. The bank robbery was numero uno. The anchorman smiled as if bank robberies were a lot of fun. "The Capitol Hill branch of Seattle Trust was robbed today . . . and two people were killed. Deborah Wallings is standing by live. Deborah?"

Something heavy fell into my stomach. Killed? Deborah Wallings live?

I struggled to my feet and ran to the window. Sure enough, a TV crew had set up in front of the bank, and Deborah Wallings was gesturing towards the front door. I rushed back to the TV set and cranked the volume up.

Deborah was blonde-haired blue-eyed perfection as always. ". . . Frank. The robbery was carefully planned to coincide with the noon rush hour."

My mind boggled. "Carefully planned?" Where'd she get that? Regardless of where she got it Deborah continued. "Shortly after twelve, two unidentified white male suspects came through the door. One pointed a gun a teller Cindy Hall, and ordered her to empty the till."

At this point they put a shot of Larry on the screen. The blurry black and white security photo made him look even worse than usual. He clutched the .38 in his right hand while a joint drooped from the corner of his mouth. Jeez! The idiot even smoked while robbing banks!

I felt disconnected, separate somehow, until my picture flooded the screen. The shot was crystal clear and better than the one in my high school yearbook. I was staring upwards, almost directly into the lens, looking stupid as hell.

Deborah droned on. "The second man functioned as a lookout and may or may not have been armed."

Now the picture dissolved from the shot of me to Deborah. She looked smarter than I had.

"After collecting more than a hundred thousand dollars in cash the two men fled south on Broadway. They split up after a block or so. One jumped onto a metro bus— and the other disappeared down a side street. Seattle police spotted him ten minutes later and gave chase. They caught him in the alley behind the Payless drugstore."

Now the shot dissolved to an alley and a blanket-covered corpse. All you could see were Larry's dirty Reeboks sticking out from one end of the blanket. Suddenly it came crashing home. Larry was dead. Really dead. Pushing-up-daisies dead.

I felt a lump form in the back of my throat. Larry was an idiot, but he was *my* idiot, and we'd been friends since the third grade.

The camera zoomed back to show Deborah. A pair of medics were loading a second body into the back of an ambulance. How did they do that? Oh, this part was taped. The taped Deborah looked sad.

"Police say they ordered the suspect to halt. He turned, pulled a .38-caliber revolver, and fired a single shot. Then, in what police describe as a 'one in a million' occurrence, the suspect's bullet ricocheted off a building, and hit Officer Philip McCutcheon in the head. He was pronounced dead at Harborview Hospital.

"McCutcheon's partner, Officer Kline, returned fire and the suspect fell. She will remain on administrative leave until a shooting review board is convened and their investigations are complete. Seattle police and FBI agents are searching for the second suspect. Frank?"

A dead police officer? The FBI? Oh shit, shit, shit. What the hell had I done?

Frank appeared on the screen, one eyebrow carefully raised. "Thank you, Deborah. One question before you go . . . what about the money? Did police recover it?"

Deborah shook her head. "No, the police found no sign of the money, and assume that suspect number two has it. Interestingly enough, sources close to the investigation say that the suspects got away with an exceptionally large haul. It seems there was an unusually large amount of money on hand . . . much of which was close to Cindy Hall's window when the robbery occurred."

Frank shook his head at this sad turn of events. "Thanks, Deborah. We'll be back for an update at 6:30. There was a fire today . . ."

I turned the TV off and sat there trying to absorb what had transpired. Larry and I had robbed a bank. Larry was dead. A police officer was dead. The FBI was looking for me. The FBI! What the hell was I sitting around for? Come to think of it, why weren't they knocking on the door?

The phone began to ring. I started to pick it up and stopped. Who was it? The FBI? Mom and Dad? They love Deborah Wallings. Mom thinks she's "cute." Oh god, what would I tell them?

The phone continued to ring as I stood up and looked around. There was Larry's wallet, laying on the card table where he'd forgotten it for the last time. That would explain why they weren't beating the door down. I grabbed it and looked inside. It contained little more than some scraps of paper, a ticket stub, and a driver's license. I threw it on the futon. Poor stupid Larry. The phone quit ringing.

My brain kicked in. I needed clothes. Clothes and money. There wasn't much time. The cops would arrive any minute now. They'd arrest me, find me guilty, and send me to prison. All in about fifteen minutes. Not if I could help it they wouldn't!

I grabbed some dirty laundry and stuffed it into a blue gym bag with ALASKA AIRLINES stenciled across the front.

Walking over to the makeshift bookcase, a surefire place to hide things from Larry, I grabbed *Hidden Hawaii, An Adventurer's Guide* and opened it up. The twenty was right where I'd left it. Some pit spray, my shaving kit, and Larry's portable CD player. I was ready to go.

I slipped out the door, took the back steps two at a time, and walked away. There wasn't a cop in sight.

Parking on Capitol Hill is next to impossible so my car was six blocks away. It's a red 1994 Honda Civic, not fancy, but as Dad would say, "dependable."

It was my graduation present from high school, a reward for my 3.5 grade average, and supposed to carry me through four years at UCLA. Unfortunately I dropped out after two and moved in with Larry. A mistake if there ever was one.

The Honda started like always and I battled my way out from between a couple of old beaters and oozed my way towards 15th.

I felt safe now, rolling along the city streets, wrapped within the wonderful cocoon of privacy that surrounds a car in traffic. The feeling is largely illusionary of course, since people can see you in there, picking your nose, and scratching your pits. But it *feels* private and I needed that.

Time passed and I went nowhere, driving aimlessly around the city, trying to make a plan. I wound around Queen Anne, over the Ballard Bridge, and out past Golden Gardens.

I knew I should be doing things, like changing my appearance, finding new plates for the car, and putting some miles between Seattle and me. The last was especially difficult since it would take some money, and outside of the twenty, and six more in my wallet, I was flat broke.

It was kinda funny in a way. I mean here I was a bank robber—without any of the stuff you rob banks for!

And that got me to thinking . . . Where was the money anyway? The "more than a hundred thousand dollars" that Larry had toted out of Seattle Trust and stashed somewhere? Maybe I should look for it.

I abandoned the thought as quickly as it came. No, if it was that easy the police would've found it.

I passed a 7-Eleven convenience store. A pay phone sat out front.

Of course! The answer was simple. I'd call Larry and ask him where the money was. He'd tell me, I'd get it, and presto! Escape time.

I slammed on the brakes, made a highly illegal U-turn, and pulled into the parking lot.

It was dark by now, but a carefully placed spotlight lit up a banner advertising 16-ounce Big Gulps, and there was a guy pumping gas into one of those giant 4 X 4 pickups. The kind with a winch, off-road lights, and nary a scratch.

More than a little paranoid, I looked around to make sure no one was watching, and backed into a parking space. Even amateur bank robbers should be ready for a quick getaway.

The phone booth's bifold doors squeaked as I pushed them open. I turned my back to the street. No point in showing my now famous mug.

Someone had scribbled all over the instruction card
mounted over the phone but I didn't need it. Who could
forget AT&T's "Call Heaven" ad campaign? Complete with
grandchildren talking to recently departed grandparents
and a celestial choir? It brought new meaning to "Reach
out and touch someone."

I used my right index finger to punch the buttons.
C-A-L-L H-E-A-V-E-N. It rang three times before an
operator answered. "AT&T operator . . . Billing please."

I was ready for that one and gave her my parents'
telephone number and four-digit pin code. Just one more
abuse of their trust. There was a pause followed by a
recording. "Thank you for using AT&T. Please stay on
the line. A disincarnate operator will take your call and
send for the party you requested."

I settled in for a long wait. I'd seen plenty of news
stories and knew how it worked. Disincarnate operators,
or D.O.'s as they're called in the telecommunications
trade, are volunteers. They do what they do for the
same reasons that people on this plane of existence staff
hot lines and collect food for the needy. They want to
help.

The only problem is that time doesn't mean much over
there. Scientists are just starting to study the differences
between the two worlds, but one thing is for sure, dead
people ignore their clocks. Assuming they have them
that is.

As a result the D.O.'s handle calls when they're good
and ready. Knowing that—the marketing folks had come
up with a bright idea: "Would you like to hear Dr. Ruth
interview Caligula? If so, press one. A charge of ninety
cents a minute will be billed to your card. Or how about
Genghis Khan? Were you a member of the horde? Press
two to hear some of the Khan's favorite war stories . . ."
And so on until you could barf. A full ten minutes passed
before I got an answer. Unfortunately it was in Chinese.
I spoke very clearly and distinctly as if that would make

a difference. "I am sorry. I do not understand. Do you speak English?"

It was apparent from the ensuing gabble that he didn't. Another ten minutes passed. During that time a rather large man who probably ate anabolic steroids for breakfast, lunch, and dinner approached the booth, paced back and forth, gave me a series of dirty looks, and eventually went away. I gave a sigh of relief.

Twenty seconds later a woman came on the line. "Hello. This is Mary . . . How can I help you?"

A chill ran down my spine. I opened my mouth but nothing emerged. A dead person. I was talking to a dead person! Or would be if I could make my voice work.

"Hello? Hello? Is anyone there?"

"I'm here," I managed to croak. The phone felt wet and slippery in my hand. "I'm trying to call Larry Lewiston. He died earlier today," I added stupidly.

Mary's voice was calm, professionally soothing, and carried just the slightest hint of a southern accent.

"Thanks hon, that means your friend is still in transition. It's still a bit early . . . but we'll give it a try. People adjust a lot faster now that they know what to expect."

"Thank you," I replied hoarsely and settled back to wait. I wished I'd had the foresight to buy a cup of coffee and felt the simultaneous need to pee.

A full twenty minutes went by before Mary came back on line. And a good thing too . . . since my bladder was about to burst.

"I found Larry. But be patient hon . . . He suffered a rather traumatic death—and it takes time to adjust."

No shit, I thought, and what about the cop? How does *he* feel?

But she made it sound so reasonable, so ordinary, that I found myself responding in kind. "Of course . . . thanks Mary."

Much to my surprise Larry came on line a second later. The style was his, but the voice was different, the product of a speech synthesizer buried in the telephone network. It was weird to think Larry was out there, separate from his body, but still him.

"Hey dude, is this weird or what?"

"This is definitely weird," I replied. "How you doin'?" There was a pause as if Larry was thinking.

"Well, I don't know yet, dude, this place is different ya know? I mean you can create a cigarette by thinking about one . . . but you can't light the damned thing."

"Bummer," I said with what I hoped was the right amount of sympathy. "Well, I'm sure you'll get the hang of things pretty soon. What was it like?"

"What was what like?"

"Dying, Larry. What was dying like?"

"Oh, that. It's just like they say, dude . . . You kinda rise up outta your body, there's this tunnel of white light, you float through and there you are. Mom didn't come—but Grandma did."

"What about the cop?"

"Cop?"

"Yeah, you know, the one you shot."

"He's pissed, dude, real pissed, but that's karma for you. The dude had it coming. It seems he offed somebody in a previous life or something."

"So that makes what you did okay?"

"No," Larry responded, "not according to the welcoming committee. But you know me—I'll find a way to beat the rap."

"That's just terrific," I said, watching a police car pull into the parking lot. "Except that it won't help me . . . The fact is that Officer McCutcheon died during the commission of a felony. A felony *I* participated in. I'm wanted for murder, Larry. A murder you committed. So tell me . . . what happened to the money from the bank job?"

Two cops got out of the patrol car, hitched up their gun belts, and strolled towards the 7-Eleven. A doughnut break. I wanted to pee real bad.

There was a long silence.

"Larry? You still there?"

"Yeah dude, I'm here, but I've gotta think about the money . . . I don't have a handle on all this stuff, but there's my karma to think about, plus yours. I mean that money doesn't belong to you, dude. Maybe you should turn yourself in."

One of the cops said something to the other and started in my direction.

"Turn myself in? Listen goddamn it! I wouldn't be in this spot if it weren't for you! I was high . . . I didn't know what I was doing."

The cop was closer now. He pulled something out of a pocket and looked at it. A phone number? A photo of me?

Now Larry's voice took on a supercilious quality. The words sounded as if they had been uttered by someone else. Someone Larry had heard very recently. "Hey, dude, each of us is responsible for our own actions. No one forced you to rob that bank."

The policeman was just steps away. He looked up from the paper and frowned.

"Cut the crap, Larry, and tell me where the money is . . . I need it."

Larry laughed. "Screw you, dude." Then there was a click followed by a dial tone.

My heart beat like a trip hammer as I hung up, opened the door, and mumbled to the cop.

I waited for him to say something, to grab me by the arm, but he nodded and stepped inside.

I circled the building, checked to make sure that the cops couldn't see me, and emptied my bladder by the dumpster. Something caught my eye as I zipped my pants. A red Civic, which, except for the PEROT FOR PRESIDENT bumper sticker, was identical to mine. The fact that it was parked next to the store's back door suggested an employee.

I took a quick look around, hunkered down behind the Honda, and used my Swiss Army knife to undo the rear license plate. Seconds later it was safely tucked inside my jacket and I was walking away.

The cop car was gone, and moments later, so was I.

The first thing I did was find a poorly lit residential street and remove the license plates from my car. Then I screwed the stolen plate to the rear bumper, hoped no one would notice the fact that the front plate was missing, and took off.

The next half hour or so was spent in more aimless driving. Damn that Larry! Handing out sanctimonious garbage like he was an angel or something. It didn't make sense. Geraldo Rivera had interviewed everyone from Joan of Arc to George Washington. They all said the same thing. You're the same person after you die. So, if Larry was a selfish jerk at the moment of his death, he still was.

That being the case, he didn't care about his karma, or mine. No, he cared about something else . . . But what? Then I had it! The rotten sonovabitch cared about the money! He had plans for the money, and didn't want to give it up!

I slammed on the brakes, scared the hell out of the elderly couple in the car behind me, and pulled over to the curb. That was it. Larry had plans for the money. Plans that didn't include his old buddy Greg. But what plans? What could a dead man do with a hundred thousand in cash?

Then it hit me . . . The sneaky bastard was going to come back and get it. All he'd have to do was reincarnate, arrange for someone to call him when he reached the age of eighteen, and pick up the money.

No, wait a minute. Damn! He could call one of his slime-ball friends, have him retrieve the money, and invest it! The better part of a hundred thou sitting around, collecting interest! The thought made me sick.

I cruised northwards along old Highway 99, spotted a run-down motel, and pulled in.

A beefy woman with a full head of curlers answered the door, accepted the phoney name I gave her, and directed me to unit six. I half expected her to ask for money in advance, but I guess the combination of my clean-cut looks, and late model car put her at ease.

The room was small, badly in need of paint, and smelled like the bottom of an ash tray. I opened a window to let in some air, collapsed on the lumpy mattress, and fell into a troubled sleep. I woke up with sunlight in my eyes and rolled over. My eyes snapped open. The bank robbery, Larry's death, and the phone call . . . It hit me like a ton of bricks. For a moment there I felt horribly, intensely sorry for myself, certain that no other human being had been so sorely mistreated.

That feeling began to wane however as I thought about Larry and his refusal to give me the money. Anger flooded in to replace the self-pity. I gritted my teeth. Damn the bastard! To hell with him! I'd find the money and return it! That would fix his wagon . . . and cut my karma to boot.

I rummaged through the Alaska Airlines bag, found my shaving kit, and entered the bathroom. There was a tiny mirror on the wall. The face that stared back at me from the mirror was different somehow. Brown hair, what one girl had called "sensitive eyes," and a determined mouth. Yes, that was it, a determined mouth. Larry had given me a purpose, something to accomplish, and by god I would!

Breakfast consisted of a non-fat, no-whip, coffee mocha plus two maple bars and the *Post Intelligencer*. A plane crash had pushed the bank job below the fold with more inside.

They had identified both Larry and me, located our apartment, and searched it. There was even a quote from my mom, something to the effect of "We don't know why Greg would do such a thing—and I feel terribly ashamed."

Poor Mom. I felt the tears push up and threaten to cascade down my cheeks. I wanted to run to the nearest phone, call my parents, and beg their forgiveness.

But that would be stupid. The police might be tapping their line, or who knows? No, I'd get even with Larry, and then look for a way to contact my parents.

Determined to be tough—I took another bite of maple bar and paged my way through the paper. Maybe Dilbert could make me laugh.

I was almost there when a photo caught my eye. It was a shot of a young woman, pretty, and disturbingly familiar. Then I had it. Kathy Keenan! A cheerleader at my high school—and the object of considerable adolescent lust.

There had been a time when I would've given anything for the chance to hold one of her perfectly manicured hands, to look into her big blue eyes, and hear the sound of my name on her lips. But that was impossible since Kathy had existed at the most rarified heights of our pubescent social structure, and I, if not at the very bottom, was close enough to see it, and know those who dwelt there, Larry being one.

Yes, I showed for all the games, not because I cared who won, but because of Kathy's legs. And when I cheered, it was for her, not the team.

So I read the article fully expecting to hear something good. So it was a shock when I discovered that Kathy had cancer, was expected to die soon, and was taking part in a new "transition" program for people with terminal diseases.

Kathy Keenan die? Impossible! I could see her in my mind's eye, wearing the sweater with the red letter "L" on the front, and that short white skirt. For years she'd been an important part of my fantasy life. Now she was dying, heading for the other side, going with Larry. Wait a minute! I had an idea . . .

I crammed the last bite of maple bar in my mouth, washed it down with a gulp of lukewarm mocha, and headed for the door. I had a crazy idea, a truly crazy idea, but so what? My whole life had turned to shit.

It took twenty minutes to find the hospice, park the car, and work up the nerve to ring the bell. It was an older house, a mansion once, located just north of the university. There were maple trees all around, some shabby shrubs, and the last of summer's flowers.

The house seemed to radiate a dignified peace, as if it was special, and knew it. There was a brass plaque on the front door. It read GATEWAY HOUSE.

I pressed the bell and heard a distant chime. A few moments later the door opened to reveal a pleasant-looking woman in her late thirties. She had black hair quickly turning to gray, intelligent eyes, and a sensitive mouth. Something about the clothes she wore indicated a lack of interest in worldly things. She smiled. "Yes?"

I felt suddenly paranoid. What if she recognized me and called the police? Or worse yet, what if Kathy refused to see me? After all, why should she? We'd barely known each other in high school. "I'm here to see Kathy Keenan."

The woman nodded encouragingly. "Is Kathy expecting you?"

"No, I'm afraid not. I knew her in high school, and read about her in the paper, I . . ."

"You wanted to see Kathy before she makes the transition . . . Quite understandable. Your name?"

I swallowed hard. If I gave the woman my name she might recognize it, but if I didn't, Kathy wouldn't see me. "Greg Altman."

The woman put out her hand. I shook it. "I'm Florence. Please come in. Have a seat in the library while I track her down."

The woman ushered me into a room full of books, freshly cut flowers, and comfortable furniture. Light streamed in through leaded glass windows and splashed on a well-worn oriental rug.

I had no more than taken a seat when an elderly man in

a wheelchair rolled in. His eyes lit up when he saw me and the motor made a whirring sound. Little tufts of white hair stuck out of his head at odd angles, his skin had a sickly pallor, and he smelled like unchanged diapers. But his eyes were clear and his voice had a cheerful ring. "Hello, son. Are you goin' belly up? Whatcha got? Some kinda cancer?"

I forced a smile. "No, not that I know of . . . I'm here to see someone."

"Oh," the old man said, obviously disappointed. "I'm gonna check out any day now. Can't wait. Phoned ahead. Got all sorts of friends and relatives over there. A lot of the guys from Korea. The ones that didn't make it back. Hey, the folks here in hospice are giving me a party this afternoon. You wanna come?"

"Thanks," I replied, "but I'll be gone by then."

"Okay," the old man replied. "Suit yourself. In the meantime I'm goin' out for a smoke. I mean why not? What's it gonna do? Give me cancer?" The old man cackled gleefully and wheeled himself out of the room.

After that I just sat there for a while and enjoyed the sunlight that pooled at my feet. For the first time since the robbery I was almost happy. Her voice caught me by surprise. "Greg? Greg Altman?"

I stood and turned. She was thinner, much thinner than I remembered her to be. The gray jogging suit hung in loose folds around her body. She wore a hat too, a Diane Keaton thing, to cover the fact that her hair had fallen out. The thick blonde hair was no more.

But it was her face which captured my attention. The face that I'd secretly studied during home room, stared at in the halls, and watched from the bleachers. It was still pretty, but more mature somehow, as if she'd learned a great deal since our senior year.

Kathy smiled and held out her hand. I took it and felt a tingle run through my body. Here she was, dying of cancer, and she could still turn me on. "Hello, Greg, it's been a long time." Now that she was here, I felt silly, unsure of what to do or say. She squeezed my hand to remind me that I should let go. I did.

"Hello, Kathy. I read about you in the paper. I . . . I . . . god I don't know . . . I wanted to talk to you that's all."

Kathy nodded as if my desire to talk with her was the most natural thing in the world. "I'm glad you came. Sit down. I'd invite you to my room, but I share it with someone else, and she's close to death."

Kathy said it as if death were the most natural thing in the world, and come to think of it, I guess it is.

She curled up at one end of the couch like a little girl in her daddy's chair, while I sat at the other, basking in her presence.

We talked about the old days for a while, about high school, about our classmates. It didn't work too well, since we'd hung out with radically different crowds, but it was common ground of a sort.

After that came the story of her short-lived marriage to some jock, a glowing description of her four-year-old daughter, and the sad story of my rather truncated college career.

Then there came a pause, a point where the past was all used up, and the conversation should turn to the future. But I didn't know how to do it, how to broach the subject, how to tell her what I wanted.

Much to my surprise Kathy did it for me. "Greg . . . maybe it's none of my business . . . but you were in this morning's paper. You and that Larry guy. The one who spray painted the front of the school. They say you robbed a bank . . . and killed a policeman."

The words came as a shock. My god! She hadn't said a word . . . Or had she? For all I knew the police were on the way. I started to rise but she stopped me. "No, Greg . . . I didn't call the police."

She smiled. "Outside of my mother . . . and some distant relatives . . . you're the only one who came to see me. I had to know why."

There was a long moment of silence during which all sorts of things bubbled up inside me. Finally the words came spilling out, everything, the way I'd worshipped her from afar, the robbery, my conversation with Larry, everything. By the time I had finished, there were tears streaming down her face, and I felt terrible. But she wiped them away and held my hand.

"Don't feel badly, Greg . . . you've made me happy in a way that no one else could . . . I simply wish that sixteen-year-old girls were smarter, that's all. We're kind of similar you and I. Lots of potential and nothing to show for it."

Well, that seemed to say it all, and we just sat there for a while, holding hands, and thinking our separate thoughts. That's when I made my proposal. It was simple. Once Kathy arrived on the other side, she would find Larry, and raise the subject of the bank job. And Larry, being more than a little susceptible to female flattery, would spill his worthless guts. That's when Kathy would call the police, tell them where to find the money, and turn me in. There was a reward for my capture, that's what it said in the paper anyway, and the money would go to her daughter.

Not bad, huh? And guess what? The whole thing went without a hitch. Slower than I would have liked—but smooth. Weeks passed before Kathy died, passed through orientation, and located Larry. Weeks during which I lived on the little bit of money she gave me—and passed the time watching myself on *America's Most Wanted*.

But finally it was over. Kathy got the information, passed it to the police, and told them where to find me. I was arrested, charged with murder, and pled guilty. Not only that, I told them I wanted to die, and the sooner the better.

Well, you can imagine the furor. I was the toast of the tabloids. The criminal justice system was in a quandary— since no one had figured out what to do with the death penalty. I mean, where's the penalty? Not to mention the fact that folks on the other side were sick and tired of having the freaks and weirdos shipped over to them.

But the law's the law, so they have to kill me, and today's the day. I talked to Kathy just yesterday, and she's waiting for me, along with that son of a bitch Larry.

Just wait till I get over there! I plan to kick his ethereal butt! As for Kathy, well, we plan to spend some time together. Give me a call sometime . . . I'll let you know how it turns out.

A Watery Silence
Billie Sue Mosiman

June 4

I have been five days dead.

Nietzsche was right. God is, also, dead. Or God never was. If there were a God, he wouldn't have let humankind suffer in this manner. I would have rather there had been a God in heaven and a Lucifer below, I would have rather burned on red-hot coals for my sins for eternity than to live this everlasting death.

I'm leaving these pages for the living so they will know what they face if they join me. No one before me has chronicled what this life-in-death is like and it's important for the world to know.

The plague that swept across continents and infected millions has also infected me. So far as I know I am the only one who *understands* my predicament. I'm searching for another. I don't want to be alone much longer. I fear my mind is slipping, has slipped, will continue to slip, into madness.

It all began five days ago.

I lifted my arm just now and brought my flesh close to my face. I pressed my nostrils directly against the skin, felt its tightness against my cheek, slid out my tongue and tasted. It is a little sweet, my flesh, not very salty, and cool. Cold. There is the faint scent of some bits of me rotting down below the layer of muscle. I am corrupting, but at a slower rate than I would have thought. Especially in this tropical climate. Miami, Florida. A splendid paradise for dying.

After lying dead for five days, an uninfected man would have bloated, stiffened with rigor mortis, and gone soft again, turned to jelly, gaseous and purple as a plum.

It was Saturday when I died. In May. When I had everything to live for. But we all do, always. I tell you this, and you must remember it every moment you live and draw breath. *There is everything to live for*. Treasure every second. Lift up your eyes and see the sun and touch your loved ones and capture and hold onto any little joy that burbles in your heart. Life is never so bad that death—any death, but particularly this death—could ever be thought remotely preferable.

Saturday. "Carrie," I said. "We must have milk for the baby." My daughter had barely survived for eight days on water strained from oatmeal and she needed more nourishment. I couldn't stay barricaded in the house any longer.

Carrie begged, "Please don't go outside, please don't leave us. The provisions will be here on Monday." Teardrops collected on the lower rims of her eyes. I wanted to take her into my arms, but I couldn't, not this time.

The army truck would bring our neighborhood milk and cheese and meat and vegetables, enough to last another month, but it never did, it never lasted, not for a growing child. Margaret is just four months old. I delivered her myself, held that tiny wonder in the palms of my hands and saw her take her first breath, held her against my chest and felt her heartbeat flutter wildly, fighting to live. Carrie had no milk, her malnourishment drying her breasts before the baby could gain a hold on life. I couldn't stand to watch Margaret waste away, grow listless, her blue eyes fading to slate, her lips blindly, softly sucking at the stained water when I could do something, by God, I was her father, wasn't I? I couldn't let her die, could I?

But I have to make you understand this. I didn't want my daughter to die, but there was more than her life in the balance. I wanted her to live for *me*. I knew if the baby died, Carrie would soon follow. She was already slowly losing her mind, and with the baby's death, I knew she would give up. In the end I would be living alone in an echoing house, alienated from any human touch or voice or kindness.

Carrie threatened, "I'll call in and report you! This is abandonment, you can't leave me alone."

She was so afraid of losing me to the zombies. I couldn't let her know my fears of losing first the baby and then her, so I said go ahead, call, turn me in, have me put into some prison camp for leaving the house, then *she* could watch our baby die alone, if that's what she really wanted, goddammit.

It took that kind of cold fury to deal with Carrie those days. She didn't listen unless I turned my back on her and spoke with a rough edge.

I took a thirty-ought-six with me and a machete hanging from my belt. I thought I could protect myself, make it to downtown Miami and back again. I forgot the car wouldn't start. Carrie's pleading had made me lose all sense of reality. Battery dead. I should have known, I *must have* known, but I only wanted to find the milk and watch the light return to my little girl's eyes so my family, my *sanity* could once again be secure.

And I wanted to be outdoors. I was stir crazy, itching all over to be out in the sunshine, to feel the ocean-washed breeze on my face, to smell the mimosa, to touch the grass, to pretend, just for a little while, that the world was as it had been once.

I had to walk. It was four miles. I made three of them before I was attacked.

Surrounded by monsters who lusted to bring me down.

I killed a few, not nearly enough. They came from abandoned houses and buildings. They came from broken storefronts and the front seats of wrecked cars still littering the curb sides. They crawled from bushes and from beneath porches and fell from trees like writhing snakes. The sounds they made were worse than anything I ever heard outside our house where they scratched pitifully against the doors and boarded windows at nights, moaning unintelligibly. The sounds I heard when they had me flat on my back and unarmed were deep growlings and stirring grunts of hunger. They filled my head so that I couldn't hear my own screams.

I don't remember the dying part. If there is a God that's all the good he managed to lend me. I woke feeling . . . different. Oh, very different. Numb. That hasn't changed and I don't expect it to. My limbs are like lead weights and I've not yet learned how to make my legs and arms swing the way they should. I can't yet pass for a living man. I'm still trying to learn how.

My vision was strange. I had trouble focusing. At first my eyes watered and tears ran down my face because of the sun. My nose wouldn't stop dripping; it was as if I had stuffed truckloads of cocaine up my nostrils for a solid year. For some time I lay on the sidewalk where they'd left me, trying to believe I had been granted a reprieve. I was still alive.

So what if my flesh felt wooden and I couldn't see clearly? What matter was it that when I tried to move, my joints popped and it felt as if my ligaments were being stretched to their limits? I feared to feel for my heart, to check for a pulse. I feared to bring my hand to my mouth to see if I could discern air rushing from my lungs.

I had to be alive. I was thinking. I knew what had happened to me. I had a memory and a past. Zombies didn't think. We all knew that. They were automatons, hardly more than corpses in motion, possessed by the virus with an instinct to move and keep moving, to destroy the living, and to eat. If their brains had died and mine had not, then that was proof! I was not hungry in the least, not for food or for the flesh of my kind. Why should I doubt my good fortune, why check my pulse, feel for my heartbeat? I would not tempt fate, never again. I would get up and hurry back to my home, there to stay behind the walls until the army told us it was all right to come out. If it took two more years of waiting—the time minimum we'd been promised before there was a vaccine available—I didn't care, I'd never venture out again.

I could move a little, though the creaks and cracklings of my bones sent small thrills of worry through my brain. My clothes were torn and there was a nasty rippling series of bites on my legs and arms, even one on the back of my neck, and I could see congealed blood, but I wouldn't think about the infection. I thought I must be immune. The only immune man in all the world because I was alive, surely I was alive for I felt alive. Dead wasn't just a numbness and a watering of the eyes and a few ligament strains, was it? Wouldn't my soul have fled had I really died? Wouldn't I be traveling through a tunnel toward light and peace and find those who had gone before me . . . my mother, my father, my two brothers, my grandparents?

Death could not be so simple as this.

Yet it was. It was.

But I didn't know that—or admit the possibility—for most of Saturday and Saturday night.

June 6

I crept to my house today. It was the first time I'd been back since my death. For days I couldn't do anything, but hide in shadows and dribble and beat the palms of my hands against my forehead. Once at my house, I joined the others at the door and stood there patting, patting at the wood, pressing my cold face there, moaning, trying to cry.

I cannot cry. I would weep all the time if I could. My eyes won't water anymore. My nose is dry. My juices are building inside, that's all I can think. Seeping all together inside, commingling, organs and blood coming together in one wet soggy mass.

Oh sweet Jesus.

I could not bear to speak, to tell Carrie inside that it was me, that I had joined in the ranks of the dead, and that I could never again be with her or see my daughter's face. For she'd not have me. Though I'd never hurt them! I have noticed a hunger awakening, but I intend to ignore it. Forever. I hope never to sink so low as to feel a compulsion to betray my own kind, to cannibalize them. But there's no way for Carrie to know that or to trust me.

I had thought—let me tell you—I had thought the zombies created by the infection that took their lives yet let the bodies walk and terrorize the rest of us . . . I had thought there must be a soul and their souls had left them. I am not so sure now. I think there must not be a soul since there is no God, there is no hereafter, no tunnel of light, no meeting with dead loved ones, and no reward, good or bad. There seems to be nothing, but this aching, this wondering horror at what it has all come down to, this sad, unconquerable impetus to go on no matter what. And this gently gnawing hunger for the taste of blood on my tongue.

There was real death and darkness before the virus that has decimated the world and now there is walking death that has taken its place. But there is no soul.

I wish I didn't have to tell you this.

I wish it were not true.

I would die forever and enter that darkness except there is something that causes me to nurse the wish to survive. At all costs. Even though I am cold and numb, I cannot cry, and I cannot find joy again. I still want to go on with this tired old beaten body for as long as I can. You see, I have this hope. A small one, but it keeps me out of the soldiers' line of fire and away from the depots where they congregate in platoons readying for search-and-destroy missions. My hope is that there might be another zombie like me. Somewhere. One who understands that he or she is dead and what it means. If there is just one more of us, it might portend a change in the direction the virus takes. Perhaps . . . there could be a reversal? A coming alive again?

No. I don't suppose that would happen. The blood is clotted and impure. The heart rots and curls into a knot. Each night I lie down to rest (not sleep, for I do not sleep), my muscles contract, and I'm forced to stretch them out again before I can even walk. I know this will never be put right again. Nothing modern medicine could invent would make the physical entity pink and pliant and warm once more.

But something makes me careful. I feel this powerful craving to preserve myself. I believe I have discovered something important about the infection. Part of the reason men who are dead still walk and become dangerous is that they are propelled by instinct. The instinct to survive. Even unto and beyond death. It is as if they walk in their sleep, hunting for relief. Or revenge for the injustice done them.

But why can they not think any longer? Or why can I? There is no fresh blood circulating in my body. I did finally check, late that first night, huddled with my coat pulled around my neck while cowering, fearful, waiting in the night behind a tall hedge of blooming hydrangea. My fingers brushed against the artery at my throat, the carotid, and I jumped as if I had been branded. Fear caught me round with steel bands and for some seconds I couldn't move. I didn't want to know! Not for sure.

But it was too late. I had already felt the stillness there. The perfect quiet. My blood was not rushing through that artery or any other. And hunched there in the dark, scared of the many shadows slipping through the trees and around the sides of the buildings, I realized with a shock that I had not taken a breath since I woke. My chest had never expanded, had never even moved except with exertion when I twisted or turned or pulled myself up.

I lay then, down on the spongy wet grass behind the wild blue nodding heads of hydrangea, and pushed my face into the earth, and for the first time moaned just like the rest of them, the dead ones, moaned deep, without air, with sheer misery vibrating the vocal cords.

I was one of them. It was true. There could be no greater horror.

Why, why, why? Why me? I wanted to be like the others, unknowing, hardly more than amoebas squiggling around, hunting for someone somewhere to halt them in their tracks, to cut off their heads or blow them to pieces so they could never move again.

If there was a God who had let this plague overtake us, it was terror enough that he allowed us to walk when we should be resting in peaceful graves, but to let me know it, oh no, that was impossible. I beat with my fists against the damp dewy earth and cursed him, cursed the thought of any god who might let me suffer this most unholy of unholy hells.

June 7

I slipped a note today beneath the door of my home. The brainless ones tried to stop me. They pushed and pulled and tried to take it from my hand, but I held them off. I wanted to say goodbye. That's all. I wanted to leave something behind saying that I loved them.

I didn't tell them I am one of the dead. I couldn't go that far. When these pages are found they might know then, but not yet. I just told them that I had to be away. The army recruited my help and I could not come home again. Maybe for years. Maybe never. I told them to stay

inside and obey orders. Never to come outside without
an army escort.

I told them to be brave and that one day I hoped we'd
be together again.

I told them I loved them. I would always love them.

Afterward, I wandered toward the edge of town, sorrow
the guiding force. There is nothing else to do, nowhere
else to go except away from the city. Downtown is empty
except for the military. The army controls everything. The
power plants, the telephone company, the farms, the
deliveries to those few living urban dwellers who are left
in their prison homes.

I couldn't follow the freeway until I learned how to walk
better, how to control the jerky movements of my
extremities. I knew I wanted to go south, toward the islands.
I wanted to leave the country. But I would have to learn,
very quickly, how to pass for human to ever make it to
Key West.

There are people on the roads because the troops are
there, coming and going, always on the move, hunting
down zombies like rabid dogs, making deliveries of the
goods that will keep civilization running for a little while
more.

I tried concentrating on my legs, my feet. The contractions,
when I rise at dawn, draw my fingers toward my wrist, my
thumbs toward the palm, my feet outward, toes curled under,
my arms bent at the elbow up toward my face. Each time
this happens, it comes on slowly, while I'm immobile, and
I fight it, but unless I get to my feet and begin moving, it
always works this way. I expect this is a form of rigor mortis,
returning, trying to make me like the real dead.

When I work really hard at it, I can get all my parts to
move naturally. Pick one foot up, set it down, pick up
the other, set it down. I found a way to do it in a small
loping way, as if perhaps I had a hitch in my hip, or an
old war wound.

Then I had to work on my arms, forcing them into a

looseness so they would swing in rhythm with my strides.
Flexing my fingers is the worst thing of all. The bones
pop and I don't know for sure, I'm not conversant in
anatomy or pathology, but I think those bones are breaking.
Over and over again. The thought . . . as I flex and
stretch . . . makes me want to scream.

It took miles and miles before I could learn to walk
decently. Every time a convoy passed I had to duck into
the palmettos and lie flat on my belly, eyes braced on
the ground. Then up again, working at it, finding it easier
the more I tried. I believe the only reason the others can't
do so well, why they stagger and stumble and walk stiff-
legged is because they cannot think, their brains are dead,
so they can't concentrate the way I have managed to do.

When I reached Interstate 95 it was like being drawn
into an exodus. Whole families streamed north and south.
They passed one another on each side of the freeway,
staying clear of the rolling refrigeration trucks and the
lines of green army jeeps. Again I brought my arm to my
face to see how I smelled. I can suck in air and let it out.
I can smell and taste, see, hear, and think. But I am corrupt.
More and more each day. And I cannot speak. I have
decided to pretend I am mute. I have no other choice.

I keep a small pad and a pencil for writing notes. I took
it, this notebook, a knapsack, fresh clothes, deodorant,
soap, a washcloth, a pungent aftershave, and a flashlight
from a deserted house. It was there I cleaned and bandaged
my wounds. I put a large adhesive bandage on the bite
at my neck. If someone asks about it, I'll just say it's a
boil. Lack of iodine, you know, not enough salt in my diet.
None of us get enough salt these days, or sugar, or coffee,
or tobacco. Or milk for our children, never enough milk.

My plan, what there is of it, is to flee Key West to Cuba.
There I might find a ship or plane that will take me to
Europe or South America. Or Mexico. I'd like to go to
Mexico. There haven't been any reports from that country
in months. Maybe things are better there. We have been

told the plague is everywhere, it's worldwide, governments are in chaos, but I cannot mingle with humans much longer. I expect it will be an easier task to search out someone like me in some place where the army is not in such tight control.

Already there are sores erupting behind my knees, between my toes, in my crotch, and beneath my arms. Places where air does not circulate enough.

I won't be able to pass as the living forever. I will make my escape and my search now before I have to begin repair on all these putrefying body parts.

I have been dead a week.

June 8

There were some men and women traveling alone. I didn't stand out so badly. I kept my distance as best I could. I had to concentrate. I had to keep my eyes lowered so the soldiers and the passersby could not see that my eyes are sunken and they have no sheen. No moisture. It is getting more difficult to close my eyelids. I haven't any pain, but the grating of lid on eyeball is unnerving. Like sandpaper over old dry wood. I can actually feel them grinding down when I try to blink.

And the sun is terrible, a fiery ball hanging overhead burning, scorching my back and shoulders, the top of my head. I should have taken a hat. I've been so stupid. I often catch myself gazing longingly at the refrigeration trucks. I could lie down and let the cold halt the deterioration of my cells. I could let the frost cover me over like silken threads.

A stranger came alongside to walk with me a ways. I was grateful there was little breeze to waft my scent to him. He tried to hold a conversation just as I feared he would.

"Goddamn shame we're run out of the cities," he said.

"The damn military thinks they can tell us when to take a crap and when not to. Myself, I'm going down to stay in my old fishing camp at Duck Key. Got enough ammunition here"—he hooked a thumb over his shoulder at a shopping cart he hauled behind him loaded with goods—"to blast any crazy dead fuck wants to mess with me."

I nodded. Took my pad and pen from my shirt pocket and wrote, "I'm sorry, I can't speak. I had an operation. Cancer."

"Well, hell, that's too bad," he said. And then he proceeded to bitch about everything under the sun for the next two hours while I nodded and plodded and concentrated on keeping my feet in time with his and my fingers loose. And my gaze down.

I would have liked to tell him. Tell him *shut up!* You're alive so don't complain, not about anything. Try feeling some kind of elation now. Feel some joy and love because dead isn't dead and being alive is all there is, no matter how bad you might think it is, and there is no God, THERE IS NO GOD.

I told him nothing. I was a sounding board while the day waned, the sun sunk to the horizon, and the families drifted off into the grasses to build summer cooking fires. Still the trucks rumbled past, armed guards eyeing the crowds that lined the pavement.

Finally my companion gave out. I waved goodbye while he called at my back, "You be careful out on the road when it's getting dark! Don't take any shit offa them assholes who come stumbling outta the dark, hear?"

I waved. I went forward at a pace that would have winded a living man and put distance between me and anyone else who looked as if he might want to join up for a little chat.

I'm writing this by firelight. All alone now. I see other fires from here, but the people are tiny black midget shadows moving about beneath a full moon. The trucks are fewer, the night is coming on thick and deep. Crickets chirp nearby, a reedy chorus, and bullfrogs croak down in the ditches. There are a few fleecy clouds overhead. A thousand stars shining down on this desperate planet.

I stare at the open sky and wish to feel some kind of pleasure. I try very hard to feel something besides this cloak of loneliness and utter hopelessness. It's as if the numbness has also reached my heart and turned it to stone.

Nothing comes to me, nothing enters into my thoughts, but dread. That and the creeping pain of hunger radiating from my belly outward to all my parts. I thought perhaps for a time that I could actually take food, but one bite of an orange from a grove tree taught me better. It made me retch and a ghastly trembling took hold of me so that I thought my stomach would come up my throat into my mouth and be expelled onto the ground.

I know what the hunger means. I know what would satisfy it. And before I ever do that, I would rather stand before the army snipers and point to my head.

If I could sleep, I might dream of life the way it was before and for a while escape myself. As it is I can barely keep a flicker of hope burning as the hours lumber by, trickles of sand in an hourglass.

As I sit and watch, the fires burn down. The dark creeps closer. The moon rides high over the world.

At least I have an expectation of tomorrow crossing the long bridge over the aqua waters. Halfway to Key West.

I miss . . . everything. I curse this new death and I cannot tell you how much I wish I could blot these last days out, make them vanish, and return to my little dark house where my only trouble was to ration the milk until help arrived.

June 9

No one accosted me today. There was cloud cover and that helped the problem of the heat. This morning there were blisters on the backs of my hands. I broke them with the needle tip of a palmetto frond. I mashed the skin flat again and wondered where I would ever find gloves before the blisters turned to festering, oozing sores.

In Key West I must do something. I've already had some looks from people on the road because I am dressed in long pants and a long-sleeved shirt. In June. In Florida. I don't let their curious looks bother me. I am beyond the worry of social ambiguities. I don't look right? I may be mad? I want to shout at them: *Fuck this shit, this dead dead dead shit! You'll be like me before long.*

Just before dawn I traveled far into the palmetto and grassland hunting for zombies. I found a half dozen lying on their backs, mesmerized by the moonshine. I shook them. I brought out my pad and wrote, CAN YOU READ THIS? They tore at the paper and tried to stuff it into their mouths. They were mindless creatures. And hungry, always ravenous. But they all know I'm one of them. I don't know how. I can fool humans so far. But not another dead man. Can they smell me, do they know from my eyes, can they sense my blood lies cold in my veins? I don't know. I don't want to know. *Fuck* knowing how they recognize me.

I came back to the highway in time for sunrise and moved into the stream of travelers south. Keeping my distance. Keeping my eyes down before me, watching the gravel roadbed beneath my feet.

I will go out again tonight hunting one who might read my message. I've made it to Marathon Key. There are a few lights, a few houses boarded against intruders. The crowds pass north and south, it seems neither stream of people know what they're doing, they just feel safe with the military on the roads to protect them, and after all, they're in the open, breathing fresh air, doing something more than lying in wait behind walls, hoping for a change, hoping the television will come on again and play their favorite shows.

I despair. But it could change, couldn't it? Might I find a friend, someone to talk with, someone to commiserate about what it all means? It's what keeps me going.

I will steal gloves tomorrow.

Tonight I will wrap bandages against the seepage behind my knees. And I'll wash my clothes and my body in Gulf waters.

The flies are thick. They love me. The ants and black gnats love me.

All the little hungry things love me.

June 10

Key West! I've made it this far without detection. I fear I am beginning to smell something dreadful. Despite my bath, my washed clothes, the deodorant and aftershave, I notice people shying from me. Not in any rude noticeable way, just drifting back behind me farther or moving slightly faster to get ahead of me. A cloud of black flies hovers all around. They get in my face, crawl into my nose, ears, mouth. I hate them and it makes me want to slap myself all over, like a comedian into the worst physical comedy routine, hurting himself just for one more laugh.

Now I must find a boat. To steal. There's nothing I have I could barter for a trip even if I didn't know I'd be found out because of my smell. Tonight I'll check among the zombies for one sentient. And then I will take a boat and leave this land.

There must be someone . . .

Please. Someone.

June 11

Here I am on the open sea. I'm afraid I've done something unspeakable. I threatened another man's life. I made the captain of this ship take me off the island. I thought to go alone, but I was afraid I'd be lost at sea. I've only been motorboating off the coast of Miami and down through the canals in Fort Lauderdale. I'd never make it out of the sight of land. I don't really mean to hurt this man. Unless he makes me.

His name is Bailey. Raymond Bailey. He was tied at the dock I haunted and about to set sail himself. Fishing, he said, but come to find out his hold was packed with weapons and supplies. Gunrunner. Guns and drugs are the most expensive commodities in the world now. As if making money means anything. He says it's not the money, it's the principal of the thing. He fancies himself a savior, a man bringing help to those less fortunate than the paranoid Americans who were prepared for this world event with guns in every home.

He was on his way to Cuba anyway. I'm just a passenger, though he'd like to throw me overboard.

I tried to explain. *I feel*, I told him. *I'm not an animal.* I am a man just as he is, and through no fault of my own I have become this dead thing. But I'm not like the other zombies. I am a new breed. I might be one of a kind. I *control* the hunger. Won't you try to understand this, you cocksucking moron?

Couldn't he help me?

He tried to blow my head off. I wrestled the gun from his fist and knocked him to the deck while the wheel spun and the boat circled in the moonlit ocean as we scuffled.

I let him up and then I bent over and grasped my knees and tried to scream. I wanted to scream in frustration so loudly that he would understand my anguish, my frustration, but what rushed out through my dry throat and shrinking vocal cords was a harsh rasping whine that scared even me until I quit it. When I stood up, Raymond had climbed to his feet and gotten hold of the wheel. I could see his shoulders twitching, and his head wobbling on his neck. He had wanted to kill me.

"All right," he said. "You want to go with me, just stay downwind, out of my face, you understand that? I think you ought to throw yourself into the sea and be done with it, but if you want to go to Cuba, fine, we're on our way. But stay away from me. The next time you lay hands on me you'll have to kill because I won't have it. I just won't have a dead man touching me again."

I sat against the door leading into the cabin and watched him. He worked the little boat through the waters without ever glancing at me. A terrible longing came over me as I sat, staring. I thought of his arm, the hair there golden, the *blood* beneath the skin hot and red and ripe. The hunger seized me to take him. To possess him. To eat and to drink him as if he were a succulent pig roasted and stuffed and laid on a platter for me alone.

I shuddered. The thought of eating this way, so repellent before, seemed to be changing inexorably into something that was not so wrong, so bad, so diseased. What can I do! To deny the urge is the last vestige left of my human morality. If ever I give in to the seductive clamor for human flesh, I will be lost, even to myself.

I began writing in this notebook to take my mind from the low rumble in my stomach and he heard the pencil scratching over the paper and he stiffened. I know what he thought. That I was about to pounce, I suppose, catch him unaware. Eat him for supper. How close we came to that he'll never know. But he would not talk to me and he drank whiskey, and once I saw him deliberately spill some of it on his clothes. Probably to keep my scent from making him vomit.

I am in terrible shape now. I can't take off the gloves I found. Skin came off with them when I tried.

I wonder if I will disintegrate and know it. Watch it happen bit by bit, see my flesh fall from my bones, and then will my skeleton walk, will it long for companionship, will this ever ever end?

If I could just . . . give up.

If I could just . . . let Raymond Bailey blow a round through my head.

I don't know why I can't, why I want to keep going.

I must be insane.

I know that I am.

June 27

So much happened. I can't put it all down. I don't have time. Raymond got me to Cuba and I was smuggled onshore in a case of rifles. I spent a week looking for a zombie who might have a working brain. No one. No one. A family by the name of Valesquez was coerced . . . I forced them . . . to take me with them to Mexico. I still believed that somewhere I'd find a companion.

Oh, it was an awful time. One of the Valesquez boys, six years old, died on the trip from a high fever. There was such uproar and breast-beating. They held a religious service and performed a hasty burial at sea. They were afraid I would turn the child into a zombie. They circled round me, holding up crosses as if I were a vampire to be held at bay by the Christian symbol, and I laughed, I made a laughing face, because although the heat of the hunger now so often tortures me, I fight valiantly against the desire to harm anyone, especially the quiet dead, especially them, the lucky ones.

In Mexico I had to stay hidden and only come out at night. My feet, you see, are falling apart. Both my small toes are gone, and the others are following suit each time I dare to remove my shoes. And my hands, they're a mess. My gloves make squishy sounds while I try to write this. My face, oh Jesus, if you could see my face. Great chunks are missing. I have tried everything. Bandages. Tape. Staples. The skin is too thin and tender. Nothing holds. My testicles were lost on the boat over. I dropped them gently into the sea when no one was paying attention to me. Also my nose is gone, thrown to the sea, bait for fish. Although I can't smell anything anymore, I know I must be a pit of vile odors. I can't even get close to the towns any longer. Their dogs come out, lunging and snapping, hoping to tear me to pieces.

A few days ago I met one person who made me feel that all of this bother and searching and hoping was worthwhile. I lay resting out on the plains outside a small village. I heard a rustle and thought it a rattlesnake slithering across the sand, but when I sat up there crouched not three feet from me was a young girl who might have been twenty. She was dressed in rags and dishwater blond hair hung in front of dark, haunted eyes.

"You're a zombie, aren't you?" she asked. She was not Spanish, but American.

The question was so startling that I could just dip my head a little in answer.

"I've seen you out here walking in circles, pacing at night. Do you understand what I'm saying to you?"

Again I nodded, but more vigorously. I grabbed for my pad and pencil. I threw a couple of sticks on the fire and motioned her forward. On the pad I wrote, *Why aren't you afraid that I'd attack and kill you?*

She said, "I don't know. I just watched you for a while and it seemed to me that you aren't like the others."

I'm not! I wrote quickly. *I was killed and infected, but I am just the same as I was when alive. I don't understand it and have come all this way from Florida trying to find another one like me. Have you met any?*

She shook her head slowly. "You can't talk?" she asked.

I wrote, *No. My vocal cords are no good and my lungs . . . well, I have no air in them.*

She did something incredible then. She crept even closer to me and she reached out and she placed her warm hand on my shoulder. She said, "I don't think I could have ever thought of something so terrible as what you must be going through. I've traveled three thousand miles, and I've seen dead children in piles waiting for burial, I've seen bombed out cities, and whole towns on the move with just what they could carry on their backs, but to be . . . dead . . . and to know it . . . I am sorry, I'm really so sorry. The others, the ones who don't know, they must be better off."

I lowered my head and stared at the pad and pencil in my hands. My fingers trembled when I tried to write another note. I had to get a firm grip on the pencil.

Will you stay with me the night and just talk to me? I won't hurt you. If you'll just talk to me, I'd be so grateful.

And she did. She had me lie on my back. She took one of my gloved hands and despite how my scent must have made her want to gag, she sat beside me all through the darkest hours and she talked to me about her family, her travels, her hopes for the future. She had a bright optimism that made me glow, that made me forget, just for a while, that I had nothing whatsoever to look forward to. She even made me forget that I was ravenous and that without the greatest exertion of will, I would turn on my side, grab her in a vise unyielding, and bite a chunk from her smooth white fragrant abdomen.

When I thought of chewing, of swallowing, of satisfying that burning need that glowed like a large red ember in my belly, I wrenched my thoughts back to the girl's soothing singsong voice, remembering, with her tales, what it was like to be a man. To hear a woman talk to me in that tone of voice reminded me when I would reach out and take the globe of Carrie's breast into my palm, suck her lips, separately, between my lips, feel her strength beneath me in her heat, rising to meet me, clutching me as she peaked, riding down the escalator into the abyss of surrender . . .

After the girl left, no one came to the plains again. I have spent days and nights rolling across the sand, holding myself, the hunger so deep it's a scream locked inside me, a claw scraping through my innards. I am afraid now. I know it has gone too far. I would eat now, if given opportunity. If the girl comes back, I will tear her limb from limb and feast. There is no help for it. I'm driven by such tremendous need that when I think of Carrie now, I think of consuming her. When I think of Margaret, I think of what a small, pure, tasty feeding she would be. I would murder and eat that which I had left to protect, that which brought me to this place and in this condition.

I am now truly as obscene and irresponsible as any other of the dead.

It has come down to this.

As I hunger, so am I hungered for. Now it's the coyotes who want me at night. Wolves. They come down from the hills and howl at me where I've climbed a tree. Flies have laid eggs in my crevices and I crawl with little white blind . . . I can't say it, I can't write it, I can't think it . . . I have always abhorred wiggling, squirming, segmented things.

There are zombies here as there were in Cuba. I saw them, but the girl told me so, too. There are millions of them. More than live humans. The towns are dead. Stinking. People are on the move everywhere. People kill to get what boats are left. Rafts set sail with dozens on them. All the planes have disappeared from the country. Children are orphaned and have joined into gangs. They are worse than the military in the States, worse than the wolves even. They don't care if you're alive or dead, they shoot to dismantle you.

I've made up my mind. I'm going to let them.

Shoot me.

I commit not suicide, for that's for the living. I commit deathicide. I simply walk out into the open and let them explode with impunity this dead body.

There aren't any zombies like me. But I am becoming one of *them*. I either die to this world or I turn on men and I eat. I'm the only one who ever knew what this is like and I am coming to pieces before my very eyes.

I have no ears. My hair fell out. My eyes are going. I

can hardly see to write this. My dwindling muscles have contracted and my bones been broken a thousand times over. I stumble when I try to walk. It is only my brain that knows anything and what it knows it is tired of knowing. There is no pleasure, no curiosity, no hope, no reason to keep going.

The best I can do is go into that forever darkness where I won't worry about being alone again. I'm placing this notebook in an envelope and will hold it to my chest as the gangs shoot my head into tiny bits.

What becomes of my testament is not of my concern after tonight. I could have sent it to the president in Washington, D.C. He's a good man trying to keep a nation together, though I could tell him it's no use. He would never tell the people, he couldn't, I understand that, and it doesn't matter that much to me anymore. I thought I could find a way to go on, find a reason why this has happened to me, that my survival might help in stopping the plague, or that at the very least I could provide an enlightenment about life after death, but I don't think so now. It appears it was futile to ever begin this long trek across miles and oceans.

I don't mean to sound like suffering Jesus or the tortured Job. I thought I could still find a shred of happiness or some meaning, even a tiny pleasure left to me, but I should have known better. I can do one thing. I can tell you to *stand and fight*. The armies will fall eventually. You'll be on your own. Order will give way even more and there will be nothing but chaos, enemies, and insanity. If you don't fight to the end, are you worthy to be called human?

There has never been a plague like this one and there never will be one again because this is the last. You know they don't understand how the virus mutates and defies all efforts to contain it. As soon as something is tried, the virus changes, finds a way to survive, grows ever stronger and impenetrable. The promised vaccine might work and it might not. None of the "cures" worked, did they? As expensive as they were and no matter how much pollyanna-hopeful-bullshit scientific hype you heard about them, they *did not work*, did they?

You should be ready if the vaccine doesn't work either. The world we have known might truly return to the pristine beginning of time when it was but a revolving ball of watery silence spinning in space.

If you fight and if you survive it unscathed then there might be a slim possibility there really is a God. I hope there is. I pray there is. For all our sakes.

Unfortunately, my earnest opinion—and please feel free to disregard it because I don't wish to leave you without all hope, that was never my intention—but it just seems to me, in this hour before my real true death, that Nietzsche was probably right.

The son of a bitch.

Basic Training
Mark L. Van Name

Week 1, Day 1

I knew I wasn't supposed to look anywhere but straight ahead, but I wanted to check down the road to my right, to see if Mom was still there. After she dropped me off everything happened so fast that I didn't even know if she had left yet or if she was still watching me. I sorta wanted her to watch me, but I sorta didn't, because she had started crying when the men yelled at me to get in line, and that had made me feel like crying and I knew I shouldn't cry. Daddy taught me that. Men don't cry. Now that he was gone I was supposed to be the man.

But I still wanted to see her, and Sergeant Minola sounded like he was yelling at some kid at the other end of the line, so I turned and looked.

She was gone. I couldn't even see her car, and that made me mad and it made me want to cry and I wished she was still there.

Then he was screaming in my ear, and it all happened so fast that I couldn't tell what he said at first even though his voice was loud.

". . . some kind of hearing problem, Private?" He yelled louder. "Is my voice not clear enough for you?"

"No, sir!"

All of a sudden he was right in front of me, leaning into my face.

"Do I look like I sit around the office all day, playing pocket pool and having lunch at some air-conditioned officers' club?"

His face was the color of old cardboard and looked as hard as wood. The muscles in his neck and his arms stood out as he leaned over me, and I could not imagine him ever sitting around. "No, sir!"

"Then stop calling me sir! I work for a living, boy. You call me Sergeant! Do you understand me?"

"Yes, Sergeant."

"No wonder you have a hearing problem, Private. You don't talk loud enough to wake an ant sleeping on your lips." He stood up and backed away. "Now, do you understand me?"

I yelled as loud as I could, "Yes, Sergeant!" I was so scared my hands were shaking. The noon sun was so hot I was drenched with sweat, and I felt like I was going to throw up. I didn't want him to see any of it, I didn't want him to keep yelling at me, I didn't want to be there. It wasn't fair. None of the other boys I knew had to join, none of their fathers had died in this stupid war and made them have to become soldiers.

"What's your name, Private?"

"Larry, sir, uh, Sergeant."

"You don't get it, do you, boy?" He leaned again into my face. I could see the hairs in his nose and tiny scars like craters on his cheeks. "I don't give a rat's ass what your first name is. I don't care who you were or what you were back in that sorry excuse for a world that brought your sorry excuse for a recruit ass to me. What you are now is a private in my corps. Your first name is 'Private,' and your last name is something I'm only going to learn because I have to have some way to refer to your worthless self. Now, what is it, Private? What's your name?"

I wished he would stop yelling at me. It made it hard

for me to talk, to think, even to stand there. I had to work my throat so I could talk. "Private Burger, Sergeant."

"Burger, huh? You some kind of cheap sandwich I'm gonna chew on, get sick, and spit out like those cheap rat burgers they sell across the bridge in Tampa? Is that what you are, boy?"

I didn't want to get mad, but he kept screaming at me and so I yelled back, "No, Sergeant!"

He nodded, stepped back, and walked to the center of the boys to my left. I could barely see him out of the corner of my eye.

"Let's get some things straight here," he said. "None of you like me, and I don't like you. I normally wouldn't cross the street to piss on worthless punks like you if you were on fire. But you are no longer just punks. You are part of my militia, and you are mine. You may have had mommies and daddies once, but now all you have is me and each other, and none of you is worth a damn without me. I am your world, the last thing you'll see before your miserable bodies fall asleep at night and the first thing you'll see when I drag you out of your bunks in the morning. Do you understand me?"

"Yes, Sergeant!" We all yelled, and the sound was so loud I almost jumped.

"I can't hear you!"

I took a deep breath and screamed as loud as I could, "Yes, Sergeant!" We didn't all finish at the same time, but it was close enough that the noise was amazing.

"My job is to train you to fight, and I will do that job. This war is the big one, and the heathens are playing for keeps. Winner takes all, and we will win because God is on our side. But the heathens are tough, don't mistake that. When I joined up ten years ago, we never would have taken kids your age, but now we're fighting here and in almost every town across America, and we can't afford to be picky. So I will teach you, and you will fight them and keep on fighting until we have killed them all for the glory of God and the corps. Do you understand?"

I didn't, but I knew the answer he wanted and I was sure not going to say anything else. "Yes, Sergeant!"

He took off his hat, tucked it under his left arm, and with his right pulled a cord from around his neck over his head. It was a necklace, a dark brown leather cord holding many smaller pieces of less dark leather. He held it in front of him as he walked back and forth in front of us.

"There is nothing pretty about killing, but there is also nothing magic. The heathens are men, the devil's men, but still men, and you can kill them as easily as they can kill you. And they will kill you. Unless you kill them first. Which I will train you to do." He stopped in front of the boy next to me, a black kid a little taller than I was. "Do you know what this is, Private?"

"No, Sergeant," the kid said.

"It's my ear collection, Private." He stuck it in the kid's face. "Right ears only, one ear for each heathen I killed, more than two dozen before I got called back from South America to teach worthless pukes like you."

I couldn't help myself. I turned my head for a better look. The ears didn't look like ears, more like shrunken leather Brussels sprouts, but as I looked closer I could see the folds and bends of an ear in some of them. I wanted to grab my own ears, make sure they were still there. I felt sicker and shakier and the air seemed heavy.

"Do you have a problem, Private Burger?"

I knew I shouldn't say anything, but I couldn't help myself and as soon as I started talking I couldn't stop. "It's gross. I don't wanna see it. I don't wanna be here. I'm scared and I wish you'd stop yelling at me . . ."

"Burger!" He was in my face, screaming, and I still couldn't stop.

". . . and I don't know why my dad had to die and do this to me and . . ."

"Burger!" He was even louder this time, but I couldn't stop.

". . . I wish my Mom were here and I wanna go home and . . ."

He hit me in the stomach. I didn't see it coming, but one minute I was screaming and the next I had no air and I was falling down and holding my stomach. I kept trying to breathe but somehow no air seemed to get in. The road was hot and rough and scraped my cheek and my hands, but I couldn't get up.

"You will not panic, Private Burger. You will not talk unless I tell you to talk, and you will stop when I tell you to stop. Do you understand, Private Burger?"

I nodded my head and squeaked out a "Yes, Sergeant," that I could barely hear. I hoped it was enough for him, because I didn't think I could be any louder.

"How old are you, Burger?"

My stomach felt like a hole in my body, and my throat burned. I sucked in a little more air, enough to answer a bit more loudly. "Ten, Sergeant."

"Well if you want to live to see eleven, Burger, you better learn these things, and you better learn 'em fast. Now get up and stop dirtying my road."

Week 1, Day 4

My legs were shaking as I struggled to hold them together and six inches off the ground. The muscles in the tops of my thighs and my stomach were on fire from the strain of the leg lifts. The world narrowed into the pain in my legs, the sun blazing into my eyes, and the sound of Minola's voice. I could hear his boots clacking on the pavement, but I couldn't see him.

"Apart." His voice sounded distant, but clear.

Keeping my legs above the ground, I spread them as far as I could. Simply being able to move relieved the pain for a moment, but then it came back worse than before. I wanted to reach down and lift my legs with my hands, but the bootprint on my uniform sleeve and the dull ache in my left arm reminded me of the penalty for that particular cheat. I gritted my teeth, closed my eyes, and concentrated on blocking out the pain and keeping my legs up.

"Together."

I moved them back together, grateful again for the momentary movement. This was our tenth repetition, the last one. We always did ten. If I could hold out until Minola called the last movement, we'd be done. It was dinnertime, so I'd get to stand up, escape to the mess hall for half an hour, relax. All I had to do was finish this one.

"Down."

Yes! My stomach felt like it would cramp and I wanted to grab it, but I kept my hands under my head. My legs twitched and I sucked air, glad to be done. I was sure I could not have managed another.

"Up."

I couldn't believe it. We always did ten. I wanted to shout, but I clamped my jaw shut and only grunted as I lifted my legs. I heard a lot of other grunts and gasps, but no words; we had all learned.

"I know what you pukes are thinking," Minola said from somewhere closer but still behind me. "We did ten, so we should be done. It's not fair. Well, you're right; it's not fair. Tough shit. Sometimes you have to push a little harder. Now, apart."

Even spreading my legs brought no relief. The shaking was worse, and I wasn't sure I could go on. I had counted on stopping, and now I had nothing left. I felt tears in the corners of my eyes, and I shook my head to make them fall out. I'd be damned if I would cry again in front of him. I might not be able to do these leg lifts, but I would not cry. That much, I could control.

"Together."

I couldn't do it. I tried, but my legs fell, and then Minola was staring down at me.

"Stand up, Burger!"

I stood to attention and faced him.

"Why did your legs fall, Burger?"

"Sergeant, I couldn't keep them up, Sergeant!"

"Bullshit. Look around you, boy. Do you see any other legs on the ground?"

I looked. Everyone was shaking, and some of their legs were almost touching the concrete, but all were above the ground. I couldn't believe I was the only one.

"That's right, Burger. They're doing it. You could have done it, but you gave up. You made up your mind you were done, and so you were." He stepped back. "Down! Fall in! Now!"

Everyone scrambled to line up in our usual formation. We dressed our ranks, left arms touching the guy to the left, right arms touching the guy in front, and then we snapped to attention.

Minola stood in front of us, arms crossed behind his back, the creases in his uniform, as always, so stiff they appeared to be carved from an unbelievably pure-green granite previously unknown in Florida. "It seems Burger decided to give up early on leg lifts. That means he didn't finish his exercises, so he needs to do a little more before dinner. And, as I keep trying to pound into your worthless skulls, you are supposed to be a team. If one of you doesn't finish, none of you have finished. So, you can all take a few minutes from your dinner break to double-time it down to the end of the compound and back."

Everyone groaned. I could feel them looking at me. We only had thirty minutes to eat, and this run would take ten of them. My fault, not theirs. Mine. I wanted to die. "Sergeant, request permission to speak, Sergeant!" I had to try.

For a second, I thought I saw him smile, but then it was gone. "Go ahead, Burger."

"Sergeant, this is my fault and the others should not have to run, Sergeant!"

He walked in front of me and bent into my face. "You don't get it, do you, boy? Listen to me. Read my lips. You are part of a team. If you fail, the team fails." He moved away, back in front of us. "If any of you fail, the team fails. You must be able to depend on one another absolutely, without doubt, because anything less will get you killed. Do you understand me?"

"Sergeant, yes, Sergeant!"

"Good. Left, face. Double-time, march!"

We ran in formation. I didn't see Minola in his usual spot to my left. Then, I heard his voice from behind us.

"The sooner you pukes finish this little run, the sooner you eat."

We trotted on. My legs felt like weights, but I was glad for the chance to be doing something. Maybe if I sat alone in the mess and stayed out of everyone's way, they'd forget me. Johnson and Gonzalez liked me, maybe they'd even sit with me. It wouldn't be so bad. All we had to do was make it to the storeroom at the other end of the complex, turn around, and run back. We did it many times each day. I wouldn't let them down this time. I could do this.

As we neared the storeroom and the point for our turn, I noticed a few of the bigger guys in front of me had slowed a bit. When I tried to slow, Johnson, the guy behind me, pushed me forward. I could barely keep running in the space between him and them. We started into the turn, and I felt a hand in my back and I stumbled and then I was on the ground and boots were kicking me. I covered my face and curled into a ball, trying to protect myself. I don't know how many people kicked me, but it was over fast and the platoon was moving on. My shoulders and neck and legs and stomach and ass hurt, and I tasted blood. The platoon was running away from me.

They were all I had left, and now I was losing them. Fuck that.

I got up and ran after them. I dusted my uniform as best I could as I ran. I didn't even try to run as Minola had taught us. I didn't care about my legs or my stomach or the blood in my mouth. I sprinted after them.

I caught them halfway back to Minola and fell into my position. No one spoke to me, and I didn't say anything.

When we were about to pass him, Minola called, "Platoon, halt!"

We stopped, everyone at attention and sucking air.

Minola looked at me but did not come closer.

"Burger."

"Sergeant, yes, Sergeant!"

"What happened to your uniform? You look even more like shit than usual."

No one moved, but I could feel them all watching me.

"Sergeant, I tripped and fell, Sergeant!"

"I see, Burger. What made you fall?"

"Sergeant, I was clumsy, Sergeant!"

He stared at me for a minute, then looked away. "Go clean up, then join the rest at mess. Everyone else, fall out. Back here in twenty minutes."

"Sergeant, yes, Sergeant!" we all shouted.

I ran through the group to the barracks. I figured if I changed fast I could still grab a bite. No one pushed me as I cut through.

Week 3, Day 5

The ceiling fans in the old warehouse bathed us in a slight breeze that was a wonderful relief from the unrelenting heat outside. The building smelled faintly of plastics and more strongly of sweat. We sat along the edges of a large square of faded blue workout mats. We were lined up in order of size, from Hughes, who at 16 and somewhere around six-four was a little bigger than Minola and everyone's pick as the guy most likely to be able to take the Sergeant, to Gonzalez, three seats to my right and a good couple of inches shorter than I was. Minola stood, shirtless, in the center of the mats and held aloft a gleaming bayonet.

"What is the spirit of the bayonet?" he asked.

"Sergeant, to kill, Sergeant!"

Minola granted us a rare full smile. "You've learned the words. I've let you hold the weapon. Now it's time to learn to use it." He walked along the border of the mats as he talked, now keeping the bayonet at our eye level. "This war is not like any movie you've seen. We're not charging up hills. We're not humping through a jungle. We're going from door to door, down streets, into buildings, fighting the enemy in our very own cities, cities their presence disgraces. Less than a mile away from the edge of this compound are heathen neighborhoods, perfectly good houses and streets infected with the devil's servants. Up to now, we've had to put up with them, because we haven't had the manpower to deal with them. Now we do: You. It's going to be your job to clean those neighborhoods. You won't have guns, because neither we nor the enemy in those houses have any ammo for the few guns we have. Ammo is too precious for untrained pukes fighting rear actions. We have to save it for those on the front lines. Which is why," he lifted the bayonet over his head, "you must become very good at both using your bayonet on others and defending against it yourself."

He put the bayonet in a bag at one edge of the mats and pulled out a black rubber replica. "So none of you darlings accidentally slices himself and messes up my nice mats, we'll practice with this rubber version. You attack, I'll defend. Who wants to start?"

Nobody spoke.

"Don't be shy, boys. This is your chance to hit me with something hard. Surely at least one of you babies has wanted to hit me."

Everyone had wanted that, and he knew it, but no one

said a word. I sure wasn't going to volunteer. I had learned that lesson, and so had everyone else.

Minola laughed, a sound I rarely heard and one I was pretty sure I didn't like. "Okay, then, I'll pick. Hughes, on your feet, front and center."

"Sergeant, yes, Sergeant." Hughes went to the center of the mat and stood at attention in front of Minola.

"Relax, Hughes. When you're on this mat, you can stand any way you want. Take this weapon, and let me know when you're ready."

Hughes took the practice bayonet, backed away, and checked it out. He flipped it from hand to hand a few times, smiled, and settled into a half crouch.

Minola, in a similar but slightly wider stance, never looked away from him. His face was calm, his mouth slightly open. The muscles in his chest and stomach moved in and out in an unchanging, slow rhythm as he breathed.

"Sergeant, ready, Sergeant!"

"Then have at me, boy. Try to cut me."

Hughes, the bayonet in his right hand and that arm slightly bent, slowly edged toward Minola. He moved the bayonet from side to side in an arc about a foot and a half wide, no fast motions, everything under control. Never taking his eyes off Minola, he drew closer to the sergeant. He looked good to me, and I began to believe he might have a chance. Seeing Minola get hurt a little would be fine by me.

Minola didn't move. Nothing in his expression changed, and his breathing stayed the same.

Hughes thrust the bayonet slightly at Minola, not far, just a few inches.

Minola didn't react.

Hughes moved a little closer, and then suddenly he stabbed right at Minola's chest.

Minola wasn't there. He was to the side of where he had been, grabbing Hughes' arm, doing something with his feet, and then Hughes was on the ground and Minola was on top of him. Minola's knee pinned Hughes' back as he bent Hughes' arm backward until Hughes grunted in pain and dropped the bayonet. Still holding Hughes' arm with one hand, Minola picked up the bayonet with the other, dragged its sharper side across the back of Hughes' neck hard enough to leave a bright red line, then stood. Hughes rolled over and held his right arm with his left hand.

"Too obvious, Hughes, and too much weight on your front foot. You thought your size and a little experience with a knife would be enough—dumb. A move like that'll work only on someone with no training, and the heathens do train. Get back in your position. Who wants to be next?"

No one volunteered, so Minola ordered Langdon, a tall, wiry kid about fourteen with hair so blond his buzzed head looked bald from a distance, onto the mat. Langdon tried a different approach, dancing back and forth a lot and thrusting the bayonet at Minola's head each time he drew closer, but he lasted only a tiny bit longer and fared no better. On one lunge Minola seemed to fall, his leg shot out, and Langdon went down. Minola was on him instantly, taking the rubber bayonet and dragging it across Langdon's throat.

Two other guys also ended up with red throats, and then Minola called my name. I thought I was going to throw up as I walked to the center of the mat. I had been in a few short fights, but always with kids my size or only a little bigger, and never with a weapon. The bayonet felt foreign and I wanted to throw it away and run, but I knew that wouldn't work. I gripped it tightly, bent my legs, and hoped he wouldn't hurt me too much. I swung the bayonet lightly in his direction, hoping he'd maybe just take it away and I could finish without having to hit the mat or feel him drag the rubber blade across my throat.

He didn't move. Though he was staring at me, I couldn't sense any reaction in his eyes or his face. I wondered what he was seeing.

I swung the knife again, a little faster this time.

He slapped my face. I never saw the hand coming. "Is that all you can do, Burger? What a worthless baby you are."

He slapped my face again. "What are you waiting for, Burger? Your mommy to come save you?"

My face burned. I was having trouble breathing, and I shook my head. I wanted to hit him, hurt him.

He slapped me again, harder than before, stinging my face and snapping back my head. "Is this how your daddy died, Burger? Does being a worthless pussy of a mommy's boy run in your family?"

I couldn't stand it anymore. I yelled and charged him, the bayonet aimed right at this throat. I wanted to slice it open, shut him up, not have to take any more from him, kill him.

I was on my back on the mat before I knew what had happened. He was sitting on me, his knees pinning my arms, one arm over my mouth so I could barely breathe, the other pushing the bayonet into my throat. I was afraid he was really going to hurt me.

Without breathing hard, with no emotion in his voice, Minola said, "Anger can help you, but only if you control it. Burger got mad and lost control. I stayed in control." He dragged the bayonet across my throat, then got off me. "Now, he's dead, and I'm alive. Back to your position, Burger." As Minola talked, he walked the perimeter of the mat, locking eyes briefly with each of the guys in the platoon. "You may think you're better than Burger, that you'd never get mad or lose control. You're not. Everyone loses it if the wrong thing happens to them. I can and will tell you never to get mad, to stay under control at all times. I can even teach you how best to maintain that control by focusing on your target and keeping your breathing easy.

"None of that training, though, will totally prepare you for what you will feel when the action is real, when the men you're hunting are also hunting you, when you either have to kill them or let them kill you. Only that experience will teach you those feelings, and once you've felt them—and you will, there is no way not to—you'll spend the rest of your life wishing you could get rid of them. But you won't be able to, and that's a cost you're gonna have to pay.

"Unless, of course, you die. Which is what this training has a chance of helping you avoid. When the craziness of combat hits you, this training and the other guys in your unit will be all that can keep you alive.

"I know you don't understand a fucking word I'm saying, but it's my job to tell you anyway. So we're going to do the only thing we can do that has any chance of helping: Practice. We're gonna practice until we get it automatic and right, until you learn how to attack and defend and stay in control while doing each.

"Johnson, you're up."

Week 5, Day 2

On my second day as the leader of Charlie squad, Minola assigned us to the obstacle course and left us alone there for an hour. We had a goal time of ten minutes flat. Our previous best was a little over ten and a half, but we'd logged that result last week, so I was sure we could hit the goal this time. After three tries, though, we were sucking wind, dirty, bruised, and still 15 seconds over. "We've gotta try again, guys," I said. "We've got less than half an hour to get rid of those fifteen seconds."

Langdon, the tallest of my squad members, said, "Bullshit. Tell Minola we made it, and let's catch some rest while we can. Right, guys?"

Gonzalez, who was having the worst time of the group, nodded in agreement. Peters and Johnson looked down, carefully not agreeing or disagreeing, waiting to see which way it would go. I knew Gonzalez would do the right thing if I pushed him, but Langdon could be a problem. Agreeing with him meant letting the team fail. Taking it to Minola would label me as a snitch. The only way out was to make it happen.

"Wrong, Langdon," I said. "If the Sergeant says we do it, we do it. We follow our orders."

"The only thing between us and those orders being done is you, dickhead," he said. He stretched to his full height and stared down at me. "If you could stop kissing up because Minola made you squad leader, you'd write ten minutes on the score sheet and leave us the fuck alone." He turned his back on me and started to walk away.

I was not going to let this happen, not on my watch. "Fall in!" I yelled.

The other three slowly lined up and stood to attention. Langdon stopped walking but did not join them. The others were watching me, though trying not to be obvious about it.

I walked slowly in front of Langdon and stood as close to him as I could without touching him. I craned my neck so I could look directly into his eyes. I silently counted to five and calmed my breathing as best I could. "Here's how it is, Langdon," I said, slowly and clearly, never looking away from him. "I'm squad leader. You may not like it. I don't know, and I don't give a shit. It's my job now to lead this squad, and it's your job to be part of it. This squad is a team, and you will not let this team down, and I will not dishonor it by lying." I wanted to yell, but I kept my voice level. "This squad is going to run this course until we do it in ten minutes. We can get it this next run, or the one after that, or ten runs later, but we will get it. We can all run it together, or we can carry your worthless unconscious ass on our backs while we run it. But we will do it. It's your call how."

Langdon stared at me for a few moments, then shook

his head and joined the others in line. "Fuck it," he said as he snapped to attention, "let's run."

"I can't hear you!" I said.

"Let's run!" he shouted.

We took our marks, and on my command, we ran.

Week 7, Day 5

At 04:30, my squad crossed the Ninth Street DMZ about thirty yards below Twenty-Second Avenue, three quarters of a mile from the southeast edge of our compound. Cutting and tying back the razor wire took only a few minutes. No patrols were anywhere in sight. We hadn't hit the heathens in this part of St. Pete in months, and our recon teams knew they had become careless and rarely patrolled it in the early morning hours. We were due back by 05:15, almost an hour before their first patrol ever passed this area.

Once all five of us were through, we split into our teams and sprinted to the shadows on either side of Twenty-First Avenue. I took point and kept to the right side of the street, the side on which our target house sat. Gonzalez and Peters followed on the same side, with Langdon and Johnson staying parallel with them across the street. The other five squads in our platoon were doing their first forays at the same time in different spots around the city. If we all did our jobs well, by sunrise the heathens would find themselves down six key adults, and we'd all be back at the compound.

We were about a quarter of a mile due west from the home of our targets, a man named Sam Kaplan and his son, Tim. Kaplan ran a warehouse that was a major food and weapons depot for the heathens in this part of the city. Supplies were so tight that he was the only local with all the necessary access codes. Taking him out would mess them up for a couple days, enough time for more missions.

Our briefing notes said he and his son left their house each morning about five so they could arrive well before any of their customers. Our job was to take them just outside their house and then get back home safely.

Only a few streetlights still burned in this area, and we had plenty of time to cover the quarter mile and secure our positions, so we never had to leave the darkness for more than a few seconds. Even so, we moved carefully from bush to tree to dead car to house corner, always staying spread out and in the shadows, checking for trouble at each stop. Never assume, Minola said. Take all the time the situation offers you. A few cats ran near us, and one even hissed, but no one seemed to notice. My heart was pounding and I could feel the sweat all over my upper body, but no lights came on, and no heathens attacked. Each time I stopped to check the area, I tried to take a slow, deep breath. The grass was a bit damp from an earlier rain, so the air was clear and fresh.

The only real dangers were the streets. Once we were over Ninth, we had to cross three more to reach our target. As point, I was the first to take each of them. I'd hold in the covering shadows on the near side until I had checked each house with a street view, then I'd dash across, grab the nearest cover, and check all the houses again. Only then would I wave over the others, who crossed all at once. Nothing fancy, everything by the numbers. When we were all safely over the last cross-street, I waved us down and counted off two minutes on my watch, making sure. Nothing stirred. No one followed. Time to get in position.

The target house was the third one down. I looped around the rear of the nearest house and paused to make sure Langdon and Johnson had crossed safely. When they had, I made my way through backyards to the far side of the target. Gonzalez and Peters showed up a few seconds later. I doubled back to make sure Langdon and Johnson were in position on the other side. They were. By 04:44, one minute early, I was back in my position, and we were set to strike.

Conditions were pretty good for the assault. We had enough moonlight to see the targets, but not so much we would be obvious. One streetlight shone on the same side of the street a few houses down, but no other lights illuminated the block. Some lights were already on inside the small, one-story building, which was also good for us: harder for them to see out into the relative darkness.

I replayed the plan in my head, making sure I was missing nothing. It was simple and, Minola had said, intentionally overkill because it was our first mission. Langdon and Johnson were to take the two targets from behind, Langdon on the big one, Johnson on the smaller. They were to cover the targets' mouths to stop any noise and at the same time go for their throats. Gonzalez and Peters were to lag them by a step and attack from the front. Their targets were the hearts. Two hits per target within a second or two, and they should go down fast and quiet. I was coordinator and secondary backup. We would hit them as they turned down the sidewalk, get it all over in only a few seconds, and head back to the extraction point on our side of the DMZ.

Waiting was harder than it had been in the drills, harder than I had thought it would be. The night seemed louder, busier, the longer I leaned against the house's side. Crickets, frogs, odd animal rustlings, our own breathing— every noise seemed a possible warning to our targets. The house was insulated well enough that I couldn't hear any of the activity that had to be going on inside it, and that made me nervous. At the same time, that insulation was also protection, because they couldn't hear us. I kept my eyes on the front of the house and worked on calming myself, slowing my breathing. I flashed a thumbs-up to each of the teams, and both gave me the same.

Lights in the rear of the house snapped off right at 05:00. A few seconds later, the lights in the front went out, and the door opened. Two figures, one about six feet tall and the other about my size, stepped out. The larger turned back to the door and locked it. As they stepped out from under the slight overhang of the house's ceiling the light from the streetlight down the block gave me a brief glimpse of their faces. They looked tired but otherwise normal. If they knew we were there, they sure weren't showing it. The larger put his arm around the smaller, and they started walking.

When they turned right on the sidewalk, I twirled my finger in the go signal. Langdon and Johnson, bayonets drawn, darted from the other side of the house. The sound of their boots on the sidewalk was like shots going off, and for a second I wanted to run in fear that someone would hear, but then it was our turn to move and without thinking about doing it I was waving us forward. We charged, and I could see surprise come across the faces of the targets as we appeared from the side of the house. A second later, Langdon and Johnson were on them, Langdon taking the taller and Johnson the shorter. Each had his bayonet in his right hand and grabbed at the head of his target with his left.

Everything had felt slow, but now everything sped up and we moved without thinking, the training taking over. Langdon's hand closed on the man as Peters and I were still two steps from him, but the man spun away from Langdon's grip and avoided his bayonet. Langdon stumbled, and the man kicked him and then drew a knife, not as large as our bayonets but respectable. He waved the knife at Johnson, who let go of the boy to protect his forward arm. The boy also drew a knife as he ran for his father.

Then Gonzalez, Peters, and I reached them. Their backs were now to us, and before they could turn we were there. Gonzalez went after the boy, Peters and I, the man. Peters caught him in the side, and as he turned I grabbed his hair, pulled down his head, and drew my knife across his throat. I felt it bite and catch for a second, then it came free smoothly. The man flailed as his blood spurted on Langdon, who was pulling his knife from somewhere in the man's chest. When I was clear, the man fell backward, right beside me.

I checked the others. Johnson and Gonzalez were straddling the boy, who was also down. Johnson was breathing hard and holding his left arm just above the elbow. A dark stain was spreading on his uniform. Gonzalez, his eyes looking wild in even this faint light, was cursing softly. He bent and began to cut the kid's ear.

"Tie off Johnson's arm, Gonzalez," I said.

He pulled the ear off with a slight tearing sound, then stood and showed it to us, his mouth open slightly, his breathing still ragged. Johnson was shaking but still standing.

"Johnson's arm, Gonzalez," I whispered. I grabbed his shoulder and shook it slightly. "Gonzalez."

He looked at me, and his eyes seemed to calm a bit. "Got it." He turned to Johnson, pulled an elastic bandage from his med kit, and started tying off the arm above the cut. The stain wasn't spreading, and Johnson's breathing was becoming regular, so I figured he was okay.

I took a look at Langdon. He was fine and motioned toward the man's head.

"You got the throat," he said. "Your kill, your ear."

Now I was having trouble breathing, and my arms were shaking slightly. I felt sick and hot and excited and scared and knew I had to regain control. We were alive, they were dead, and that's the best we could ask for. Langdon motioned again, then Gonzalez finished and he and Johnson stood and faced me.

"Ready," they said.

They were watching me, awaiting the word. We were exposed in the light on the sidewalk, and we couldn't afford to be there long.

I bent and drew my blade across the man's right ear. I

had to saw back and forth twice, and then the sharp blade cut it cleanly free. It was damp and small in my hand. I held it up to the others, a tiny trophy dark in the gray morning, and they smiled. I was smiling, too.

I stuffed the ear in my pocket, wiped the knife on the shirt of the dead man, and gave the signal to head out.

Mrs. Lurie and the Rapture
Esther M. Friesner

It was ten o'clock of a Monday morning an even two thousand *anno Domini*, when the waters of the earth turned to blood and ruined Mrs. Lurie's washing. She stood in the basement of her lovely home in Delmont, Pennsylvania, staring into the smelly mess clotting in the tub of her Maytag, and said, "That does it. That's *it*. I'm going upstairs to write a letter to the editor." And she did.

She was still seated at her kitchen table, a Wal-Mart pad of lined paper in front of her, a Bic Stic pen held between her teeth as she searched for just the proper word to convey consumer outrage at the abuses of the utility companies, when the first trumpet sounded. It was very loud. It startled her so badly that she jumped in her chair and bit the tip off the Bic Stic. Fortunately for her, she had the presence of mind to spit it out. The tiny nub of blue plastic sailed across the kitchen, out the window, and right into the eye of a grasshopper the size of a Green Bay Packer fullback.

"Hey! Ya wanna watch it there, lady?" the grasshopper demanded peevishly. "Don't be fooled by appearances: It ain't like I'm made outa eyes."

Mrs. Lurie looked at the outlandishly sized creature. His unbidden appearance at her kitchen window alone might have been enough to send her into a mindless panic, the same for his ability to use human speech, but taken one with the other, the cumulative effect was simply ridiculous. She didn't feel the least inclination to run shrieking from the room, no matter how big he was, how hideous his moving mouth-parts, or how repulsively slick his carapace. All she felt like doing was covering her mouth with one hand and enjoying a brief giggle at the grasshopper's expense.

But that would be rude, so she restrained the impulse. Mrs. Lurie had been raised to be a civil, Christian person. Her mother's unstinting influence had left her a meticulous housekeeper, a militant guardian of the social niceties, a pillar of her church, and she was in the course of bestowing and/or inflicting the same upbringing upon her children, Daniel and Renee. Brenda Lee Oreck from down over the mountain once said, "Almira Lurie is so polite, she'd even ask a cockroach's pardon before she squooshed it." That was absurd: There wasn't a cockroach alive who'd dare set foot, foot, foot, foot, foot, or foot in Mrs. Lurie's house, and Brenda Lee ought to know better than to say so.

On the other hand, the giant grasshopper was *outside* the Lurie home, in Mrs. Lurie's garden, to be precise. All at once Mrs. Lurie suffered a very specific lower-case sort of revelation: For the monster to be leaning in over the sill of that particular window, he'd have to be standing in her prize geraniums. Oh dear. That really wouldn't do.

"Excuse me," said Mrs. Lurie. "I didn't mean to hurt you. It's just that that trumpet blast took me by surprise. It must be that Hosmer boy up the street. You know, they say he's not quite right in the head, but I'm not one to judge."

"Me neither," the grasshopper responded amiably. "That comes later, the Judgment, and I'm pretty sure they got Someone to take care of it already. Samarrafack, the Judgment comes . . . dead . . . *last*." And he laughed with a bray like a jackass.

"Mmm. Yes, well . . ." Mrs. Lurie tried to mask her

mounting annoyance. If there was a joke somewhere in what the grasshopper had just said, she failed to get it. Moreover, the creature showed absolutely no sign of moving from its place at the window. She dreaded to think what it must be doing to her flowers. A second trumpet sounded, doing nothing for her temper. She rose from her chair and stormed to the wall phone.

"I hope you'll forgive me, but I can't ask you to come in right now," she said to the grasshopper. "I'm going to call the police and have them do something to earn their pay, for a change. I have tried and tried to talk to that Hosmer woman about her son, but some people refuse to listen. This is a nice, decent, respectable, *quiet* little town, and if she thinks that they can just move in here with their Philadelphia ways and—"

"It's not," said the grasshopper.

Mrs. Lurie frowned. She had been brought up with the understanding that it was rude to interrupt. Still, allowances might be made for the grasshopper's behavior. Who could hold an insect to task for discourtesy? It was in their nature to wriggle into everywhere, including conversations, until you had the presence of mind to call the Orkin man. "It's not what?" she asked.

"Not what you said: A nice, decent, yatta-yatta-yatta town. It's toast. Wake up and smell the brimstone, lady! You know what day it is?"

Mrs. Lurie finally put a name to the irritating twang and whine in the grasshopper's speech: A New York City accent. Well, that explained a lot. That explained it all. Jerome had taken her to New York City for a weekend vacation once, to celebrate their tenth anniversary. They'd almost been killed by a heathen taxi driver, the hotel smelled like bad lemons, no one seemed capable of talking under a holler, and the waiter at that fancy restaurant had deliberately sneered at her when she'd asked him to translate some of the items on the menu. (*Moules marinieres?* What in the world were *moules* when they were at home? Mules? Moles? She wouldn't have been at all surprised, but she'd be hanged before she'd pay fifteen dollars for a plateful of marinated garden pests.)

Which brought her back to the grasshopper.

Mrs. Lurie put on her Sunday schoolteacher face, the same stern mask she donned whenever little Billy Detweiler asked one of his godless questions like *Are you sure Adam was white?* or *Why* can't *my dog go to heaven? He's a good dog!* "I know perfectly well what day this is, young mannnnn*tis*." She pursed her lips. "It's Monday, and some of us have work to do, precious little time to do it, and no reliable help whatsoever. Now if you wouldn't mind stepping out of my flowerbed, I'd like to—"

"Ha! Shows what you know, lady." The grasshopper couldn't grin, but he cocked his head to one side and flicked his antennae at her in a positively insulting manner. "It ain't Monday, it's Doomsday. Adjust." And he sprang away from the window.

"Well," said Mrs. Lurie to the now-empty kitchen. "That would explain the blood in my washer." With a calm a more classically educated person might identify as Olympian, she went into the living room to fetch the family Bible from the breakfront and make the final entries for herself, Jerome, Daniel and Renee. She smoothed her skirt and sat herself down at her *faux* Louis XV writing table, using her late father's old Mont Blanc pen for this solemn task. It was a lot more trouble to fill the heavy-barreled fountain pen with ink and wipe the nib with a square of blotting paper, but she felt that so grave an occasion as the passing away of all things earthly should not be accomplished with a Bic Stic, especially one whose end she'd nibbled off. It gave her some satisfaction to record the same date of death for everyone in the family— one of life's few memorably perfect moments, like getting an angel food cake to slide smoothly out of the baking pan or achieving the perfect hospital corner on every single bed in the house. Mrs. Lurie liked things tidy.

Duty done, she returned to the kitchen, filled the kettle with some of the bottled water from the refrigerator, made herself a nice cup of tea with *three* sugars, and sat down on the living room sofa to await the end in a suitably receptive frame of mind.

It lasted all of three minutes. Between the pangs of wastefulness she felt for having filled the teakettle with that expensive, store-bought water (Renee insisted that good, honest Delmont tap water upset her tummy, and she'd always been such a delicate child) and the pinching of her conscience over such prodigal use of sugar (she could almost hear Jerome demanding to know why she spent all that money going to Weight Watchers if she was only going to sabotage her diet every chance she got) she was unable to muster the proper frame of mind for meeting her Maker. All she could think of was her mother.

Outside the Lurie home, the sky grew dark and dreadful rumblings filled the air. A rhythmic patter began, a delicate sound that quickly swelled to more sinister proportions as tiny pellets of unseasonable hail increased in both size and intensity until the noise of shattering windowpanes on the windward side of the house made Mrs. Lurie flinch repeatedly. A fleeting regret for the fate of her garden brushed over her mind, but it was only a thought. It lacked the power of obsession that the woman's ruminations on her mother—dead lo these many years—possessed.

Mother coming to visit when Renee was born, solely for the purpose of telling Almira it was all her own fault that the child had been born via Caesarean section instead of the way God intended.

Mother staying on to help with the housework, all the time keeping up a running commentary about how she wouldn't be at all surprised if the minute she left this pigsty Almira called a home the baby would sicken and die from the sheer, overwhelming amount of filth that her lazy daughter tolerated.

Mother coming back to visit when Daniel was born—

as God intended, episiotomy, hemorrhoids and all—to let Almira know that the only reason the boy had been born vaginally was because her prenatal negligence as to diet and lifestyle had caused his head to be too small, improperly formed, and likely the harbinger of major medical problems not too far down the pike, or at least of a career in crime.

Mother doing her level best to give the aforesaid criminal career a good head start by teaching both of the children that Almira's authority as a parent had all the substance of moth spit (though she never pulled such monkeyshines when Jerome was anywhere within earshot).

Oh, one little cookie before lunch won't hurt their appetites! Children always have healthy appetites when there's decent food set before them.

You know, if you learned how to cook carrots the right way, Almira, you wouldn't have such a battle with these poor lambs over eating them.

Well, I would certainly never force my children to eat meat that looks like that! Why, it's solid gristle and bone. How did you ever contrive to turn an expensive piece of beef into a dog's dinner? Oh, the microwave? Tsk. I've heard that those things cause cancer, but don't pay any attention to me. What are your children's lives compared to saving a few minutes so you can watch General Hospital?

Oh for goodness' sake, girl, so what if Danny's playing with your good china? Let the child alone; someday he'll be all grown up and then you'll be sorry you were so ugly to him. Won't she, Danny?

And why can't I speak my mind? Since when did you become Queen of the World? I am still your mother, missy, and I'll thank you to remember it. So what if the children hear? I'm only telling you the truth. Of course if you want them to learn to lie . . . You always were a sly child, Almira.

Wouldn't you like to come stay at Grandma's house, darlings? Yes you would, my precious little angels. You wouldn't have to listen to one single, solitary word your mean old mommy has to say while you're with me, no sir, and we'd have such good times together!

Hmph! You have no idea what these children of yours have put me through, Almira. They insisted on eating treats between meals, they turned up their noses at the good, solid meals I put in front of them, and Danny went and broke the Meissen vase your poor father gave me for our tenth wedding anniversary. Couldn't you be bothered to teach him that not everything is a toy? Some day they'll be all grown up and then you'll be sorry. How could you let them get to be so spoiled?

Mrs. Lurie's hands tightened in her lap, her teeth ground together in her skull. The thoughts washing in on the tide of her daughterly meditations were definitely not the sort she'd want dogging her to Judgment. She had no idea why—with the end of all things so patently in the offing—she was thinking about Mother. A passing resemblance to the grasshopper, perhaps?

She slapped her own face, ashamed to be party to such a thought. Mother had not been all that bad—certainly not an apocalyptic monster. Early in her marriage Mrs. Lurie learned that just because you love someone dearly doesn't mean they won't annoy you to the point of fictive homicide. She loved her mother, but the old lady meddled so much when it came to raising the children that there had been times—

An undutiful vision of a daughterly foot connecting with a maternal fundament nailed Mrs. Lurie right between the eyes. She stood up and went to the window, hoping to clear her head of unfilial musings. The hail had stopped, but there were puddles of blood everywhere and three of her ornamental crabapple trees looked as if someone had left that Hosmer boy alone with a chainsaw, a book of matches, and a can of propane just a shade too long. She went back to the family Bible and flipped through the flimsy pages until she hit the section she wanted: the

Revelation of Saint John the Divine. A slight frown creased her brow. Something was not according to Hoyle.

Not that Hoyle had ever visited Patmos.

"That was a *grasshopper*," she told the Good Book. "Not a locust, a *grasshopper*. It's *supposed* to be *locusts*. It says so right here. There's not the shadow of a chance that I could be mistaken about it, either. I'm a gardener: I ought to be able to tell a grasshopper from a locust when I see one, and what's more"—she ran one finger down the page—"and what's more, my wash water wasn't supposed to turn to blood until much later. It says so right here. This isn't—isn't *accurate*. And my goodness, what in heaven's name use is a holy prophecy if it can't be any more accurate than—than—well, than that noodle-necked weatherman on the TV? This is plain poor management, that's what it is. I won't have it." She dashed out the front door, Bible still in hand, and stood on her porch, waving the book and hollering at the top of her lungs, "I am a decent, Christian woman, *and* an American taxpayer, and I *insist* on speaking to someone in authority!"

A man on a black horse went trotting by along Main Street, a pair of balances dangling from his hand. He looked out of sorts and mildly bored with his situation, but when he heard Mrs. Lurie's shouted demands he clapped heels to his steed and got the heck out of there fast. He almost collided with Jane Geist's minivan, which was stuffed full of the Geists' valuables, the three least obnoxious Geist children, and that nice young Kesey boy from the Vo-Ag high school, an obvious aficionado of physical culture who seemed to mow the Geist lawn a lot more frequently than even the most fertile growing season demanded.

Of Mr. Geist there was no sign.

Almira Lurie spared a moment to stare and sniff. "Hmph! Bold as brass and headed for the Pittsburgh road besides," she remarked. "As if *anyone* would be spared in Pittsburgh!"

"Oh, I don't know about that," said a soft voice just behind her. "They've done a lot to clean it up since the last time I was there."

Mrs. Lurie spun around quickly and got hit in the eye with a luminous feather the color of rainbows on snow.

"I beg your pardon," said the angel, whisking his wings back out of the way and grasping Mrs. Lurie's forearms to steady her. "I didn't mean to hurt you." There was a charming though unplaceable accent to his English, something vaguely European without—thank God!—a trace of Frenchness. He was tall and blond, blue-eyed and handsome in an outdoorsy way, with a distractingly well-developed musculature clearly visible beneath his diaphanous white robes of glory.

Mrs. Lurie did not notice any of this until a tad later, of course. She was still dealing with her assaulted eye. In the manner of most people who receive a blow to one eye, she had squeezed shut both in an access of mindless self-protection. Unable to see who had struck her, she snapped: "Hurt? Hmph! I wouldn't trouble myself too much with worries about merely *hurting* anyone today."

"But I always worry about that," said the angel, and he sounded so much like a whipped puppy that Mrs. Lurie opened both her eyes.

"Oh my," she said when she beheld him. (His heavenly radiance was such that no right-thinking person might simply *see* him; he had to be *beheld*. There were unwritten laws about such things.) Mrs. Lurie's heart beat more rapidly than the wings of a covey of grouse. "What are you?" she breathed. "Have you come to save me?"

The angel consulted the ThinkPad in his palm and answered, "No. I'm sorry. You don't seem to be on my list. Not that that means you *aren't* supposed to be saved at all. It just means you're not one of *my* pickups. It all happened so fast that no one could really get things in order before—" He caught sight of the look on her face as she stared at the ThinkPad and stuffed it back into the folds of his robe, guilty as a dog caught sugarmouthed in the donut box.

Mrs. Lurie pursed her lips and took her Sunday school face one step beyond its most severe expression, escalating that flinty grimace to the point where it could wring apologies and promises of reform from used car salesmen. "Young man, *what* is going on?"

"You asked to speak to someone in authority. I'm the best we could do."

A little while later, while the howls of a gigantic wolf drifted through Mrs. Lurie's kitchen and the streets outside resounded with the creak and crack of frost-heaves shattering concrete and asphalt, the angel sipped a cup of Lipton's Herbal Essence peppermint tea and spilled his ethereal guts. Mrs. Lurie gave him a platter of Oreos, all the sugars he wanted, and paid the strictest attention.

Between sips and nibbles he talked about how all the things of earth had finally reached the proper pitch of corruption to attract Divine notice. He told of the Wrath to Come and the Judgment to Follow, or perhaps it was the other way around. He spoke of sheep and goats and horses of the appropriate scriptural colors and a miscellany of marvelous beasts in supporting roles. He mentioned great signs and wonders in the heavens and the earth with the easy familiarity of a man quoting stats for his favorite baseball team. He made his entire recitation last precisely until the last bite of Oreo was gone.

"So you see," he concluded, "it really is the End Times. We didn't want to start them just yet, but we never really had a choice about it, and it *is* the Millennium. It can't be helped. Now the best thing to do is get it over with as quickly as possible; I'm sure you'll agree. No hard feelings, I hope?"

"Quickly," Mrs. Lurie repeated. "Maybe a little *too* quickly, if you don't mind my saying as much."

"Should I?" The angel looked so very all-at-sea that he might have obtained honest work as a creditable stand-in for Saint Elmo.

"You might. I suppose you ought." Mrs. Lurie had brought

the family Bible with her into the kitchen and now she folded her hands atop it on the table as if she were Reverend Edelmeyer himself, come to speak to the Ladies' Auxiliary. Reverend Edelmeyer never could simply *speak*; in or out of the pulpit, he preached and kept on preaching. So too Mrs. Lurie: "Haste makes waste, just as I've always told the children when they come whimpering to me to drive them all the way over to the Valley mall because they have to buy supplies for a school project that's due the next day but was assigned a good two weeks ago. Loose ends always show, no matter how carefully you think you've trimmed them off or tucked them in. What's slipshod and slapdash can never pass for shipshape and all squared away, even it's supposed to be the work of Heaven."

"Madam?" The angel's blue eyes swam with bewilderment, his fingers nervously reached for Oreos that were no longer there.

Mrs. Lurie sat back in her chair. "I knew something was amiss," she announced with much satisfaction. One properly buffed and trimmed fingernail tapped on the pebbled black leatherette Bible cover. "I can read *and* I can see, and it didn't take me long to observe that what's predicted in *here*"—another tap to the Bible—"and the turmoil going on out *there*"—a nod toward the Main Street side of the house—"don't gibe worth a plugged nickel. If you are going to sponsor signs, wonders, and great terrors in the heavens and the earth, the least—the absolute *least* you might do is get them right."

The angel bowed his head over his teacup and looked sheepish. "It's none of my doing," he mumbled. "I was only following orders."

Mrs. Lurie frowned, then smiled the smile of the suddenly wise. "Why, you're *German*!" she exclaimed triumphantly.

The angel's eyes were bright with alarm. "Oh! Oh no, no, I'm not German. Not that there's anything wrong with that. That is, I'm not *exactly* German. My name is Siegfried. I am—I was—a Goth." He sounded ashamed of it.

"Ostro or Visi?" Mrs. Lurie inquired.

"I beg your pardon?" There was no concealing the angel's startlement.

"Ostrogoth or Visigoth?" Mrs. Lurie amplified. "There *is* a difference, although I'm not certain it's more than geographic." That old Sunday school look flickered back into place. "I am an educated woman, after all. Just because I live here rather than in one of those huge, ugly, smelly cities doesn't mean I'm a complete hick, and I'll thank you not to assume that you can treat me as if I were ignorant."

Siegfried scratched the plumy thatch of his right wing nervously. "No, of course I would never do that." His hands were very long and very white. The nails looked as if he'd never heard of manual labor, not even to the plucking of a harp string. "I, ah, am afraid I can't answer your question. You see, it's been so very long that I've forgotten. I was one of the first converts to Christianity among my tribefolk. I don't recall where I heard of the new faith, only that it was a source of great spiritual comfort to me. I wanted everyone to share the joy I felt. In fact, I insisted on it. My kinsmen didn't appreciate my enthusiasm."

He parted the folds of his robe and revealed a gaping wound at the base of his sternum. It gleamed a moist, bright red, but the jagged edges of the opening resembled the shiny sterility of a geode more than a life-evicting injury. Cocking her head nearer the wound, Mrs. Lurie thought she could just make out the faint sound of choral hosannas emanating from it.

Siegfried readjusted the fit of his robes to conceal his badge of martyrdom once more. "Ever since then, I have been one of the heavenly host. A minor member, I admit. The saints take precedence over us mere martyrs, but I don't mind. Even if I *was* a chieftain's son." There was the touch of something hard and distinctly unangelic in his sky-blue eyes when he spoke of his vanished earthly status, but it winked away before Mrs. Lurie could be certain she'd seen it. He finished his tea in one precise, businesslike sip, then rose and said, "Well, that hardly signifies now. Nor, for that matter, does a trifling inaccuracy between what is presently happening and what was predicted." He whisked the family Bible out from under Mrs. Lurie's hands and popped it into one of the kitchen cabinets with the Tupperware cake keepers and pie takers as if it were a vital clue that might link him to a crime of some magnitude. This done, he spun about to give her a crisp smile and brightly inquire, "Shall we go?"

Mrs. Lurie wasn't about to go anywhere and looked it. "I thought you said I wasn't one of your pickups," she reminded the angel. Outside, another trumpet sounded and she could hear the screams of her neighbors, but she refused to permit herself to become distracted.

"True, but I don't think anyone would mind if I looked after you anyway," Siegfried said. "Not really." He was trying to assume the mantle of unquestionable command, but it was slipping off both his winged shoulders even as he struggled to keep it in place. He reminded Mrs. Lurie of the way Principal Bohrman always tried to bully her PTA ladies whenever their ideas for change threatened the serenity of his petty absolute monarchy. She had never stood for any such nonsense out of Gerald Bohrman and she was not about to take it from an angel. After all, it wasn't as if an angel could hold her Daniel back a grade out of spite.

Daniel. Daniel and Renee. Where were they? What was happening to them? It felt like a thousand years since she'd calmly entered their date of death in the family Bible, but that uncanny serenity belonged to the time when she'd believed that Doomsday was being run by entities who actually had a clue as to the proper way to end a world.

Mrs. Lurie stood up and faced the angel. "You're not taking me anywhere," she informed him. "Neither is anyone else. I know my rights. It's not time and I'm not going."

The angel goggled at her. "You can't mean it," he said.

One strong hand fell to her shoulder and steered her, willy-nilly, out the front door. By now, Main Street was a turmoil and a ruckus, a clangor of divers alarums and sallies. The pavement was rubble, the houses tilted this way and that, front lawns a disgrace, plaster gnomes and plastic flamingos cast down like the fallen idols of a kitsch-enriched Babylon. Almira Lurie shaded her eyes against a sudden gust of sleet and saw most of her neighbors hightailing it up the street to the three churches that served Delmont's spiritual needs.

"You see? Everyone's on the move. They'll all be gathered up in time. You might as well go now as later." If ever an angel sounded smug, it was Siegfried.

"What I see is a lot of the same people who have always run like spooked rabbits at the least little thing," Mrs. Lurie replied evenly. "There goes Jabez Roberts and his silly little wife Maureen. Even though I was hardly more than a child when it happened, I still remember with perfect clarity that during the Cuban missile crisis they piled sacks of manure around their tool shed, stuffed it with bottled Coca Cola and Campbell's cream-of-chicken soup, and barricaded themselves inside for two weeks. It was just a mercy no one was fool enough to try convincing them it was safe to come out. That man had a loaded rifle, an itchy trigger finger, and no more brains than a backhoe. When the Imbodens' sheep dog came sniffing around the door he shot that poor creature dead as a doornail." She shrugged at the memory and went back into her home.

"Yes, but this time they're right!" the angel protested as he trailed after her. "You really ought to flee the Wrath to Come. Honest!"

Mrs. Lurie wrinkled her nose in disdain. "I rather doubt that. Wrath or no wrath, I categorically refuse to follow the lead of some idiot who thinks every sheep dog is a Communist!"

In the face of such fierceness, the angel lost his self-confidence and began fiddling with his pinions once more.

"If you don't come with me, you'll—you'll—you'll be in *trouble!*" He tried to be intimidating, but not even the world's greatest Shakespearian actor had the power to make such a patently weak line sound anything like a threat.

Mrs. Lurie fluffed the sofa cushions, ignoring him. "If you want me to come away with you so badly, why all this jabber? It's a pretty poor persuasion you're offering, but it's persuasion none the less. Why trifle with trying to win my consent to go? Goodness gracious, young man, why don't you just *take* me?"

And when Almira Lurie said that, there was silence in heaven about the space of five minutes.

Perhaps there might have been silence in heaven the Biblically promised space of half an hour if the telephone hadn't rung. The angel Siegfried jumped out of his golden sandals at the sound, loose plumes scattering everywhere.

"Oh, for pity's sake, don't take on so." Mrs. Lurie gave him a pitying look and clucked her tongue as she went into the kitchen to answer it. "I can practically guarantee it's not for you."

The call lasted for ten minutes, give or take a trumpet blast from outside the Lurie house. At one point Mrs. Lurie had to cover the mouthpiece and ask Siegfried if he'd mind shooing off the pale horse, mounted by a pale rider, that had followed in the grasshopper's uninvited footsteps and stuck its gaunt head in at the kitchen window.

"My Lord, Marsha, *now* the creature's gone and chewed up that nice souvenir tea towel you brought me back from Bermuda," she said into the telephone, her voice dripping pique. "Some people have absolutely no control over their animals. The Imbodens always had that problem. There ought to be a law . . . No, I am not making this up . . . Yes, there *is* a spectral horse standing outside my kitchen window and there's an angel trying to make it go away. And doing a piss-poor job of it, I might add, pardon my French . . . Mmm, you don't say? . . . You don't say? . . . Really? Nothing at all like that happening over in Baltimore?

Huh! Well, that's a horse of another color . . . No, Marsha,
I am *not* trying to be funny. You ought to know me better
than that . . . Fine, I have to go now. Bye-bye."

Mrs. Lurie hung up the phone. "That was my sister
Marsha, the one who never married. Couldn't find a man
good enough to suit her and *now* look. Anyhow, she says
that there is *no* Doomsday in Baltimore." She gave Siegfried
an accusatory look fit to turn steel into steam. "None. Not
even the hint of one. No blood, no grasshoppers, no hail,
not even that huge, ugly, mangy wolf I saw running up
and down the street with no more leash on him than a—
" She paused and replayed her own words in her mind,
then exclaimed, "There's no wolf in Revelation!"

"Of course there is," Siegfried said, but his voice
trembled and he looked embarrassed.

Mrs. Lurie's hand darted out faster than a serpent's
tongue. The learned doctors of the Church had wrangled
for centuries over the true nature of angels, theorizing
as to the physical attributes of the divine messengers,
debating whether the winged ones' bodies were material
or spiritual. Mrs. Lurie took a more practical approach.
The creature before her had drunk deep of her Lipton
Herbal Essence and eaten copiously of her Oreos. If that
wasn't proof of his corporeal nature, it would still play in
Peoria.

The angelic ear Mrs. Lurie grabbed and twisted was
material enough for her, and the yowl of pain that broke
from Siegfried's throat didn't sound theoretical at all.

"This goes beyond the locust question," she said. "I want
some answers. I'd prefer to have them now, but if you'd
rather wait, I've got all the time in the world. I can hang
on just fine."

"There's—there's been a mistake," Siegfried panted.

"I want some answers that I don't already *know*," Mrs.
Lurie clarified. "You already told me that it's the end of
the world—which, by the way, I had pretty much figured
out for myself long before you showed up. You told me

that due to certain factors—which you managed to gloss over without getting down to specific cases—it was not going precisely according to Revelation. Fine. I could see that for myself when I consulted my Bible and I could go so far as to accept it, if push came to shove. Saint John was a man well before he was an apostle or a saint, *plus* he was a writer. You can't expect a writer to get a story precisely right, even if it's a story that's been Revealed unto him; not if it doesn't suit his way of looking at the world. My sister Marsha used to date a writer and she told me that *those* people are holding onto reality by a buttered thread. And they *will* tinker with the simplest—"

"Your—your point?" the angel inquired through pain-clenched teeth.

"My point, friend, is that Saint John might not have gotten his version of the Last Days to jibe exactly with the Divine scenario—if I can't forgive a man for confusing grasshoppers and locusts, I shouldn't call myself a Christian—but I *do* think he might at least have made some passing mention of a wolf the size of a Winnebago and the fact that there is *nothing happening in Baltimore!*" And Mrs. Lurie gave the angel's ear another twist.

"We'll get *around* to Baltimore!" Siegfried cried. "I swear we will! We'll do Baltimore and Wilmington and Poughkeepsie and—and—and *everywhere*. Just as soon as we settle this silly little conflict of interest, we can really get this show on the— *Whoa!*"

Mrs. Lurie let go of his ear so abruptly that he staggered across the rug and pitched up against the breakfront. Three Franklin Mint commemorative plates from the *Gone With The Wind* series tumbled from their places and smashed, but Mrs. Lurie's anger was far beyond the realm of supposed collector's porcelain.

"What conflict?" she growled. "Whose interest?"

That was the moment that the wolf decided to break down her front door and see if anyone tasty was at home.

He was nowhere near the size of a Winnebago and Mrs. Lurie should have been ashamed of herself for having exaggerated his size to the point where she might as well have been a writer herself. However, he *was* large and he *was* savage and his shaggy black and gray and silver coat was generously streaked with blood. Sickly greenish-white saliva foamed from his black-gummed jaws and wreathed his yellow fangs, and when he lifted his snout to the ceiling and howled he filled the living room with the reek of rotten meat. Mrs. Lurie screamed just as the beast sprang.

A fragment of "The Burning of Atlanta" flew past her nose, slicing open a gash half a foot long beneath the wolf's left eye. "Back! Back, Fenris!" Siegfried bellowed, flinging shard after shard of the shattered plates as if they were *shuriken*, the famous steel throwing stars favored by better ninjas everywhere. He coupled these first, semi-fathomable words to a stream of ugly-sounding, thoroughly incomprehensible invective that Almira Lurie assumed was Gothic. If it wasn't, then someone was going to have to work some major linguistic adjustments on the Tongue of Angels. Somehow it just didn't seem proper for the heavenly host to have a language that sounded about as sweet and soothing to the ear as rocks in a blender.

While Siegfried flung crockery and verbal abusive indiscriminately, the giant wolf eyed him askance, head lowered. It did not flee, but rather chose to stand its ground, waiting for the angel to run out of broken dishes. In the midst of the melee, Mrs. Lurie scuttled into the lee of the wedge-shaped whatnot shelf that stood in the southeast corner of her living room. From this inadequate refuge she peered out to observe the one-sided skirmish.

It stopped being one-sided the minute Siegfried ran out of broken plates. The angel stood there empty-handed, a momentary look of frustration on his face, then bared his teeth at the wolf and loosed a growl that the huge beast might have adopted for its own. The wolf stared with baleful yellow eyes and snorted loudly. Drops of warm moisture flew broadcast across the living room, spattering Mrs. Lurie. Her exclamation of distaste was smothered by a second snort from the wolf, this one accompanied by the *swish-swish* of its titanic tail as the animal turned around and departed the premises without more ado.

"You can come out now," said Siegfried, breathing hard. "He's gone."

Mrs. Lurie wiped wolf snot from her face. "Thank you," she said primly. "I'm in your debt."

"Does that mean you'll come along quietly?" The angel's warlike bearing had vanished with the wolf. He was the eager, hopeful supplicant once more.

"No." Mrs. Lurie reached for the nearest arm of the sofa and rubbed off the last of the wolf's nasal discharge with one of the lace antimacassars Mother had given her. "Not just now. And certainly not until you answer the question I asked before we were so rudely interrupted." She glanced at the now-empty doorway and added, "That's *not* going to happen again, is it?"

"Oh no!" Siegfried replied almost cheerfully. "You're not the Fenris wolf's fated prey. He won't come looking for trouble in the same place twice. I think I managed to dissuade him pretty well. Of course that doesn't mean he *wouldn't* eat you if he just happened to get a second chance at it, say if he were to run into you out on the street, for instance. Now you see, that's *another* good reason for you coming along with me right away: If you don't, you might get destroyed or devoured by one of the others. It would be purely by accident, but still—"

"What others?"

"Frost giants. Dark elves. Hel's minions. Um, that's Hel with one-*l*, not two. The personification, not the place."

And he went on from there to explain at some length exactly what the Hell (place, not personification) was happening that day in Delmont, Pennsylvania. In plain point of fact, the whole Hel/Hell opposition was the cosmic nutshell that summed things up to a nicety, although Mrs. Lurie didn't come to see it that way until some time later. Her education in matters mythological had been limited to one very truncated unit on the Greek and Roman pantheon, part of a high school English class. Her knowledge of the Norse myths and legends was virtually nil, unless a cursory glance through one copy of *The Mighty Thor*, encountered while cleaning Daniel's room, counted for anything at all. She had also once seen the old Bugs Bunny cartoon, "What's Opera, Doc?" which parodied Wagner's immortal Ring Cycle. She hadn't gotten any of the jokes, but she did think that it was somehow immoral on several counts for an unquestionably masculine rabbit to go around in Valkyrie drag trying to seduce a male human being.

"It was a very hard winter, wasn't it?" Siegfried said in the same wistful tone the town gaffers used every spring. Mrs. Lurie had often thought that it was almost as if the old men regretted having survived yet another go-around of cruel and frosty weather only to succumb just when the world itself was being reborn. "Terrible, just terrible. It didn't let up until well into April. No wonder they misunderstood."

"Who did?"

"Oh, I certainly couldn't name names." Siegfried lowered his eyes modestly. "I'm not cleared to receive that information, and it wouldn't do *you* any good to know it even if it were mine to pass along. Look, it's simple: The Fimbulwinter's supposed to presage Ragnarok and Ragnarok's the end of the world according to *some* people. One of them just got the bit between his teeth a little early and gave the go-ahead without pausing to think, that's all, and mucked it up for the rest of us."

"Ragnarok?" Mrs. Lurie echoed. "That's not one of the ways *I've* heard you're supposed to pronounce Armageddon." She pronounced it *arm-a-jed-don*.

"I always preferred saying it with the hard g myself,"

Siegfried confessed. "It sounds so much more menacing that way. But soft or hard, it's nothing but trouble, and trouble made worse than it needs to be." He spread his hands wide, helpless. "Bureaucrats. What can you do?"

What Almira Lurie could and did do was scream. She let fly with a window-rattling, inarticulate, feral roar that nearly knocked the angel into the next room and made him cup his hands protectively over his already smarting ears. "What was *that* for?" he demanded.

"*That* was for making me worse ferhoodled than I was before I met you," Mrs. Lurie snapped back.

"Ferhoodled?"

"Confused. Bewildered. No, those words are too tame. Better make that completely confounded! I am a simple, decent, churchgoing woman. I have tended my home, looked after my husband, raised my children and, God for my witness, respected my mother above and beyond the call of duty. I am at the very least entitled to a clue, and if you continue to give me the runaround, you can go peddle your butter and eggs somewhere else. Maybe you think that all this foofaraw you've been spouting counts as an explanation, but not in *my* book, it doesn't; not by a long shot. I want answers and if I can't get them from Heaven, I'll get them from Hell!"

It was a brutal thing Mrs. Lurie said, and quite out of character, but she'd been pushed to extremities by the doings of the day. Even as the words left her mouth, she regretted them, but before she could express her repentance there was a flash of flame, a fall of rust-colored ashes, and a lithe, lissome, utterly luscious young woman appeared in the middle of the Lurie living room without a stitch of clothes to cover her shame.

"Hi," she said, waving one webbed hand, pink as a bunny-rabbit's nose. "Who wants sex?"

"Er," said the angel.

"Then it must be you." The nymph glided across the floor to enfold Mrs. Lurie in a sinuous embrace. A rank

yet seductive perfume arose from her flesh and the rich
fall of her copper-colored hair shuddered with independent
life not readily ascribable to cooties. It curled and twisted
down the creature's back, then snaked up to pour its
scented mass over the two women like a satin tent, hiding
them both from view.

Under the tent, something went *crack*!

"Ow!" The naked apparition jumped away from Mrs.
Lurie, hand to cheek, eyes wide with reproach. "You—
you *slapped* me!"

"Try those monkeyshines on me again and you'll get
worse," Mrs. Lurie snapped. "The idea!"

"If you don't want sex, why did you summon me?" the
creature demanded.

Before Mrs. Lurie chose to answer, she leaned towards
her new visitor, sniffed vigorously, and made a face. "That's
brimstone I smell," she decreed. "You stink of brimstone."

"Well, *duh*." The creature jammed fists to hips and rolled
her eyes in just the way Renee always did when her mother
committed one of the nine billion parental blunders for
which all teenagers were constantly vigilant. "I'm a demon.
What did you want me to smell like? A daisy? As a matter
of fact, I happen to be a succubus, and one of the best in
the business. The name's Cheryl."

Siegfried pursed his lips. "Cheryl?" he repeated, scorn
oozing from every syllable. "What sort of a name is *that*
for a succubus?"

There is no contempt to rival Divine contempt, and
Cheryl felt it. She reeled from Siegfried's disdain as from
a blow. "Okay, okay, so I'm not a succubus; I'm just
apprenticed to the trade. I haven't been at this long—
only since the sixties. Me and my best friend Mary
Margaret Halloran got kinda carried away fooling around
with a Ouija board and the next thing I knew, I was up to
my tits in a lake of fire."

Mrs. Lurie frowned. "I don't think that's supposed to
be a feature of Ouija boards."

"Yeah, well, Mary Margaret also thought it'd be so cool if we did some other stuff before we used the board."

"What sort of 'other stuff'?" Siegfried asked, his face an open battlefield between moral superiority and blatant nosiness. "You didn't . . . make a sacrifice to the Powers of Darkness, did you?"

Cheryl nodded. "Bingo on the first try. It was *her* idea: Mary Margaret's, the dumbass cow. She wanted us to take one of her little brother's pet goldfish and whack it with the planchet so it squished, but—*eeuuwww!*" The apprentice succubus shuddered. "I mean, just thinking about it after all these years makes me want to barf."

"Then you didn't sacrifice the fish?" Mrs. Lurie asked.

"Kind of. Kind of not. I yanked an anchovy off the pizza we were eating and made Mary Margaret agree to use that. It's the thought that counts."

"Obviously," Siegfried said, sanctimonious virtue personified. "Or you wouldn't be as we see you now."

"Ah, clam it, Harpboy," Cheryl snapped. "I wouldn't be anything *like* you see me now if Mary Margaret's old man had ever bothered to run a safety check on their furnace. Stupid thing blew sky high just when we were fooling around with the anchovy, and next thing I knew—*kapow!*—Satanland, and dabbling in the occult when you die's just like holding a fistful of E tickets. Even if all we were using was a crappy Ouija board Mary Margaret bought at fuckin' Woolworth's."

Mrs. Lurie slapped the demon's face a second time. "I don't care if you were born and bred in Lucifer's armpit, young . . . woman, you will *not* use that kind of language while you are under *my* roof."

"Yes'm."

"So that was how you came to be a lost soul," Siegfried said. "But to leap from that unhappy state to a place in the lower echelons of the infernal hierarchy in less than half a century! It is an advance of such rapidity as to be unheard-of, barring some great inherent talent for pure evil. This I doubt you have."

Cheryl gave him the finger, but quickly, just in case Mrs. Lurie was watching. "So you're right. So sue me."

The angel raised his eyebrows. "Well then, how *did* you—?"

"Plea bargaining. Soon as the two of us woke up and found ourselves in Heeee—" a nervous glance at Mrs. Lurie, "*heck*, Mary Margaret started sniveling and wailing and yowling that it was all a mistake, everything was my fault, she didn't belong there. Then she reached down her blouse and pulled out her Saint Jude medal. That was enough for the guy at the desk; he shipped her right off to Purgatory with a warning, the back-stabbing little bitch. Dumb jerk didn't bother checking his records before he did it, though, so when he finally did look up the record and he saw she'd lied and it really *was* all her idea, he knew he was screwww—in big trouble. So then he asked me if I'd mind keeping my mouth shut, and I asked what was in it for me if I did, and he said he could fix it so I wouldn't have to be a tormen*tee*, I could be a tormen*tor*, but I'd have to hire on as an apprentice for starters, and I said sure, why not, it beats the pants off being the main feature at the eternal barbecue." She spread her hands wide. "And now you know the rest of the story. So. Who wants sex?"

Mrs. Lurie's lips had pursed in disapproval so many times since this strange day had begun that by now they fell into the grimace smoothly and naturally, as if some unseen cosmic hand had them on a drawstring. "Amateurs," she said, regarding Cheryl. "Well-meaning incompetents," she said, shifting her gaze to Siegfried.

"You thought I was competent enough when I was saving you from the Fenris wolf," the angel shot back.

"Perhaps you were," Mrs. Lurie allowed. "However, I'm beginning to wonder how much of your success in that arena is ascribable to your ethnic roots rather than your angelic powers. Just where *do* you rank in the celestial hierarchy?"

"I thought I told you: I'm a martyr," Siegfried replied, but there was a certain evasiveness in both his tone and bearing. A number of maternal alarms went off in Mrs. Lurie's head all at once. This was like the time she'd confronted her boy Daniel with the inevitable question that comes to the lips of all mothers of adolescent males, namely, *What were you doing in the bathroom for so long?* Daniel had claimed a bad hair day as his excuse, but she'd seen through that polite sham and forced him to reveal his stash of *Playboy* magazines under the laundry hamper before she let him off the hook. She hadn't even needed to say much to wrest a full confession from her son; she'd simply looked at him and said, one eyebrow raised, "Oh?"

So now too she settled the bright, all-piercing eye of female skepticism full on the angel and remarked, "Really."

It wasn't a question. It didn't need to be. Siegfried squirmed like an angleworm feeling the first nip of cold fishhook steel probing its innards, but he stuck to his original account of things.

"Yes, *really*," he said with a bit too much force for someone secure in their mastery of the facts. "I was an early convert to Christianity, but my tribefolk disapproved and they massed against me in great numbers and killed me for it. Is that so very hard for you to accept?"

"Who said anything about not accepting your story?" Mrs. Lurie replied with a maddening degree of serenity.

"Yeah, except for the part where it's a crock," Cheryl said.

"Be silent, diabolical whore!" Siegfried thundered. "What would you know about such holy matters?"

Cheryl chuckled and slowly held out her tightly closed hand. As the fingers uncurled, still another trumpet sounded outside, and the sound of many large, flaccid objects hitting the pavement. Mrs. Lurie pondered whether or not she really needed to know how Doomsday was

progressing, but given the slack and imprecise nature of
the proceedings so far, she resisted the temptation. She
knew it would only upset her if she went to the window
and saw Delmont shuddering under some uncanny
meteorological assault prophesied nowhere—a rain of
manatees, for example. Bad enough to have the world
coming to an end without having to put up with too many
additional surprises. Instead she chose to focus her
attention on whatever nasty little surprise Cheryl had just
revealed.

It was the world's teensiest personal computer, a fire-
engine-red machine little bigger than a price tag, a perfect
miniature version of the laptop model Mr. Lurie used to
keep his sales records in order on the road. "My goodness,"
Mrs. Lurie said, eying it closely. "How do you ever manage
to hit the right keys? With a needle?"

Cheryl chuckled. "Not a problem. I may be just an
apprentice succubus, but I rank high enough to have my
own summer intern." She snapped the fingers of her other
hand and a mustard-yellow imp blipped into sight, looking
much like a cross between a sparrow, a shrew, a gecko,
and Marlon Brando. Muttering hideous blasphemies, the
hellish thumbkin leaped upon the minute machine and
began pounding on the keyboard with the fury of a
thousand full-sized demons.

The succubus sighed. "When you're *quite* through
playing Tetris, Billy, I've got some actual work for you.
Call up all records of early martyrs and see if you can
find the straight dope about—what did you say your name
was?" She had the gall to give Siegfried a wide-eyed
innocent look and even went so far as to bat her eyelashes
at him.

"I didn't," the angel retorted coldly. "Not to you."

"Oh well, no biggie." Cheryl shrugged. "We can just
run a scan check on all visual IDs on file. Hey Billy, check
out www.martyrs.org for starters." She showed Mrs. Lurie
a mouthful of brilliantly white teeth, only slightly pointed,

and added, "Heaven's got the libraries, but Hell's got the network access."

Siegfried's hand came down hard on Cheryl's, smothering the impgeek and his machine. Over the trapped fiendlet's impotent squeaks of rage he said, "Is this really necessary? You and I may be adversaries, but in view of the present circumstances, we ought to band together, make common cause. That's supposed to be *our* Doomsday out there." He jerked his head towards the windows.

"Gotcha." Cheryl winked at him so lasciviously that the angel jerked his hand away as if she'd just given him an acid manicure. "Hey, don't sweat it too much, Harpboy; it's gonna be ours in the end."

"You sound confident," Mrs. Lurie remarked. "From what I've heard, there are legions of pagan gods and monsters arrayed against you. I can't offer any opinion as to your chances against the deities, but judging from the one monster I *have* seen, you have your work cut out for you."

Cheryl made a derisive sound with her lips, as if she meant to blow away all of Mrs. Lurie's words on a single gust of scorn. "Work? Big deal. I've got the inside dope on this snafu." The apprentice succubus breathed over the miniature computer and the fiendlet in her hand; both vanished in a puff of sulfurous smoke the virulent color of orange Kool-Aid. "It all comes down to simple mathematics: highest body count wins."

"Body count," Mrs. Lurie repeated. She had never liked the sound of that phrase. She had grown up in the sixties, and those two words had played too large a part in too many evening news broadcasts. She'd gone to school with some of the boys who made *body count* mean something more than an overpaid, overgroomed anchorman's detached recitation of figures. She couldn't do much about the situation then, but she'd see herself working a streetcorner in Hell right next to Cheryl if she didn't take some action now.

"Young man," she said, looking Siegfried right in the eye, "I demand that you tell me the truth. The *whole* truth."

"As if I could do anything less!" Siegfried struck a wounded-to-the-quick pose, an affectation that swiftly withered up and blew away under Mrs. Lurie's gimlet eye. "What do you want to know?"

"Am I correct when I say that there are two different stripes of Armageddon going on here in Delmont at the moment?"

"Whoa. *She* catches on quick. *Not*." Cheryl was pleased to give her best adolescent sarcasm an airing.

In ordinary circumstances Mrs. Lurie might have overlooked the sass—she only corrected other people's children when property damage, actual or potential, was involved—but her nerves had been under some strain. She smacked the succubus' face yet again. It was getting to be a tedious yet strangely satisfying habit. After all, the girl *was* a demon, even if only an apprentice to the trade. The Reverend Edelmeyer had often mentioned "muscular Christianity," and Mrs. Lurie rejoiced in finally having the opportunity to practice the same.

"I am merely attempting to comprehend the situation as it stands," she informed the trainee succubus without apology. "If you don't know *where* something's broken, you can't hope to fix it."

"Fix it?" Cheryl repeated, hand to cheek. "Like . . . fix *that*?" She waved her other hand at the windows just as something huge, blue and hairy went lumbering past, shedding icicles and muttering gutturally.

Siegfried went to the window for a better look. "Oh dear. A frost giant. They've brought on the big guns now."

Mrs. Lurie chose to ignore the angel's whinging and concentrate on the succubus. Although she didn't like to admit as much—being a good churchgoing woman and all—she'd noticed that in full many a Sunday school tale, the forces of Good tended to sidle away from giving a body direct answers more often than not, whereas the forces of Evil had a refreshing-if-deplorably-applied directness to them. "Yes, *fix* it," she told Cheryl. "In case it hadn't crossed your mind, I have quite a stake in seeing to it that the world does not end today."

"Beauty parlor appointment tomorrow?" The succubus smirked, but she also jumped well out of reach of Mrs. Lurie's face-slapping hand.

"What a fool you are," said Mrs. Lurie, and turned her back on the succubus.

"Hey!" Cheryl took instant umbrage at the slight. She rushed up behind Mrs. Lurie and tapped her on the shoulder, trying to make her turn around. "Hey, who gave you the right to say that kind of stuff about me, you— you—mortal!"

Mrs. Lurie continued to snub the importunate demon, returning the grace of her regard to the angel. Playing one against the other with her attention as the prize was a strategy she'd long used with her own children. It wasn't very nice, she knew, but it did keep their grades above C-level. "Siegfried, dear, how would you describe someone who not only can't recognize a much-needed ally, but who purposely, childishly tries to alienate him? *Or* her. I mean, *I'd* call that person a fool, but I'm only a housewife. What do I know?"

"Er, um, that is—" Siegfried fidgeted, uncomfortable in his abruptly assigned role of buffer zone.

"What kind of ally are *you*?" Cheryl demanded, tapping on Mrs. Lurie's shoulder harder still. "Oh yeah, sure, it doesn't take a rocket scientist to figure out why you don't want the world to end today: You don't wanna die. *Very* deep, *very* noble motivation, and *big fucking deal*. It's gonna end sometime, and you can't do a thing to stop it, can you? *Can* you?" She gave up pounding on the woman's shoulder and instead tried ducking around to thrust her question right into Mrs. Lurie's face.

Mrs. Lurie simply turned away again. It was almost the identical tactic she had used on Renee when her daughter

had announced her intention to wear lipstick to school
and *no one was going to be able to stop her*. Renee had
worn lipstick to school for the better part of a week, and
for the better part of that same week Mrs. Lurie had
behaved as if the forbidden cosmetic had rendered the
girl invisible. In the end the lipstick had gone into the
trash and Mrs. Lurie's eyesight was miraculously restored
thereby. And if Renee slouched around the house for two
weeks after that with a grouch on that a grizzly bear might
envy, her mother felt it was a small price to pay for having
saved the child from looking cheap and trashy, to say
nothing of the fact that the shade of oversilvered pink
she'd chosen also made her look like the star attraction
at a three-ring funeral.

Of course Renee was no succubus.

"Ow!" Mrs. Lurie leaped for the ceiling, batting at her
behind. The lizardlike creature that had so abruptly
attached itself to her backside held on with every tooth
in both its heads and refused to let go until Cheryl stuck
two fingers in her mouth, calling it off with a shrill whistle.
The moment it hit the floor a hefty swordblade descended,
slicing it in half lengthwise.

Cheryl glared at Siegfried. "Was that necessary?" she
demanded, pointing at the bisected monstrosity now
bleeding an effervescent ochre liquid all over the carpet.

"Was *that*?" Siegfried countered, pointing at Mrs. Lurie's
behind.

As for Mrs. Lurie, she craned her neck at a painful angle,
trying to assess what damage had been done to her skirt,
gave up at last, and marched herself to take a stand between
the two supernatural beings. Her right hand darted out
to cup the back of Siegfried's head at almost the same
instant as her left hand did the same to Cheryl's. Then,
with a thunderous report that all but drowned out the
sound of yet another of those irksome trumpets, she
brought the two skulls together smartly.

Cheryl sat down hard, stunned and blinking rapidly.

Siegfried, who came from more resilient stock—thicker headed, anyway—stood gaping at Mrs. Lurie. "You dare thus treat a holy messenger?" he exclaimed.

"Says you." Mrs. Lurie's mouth had grown tight with disapproval and annoyance, and was growing tighter by the second. Somewhere outside on the streets of Delmont there were signs and portents of doom, yet none that promised so great a measure of suffering before death's kind release as the expression on that simple housewife's face at that particular moment in time.

"A holy messenger?" On Mrs. Lurie's tongue the words acquired a coating of cold cynicism that cut them off from all hope of credibility. "Then why did you prevent that little yellow demonling from calling up your records? Holiness means never having to sweep the dirt under the rug. There's more to you than meets the eye, Siegfried, but that doesn't mean it's all fit to print. Is it." It was another of those no-question-about-it questions, the sort that were more dare than interrogation.

Siegfried's fair skin colored up nicely. "I have nothing to hide. I showed you the mark of my martyrdom. Do you think I faked that?"

Mrs. Lurie waved her hand, dismissing the angel's protests. "Keep your secrets. They don't interest me. Just don't take me for a fool, that's all I ask."

"A fool? You?" The succubus uttered a sharp bark of laughter, but one glance at Mrs. Lurie's face made her turn it into a phony-sounding cough in short order.

Siegfried scowled and gave Cheryl a sharp nudge in the ribs with his elbow. "Stop that," he hissed. "Do you want to remain an apprentice for all eternity?"

"Hell, no," Cheryl snarled back out of the corner of her mouth.

The two supernatural beings might have been trying to keep their voices inaudible to anyone save each other, but if so, they failed. Mrs. Lurie's brows rose and her eyes brightened with speculation. However, all she said was, "All right. You've more than made your case. I'll come quietly."

Siegfried and Cheryl went simultaneously wide-eyed with such precision that it looked as if they'd been rehearsing double takes in some otherworld No Man's Land. "You will?" Siegfried gasped.

"I might as well," Mrs. Lurie replied, to all appearances calm, self-contained, and graciously resigned to her fate. "Although I'm afraid you haven't been much help to me as far as explaining matters, I think I've managed to piece together the situation. Correct me if I'm wrong, that's all I ask: Saint John's text is only *one* script for the world's end?"

The angel nodded. "Of course it is the only *suitable* version," he added dutifully (and not a little self-righteously). "The one that really *ought* to be the universally accepted criterion for bringing all things to a close, but still—"

"Yes, yes, yes." Mrs. Lurie dismissed Siegfried's celestial jingoism out-of-hand. "And yet other peoples—your own included—have other theories for how all this will ultimately be swept away?" Her arms spread wide.

"All this?" Cheryl looked around. "You mean the Norse gods are gunning for your living room?"

Siegfried gave her another shot to the ribs and a will-you-just-shut-*up* scowl to go with it.

"It was a *joke*, Harpboy," the succubus grumped.

Mrs. Lurie ignored the byplay. "So," she said. "Somehow, certain circumstances were set into motion causing certain . . . people? . . . beings?"

"Powers," Siegfried provided.

"Powers, yes, thank you." Mrs. Lurie acknowledged the correction with a smile. "Certain powers came to believe that the signs were right to initiate the end of all things and they went ahead without asking anyone else what they thought."

"My father's gods always were portrayed as being impulsive," Siegfried remarked.

"They're not the only ones," the succubus said. "I got a wrath-smitten fig tree you oughta see. Just because it wouldn't bear fruit when *Someone* I could mention wanted—"

"You *would* bring up that . . . minor incident." Siegfried attempted to laugh it off. "One of your kind would never understand the motivation behind such a—"

"Hey, if you don't like *that* one, I got a dozen other assorted smote-quotes from either Testament you prefer," Cheryl countered.

Mrs. Lurie made unnecessarily loud throat-clearing noises. "As I was *saying*—" She gave the paranormal pair a look of gentle reproof for their interruption. "What you call Ragnarok was set in motion, causing the, um, sponsors of the Book of Revelation brand of Doomsday to initiate their version because if they waited for the *proper* time, there'd be no earth left over for them to destroy. Correct?"

"It *is* the proper time," Siegfried said stiffly, a company man to the end. "The Millennium has been widely acknowledged to be the point at which—"

"Of course it has, dear; of course it has." If familiarity didn't breed contempt, it certainly did nibble away at awe. Mrs. Lurie seemed to have fallen into the habit of waving aside anything the angel had to say. Understandable, naturally: Once you'd seen an angel dip Oreos in peppermint tea, it was difficult to resume thinking of him as a dread and fiery messenger of divine favor and/or punishment. "Let's just say that mistakes were made and no one's willing to admit to it, so now the whole nasty pickle's going to be resolved in small right here, Revelation versus Ragnarok. The version of Doomsday that destroys more of Delmont— as reckoned by body count—will be declared the winner and get to take its show on the road to devastate the rest of the earth, including Baltimore." She glanced from angel to succubus and back as calmly as if she'd just given them her grocery list. "That's it, isn't it?"

"Er, yes," said Siegfried.

"Dead on," said Cheryl.

"The end of the world, my, my, my." Mrs. Lurie sighed, though not with any grief or regret. "The end of bodily existence and all it entails. No more sickness. No more sorrow. No more sleepless nights. No more sex. No more wrestling with our inner demons or"—she winked at Cheryl—"our outer ones." She smiled at her guests and concluded, "Poor dears, you'll be out of a job forever."

The angel and the demon began to speak all at once, yet strangely enough neither one found a single word to say. Mrs. Lurie continued to smile. Outside, the pandemonium of contending Doomsdays made the streets of Delmont hellish and then some with the clash of swords, the clatter of hooves, the roaring of dragons and wolves, and the intermittent patter and thud of various inauspicious objects tumbling from the skies. But inside, Mrs. Lurie's living room was an anomalous isle of tranquillity in a sea of weirdness.

Mrs. Lurie was the one to shatter the silence: "I'm glad that's settled. Now we make a deal."

"A deal?" Siegfried's blonde brows rose like a pair of wings that had forgotten their angel.

"A deal!" Cheryl clapped her hands together with glee. "Now you're talking *my* language! I *like* you, lady. Okay, so what do you want? Oh, wait a sec." She snapped her fingers and a long scroll of closely-written parchment appeared in midair between them, its borders edged with foul-smelling flame. "I know we don't have a lot of time left, but you just sign this and I guarantee you that your last moments on earth will be *so* incredibly to-die-for that you won't even mind, well, when you've got to die for them. But you gotta go sometime, right?" she added hastily, seizing the contract and shoving it at Mrs. Lurie.

Mrs. Lurie fixed her gaze on the hellish compact and assumed a peculiar air of concentration. Within moments the document—previously on fire but unconsumed—fizzled into a pile of ashes at her feet. She toed the still-steaming embers and nodded, gratified. "I thought so," she said.

"How'd you *do* that?" an amazed succubus asked.

"It's a sign," the angel said, leaping in to seize the moment. "A sign that this woman is of the elect, the souls who will undoubtedly be saved when the final trump is sounded and the sheep are separated from the goats. It means she's supposed to come with me. *Now*." He flung out his hand, most likely intending it as an invitation to Mrs. Lurie. Whose fault was it that instead it looked as if he were striking a *ta-daaah!* pose?

"You know," said Mrs. Lurie, "I never did think much of sheep. They're fairly stupid animals, too easily led. Goats, on the other hand, have little more to recommend them. Not all choices are either/or. That includes Revelation or Ragnarok, to my way of thinking. Why only *two* contending Doomsdays? And why *these* two? It's not as if the Germans *did* take over the world. Why not something Japanese in the way of End Times? Or Native American? My Daniel once did a wonderful school report about the Aztecs; they had the world ending four or five different ways, one right after the other, like frames in a bowling match. Well?" She looked at the demon and the angel.

"Er, what was the question again?" Siegfried asked.

"I think she wants me to take her bowling before she signs away her soul," Cheryl whispered. "Not the greatest choice, if you ask me, but who am I to argue? The customer is always right." She made a graceful gesture of dark sorcerous meaning and a pair of battered red-and-blue bowling shoes appeared on her feet.

"There really *was* no question," Mrs. Lurie told them. "None that either of you could handle, anyway. I've got all the answers I need. There's only one." She toed the now cool pile of ashes once more. "I'm the one in charge here."

Siegfried snorted. Cheryl broke into a storm of laughter. It was infectious as well as diabolical, and soon the angel had shucked his shell of self-righteous indignation and was laughing along with her.

"*You?*" the angel wheezed through tears of mirth. "In charge of what? The PTA bake sale?"

"Easy to see how you could confuse that with being the master of cosmic forces beyond the control of mere mortals," Cheryl snickered, then gave up all restraint and howled with laughter.

"Stop that," said Mrs. Lurie. And they did. Dead. Cold. "See?"

Cheryl brought her hands together and when she pulled them apart again she was holding a cardboard sign that read: WHAT *is* THIS SHIT? Mrs. Lurie pursed her lips and the last word was transmuted into: SHINOLA.

"This . . . situation is precisely what it seems," Mrs. Lurie told her. "As I said, I'm in charge. As are my neighbors, my friends, and every other living human soul within the borders of Delmont. It's all quite logical. I figured it out myself, and I didn't even do all that well in math. This was the clincher, when all I did was reject your contract utterly, from the heart, with *this* result." She indicated the ashes still mounded on her living room carpet.

A passing thought jerked her up short: "Oh. Wait just a moment. There's just one last thing I need to check." She hastened to the front door, opened it and looked out. By the time she'd closed it again and returned to the immobilized angel and demon there was no agency, human or otherwise, capable of taking that smug smile off her face.

"I was mistaken: *That* was the clincher," she said. "Out there. The streets are a disaster, the roads are all buckled and cracked and chasmed, the houses are tumbling or shaking or already fallen over, the people are rushing back and forth in a panic, fleeing monsters of every flavor and variety, but do you know what's missing? The dead. Giants and wolves and multiheaded dragons running rampant, and I *think* I saw a sperm whale buried nose-first in

Gretchen Fowler's front lawn, but no human casualties.
Not a one. That's either the worst case of incompetence
I've ever seen at work, or else it's not incompetence at
all. It's impotence."

The demon and the angel both discovered a sudden
fascination with the ceiling of Almira Lurie's living room.
She allowed them the luxury of not having to meet her
eyes.

"Faith," she went on, "is widely agreed upon as better
than a bulldozer for all large earth-moving projects. I'm
not about to chop logic with either one of you as to the
relative powers and differences between faith and belief,
but I will say this: *Something* at work here today isn't
operating according to Because-I-said-so rules. It's asking
for *cooperation*. The elect are supposed to be swept up
into heaven just as the damned are supposed to be shoved
into hell without playing *Mother, May I?* first. If it were
otherwise, *you*"—she pointed at the angel—"wouldn't be
trying to persuade me and *you*"—it was the demon's turn—
"wouldn't be trying to seduce me. I *am* in charge of what
happens here, in both the long and short runs. And for
that matter, so is every other human being who's still within
the town limits, only none of them know it yet."

"It *is* kind of difficult to realize that you're self-
empowered while you're running away from a frost giant."
Cheryl gave Siegfried a nasty look while she said that.

"Now see here—" the angel began indignantly.

"No, *you* see here!" the succubus snapped at him. "She's
right. She figured it out, loopholes and all. Man, I am
sick to death of loopholes: big enough and a cow like Mary
Margaret Halloran can shimmy through 'em, but small
enough so all that's left for me is an opening just the right
size to put my head through and then they tighten the
noose. Well, no more. She's right," she repeated. "There
is no direct, hands-on, claws-on, fangs-on slaughter allowed
on this playing field. No shanghaiing allowed, a press-
gang-free zone. We're just supposed to *recruit* the marks

for good old Judeo-Christianity, and for what? If we lose, the visiting team gets to take their version cross-country and trans-global. The world will end, our kind will be out of a job, and if there is such a thing as an after-afterlife, we'll spend it either kicking ourselves or being bored to tears."

"But the Aesir won't win," Siegfried protested. "They can't. That is . . ." He grew thoughtful and fell silent.

"Don't flatter yourself," Cheryl snarled, reading his thoughts without benefit of clairvoyance. All demons received a crash course in doping out human nature as part of Basic Training, and it applied even if the human in question had been elevated to angelic status. Something of the old Adam always managed to hang on by its teeth and hide under the robes of glory. "This isn't a win-win situation for you, no matter what you think. You won't be able to weasel your way into the good graces of the Aesir, Harpboy. Your father's old gods won't *want* you back. You sold out to our side a long time ago. Anyway, the only mortals that crowd ever took an interest in were warriors who died gloriously in battle."

"*I* died gloriously!" Siegfried countered. "I died fighting for the one true faith!"

"I think Cheryl's right, dear," said Mrs. Lurie. "As true as that may be, it still won't impress the other side."

"It doesn't matter." Siegfried brushed invisible dust off his sleeves. "They won't win. We will."

"And lo, you and I will still be out of a job," Cheryl riposted. "Just like she said *again*. Who needs heavenly messengers when there's no one mortal left to accept delivery? Who needs demons when there's no more candidates for damnation? We'll get to fly or fry through tedium everlasting, unless Someone decides that since game's called on account of Armageddon, we're obsolete, and simply wipes us off the playing board."

The devil is said to be able to argue Scripture, but Cheryl's diatribe pretty much took the cake. Siegfried's face paled then flushed as the waves of realization, denial, acceptance, and dread broke over his spirit sequentially.

"*Scheiss*," said the angel.

Mrs. Lurie knew enough German to recognize her window of opportunity even if it didn't have gingham curtains and a giant grasshopper leaning on the sill. "It doesn't *have* to be that way," she said.

"Oh yeah?" Cheryl jammed her fists to her hips. "You just finished convincing us that win or lose, we lose. So what other way do you think it *can* be?"

Almira Lurie smiled with that same dimple-heavy breed of personal charm that had inveigled her Jerome into asking for her hand in marriage without receiving the reciprocal right to put *his* hands anywhere he damned pleased. "Winning isn't everything, especially not in *this* case, and I don't think you need me to tell you that losing is flat out *nothing*. But who says every choice you make in your life has to be Coke or Pepsi. Sometimes you've just got to reach for the Seven-Up."

"Of course you do," said Siegfried, who had the bright, blank stare of one who is completely clueless but will die before fessing up to same. Like most angels, he would have made excellent middle management material.

"Huh?" said Cheryl, who already being damned and naked didn't have much left to lose by way of personal pride and thus didn't give two shits in a handbag if she appeared ignorant.

"Just get in the car," said Mrs. Lurie.

And so it was that this simple housewife found herself arbitrating the fight between the forces of Heaven and Hell as to who got to ride shotgun in her dependable old Chevrolet Celebrity station wagon. Siegfried argued that he needed the room for his wingspan, Cheryl insisted that she needed it to accommodate her huge quantities of hair.

"Stop behaving like children," Mrs. Lurie told them severely. "Siegfried, the front seat offers extra *leg*room, not *wing*room. Your wings would fit much better if you lay down on your tummy back in the cargo area. Cheryl, I'm sure you can't help it, but you do smell like rotten eggs and gone-over Chanel Number Five, and I'm afraid it's just too much for one little pine-scented air freshener to handle, so you're not going to set foot inside my car at all. You're going to ride on the roof, thank you very much."

"The roof's a *much* cooler place to ride than the cargo space any day," Cheryl decided. "*I* ain't no sack of groceries." She stuck out her tongue at Siegfried before gleefully scrambling up to lay hold of the luggage rack and strike a gargoyle pose. It would've looked better if she'd remembered to get rid of the bowling shoes.

"It's certainly the perfect place for a baggage like you." Frost enough to beget a score of Norse giants crusted itself over the angel's sarcastic reply.

Mrs. Lurie clapped her hands together sharply. "Stop it, you two. We're all on the same side here. I won't stand for any squabbling. Once we've settled matters, you can skin each other with blunt butter knives, for all I care. Until then, I want cooperation and I want it *now*."

She got it, too. With an angel behind her, a demon over her head, and her blue plastic purse on the seat beside her, she did what any sensible Christian woman would do in a similar time of trial: She drove straight to church.

Most of the people of Delmont who had been unable to escape from their tormented town had chosen the churches as the best sites to hole up until Doom cracked or the Fenris wolf had them for brunch. The first place Mrs. Lurie's station wagon of otherworldly wonders stopped was at the Lutherans'. Mrs. Lurie didn't attend Delmont Lutheran herself, but she knew that there was no reason to race to save her own church ahead of the rest. Everything she knew reassured her that it would likely be the last to fall to the encroaching forces of competing Armageddons; the Reverend Edelmeyer would see to that. If the End Times required human cooperation, consensus, and consent to occur, they weren't going to get any of the above from *him* too fast. That godly man could be very stubborn, as well as very good at ignoring circumstances he found to be unorthodox or just unpleasant. He had once confronted an entire squadron of motorcycle toughs who came roaring into the community picnic grove during the big Fourth of July celebration. He dealt with them by facing them fearlessly, refusing to acknowledge so much as the possibility that they might be capable of violence, and suggesting they'd be happier if they went elsewhere. They departed like Harley-riding lambs.

Of course it didn't hurt that the Reverend Edelmeyer also just happened to mention that the community grove was "dry" but that the nearby town of West Altdorf always had plenty of beer on tap at *their* picnic.

Mrs. Lurie and her aides found the Lutheran church besieged by half a dozen scraggly-looking dark elves on the south side, one of the Four Horsemen—probably War, judging by the spiffy uniform—on the north, locusts with the bodies of horses, the teeth of lions, and the crowned heads of men on the east, and Mr. and Mrs. Imboden on the west, where the main entrance faced the street from the top of a steep flight of granite steps. Mrs. Imboden was holding a squirming Corgi to her bosom while Mr. Imboden pounded on the closed doors and hollered that after all the money he'd given over the years to the Building Fund someone had damn well better let him inside.

While he banged away and his wife whimpered and the Corgi snuffled and barked and howled with embarrassment, the dark elves took notice. Four of them nocked arrows to the bows they bore while the fifth and sixth ambled over to confront the Imbodens. The elves were smiling, if you could ascribe a friendly intention to that sharklike baring of teeth. One of them began to address Mr. Imboden in a low, cajoling voice. Mrs. Lurie was just letting Siegfried out of the back of the Celebrity when the angel, overhearing the elf's words, stiffened to the very tips of his pinions.

"You cursed *liar*!" he roared, and charged up the church

steps with fists clenched. He was upon the elves before
they could blink, and before their four backup companions
could pull back their bowstrings and let the arrows fly.
With a single backhanded blow, Siegfried knocked one
elf down the steps, then seized the other by the front of
his tunic and proceeded to slap him silly, all the time
muttering, "—colossal *nerve* to tell these sheep that they'll
go straight to Valhalla if they come with you . . . As if they
had the faintest idea *what* Valhalla is . . . entrance
requirements . . . Try telling a retired hardware store owner
he's got a chance in Hel's domain of being taken for a
mighty warrior who's died nobly in battle . . . say nothing
of his wife and the dog . . . Nasty, lowdown, rotten, lying
elves . . . Piss on the truth as soon as look at you . . ."

By this time the other four elves had recovered themselves
enough to send their arrows soaring. Two of them went
right into the angel and were immediately transformed
into rays of mystic effulgence in unflattering shades of
purple. The remaining two sank their glittering black heads
deep into the heart of Mrs. Imboden and the rump of her
Corgi.

The Corgi yelped and leaped out of Mrs. Imboden's
arms. As for his mistress, she never noticed his abrupt
departure. Eyes glazed, mouth agape, she sank to her knees
on the steps of the Lutheran church and toppled over
against the sealed door.

A great silence came to settle over the scene. The elves
scattered, slipping from sight between the privet hedges
bordering the church lawn, snatching up their comrades
as they fled. Shocked, Siegfried allowed them to snag and
bear away the elf he'd been slapping around. The
apparitions that had been besetting the church building
on the other fronts decided that this might be a pretty
good time to go see how things were progressing over by
the Methodists. Mr. Imboden let out a moan of despair
even louder than the one he'd uttered more than thirty
years ago when Jabez Roberts had plugged his sheep dog.

He threw himself across his wife's body, weeping. Cheryl knelt beside him, a soft, alien expression of compassion on her face.

"She's gone," the succubus whispered, her voice breaking with emotion. "Your faithful, devoted wife is gone. Alas." She sighed deeply, then thrust Mr. Imboden's face into the pillowy valley of her breasts. "So, you want sex?"

Mrs. Lurie brought her blue plastic purse down on Cheryl's head like the still-in-a-holding-pattern Wrath of God. Then she stood over Mrs. Imboden's body, got a good, two-handed grip on the elfin shaft protruding from her chest, and gave it a healthy yank. It came out with no trouble and it left not so much as a rip in Mrs. Imboden's blouse to show it had ever had the effrontery to pierce that honest matron's bosom.

"Why, thank you, Almira," said Mrs. Imboden, smiling up at her. "I always did tell your mother that you were such a *nice* girl, no matter *what* she said."

Shortly thereafter, the good folk of Delmont had reason enough and more to agree with Mrs. Imboden's character assessment of Almira Lurie. With Siegfried's help, she and the others in her party gained entry to the Lutheran church. While the angel set the torn-away door gently to one side on the lawn, she marched up the aisle between rows of pews where her fellow citizens prayed and cowered and trembled, she took the pulpit from that skittish young minister, the Reverend Packer, and said a few terse sentences into the sound system concerning the purported End Times. She only told the congregation what she'd seen and what she'd learned concerning Delmont's options, but it was enough.

The sound of frantic prayer ebbed and faded like an outgoing tide. The people lifted up their eyes, for the first time daring to hope. The Imbodens, being senior citizens, took a while to join Almira up at the front of the church, but when they did, they added their say to her testimony. It was most impressive when Mrs. Imboden showed the

very arrow that had been powerless to take her life by
force, and even jabbed it into her hand a couple of times
for effect, smiling as if she were a Mary Kay Cosmetics
rep demonstrating a new eyeshadow. Unfortunately Mr.
Imboden ruined his wife's fifteen minutes of fame by
adding a few gratuitous comments about what the Building
Fund Committee could do with their next solicitation letter.

An anonymous Doubting Thomas from somewhere
towards the back of the church raised the question of
Mrs. Lurie's credibility, but he was promptly quashed
by Siegfried. The angel stepped up to the mike, tore
asunder his robes to flash his radiantly bejeweled heart
of martyrdom as if it were an American Express card,
and exclaimed, "Hear her, O ye peoples of the earth, for
the Last Times are not come upon you unless you so
desire, and the End of All Things will not touch you unless
by your own volition you bring it down by your own
surrendering of faith!"

"Besides, a schoolchild could tell you that the Millennium
actually begins in the year 2001, not 2000," Mrs. Lurie
added, pushing Siegfried gently aside and reclaiming the
microphone. "So it can't be now: It's too early. It wouldn't
be proper. I'm surprised no one thought of that. Everyone
go home and for heaven's sake, don't pay any more attention
to these silly creatures that've been turning our town on
its ear. They're just like tantrum-throwing toddlers: If you
ignore them, they'll get bored and stop it. Or would you
like word of this to get back to West Altdorf?"

Well, that did it. No one wanted that nest of gossips
and tattletales to get their flapping jaws around any of
this, oh no! Within minutes the members of the Lutheran
church were streaming down the steps and hastening home
as directed, or else going forth to spread the truth of things
unto all the other churches and miscellaneous shelters
and refuges of their town. Siegfried and Cheryl went along
to lend their voices in support of the newborn *Just Say
"No" to Apocalypse* campaign. With the angel's help, Mrs.

Imboden managed to recover her Corgi, who was still elfshot in the butt. The dog's buoyant demeanor despite its fey arrowhead wedgie lent much weight to the argument that Doomsday—of whatever sect, culture, or flavor— need only bother you as much as you cared to let it. If even a dog could deal with the situation, could the people of Delmont do anything less?

As for Mrs. Lurie, she got back into her station wagon and drove to the town school. The False Prophet was stationed outside, leaning against the flagpole, waiting for his big chance, but Almira soon sent him packing.

"They're not going to listen to anything you have to say anyhow, you know," she told him. "You look too much like Principal Bohrman."

As she had expected, the children of Delmont were all crouched under their desks or huddled up in the classic duck-and-cover A-bomb drill position out in the halls. No one stopped her as she paced up one corridor and down another to find her babies and take them home.

She had Daniel and Renee at the kitchen table while she made them a nice afterschool snack when she heard— even above Daniel's whining that there were no more Oreos—a knock at the front door. It was Siegfried and Cheryl. The succubus looked different, somehow; Mrs. Lurie couldn't quite put her finger on it. Then it struck her: Cheryl wasn't naked any more. In fact, she was wearing a set of robes that were almost as shining as Siegfried's.

"Hi," the former demon said, blushing a very pretty shade of pink. "We're headed for home, but before we leave, we wanted to thank you for what you did for us. And we thought you'd also like to know that everything's all settled now. Oh! And I almost forgot: I got kicked upstairs for spending too much time in the company of *this* big lug here." She squeezed Siegfried's hand affectionately. "Heeee . . . *Heck* wouldn't have me."

"Mercy sakes, *that* was a quick redemption," Mrs. Lurie remarked. "I don't think it's been half an hour since I saw you last. It's a comfort to know that even the most fallen soul can still hope that faith and prayer will swiftly move the Almighty to—"

"Oh, it wasn't any of that," Siegfried cut in. "It was all the extra points she got for helping us clean up the town."

"Clean . . . ?"

"Certainly. Once the Powers That Be realized that you mortals understood what was going on, They knew there was no chance of either End coming out on top, so they called it all off, just the way you said they would. They're gone now—the frost giants, the Dragon, the dark elves, the Beast, vengeful Hel herself, the Four Horsemen— all the players. A few of us stayed behind just long enough to tidy up."

Mrs. Lurie stuck her head out the door, peering past the two angelic beings. And lo, it was so. The fallen houses and the cracked pavement had all been returned to their previous state. The ornamental crabapple trees were flourishing. The people were strolling up and down the street with the same bland smiles on their faces that they always wore. Jane Geist's minivan came chugging back along the restored roadway from the general direction of Pittsburgh. It stopped on the corner to let that Kesey boy out near the half-buried sperm whale on Gretchen Fowler's front lawn.

"Oops," said Siegfried. "Missed a spot."

"Well, thank you for dropping by," Mrs. Lurie told them. "I'd ask you in, but I'm afraid the sight of you might upset the children. Besides, there are no more Oreos."

"*We'd* upset them? After all they probably saw today?" Siegfried was genuinely surprised.

"I don't want to chance it," Mrs. Lurie insisted. "Cal me overprotective if you like; I don't care. After all, I never would have put up the struggle I did if not for my children. Surrender would have been easy, but I jus couldn't. I couldn't for their sake."

"That's very noble of you." Siegfried rested one hand

on the housewife's shoulder. "If my own mother had stuck up for me as staunchly, Father would never have tossed me into that bog for a sacrifice." He sighed wistfully. "If I'd *known* he was going to do it, I never would have screamed so loudly on the way down. But he took me by surprise; no one should've blamed me for reacting the way I did. It was simply pure shock, but the Recording Angel claimed it showed a lack of faith and took off points for that, all the difference between martyrdom and sainthood—"

"You drowned in a bog? Then what about that bleeding heart you've got . . . under there?" Mrs. Lurie waved vaguely at the angel's now-covered chest.

"Standard issue for all martyrs, no matter what form our martyrdom took," Siegfried explained. "Thank God. I don't think I could stand it if I had to spend eternity covered in muck and peat moss."

"So that's why you didn't want Cheryl to call up your records?" Mrs. Lurie smiled.

"Well . . . yes."

"You really shouldn't bear such a grudge against your father. It's over. What's past is past."

Siegfried looked away, abashed.

Cheryl leaned near and gave Almira a chaste, sisterly kiss on the cheek. "If this world had more mothers like you, it would be a better place," she said. "Farewell."

"Good-bye," said Mrs. Lurie. "And please pick up the whale on your way out, won't you? It's so easy to overlook the little things. Thanks."

The heavenly messengers departed. Mrs. Lurie went back into the kitchen. Her children were still drinking milk and eating peanut-butter-and-jelly sandwiches, unaware that she had returned. She allowed herself a moment of silent contemplation to observe those two precious reasons behind her refusal to surrender to the forces of despair, destruction, and Doomsday.

Because if I'd given in, the world would have ended,

she reasoned. *And if the world* had *ended, my kids would never have had the chance to grow up. And if they'd never grown up, they'd never have been able to marry and have kids of their own,* my grandchildren. *And if I never got to have grandchildren . . .*

Almira thought of all the things her own mother had done to interfere with how she wanted to raise Daniel and Renee. She remembered how impotent it had made her feel, how angry. She looked deep within herself and found the hard, hot kernel of frustration and resentment that was still there, smoldering and festering, even after all this time. She knew that if she didn't find a way to excise it, it would devour her alive until her dying day, just as she knew that the only weapon mighty enough to destroy the ghost of her past helplessness was complete, supreme, ruthless, raw and incontrovertible *power*.

Oh yes, just wait until *she* was the grandma! Talk about power! It wasn't exactly payback, but it was the next best thing.

It was a very good thing that the angel Siegfried had left when he did. He would have recognized the look in Mrs. Lurie's eyes well enough. Maybe the Powers That Be had overlooked a little something besides that sperm whale when they'd cleared the board of—They thought—all the players.

All but one.

Mrs. Lurie looked like Hel.

With The Sword He Must Be Slain
David Drake

"If anyone slays with the sword, with the sword he must be slain."

Revelations 13:10

The Colonel had never met this tasking officer, but he was a Suit and the Colonel figured all Suits were the same. The fact that this particular Suit was part of Hell's bureaucracy rather than Langley's didn't make a lot of difference.

"Good to see you, Colonel," the Suit said as he studied the folder in front of him. "Please sit down."

He didn't get up from behind his desk, and he didn't offer to shake hands. Probably afraid he'd transfer sweat to the fine wool/silk blend of his garment. This particular Suit fancied English tailoring instead of Italian, but that was pretty standard for the Company boys too. The left half of the Colonel's lips smiled.

"Yes?" said the Suit.

"I was wondering," the Colonel said, "whether Hell is a CIA proprietary operation. Or vice versa."

"I think we'd best use our time to productive ends, Colonel," the Suit said dismissively. "The schedule is rather tight for jokes."

There was a look of disdain in his eyes. The Colonel would have liked to put the muzzle of a pistol in the Suit's mouth and watch those hard black eyes bulge when he pulled the trigger, but he wouldn't do that.

He'd never done that, much as he'd wanted to, every fucking time. The Suits with their clean hands and clean clothes were all the same. . . .

The Suit frowned again at the red-bordered folder in front of him, then transferred his attention to the Colonel. "What's your physical condition?" he said. "This says you were—"

"I'm fit," the Colonel said curtly. His ribs were taped. He'd blocked the obsidian-fanged club, but the blow had driven the flat of his own weapon, a similar club, into his side. Adrenaline had hidden the pain while the Colonel buried the butt of his club in the solar plexus of the squat giant who'd struck him and then broke his neck with the edge of his hand; but the pain was back now, every time he breathed.

"Colonel, if you're not—"

"I said I was fit!" the Colonel said. "I can execute your Goddamned operation better than anybody else you can hand the job to!"

The Suit gave him a cold smile. "Yes, you will have your joke, won't you?" he said. "Very well."

He shifted one, then two sheets from the right side of the folder to the left and said, "You'll be inserted with a twenty-man team to eliminate an Enemy base. We believe it's a medical unit, but there'll doubtless be a security element attached. You should be fine if you execute a quick in-and-out."

The Suit flipped another page. *You'll be fine, you smug sonuvabitch,* the Colonel thought, *because you won't be within a hundred klicks of the sound of gunfire. You'll be drinking in a bar with your Savile Row and Armani colleagues, talking solemnly about the strain of your position.*

The Colonel had gotten the job through an Australian friend, Macgregor. Mac was dead now, killed trying to start the motor of his Zodiac boat during some goatfuck in the Seychelles, the Colonel had heard. Maybe true, maybe not. Rumors hadn't gotten any more accurate than they'd been before things started to come apart.

The Colonel doubted Mac had known any more about the employer than he had himself. Suits were looking for people with special skills for work in the international security field—just like always. The pay was good.

The Colonel wasn't stupid; he wouldn't have survived this long without more raw brainpower than most of the Suits who tasked him. He'd realized a long time ago that the pay was just an excuse. He was doing this work because the only time he felt alive was when he *was* doing the work, and he wasn't ready to die.

When the Colonel figured out who his employer was, he didn't much like it. But neither did the knowledge make any real difference in what the Colonel did or how well he did it.

"Here's the map of the terrain," the Suit said, handing over a folded document. "You can study it as long as you wish, but it can't leave the room, of course."

"Of course," the Colonel said. Suits were always jealous of their secrets, their Sources and Methods. A captured map might tell the Enemy what we knew and how we'd learned it. In this particular case, the Enemy being who He was, that was even funnier than the usual Suit bullshit.

The map was satellite imagery overlaid with contour lines and elevations noted in meters. A hollow triangle marked the objective. The satellites hadn't been up for the past six months, though the Colonel was losing track of time. Still, the mountainous terrain itself wasn't likely to have changed much.

There were no landmarks familiar to the Colonel. He waved a corner of the map to the tasking officer. "Where is this?" he asked.

"The operation doesn't require that you have that information," the Suit said coolly.

The Colonel looked at him and smiled. *Eyes bulging outward. A spray of blood from the nostrils as the bullet acts as a piston in the chamber of the skull.*

He went back to studying the map.

"You'll insert by air," the Suit said. "The vehicle will remain under your operational control and will extract you at the completion of the mission."

"Enemy forces?" the Colonel said, his eyes on the map.

"In the region as a whole, considerable," the Suit said. He shrugged. "Brigade strength, we believe. But the site you're to eliminate should have no more than a platoon present for security. The Enemy won't be able to bring greater forces to bear in the time available—if you do your job properly."

"Yes, all right," the Colonel said. He stood up and handed back the map. The right knee caught him as it always did, the calling card of a paradrop into bamboo when he was nineteen and thought he was indestructible. "I'm ready to meet my unit."

The Suit replaced the map within the folder. "Very well," he said. "One of the service personnel is waiting outside the door. He'll lead you to your men."

The Colonel paused before touching the doorknob and looked back. Maybe it was the "if you do your job properly" that made him angry enough to say, "Does it bother you to be working for the losing side?"

"I beg your pardon?" the Suit said. He looked genuinely puzzled.

"This is the battle of Good against Evil," the Colonel said. "Evil loses, right? And don't try to tell me we're the forces of Good!"

"Certainly not that," the Suit said with a faint smile. "What a concept."

His smile hardened. "But for the rest, Colonel, you're quite wrong. Good doesn't defeat you." The Suit shook his head. "What a concept!" he repeated.

The Colonel stepped into the hallway where the silent

servitor waited. He didn't know how to take what the Suit had just told him, so he didn't think about it.

He had a lot of experience with not thinking about things.

The troops were camped under a metal-roofed shelter at the edge of thorny scrubland. Fiber matting hung from the rafters on the south side as a sun shade. There were low platforms around the edges where the men would lay out their bedrolls at night. Now they used the platforms as seats as they cooked on a pair of small fires burning on the dirt floor in the center.

The man who noticed the servitor guiding the Colonel toward the shelter jumped up and called to the others. Chattering with high-pitched enthusiasm, the troops spilled out to stand in a single rank to greet their new commander.

The air was hot and dry. The outline of the mountains in the eastern distance was as unfamiliar to the Colonel as the topographic map had been.

"Sir!" said the man at the left end of the line of troops. He threw the Colonel a British-style salute, palm outward. "I am Captain Sisir Krishnamurtri of the Telugu Resistance Army. My men and I know you by reputation. We are honored to serve with you!"

The Colonel returned the salute with the edge of his hand out the way he'd learned it too many years ago. Instinctively he sucked in his gut. He was in good shape— "great shape for a man of his age," people said—but he knew the difference between that and nineteen.

The servitor knew the difference too. They never spoke, these hairless, sexless nude figures who performed administrative duties for the fighting forces, but they had minds and personalities. This one smirked when he saw the Colonel pretending to be more than the decayed remnants of what he once had been.

What made it worse was that the troops were so absurdly young themselves. Captain Krishnamurtri was probably twenty-five, but the Colonel doubted any of the others

were out of their teens. Several on the far end of the line
were fourteen at the oldest, boys hopping from one foot
to the other with their eagerness to go out and kill.

Telugus were South Indians, the Colonel thought, though
he'd never heard of a Telugu Resistance Army. They were
small, dark folk, barefoot and wearing dhotis wrapped
around their loins. Krishnamurtri had put on a short-
sleeved khaki shirt as a sign of his rank when the Colonel
arrived. Their red sweatbands were probably a uniform.

"I'm pleased to be working with you too, Captain," the
Colonel said. That was a lie, but it was a very familiar lie;
and God knew he'd commanded worse. In Sierra Leone,
for instance . . . "Send the men back to their meal while
you brief me on your unit."

God knew. The Colonel smiled at his accidental joke.
Black humor was the only kind of humor there was in
the field.

The platform at the east end of the shelter was eight
inches high, twice that of the others. It provided a dais
on which Krishnamurtri and the Colonel sat—the Telugu
squatting, the Colonel with his left leg crossed and the
right straight out in front of him because the knee hadn't
bent properly since the day bamboo splintered its way
through the connective tissue.

"First off," the Colonel said, "how many of your men
speak English?"

A young soldier came over with two small glass cups of
tea on a brass tray. There was a sprig of mint in either
cup. He bowed, set the tray down between the officers,
and scuttled off.

Krishnamurtri picked up a cup and offered it to the
Colonel. "Them?" he said. "None, they only speak Telugu.
They're merely field workers. I am a Brahmin. Without
me they would be nothing. You will tell me what to do,
Colonel, and I will see that they do it."

The Colonel sipped his tea. It was sweet and hot, hotter
even than the steady wind out of the west.

He'd seen it too often to be surprised any more: local officers who thought their men were dirt. That's what they were in truth, often enough, thugs good for nothing but to smoke *khat* or whatever the local drug of choice was and carry off girls to rape for the next week or so until they got tired of them.

But the officers were even worse to any eyes but their own. If the Colonel could speak Telugu or the troops knew English, he wouldn't have kept Krishnamurtri around even to wipe his feet on. That wasn't an option—it usually wasn't—and anyway, the other side was usually just as badly off.

Even now. This was the Colonel's third operation for his present employer, and the quality of the opposition had been well short of divine. He smiled again.

Before the Colonel could ask about the unit's training and experience, a vehicle sailed out of the western sky as slowly as a vulture and landed beside the shelter in a shimmer of static electricity. It was a narrow, flat-bottomed craft more like a toboggan than an aircraft. It was open-sided except for the exiguous cockpit in front where a kneeling servitor drove. The Colonel had never seen anything like it before.

The servitor got out, pointed an index finger at the weapons lying on the rear deck, and walked away without a backward glance. The Telugus chirped with amazement as they gathered around the vehicle.

"An air sled!" Krishnamurtri said. "And look, they're giving us ion guns too, enough for all of us! This is because we serve with you, Colonel. We are honored, greatly honored!"

The Colonel got to his feet with the care his ribs and his many previous injuries required. He kept a straight face as he stepped out of the shelter. He'd never heard of air sleds *or* the ion guns which the delighted Telugus were now waving in the air. He didn't suppose it mattered.

On his first operation for the present employer the Colonel's troops had been mostly Nigerians. They'd been armed with a variety of World War II weapons: Enfield rifles and Tommy guns, with American pineapple grenades and a Danish light machine gun, a Madsen, that took 8-mm ammunition instead of the .303 that the rifles used.

Riddle had been assigned as his XO on that operation. The Colonel had worked with him before, on Bouganville. Riddle knew his business, right enough, but he was a nasty piece of work. He liked his boys as young as possible and screaming, even when they were prostitutes and already, as Riddle put it, stump-broke. The Colonel hadn't been sorry when the bunker Riddle threw a grenade into blew up and took him with it. There must have been a ton of explosives stored inside.

You could call the operation a success: they'd destroyed the Enemy base camp. Only the Colonel himself and a handful of his troops had survived, though.

The second operation was supposed to eliminate an Enemy command post. The Colonel had been assigned to a unit of Amerinds armed with clubs and spears. He'd worked in Latin America often enough in the past, but he didn't speak the language his troops did and they had only a smattering of the Spanish that had to serve as his command language.

They'd done their job, caught the hostile commander in his hammock with one of his wives and hacked them both to bloody fragments. Enemy forces had kept up the pursuit to where the canoes were stashed, however; only the Colonel himself and two paddlers had made it all the way back for pickup.

The Colonel examined the ion gun. It had a short barrel, a long tubular receiver, and a pistol grip with a normal trigger and a three-position safety above it. The weapon had no other controls.

He extended the telescoping buttstock, walked around the end of the shelter, and aimed through the disk-shaped optical sight toward the mountains. Telugus crowded behind him, jabbering in excitement.

The Colonel pulled the trigger. Nothing happened. He

was deliberately ignoring Captain Krishnamurtri's offered suggestions, though it was going to be embarrassing if the Colonel couldn't figure the weapon out himself.

He thumbed the rotary safety to its middle position and squeezed the trigger again. A sunburst carved a crackling path through the air. The beam traveled several kilometers, though it dissipated in a foggy cone well short of the mountains. The gun recoiled hard, like a shotgun with heavy loads.

The sighting disk went black at the instant of discharge, but purple ghost images danced on the retina of the Colonel's left eye. He'd have to remember to close it in the future, fighting a lifetime's conditioning to shoot with both eyes open in order to be aware of his surroundings as well as his sight picture.

He turned the safety straight back, to its third position. He sighted, closed his left eye, and squeezed. His feet were braced and the butt was firmly against his shoulder. Even so the discharge rocked him backward.

The flash lit the entire vicinity. The Colonel had aimed well above the nearby vegetation, but it still exploded into flame. The weapon ejected a silvery tube from a port in the underside.

The Colonel lowered the weapon carefully; its muzzle was white hot. "All right," he said to Krishnamurtri as the other troops capered behind him, thrilled by the display. "Do we have a driver for the air sled?"

The Colonel checked moonrise against his watch, then velcroed the field cover over its face. The fabric both protected the crystal and concealed the luminous dial. This was a bright night, but habit and the awareness of how often little things were the difference between life and death kept the Colonel to his routine.

He settled onto the right front of the vehicle beside Rao, the pilot. There were no seats. The Colonel's stiff right leg stuck out the side at an angle.

"All right," the Colonel said. "Take us up." Krishnamurtri, squatting immediately behind Rao, relayed the order as a short bark.

Rao had circled the base camp alone to prove he could fly the air sled. As they staggered into the air with a full load of troops and equipment, though, the Colonel knew they were in trouble.

Because they weren't rising as fast as Rao thought they should, the Telugu shouted at the vehicle and jerked back on the simple joystick control. The bow came up—too sharply. The sled apparently couldn't stall, but it *could* slide backward if the angle of attack was too sharp. It started to do that.

Krishnamurtri pounded Rao on the top of the head. The troops in back babbled with surprise and fear.

The Colonel put his big right hand over the pilot's and rolled the joystick forward. The stick slid in on its axis also. That in-and-out motion controlled the sled's speed, as the Colonel realized when they slowed. They'd almost mushed out of the air before he hauled up on Rao's hand and the stick.

The sled's nose dipped. They accelerated in a rush toward the ground. The Colonel eased the stick back carefully, fighting Rao's urge to haul them up hard. The vehicle lifted smoothly instead of crashing through the scrub, shedding pieces of itself and the men aboard.

They leveled out and started to climb gently. The Colonel took his hand away from the joystick. He patted Rao on the shoulder.

He turned toward Krishnamurtri. "Tell him that easy does it," he said. "With a load like this it's important not to overcorrect."

Krishnamurtri shouted another string of Telugu abuse at Rao. The Colonel couldn't do anything about that, but when Krishnamurtri raised his hand to hit the pilot again he caught the captain's wrist.

"Stupid peasant!" Krishnamurtri muttered as he subsided.

The Colonel rode with his right leg sticking out in the airstream. His ion gun pointed at the scrubland, ready to fire individual bolts. Because of where he sat in the vehicle, he held the grip with his left hand. The right was his master hand, but he'd learned long ago to use either as circumstances dictated.

The Colonel had flown helicopters in the past. He'd never had formal training, just a quick-and-dirty grounding in the basics. There'd been time to spare and the pilot wanted somebody who could grab the stick if he was shot in a place that was incapacitating but not fatal. (The pilot didn't care *what* happened to the bird if he'd already bought the farm.)

That particular operation had been a dream—the team extracted before anybody on the ground knew they'd had company. Three months later, though, a different pilot took a .51-cal round through the throat and sprayed his blood all over what was left of the cockpit while the Colonel flew them back to the base. They'd pancaked in from twenty feet up, but that wasn't the Colonel's fault: another round had opened the tank. The turbine died when the last of the jet fuel leaked out in the airstream.

The Colonel figured he could fly the air sled if he had to—fly it better than Rao, at any rate—but he couldn't both fly the bird and conn them in at low level the way this insertion had to be made. Besides, the controls were on the left side of the cockpit; they'd have to land for him and Rao to change places, which meant circling back to the base to find a cleared area. The number of ways that could go wrong made the risk at least as significant as letting Rao continue as pilot.

The Telugu seemed to have gotten things under control after the rocky start. The sled's speed built up until they were belting along at close on ninety knots by the Colonel's estimate. They could have done with a proper windscreen, though the reverse curve of the sled's dash panel did a remarkably good job of directing the airflow over the pair in the immediate front of the vehicle. Buffeting was much worse for the common soldiers farther back.

The Colonel gave his usual half-mouthed smile. Rank hath its privileges. In this case, the privilege of taking the first round himself if they happened to overfly an Enemy outpost. God knew Enemy troops should've been patrolling well out from their bases in the mountains.

But even if the local commander knew what he was doing, his subordinates might still have ignored his orders or simply done a piss-poor job of executing them. You couldn't assume that the Enemy was ten feet tall, any more than you could count on the Enemy not knowing his ass from a hole in the ground.

The air sled continued slowly climbing. He'd told Rao— told Krishnamurtri, at any rate—that they needed to stay within ten feet of the treetops; they were up to thirty by now and going higher. Rather than go through the Brahmin, the Colonel tapped on the top of the dashboard to get Rao's attention and mimed a gliding descent with his right hand.

Krishnamurtri immediately shouted at the pilot and slapped the back of his head. Rao looked around in wide-eyed amazement. The air sled yawed; the troops in the back cried out with fear. They had a right to be afraid: the sled didn't even have a grab rail. The Colonel was more than a little surprised that they hadn't lost somebody during the wobbling takeoff.

He put his hand over Rao's again, steadying the Telugu instead of trying to take control, and said to Krishnamurtri in a clipped, very clear voice, "I'll handle this if you please, Captain. And I suggest that you not hit our pilot again while we're in the air. A Claymore mine isn't in the same league as an air crash for shredding human bodies. As I've seen many times."

God knew he had.

The air sled stabilized. They flew on without further incident until the ground beneath changed abruptly from rolling scrubland to fractured terrain where rocks stood up in sheer-sided walls from the softer earth beneath. Rao pulled back on the joystick. He was adjusting his altitude instinctively by the mountains on the horizon rather than the broken hills immediately below the air sled.

The Colonel tapped the dashboard and again mimed a descent. Rao glanced at him sidelong and adjusted the stick only minusculely. The sled continued to rise, though at a flatter angle.

"Tell him to follow the gully to our left!" the Colonel said to Krishnamurtri. The sled's drive mechanism made no sound other than a low-frequency hum and an occasional pop of static electricity, but wind rush meant words had to be shouted to be heard. "We need to be down below the level of the gully's walls!"

The Brahmin nodded several times as though he understood, but he didn't say anything to Rao. "Well, tell him!" the Colonel said, wishing he spoke Telugu.

But why stop with a little wish like that? He could wish that he had a team of Special Forces instead of Third World farm boys qualified as soldiers by the fact that they wouldn't fall over if you leaned a rifle against them. He could even wish that he'd lived his previous life in a fashion that didn't have him now commanding troops on the side of Hell in Armageddon.

The Colonel smiled. "Tell him," he repeated. His voice was no longer harsh, but Krishnamurtri looked even more frightened than before. Maybe it was the smile.

Krishnamurtri spoke to the pilot without his usual hectoring violence. Rao looked at the Colonel with a desperate expression. The Colonel put his hand over Rao's and gently forced the joystick forward.

"Tell him he can slow down if he has to," the Colonel said to Krishnamurtri. "But not too much. Remember, if we don't do this fast, they're going to do us."

He smiled. "Just as sure as Hell."

❖   ❖   ❖

It was mostly bad luck.

The Colonel had a phenomenal talent for correlating maps with real terrain at ground level; practice had honed an innate skill. Nevertheless he had to concentrate to guide them along the route he'd planned after ten minutes with an aerial photograph, and he wasn't paying much attention to the Telugus. After the fact, he wished that he'd remembered to warn Rao that the gorge they were following took a hard jog to the left, but there was only so much you could do.

Rao tried to go over the sudden barrier instead of banking with it. That might have been all right if the sled hadn't been so heavily loaded; as it was, they were going to clear the rock but not the thorny trees growing on the creviced top.

The Colonel acted in a combination of reflex and instinct, two of the supports that had kept him alive longer than even he could credit when he looked back on his life. He thumbed the ion gun's safety to position three, rock and roll, and triggered the weapon.

The ion gun's discharge dazzled the night. Trees vanished and the limestone slope beyond glowed white under the lash of the beam. The air sled sailed through a momentary Hell of furnace-hot air. The troops were screaming.

Ash flew into the Colonel's eyes when he opened them after shooting. He blinked furiously to clear them so he could see again.

Rao fought the sled under control, then clapped the Colonel on the shoulder with a cry of delight. The Telugu was thrilled to still be alive.

"Watch your—" the Colonel said, unable to see clearly himself but aware that this was no time for the pilot to be thinking about dangers already past.

Rao curved back over the lip of the gorge they'd been following. The air sled dropped precipitately as it left the updraft from rock heated by the ion blast. The back end ticked the ground hard enough to throw the rearmost

Telugus overboard. Without their weight, the nose tilted sharply down.

Rao screamed; the Colonel hauled his hand fiercely back on the joystick. Neither man's action made any useful difference. The sled scraped along the rocky soil, disintegrating as it threw its passengers off to either side.

The Colonel bailed out at the first hop, before the sled started to tumble. He curled into a ball and hit rolling; there wasn't a good way to smack the ground at forty knots, but he'd done it before and survived.

He clamped the ion gun to his belly. The barrel was searingly hot from firing, but the Colonel's instinct to cling to his weapon was stronger than any pain.

He skidded to a halt well down the slope and paused a moment before he got to his feet. He'd once seen a man leap from a C-47 as it bellied in on a grass strip. The fellow would probably have been all right if he hadn't tried to stand up before he'd come to a complete stop. Momentum flipped him in an unexpected cartwheel; he broke his neck when he came down again.

The Colonel had seen people die in some of the *damnedest* ways. God knew he had.

He checked himself over. He didn't seem to have broken any bones. His left elbow had taken a knock, but it bent and straightened all right. His ribs felt like there was a white-hot sword in his side every time he took a breath, but there was no blood in the phlegm when he cleared dust and soot from his lungs in a wracking cough. Pain had never kept the Colonel from moving when his life depended on it. His life certainly depended on moving now.

There'd been a box of six reloads along with the ion guns; five remained after the Colonel tested the weapon. He thrust one of the silvery tubes into the receiver now and turned the safety back to single shot. The Colonel had taken all the reloads himself since he hadn't been with his troops long enough to know which men might be trusted with extra ammo.

Probably none of them. Christ, what a mess. Ten klicks
into hostile territory with twenty farmers, no commo,
and no transport but their own feet. The Telugus—
Krishnamurtri included—didn't even have boots.

The Brahmin sat weeping. He seemed healthy enough
except for scrapes.

Rao lay on his back, whimpering as he tried unsuccessfully
to breathe. The pilot had separated from the air sled only
moments after the Colonel did, but a blow from the joystick
had crushed his ribs. Rao's chest quivered, but without
the rib cage for an anchor his diaphragm couldn't suck
air into his flailing lungs.

The Colonel shook Krishnamurtri. When that didn't
rouse him, the Colonel slapped him hard. "Get the men
together," he ordered. "Tell them we're hiking back to
base. Anybody who can't march gets to make his own peace
with the Enemy, but I haven't seen much sign of heavenly
mercy in the past."

Krishnamurtri looked at the Colonel in sick amazement.
The Brahmin's teeth had cut his upper lip in two places,
either during the crash or when the Colonel slapped him.

"Look," the Colonel said in a soft voice. He slid out
the double-edged knife he wore in a sheath sewn to his
right boot. "If you can't talk to these people, you're no
good to me at all."

Krishnamurtri crawled backward in a sitting position,
his eyes on the Colonel. He shouted orders in high-pitched
Telugu.

The Colonel half walked, half slid, the twenty feet down
to Rao. The Telugu watched in sick desperation. His lips
moved, but he had no breath to form words. He couldn't
have spoken a language the Colonel could understand
anyway.

The Colonel had heard the words often enough, in at
least a score of languages. God knew he had.

The Colonel thrust the bootknife behind Rao's left
mastoid and drew it expertly around to the right, severing

the Telugu's throat to the spine. He stepped back, clear of the spurting blood, and tugged the pilot's dhoti off to wipe his blade while the body was still thrashing.

It wasn't the kind of help Rao had wanted, but it's all the help there could be: a quick death in place of the slower one of suffocation.

Krishnamurtri was on his feet, calling orders with increasing confidence. Men were moving among the trees and brush. At the bottom of the gorge, vegetation burned with an occasional blue electrical splutter to mark where the air sled had come to rest.

That fire and the one the Colonel had lit with his ion gun would mark his unit for the Enemy, too. They didn't have a prayer of getting out of this goatfuck. Not a prayer.

The Colonel smiled at his joke. He sheathed his knife as he waited for his surviving men to gather.

There were thirteen of them left, twelve Telugus and the Colonel himself. Four of the troops hadn't showed up after the crash; three more had been too badly injured to march. And there was Rao, of course.

Only eight Telugus were armed. Ion guns had gone skidding off into the night when the sled tumbled. Unlike the men, the weapons hadn't walked back up the slope looking battered and worried. The Colonel didn't have time to waste searching for guns in the moonlight.

He'd left the wounded men as they were. He couldn't do anything to help them, and they couldn't tell the Enemy anything that wasn't obvious: the survivors were hiking home.

The Colonel would have killed his wounded if he'd had a reason to do so, but he'd never been one of those who liked killing for its own sake. That kind wasn't good for much. Like the looters and rapists, they were so absorbed in their desires that they didn't pay attention to the real business—till they took a charge of buckshot in the back, or a pitchfork up the bum, or a roofing tile splashed their brains across the pavement.

The Colonel had seen all those things and more. God knew he had.

He didn't hear any night birds, but frogs of at least a dozen varieties clunked and chirped and trilled from the bottom of the gorge. There must be open water, at least in pools.

The Colonel kept his unit just below the crest. It would have been easier to walk either on the ridge or down the center of the gorge. The first would have left them exposed to observers and very possibly silhouetted to a sniper; the latter was, like a trail in hostile jungle, an obvious killing ground.

Krishnamurtri objected to having to march on a surface so steep that frequently a man slid until he grabbed a spiky treebranch. The common soldiers didn't seem to mind, or at any rate they didn't bother to complain that life wasn't fair. Maybe they thought it was.

The Colonel smiled. Maybe they were right. Maybe everybody got exactly what he deserved.

Through Krishnamurtri he'd told the troops to keep two meters' interval. That plan had broken down immediately, as the Colonel knew it would. The stronger men bunched at the front of the line while the weaker half dozen straggled farther and farther behind. The Colonel had called a halt after the first hour—measured by the moon, not his watch—to regroup, and it was about time to call another.

The Colonel marched at the rear. The gorge itself provided the direction, so he was best located where he could keep stragglers from falling out of the column altogether. Krishnamurtri was immediately ahead of him.

"We'll halt in three minutes," the Colonel said. Krishnamurtri had lost his weapon in the crash. "Pass it on."

The Colonel's boot slipped; he dabbed a hand down and caught himself, but a thorn hidden in the gritty soil jabbed fire up his middle finger. The pain in his ribs had subsided to a background awareness, dull because of its familiarity.

A metallic whistle trilled behind them; how far behind the Colonel wasn't sure, but it couldn't be more than a kilometer even with the breeze carrying the sound. Not far enough.

"Cancel that order," the Colonel said, checking his weapon again by reflex. "We'll keep going till we get there."

Another whistle—this one was pitched a half-tone higher than the other—called. It was from the righthand distance, either on the opposite ridge or from somewhere within the gorge itself.

The Telugu just ahead of Krishnamurtri had been using his ion gun as a crutch; he'd torn his right thigh badly during the crash, but he was managing to keep up with the column reasonably well. Now he turned, balancing on his left leg, and aimed his weapon across the valley.

"Stop—" the Colonel said, lunging forward. He fell over Krishnamurtri who was trying to dodge back.

The soldier triggered six wild shots into the night. The first two bolts hit the tops of trees on the other slope. Recoil lifted the muzzle with each shot so that the last four drew quivering tracks toward the stratosphere.

The Telugu shot with both eyes closed. He'd probably never been told to shoot any other way.

The Colonel knocked him silly with a sidewise swipe of his ion gun. The Telugu's own weapon flew out of his hand and bounced down the slope. Plant matter as dry as the air itself caught fire at the touch of the glowing muzzle.

The ionization tracks of the six bolts trembled in the air, dissipating slowly. Each was an arrow of light pointing back toward the shooter.

"Let's go!" the Colonel said as he broke into a shambling run. Their only chance was to stay ahead of the pursuit, and God knew that was no chance at all.

As usual, the Colonel was more agile in a crisis than he could ever be with greater leisure to choose his footing. Krishnamurtri was wailing somewhere behind him, but the common soldiers stayed ahead with the ease of youth. The Colonel could see a few of his troops bounding like klipspringers across a stretch of slope scoured by a rockslide.

Despite the need for haste, the Colonel went downslope to stay covered by the trees. Nobody shot at the exposed Telugus. Another whistle called, this one seemingly from over the ridge to their left.

They didn't have a prayer. Not a prayer.

The Colonel had the map in his mind. A second crack in the rock, a crevice only ten or twenty feet wide, joined the gorge a few hundred meters ahead. Just beyond that junction was the tumbled edge of the hills, then the scrubland where an evader could choose his own direction without being channeled by the terrain. If they could make it out of the hills alive—

If the Colonel could make it out of the hills alive. He'd lost control of his unit, and anyway it had come to "Save what you can!"

It always came to that. The Colonel remembered an overloaded helicopter struggling off the roof of the American Embassy in Saigon and many similar scenes. Scenes he'd survived.

But of course, there'd come the scene he didn't survive, as sure as the sun would rise.

The Colonel smiled. Even surer than that, maybe, in these days.

An automatic weapon fired from dead ahead. It wasn't an ion gun. The distant, spiteful, muzzle blasts syncopated the projectiles' bursting charge, *Whack/crack/Whack/crack/Whack/crack*.

Ion guns replied, two or maybe three of them. Bolts traced across the sky, as ineptly aimed as those of the Telugu the Colonel had left unconscious after the second whistle blew.

The Enemy weapon fell silent after firing three rounds. The shellbursts had flickered blue-white through the vegetation, more like a short circuit arcing than any explosive the Colonel had seen before.

He understood the trap as surely as if he were within the mind of the Enemy commander.

"Go straight ahead!" the Colonel shouted. The Telugus couldn't hear him, couldn't understand the words if they did hear, and wouldn't obey if they did understand. "Shoot your way through! Don't turn!"

He reached the crevice. It led off to the left, trailing back into the hills before it ended in a spring and a pair of sheer cliffs. Rock dust still swirled where the Enemy gunner had scarred the main slope, driving the Telugus like a sheep dog snapping at the ears of his flock.

The gunner was somewhere out in the narrow wedge of rolling scrub that the Colonel could see beyond the mouth of the gorge. He might be as much as a kilometer distant. He wasn't there to stop the Telugus but merely to turn them.

The Colonel switched his safety to position three. He triggered the ion gun toward the empty landscape ahead.

The weapon spun out of his hand with a roar. Firing a third full-charge blast down the bore had eaten through the side of the barrel. Flame washed the right side of the gorge as well as the intended target.

The Colonel flung the useless gun away. He drew his bootknife and plunged into the blaze his plasma had ignited. His left hand held the tail of his fatigue shirt over his mouth and nose.

He heard the incoming artillery when he'd gotten about a hundred meters into the hell of burning shrubs. The ground was so hot it blistered him through his boots and socks.

He ran on, navigating by instinct and his memory of what the terrain ahead had looked like in the moment before he fired. The night lit blue behind him and the earth shuddered. The Enemy had blown the crevice shut, killing everyone who had tried to shelter within its narrow walls. Rocks continued to fall for more than a minute after the explosion.

The Colonel ran and then walked and finally crawled. He was crawling when a pair of servitors pried the bootknife from his hand and loaded him onto an air sled like the one that had brought him into the hills.

One of the voiceless creatures held the Colonel while the other flew. The Colonel's arms and legs continued to move because instinct, all that remained, told them to.

The Suit debriefing the Colonel was the one who'd tasked him for the mission. He made another notation in the folder on his desk and said in a detached voice, "Well, these things happen. It doesn't appear that the blame lies with you."

He put down his pen and went on, "So. How would you rate your present physical condition, Colonel?"

All Suits were the same anyway. They stamped them out with cookie cutters in Ivy League colleges and sent them on to CIA and Hell.

The Colonel smiled.

"I'm fit," he said. Pus leaked through his mittens of bandage. The damage wasn't serious: he'd just scraped the thick skin of his palms down to the flesh while crawling. His knees were in similar shape, but the bandages there didn't show beneath the loose trousers of his jungle fatigues.

His hands hurt remarkably, an enveloping throb every time his heart beat. For the first twenty-four hours after regaining consciousness the Colonel had eaten Percodans like candy,

He hadn't taken any drugs in the past six hours, though. Pain was something you got used to.

The Suit sniffed. "Well, I'm not going to argue with you," he said. "We're getting rather shorthanded, as you can imagine."

He glanced down at the folder, then closed it decisively. He looked at the Colonel with an expression as hard and detached as that of a falcon in a winter sky. "Very well," the Suit said. "Return to your quarters. I can't say precisely when you'll be called for the next mission, but I'm afraid that your stand-down this time will be relatively brief. We're approaching endgame."

"Yes, all right," the Colonel said. He stood with the care a lifetime of injuries made second nature to him.

Endgame. It was funny to think about it all being over, after a lifetime. . . .

The Colonel put his bandaged fingers on top of the desk and leaned forward slightly. The Suit looked up with the false smile that Suits always got when they thought their attack dogs might be about to slip their leashes. The Colonel had seen that look often enough before.

The Colonel smiled back. "Tell me," he said. "Tell me the truth. Do we really defeat Good?"

The Suit looked puzzled. "Excuse me?" he said. "I don't understand your question."

The Colonel blinked. He straightened, taking his hands away from the desk. He didn't know what response he'd expected, but honest confusion on the Suit's part certainly wasn't it.

"You said the Bible was wrong," the Colonel said. "You said that the armies of Good don't defeat us."

He felt the air-conditioned room pulse red with a sudden rage that wasn't directed at this Suit or even every Suit: the Colonel hated the universe and he hated himself.

The door behind him opened. Servitors slipped in quickly, ready to wrestle the Colonel down and sedate him if necessary.

"Didn't you say that?" the Colonel shouted.

"The Bible doesn't say the armies of Good will defeat *you,*" the Suit said, giving the pronoun a slight emphasis. His expression had returned to its usual faint sneer. "What a concept!"

The Colonel began to shiver. He supposed it was the air conditioning.

"Good doesn't have armies, Colonel," the Suit said, tenting his fingers over the closed folder. "Everyone who's fighting is on our side. You of all people should understand that."

The Colonel turned around. The servitors stood to either side of the doorway. There were four of them.

"I suggest you get as much sleep as you can," the Suit behind him said in a professional replica of concern. "There won't be much time, you know."

"Yes, all right," the Colonel said. He walked out of the room, ignoring the smirks of the servitors.

He had a lot of experience with not thinking about things.

Twelve Gates To The City
Margaret Ball

Alan

It wasn't exactly clear whether Achana Day was an official
holiday or not. After the Council of Sheikhs closed down
the newspaper for disseminating anti-Coastal propaganda,
and the staff of one radio station disappeared with a last
brief on-air apology for irresponsible rumor-mongering,
the people who kept the island's other radio station going
weren't doing much in the way of news, rumors or anything
else. The station now featured traditional songs and drum
dances, joyful announcements that Achana Day was
coming, and lengthy Koran readings. The Koran readings
meant nothing at all to the extensive Asian community
of Mombasa or to the few up-country Kenyans who had
remained after Achana was announced, and somewhat
less than that to Alan, who had only recently picked up
enough Arabic to figure out that the muaddhin who awoke
him every morning at dawn with a raucous call to prayer
was announcing, among other things, "Prayer is better
than sleep! Prayer is better than sleep!"

For that matter, he considered while wheeling his bike
towards the office, the Koran readings couldn't mean a
great deal to the Swahili community, because very few
of them actually spoke Arabic. However, all his Swahili
friends and acquaintances considered themselves good

Moslems and had spent hours in religious school as children and had learned to recite long passages of the Koran from memory as part of their graduation rites. So he supposed the sound of it did something for them, just as bits of the magnificent language in the King James Bible pleased his ear long after he'd quit going to church or taking any of that stuff seriously.

Alan was wheeling his bike because it was hard enough to ride through the shoulderwide alleys of Old Town on a normal day, and impossible today when the alleys were thronged with men in Western shirts and women in head-to-toe black veils, all milling around and snacking on coconut candy and jellabies and roasted corn and hoping for something interesting to happen to mark Achana Day. And he was heading towards the agency office because he was desperately curious about the effects of Achana on Garrett Mpotha's position.

The International Rural Health Relief Agency, known as "Err" to the people who worked there because of the impossibility of pronouncing its acronym, comprised a loosely organized and poorly defined coalition of small offices whose funds came mostly from France and America via the UN and whose missions were intentionally left undefined, "so that experts in local conditions may be free to choose the endeavors which will most benefit the people of the surrounding area," it said in the charter which Garrett was fond of quoting at some length. Alan had some ideas about what the Mombasa office of the IRHRA could do, modest ideas involving water quality outside the city and projects the villagers could maintain themselves, but as a Peace Corps volunteer assigned to help at IRHRA he had less than no power. Garrett Mpotha, a political appointee from up-country who couldn't even speak the complex inflected Swahili of the coast, and was proud of it, controlled the IRHRA budget with an iron hand and seldom let his two Peace Corps volunteers do more than fill out the endless paperwork involved with his projects.

Although Garrett had somehow survived the political turmoil of the months preceding the official announcement of the Coast's separation from Kenya, Alan hoped that Achana Day would mark a change in all that. Whatever you might say about the Council of Sheikhs—and whatever it was, he reflected sourly, you'd better not say it out loud—they were big on local control. That was the whole point of Achana, wasn't it? So now that Achana Day was officially here, surely they wouldn't leave a man from up-country who openly despised Swahili culture in charge of a relief agency? Garrett's power came from his relatives in the Nairobi government; now that the Sheikhs were running things, at least they'd want to have somebody from the Coast in charge.

Alan wriggled his bike wheel to squeeze between a lighted brazier with roasting ears of green corn and the legless beggar who patrolled this section of Old Town with a polished wooden bowl. A woman leaning from one of the carved stone balconies overhead called out in a high girlish voice. Alan glanced up at the embroidered scarves she was hanging over the balcony. His wheel clipped the beggar's bowl and he started to apologize, but something whacked him on the back of the head and he staggered, almost dropping the bike.

"Get out, *mzungu*!" yelled a gleeful voice behind him. "Mau Mau ran your grandfathers out of up-country and now the Sheikhs are going to get rid of your interference here!"

"Polepole, Hamid," the beggar called up, slurring the endings of his words Mombasa-style. "Mzungu huu 'sema k'Swahil' kushind' wewe!" *Cool it, Hamid. This particular* mzungu *speaks better Swahili than you,* Alan automatically translated, and wished it were true. He'd never gotten nearly as good as that researcher up-country, the girl from Virginia who lived on Linganya and spoke and thought and joked and made rhyming puns and probably even dreamed in Swahili.

He bowed over his bike to the beggar and made a reasonably complex apology for having knocked into his bowl; complex enough, anyway, that Hamid sucked on his teeth and quit hassling him. Alan bought ears of roasted corn for everybody involved and all the bystanders and eventually went on his way accompanied by cheers and good wishes, and feeling a glow of minor accomplishment. Crowds celebrating a big political change could turn nasty, and there'd been an undercurrent of worry in the Old Town that bothered him. Even among the Twelve Tribes of Mombasa, not everybody was sure that Achana was a good thing. Although nearly everybody was bright enough not to say so out loud.

Too bad Kaci hadn't been with him, Alan thought, picturing the ethereal face of his fellow Peace Corps worker at IRHRA. Then, instead of merely extricating himself from a momentarily tricky situation, he could have rescued her and demonstrated his growing command of KiMvita, the Mombasa Swahili that was so hard for up-country people and other foreigners. Surely she'd have been impressed by that. Oh, well, at least he could tell her all about it when he got to the office.

When he reached the IRHRA office, though, he didn't have much chance to tell Kaci anything. Garrett was pacing the room, lecturing them all on his plans to produce a series of educational films to teach the ignorant people of the coastal islands how to manage their resources. Halima, the Swahili girl who worked as their secretary, was looking up at him as if he had announced the Second Coming and nodding at every third word. Kaci was also watching Garrett, but Alan told himself she was just being politically wise.

"They pretty much know what their resources are," Alan said mildly when Garrett paused for breath. "Fish, coconuts, mangos, yams. Cloves, on Pemba. And ripping off the Persian dhow captains when they stop over during the season. You really think they need a movie on how to do that?" He thought it over while Garrett scowled at him. "On second thought, maybe you could give them some pointers on the last bit. Anybody from up-country who's managed to keep his position after Achana must know a lot about manipulation."

Alan was fishing for some idea of just how shaky Garrett felt, but instead he drew another lecture, this one about Garrett's wisdom in befriending the foreign aid representatives who funded IRHRA. It occurred to Alan, belatedly, that he and Kaci had usually "just happened" to be running errands or visiting villages along the coastal strip when foreign visitors dropped by to see what the Mombasa IRHRA office was doing. He'd assumed Garrett wanted to be the only one to get in on the free meals or whatever other goodies usually came with foreign visitors, but apparently it was more than that. He had so impressed Monsieur Brille and the American team based in Nairobi that the Council of Sheikhs was convinced IRHRA's money all came through Garrett's cleverness. The rest of the speech was rather vague, but Alan was able to fill in the blanks for himself. The agency budget was one piece of paperwork he and Kaci were never asked to work on; Garrett preferred to stay late at the office and make Halima stay to type up those figures. Again, Alan's assumptions had been naïve. He had figured Garrett was slipping some of the IRHRA funds into his own pocket, and that was just *desturi*—custom—and nothing you could change. Whoever was in charge of the budget would always find a way to augment his salary, and wouldn't even feel guilty about it: *desturi*. Considering Congressional fact-finding expeditions to the Bahamas and state legislature meetings on the King Ranch hunting preserve, Alan didn't exactly feel entitled to take a righteous attitude about this particular aspect of *desturi*. But it hadn't occurred to him that some of the funds had been going to the Council of Sheikhs, ever since Garrett figured out which way the political winds were blowing. Now, as Garrett held forth on his "good friend" Sheikh Ahmed Musali and his "even better friend" Sharif Hamid, Alan worked it out. There was only one reason why two conservative Islamic sheikhs would be good friends with a tribal political appointee from the hated Nairobi government. And apparently the friendship was good enough to keep Garrett in power here—for the time being.

Which would probably outlast his own time. Alan had spent eighteen months of his two years here in Mombasa, learning Swahili and making friends in the Old Town and accomplishing essentially nothing to improve living conditions in the villages. He doubted the last six months would be any better; not with Garrett still in charge and, probably, even more of their funds being funneled to the Sheikhs. Kaci, who'd only come to the office last Long Rains, would have somewhat longer before her tour of duty was over, but what difference would that make? She was far too sweet and gentle to stand up to Garrett or whoever replaced him, especially without Alan there to inject a little backbone into her.

"Now," Garrett announced, "we will all take the rest of the day off to watch the great parade and to cheer for Achana. We are celebrating a new day for the Swahili Coast, the beginning of a new world!" He looked severely at Alan. "That is much more important than niggling about clay jars and little wells."

"I never said it wasn't," Alan said mildly. It was obviously not a good time to pursue his pet project with Garrett. Besides, he was as curious as anybody else to see what kind of celebration the Sheikhs were going to throw for their official day of separation from Nairobi.

Halima, who had been studying some papers on her desk, looked back up. "But, Garrett, we have not decided about the surplus—"

"Later," Garret cut her off harshly.

Alan felt his ears twitching. "Surplus? In the budget? We haven't spent the year's funds?" Perhaps he could get those clay pots for Tunza after all.

"There is very little remaining," Garrett said quickly. "But it is true, if it is not spent the Frenchman may cut our appropriation for next year. They are so . . . finichal? Finichy? about these things."

"Finicky," Alan suggested. "Look, I could go down to Mwembe Tayari right now and order as many of the big water pots as we have funds for . . ."

"It would be impossible to arrange transport during the confusion of Achana," Garrett cut him off. "Very likely the pots would be broken before you could find a truck to take them north. I could not possibly agree to such irresponsible use of agency funds. Besides, you have not yet submitted the revised project plan which I requested, detailing the use to which these pots are to be put."

"To store boiled water," Alan said between his teeth. "Do you have any idea how many people in villages like Tunza get sick from drinking unboiled water? Kids especially. *Babies*. The people know what to do. They just can't afford storage containers big enough to hold a day's supply of drinking water."

Garrett waved his hand. "What are empty petrol cans for?"

"For turning in to get the recycling money. Besides, have you ever tasted water that was stored in an old petrol tin? If every house had a big clay pot that would hold the purified water and that would keep it cool by evaporation, they'd use it."

"Small minds, small solutions," Garrett said, not unkindly. "You Americans want to keep us using quaint Third World systems, do you not? When the water filtration plant is expanded and the pipes are sent up the coast, this problem will be a thing of the past. In the meantime, I cannot countenance using agency funds to provide these lazy villagers with common household goods. No, I have a much better idea." He beamed. "We will have a Christmas party. We will invite everybody!"

"There are two hundred thousand people in Mombasa," Alan pointed out.

"Everybody who *matters*."

"A Christmas party!" Kaci turned to Garrett. "Oh, that would be so lovely! We could have a tree, look, in this corner. And candles. And artificial snow, wouldn't that be nice, Alan? It would be just like being home for a day."

She danced around the room, slender hands flying, soft pale hair floating around her face. Oh, well, Alan thought. He hadn't really expected to get Garrett's approval for a boring project like buying clay water pots for Tunza. As long as Kaci was putting all this energy into distracting him from a fight with the boss, the least he could do was go along.

"I could string lights around the ceiling," he offered, "if we can scrounge a ladder from somewhere."

"Where would we get Christmas lights?"

"Shihabuddim Zaidi's store. He sells them to the Hindus for Diwali."

"Oh, Alan, that's wonderful! You know everything about Mombasa! I don't know what we'd do without you," Kaci exclaimed. "Between you and Garrett, I know we'll make this party a success." She glanced doubtfully at Halima. "Er—you're not—it won't offend you, Halima? A Christian party?"

"Muslims also are People of the Book," Halima said quietly, "and we honor your Bibi Miriamu and the prophet Yeshua."

"Oh, good. How do you say Christmas in Swahili, anyway?"

That stumped Halima.

"Ki-merri Ki-risimasi," Alan suggested, and Garrett sputtered.

"It is a joke, Kaci," Halima said quickly. "You see, Swahili does not use initial consonant clusters like *k-r*, so we would pronounce your word 'Christmas' as 'Kirisimasi.' But since the word now starts with *k-i*, it must belong to the Ki-class of nouns, and the adjective must agree with it. You see?"

Alan noticed his mouth dangling open and closed it with a snap. In eighteen months he had never heard Halima say anything more sophisticated than, "What code do I use on the forms 42-A?" He'd been assuming that she was just some local girl with enough secretarial training to use the office's battered 1949 Remington upright typewriter. He had also been assuming that Garrett had hired her because she was sleeping with him and the job gave her the necessary excuse to get out of her family's walled compound in the Old Town. Apparently he needed to revise some of these assumptions.

Halima noticed Alan's bemused stare and cast her eyes down. She never met his gaze directly; the traditional girls who went veiled usually didn't, and although Halima hung her black *bui-bui* on a hook behind the door during the day, she never left in the evening without swathing herself in its head-to-foot black folds. "I studied linguistics for one semester at the University of Virginia," she murmured.

"No kidding? There's this linguistics researcher from Virginia working up in Linganya. Melissa something or other. You ever meet her?"

"She was my instructor," Halima said. "I think she became interested in Linganya because of some things I told her about the dialect."

"Are you from Linganya? I thought you were Mvita."

"My father is of the Kilifi of Mvita," Halima said, identifying her father's group among the Twelve Tribes of Mvita and Kilindini who made up the original Swahili population of Mombasa, "but my mother was of the Nabahani of Linganya, and also our cousin Baraka bin Hamid lives here in Mombasa. And *he* is the son of Sheikh Hamid of Linganya."

Kaci drooped over Halima's desk. "So you don't have Christmas here? You don't even have a *word* for it?"

Halima thought. "It is not actually a topic that tends to come up when one is speaking Swahili, Kaci. And if it did, I suppose I would use the KiIngereza—the English word. But if you really wanted to keep it in Swahili, I suppose you could say, 'Siku kuu ya kualiza ya bwana Yesu Kiristi furaha.' "

"Have a happy big day of the birth of Mr. Jesus Christ," Garrett translated with a grin. "And we will! And now," he spread his arms wide as if offering them all a priceless gift, "we will close the office and go out to see the parade. This is no way to celebrate Achana Day, sitting in here over our dusty paperwork!"

"It's too hot to stand out in the sun," Kaci complained. "I think I'll just go home." She touched the quartz crystal pendant that dangled from a silver chain around her neck. "But I'll be celebrating with you in spirit, Garrett," she added quickly. "I'll meditate and send good vibrations to everybody in the parade."

Halima's face fell. "I should go home too," she said, looking down at her desk. "My family . . ."

"You want to celebrate Achana with your family, of course," Kaci said understandingly.

Alan thought he understood a little more. "If Halima goes home, she'll get stuck in the inner courtyard, cooking for the feast, while the men and boys get to go out to see the parade. Won't you?" he demanded.

"It is not important," Halima said quietly.

Kaci shrugged. "Well, you can take your choice, go with Garrett and Alan or go home. I'm not standing around in the heat for hours just to watch some people wave flags and yell political slogans."

"She doesn't have a choice," Alan said. "She can't go out on the streets alone with two men she isn't related to. You have to come with us, Kaci. Otherwise you're doing Halima out of a treat."

"I don't see what it's got to do with me," Kaci complained.

"Hey," Alan said lightly, "you're the one who keeps saying we're all mystically connected, right? All is One and One is All and we need to be in touch with the grand unity of the universe? So feel a little connection already. Come on. I'll buy you a coconut milkshake." If she let him. If he hadn't just blown any chance he ever had of getting Kaci to notice him as more than a piece of office furniture.

"Oh, Alan," Kaci said with an entrancing pout that made her lips look even softer and pinker than usual, "I didn't know you could be such a brute. But I want a *mango* milkshake, okay?" She slipped her arm through his with a little squeeze.

Maybe, Alan thought as they walked from the office block toward the corner of Kilindini and Salim to watch the parade, maybe his entire upbringing and his mother's insistence on good manners were a serious mistake. He was still ninety percent sure that Garrett was having an affair with Halima, but that didn't stop him being atrociously rude to her in the office. And bullying Kaci a little had just won him more points than eight months of finishing her paperwork and trying to help her learn rudimentary Swahili had done.

Of course, he didn't get to keep Kaci's arm once they reached Kilindini. He walked with Garrett, and Kaci followed with Halima, so that decency was served. And after half a block, Alan understood why Halima had been so nervous about going out with them at all. She had already stopped to exchange lengthy polite greetings with two cousins, an ancient Giriama woman who apparently used to either work for or belong to her family, and a gaggle of little boys who'd been let out of Koran school for the afternoon.

"Are you related to everybody in this town?" Garrett complained after the third time they waited for her to get through the required formula of greetings and inquiries after the health of every family connection from uncles to third cousins twice removed.

"I don't get how they know who you are, all covered up in that thing," Kaci said. The bui-bui tied under the chin and allowed the wearer to drop the face veil for a bit of fresh air, but apparently even that modest bit of exposure was improper for the street; every time a man from one of the Twelve Tribes approached, Halima caught up the trailing scarf of her bui-bui and held it modestly across her face, so that everything but eyes and the tips of her fingers was swathed in black.

"All these redskins look alike, anyway?" Alan suggested. Halima sputtered with suppressed laughter behind her veil. He dropped back to walk beside her and switched into Swahili. "*Ulipokaa Virginia-ni ulipenda sinema . . . How would you say, 'Western'? Sinema kama, kama . . . ya John Wayne?*"

Halima nodded. "Yes, but I like our Indian musicals better."

"*Mimi pia*—so do I!" Alan had discovered the Indian musical epic genre of films by accident, one day when he'd been willing to sit through whatever the local movie theater was showing just to get out of his stifling two rooms in the back of Mama Fatima's house in Old Town. The color and light and music and emotion pouring out of the screen had entranced him, even if he couldn't figure out exactly what the actors were singing and emoting about.

Halima's dark eyes sparkled above her veil. "How can you understand them? Do you speak Hindi as well as Swahili?"

"I could do with subtitles," Alan admitted. "I can usually get the main story line by watching carefully, but I do have this feeling there are a lot of subplots I'm completely missing. It's kind of like trying to understand a Thomas Hardy novel from the Classic Comic Books version. How do *you* understand them?"

Halima shrugged. "My cousin Noor is half Gujerati, they use Gujerati and Hindi as much as Swahili and Arabic in her household. My mother and I lived with her for a few years when I was very little, when my father was trying to save up to afford a second wife and they were quarreling too much." She giggled. "Cousin Noor spoke Gujerati and old Bibi Sanaa spoke Arabic and the boys spoke Hindi and of course Mama spoke KiLinganya, which is very different from the Swahili of Mombasa, and when I was quite small I thought everybody in the world spoke a different language."

"You may have been right," Alan said. While he talked with Halima, Kaci was carrying on an animated conversation with Garrett, trying to convince him that peace and harmony in the agency would be improved if he would just ask everybody to hold a piece of blue lace agate and meditate for a few minutes at the beginning of the day. "Sometimes I don't think I speak the same language as Kaci at all. This crystal nonsense . . ."

"My cousin!" Halima caught Kaci's arm and clung to her, turning her head away from Alan.

The slender black man who approached them greeted her with a twinkle that suggested to Alan, at least, that Halima's charade hadn't fooled him in the least. As they started in on the interminable greetings and inquiries about the health of every family member, Alan tactfully dropped back to stand with Garrett.

"Talk, talk, talk, all these damn-lazy Arabs do is talk," Garrett complained. "We will be missing the parade! Come on!" He started purposefully towards Salim Road and Alan followed. Behind him trailed Kaci, Halima, and last of all her cousin Baraka. Alan noticed without really thinking about it that they had finished the family greetings surprisingly fast, probably because Baraka was eager to get into political gossip. He seemed to think Achana was a bad sign, the beginning of the end . . . Alan couldn't follow the KiLinganya dialect; something about a prophet and a book? Oh well, some kind of local religious superstition, no doubt; perhaps Halima would explain it later.

As they approached the intersection, heat waves shimmered up from the pavement and for a moment the storefronts and cracked sidewalks seemed to be shining with a golden radiance, intolerably beautiful, and the people pressing into the street seemed to be standing on waves of shivering air instead of on hot, sticky, half-melted asphalt. Garrett fretted and told Halima it was all her fault for dawdling so, now they would see nothing through the crowd. "We would have done better to have stayed in the office," he said righteously, as though that had been his intention and he had been overruled by the others. "At least we could have seen something from the windows."

Alan was only half listening to Garrett's righteous whine. He didn't really care whether they saw anything of the parade; he'd take the average Mombasa street scene over some hastily put-together military show any day. There was a Persian off the dhows over there, buying a handful of salted nuts from a street vendor; three women in the local head-to-toe black veils, showing only delicate little brown feet decorated with dark red henna patterns; two Bajunis discussing the fishing slouched against the wall of the Ottoman Bank. It was all most unlike Ohio, and most satisfactory. If only he could draw! But even if he could have captured the shapes and colors and costumes, even if he could have somehow indicated the wavering columns of sun-heated air that occasionally cast a veil of unreality over the scene, what was one to do about the sounds—all those different languages—and the smells of roasting corn, coconut milk, curried chicken, lamb in sour milk . . . It smelled as if everybody in Old Town was planning a feast to celebrate Achana Day. Alan drew a deep breath of pure happiness and wondered what the chances were that he'd see somebody he knew in the crowd and that they'd invite him to dinner.

Horns blared somewhere far down the road, and there was an anticipatory ripple through the crowd. Some kind of music interrupted by the static of poorly wired loudspeakers followed the horns. Baraka and Halima raised their voices to continue their argument over the noise of the approaching parade. Several people in the crowd in front of them looked over their shoulders and made shushing motions; as they moved, Alan saw the boy who sold strings of fresh hot peppers in the market. "Musa!" he called out. "*Hujambo*?" Alan remembered that Musa's mother was a very good cook. She'd invited him to dinner the first time he bargained with Musa at the stall because she thought white boys who tried to speak Swahili were cute.

"*Sijambo*, Alan! *Karibu!*" Musa elbowed his neighbors aside and waved to Alan to come up to the front of the crowd.

"I spent too many years moving aside for *wazungu*," a gray-haired man sitting on the curb grumbled. "Now I don't move for anybody!" He thumped a stick on the pavement to emphasize the statement.

"But you'll move just a little, little inch for your favorite grandkid," Musa coaxed. "Besides, Alan is not really an *mzungu*. He is one of us. He speaks Swahili and he likes food with a real taste. He buys his peppers from me because everybody knows that Musa's grandfather raises the best, hottest peppers between here and Malindi."

The flattery and advertisement got Alan another inch of pavement, and by the time Musa had finished extolling the virtues of his grandfather's garden, and the grandfather had complained about the bumpy truck ride into the city for this grand parade, Halima and Garrett and Kaci and Baraka had all managed to wriggle into the few inches of space Musa made for them.

The horns and the music were nearer now. Kaci was complaining in a soft voice about being nearly squashed by the crowd. Alan felt guilty, because he was the one squashing into her rib cage, but he could hardly demateri- alize, could he? And wouldn't she rather be squished by him than by a stranger? And it wasn't his fault he was rather enjoying it, was it?

Men in green uniforms were tramping down the street now, keeping an irregular rhythm set by a leader who carried a bright green flag with the crescent moon of Islam in silver. Half of them were out of step at any given time, but they all looked tougher than hell. Alan was glad he didn't have the job of drilling them. How had the Council of Sheikhs come up with this impromptu army? There must have been a *lot* of back-room planning and maneuvering going on while he worried about water supplies for coastal villages. Of course, everybody said the Nairobi government was falling apart anyway, the Luo and the Kikuyu always at each other's throats and no attention to spare for the rest of the country, so probably the Sheikhs hadn't needed to be all that secretive.

Baraka raised his voice to make a final statement to Halima over the irregular thud of marching feet. One of the soldiers glanced at him and slowed. "You think Achana is a bad thing?"

"It is not necessarily a bad thing in its political essence," Baraka said in the precise, elaborate manner of KiLinganya, "but it is a sign of the last days as written by the prophets of the Books, and even you must have read . . ."

"Even me?" the soldier repeated indignantly. "You calling me not a good Muslim, huh! What are you, some kind of up-country agitator?" The soldier swung a clumsy punch at Baraka. His fist seemed to move so slowly, Alan felt as if everything were happening under water. But Baraka was even slower. He just stood there, looking like a helpless intellectual with those gold-rimmed glasses, and the soldier's fist slammed into his cheekbone and he went down on one knee and two more soldiers stopped, swinging their rifle butts with grins of pure joy, and the whole crowd surged backwards like a receding wave, taking Alan and Kaci with them. He heard something cracking— *oh God, that wasn't his head, was it*—and a woman's shrill scream, and then someone barking orders at the soldiers. The tidal movement of the crowd stopped and Alan pushed his way to the front. A middle-aged man in another of those dark green uniforms was telling Halima to take her cousin home before he got himself in any more trouble

"He did nothing wrong!" Halima sobbed. She was kneeling with Baraka's head in her lap.

The man looked down at her coldly. "Those who speak against Achana are our enemies," he said. "Are you a friend of our enemies?"

"He is my cousin."

"Then you have made an unfortunate choice of family," the man said. His opaque black eyes swept over Alan and Garrett. "And an equally unfortunate choice of friends. Achana is for waSwahili, not for foreigners."

The parade moved on. When the sound of marching feet was several blocks away, Baraka sat up. He moved jerkily and with difficulty but insisted that he was all right. "Of course I fell down when the soldiers hit me," he told Halima with a blindingly sweet smile. "I could hardly fight the entire army of the Sheikhs, so there was no point in standing up. What do you think I am, stupid?"

"*Punde!* Donkey!" Halima scolded. "Worse than stupid, to speak against Achana here. You should be rejoicing with the rest of us."

Baraka seemed to be having trouble standing up. Alan offered a hand and felt Baraka's full weight dragging on him for a moment; then the man was standing, swaying slightly until Alan unobtrusively slipped a steadying hand under his elbow. Baraka gave him a glance of thanks. "I think it would be better if I went to your father's house now," he said. "Before my careless tongue causes more trouble. Enjoy your happy day."

"Can you get home?" Alan whispered.

"Get Halima away," Baraka replied in an undertone. "She will be upset if she thinks I am hurt. And everything will mend in time . . . except these," he said aloud, ruefully touching his cracked glasses.

"Oh, you and your second eyes!" Halima laughed. "Those can be fixed, even if you have to send to Ulaya for the prescription to be ground."

Baraka looked doubtful about the prospect of getting

prescription glasses from Europe. Did he think the Sheikhs were going to cut off trade with America and Europe? The man *was* unduly pessimistic, Alan thought.

The heat beat down on him and the brilliance of the sun made him squint. The street scene seemed to fracture into small separate dancing pictures: Baraka leaning on Halima, an old man across the street scowling at them, more soldiers marching by. All the voices in the crowd blended and separated like a crazy braid coming undone. The old man complained in a high carrying voice that he didn't feel so good. Garrett waved a small flag—where had that come from?—and shouted "Achana! Achana Furaha!" at the top of his voice. Kaci announced that she felt sure her nose was getting sunburned. Halima quietly scolded Baraka for his pessimism. And the old man across the street staggered forward, fell into the path of the marching soldiers and spewed out a black stream of stinking, bloody vomit.

The soldiers broke step, backed up and collided with the marchers behind them who hadn't seen what was going on.

"It is ending," Baraka said from somewhere far away.

Alan was pressed back by the crowd retreating from the sick man; he could no longer see what was going on. "What is it? Isn't anybody helping him?"

Baraka gave him a pitying glance. "Do you not watch EAPTV? It is the blackspit. It began in Zaire, and now it is in Mombasa. There is no cure. Take your girl home."

Garrett had hold of Halima's arm and was steering her through the crowd. "Come on, Alan," he called over his shoulder. "Be realistic. There is nothing we can do here."

Halima

Halima told herself it was selfish to be upset about the ending of a little clerical job. She and her family still had their health and nobody had been arrested; on the day wher

Achana and the blackspit came to Mombasa simultaneously, when Baraka got in trouble with the soldiers, she would have thought that was all she could ask for.

But by now, six whole weeks after Achana, the blackspit still hadn't raged through the city as everybody predicted it would; there'd been that old man at the parade, then a handful of cases down at the dhow harbor, and then . . . nothing; only rumors, and a feeling that the plague was still with them, waiting as if it wanted permission before it ran loose. Like the green mold that grew on every surface during the Long Rains, it was always there, pervasive, threatening, and yet not *doing* anything.

And yet it had done something, after all. It had curtailed the officially mandated rejoicing for Achana, and it had frightened most people in Mombasa off the streets. The IRHRA office might as well close, after all. Garrett was hardly ever there, although Halima knew it wasn't for fear of the plague; he said loudly that the fever would never touch those who kept themselves and their lodgings clean, drank only boiled water or bottled drinks, and otherwise lived up to the standards of Western hygiene. Why else, he demanded loudly, did the black fever fall more heavily on Africans than on *wazungu*?

"There was a similar epidemic in the States some years ago," Alan pointed out. "And in Europe . . . Not as bad; most people didn't die. But it probably gave us some immunities against this form of the disease. Don't worry, Garrett, sooner or later the virus will mutate into something that won't even notice our immune system."

Garrett only shook his head. "Alan, my man, it is a practical matter. You and I, we are here to teach people how to use clean water and keep the vermin out of their houses, but do they listen? If only I had been able to finish the training film! And that reminds me—" And he was gone again, muttering something about an appointment with the Wazeer of Social Development and Planning.

Alan looked across his desk at Halima when Garrett

had bustled out of the office. He seemed troubled; did he think she would take offense? She had learned early on that Garrett was all talk and very little action.

"Don't worry," she told him. "Garrett talks about being practical, but what he really means is that you *wazungu* with your cars and airplanes and microwaves have some kind of magic. He would paint himself all over with whitewash if he thought that would give him your magic. But he knows that would be superstitious. So he talks as if he hates Africa." She thought it over. "I suppose that is a kind of white paint, actually."

"Well, we don't have magic," Alan said wearily.

Halima laughed. Sometimes he was so *young*, this *mzungu* boy from Ohio! Although she was only four years older . . . an old maid, by her family's standards. Better not to think about that. "I know that, Alan," she said. "I went to the university in America, remember? Your people have no magic . . . but they have a great deal of freedom." She stifled a sigh. "Do you think Kaci will be over her cold by next week?" She tried to ask the question brightly and as if it had no possible connection with what had gone before.

"I think Kaci intends to keep that cold going as long as there are any rumors about the blackspit in Mombasa," Alan said. "I'm surprised she hasn't turned it into a life-threatening disease that will force her to go back to America. Is that going to be a problem for you, not having her here?"

"It is already a problem." Halima sighed. If she'd been able to produce Kaci today or tomorrow, she might have talked her family around. But as it was—she would just have to give up the job. One of her brothers had "dropped in" at the IRHRA office the day before, when Kaci was out with her cold and Garrett was, as usual, off talking to politicians. His report of finding her alone in the office with some strange *mzungu* boy had set off a screaming scene that lasted well into the night.

"It was hard enough to get my father to agree that I might take this little little job," she said, "and now there is no work for me to do and it is not proper for me to stay here, and I will not have even that!" She blinked back tears. It wasn't *fair*—and that was a child's complaint. "I have a degree from an American university, I could have been headmistress of Nyali Girls' School when I came back, but my father said it was not proper for a good Swahili girl to go to live and work away from her family. Who would marry me, he said; it would be hard enough getting anybody to marry a girl who had lived in America, they would all think I had lost my virtue there." In fact she hadn't lost it until she came back; until, desperate for some work to do outside the courtyard of her father's house, she had done what was necessary to make Garrett Mpotha hire her for IRHRA.

Alan undid her by looking sympathetic rather than embarrassed.

"There is no one for me to marry anyway," Halima said, more softly. "My cousins do not want an educated woman, they want someone to make babies and grate coconuts in the courtyard. Baraka is the only man of my family I can talk to, and he must marry an mLinganya of the island so that he can take his father's place."

"There are some other people in Mombasa who've been educated abroad," Alan said.

Wazungu! They just didn't get it! "We always marry our cousins," she said flatly. "My father says there are more than enough to choose from . . . and there are . . . but *bismillah*, they are all so *dull*! So . . . there was Garrett . . . and there was this job, and at least I could leave my father's house for part of the day. And now that is all ending." She threw her bui-bui over her head and tied the strings under her chin with a jerky motion. "It is all ending. There is no food in the market, and the Sheikhs will not pay an *mzungu* electrical engineer to maintain the power plant, and no one is allowed to leave the Moslem Free Coast, even if I had anywhere to go. Baraka was right. Achana was the beginning of the end. Everything is falling apart now, and we do not know how to put it back together."

The front hem of the bui-bui dragged on the floor. Automatically, Halima tucked the top of the skirt section into the waistband of her street dress, so that the fabric draped gracefully around her instead of falling in dispirited, dusty folds. She could manage every fold and tuck in the black fabric without thinking, and these days that was the only way she *could* do it . . . without thinking. She took the face veil between two fingers and lifted it up to screen her mouth and nose. The fine black nylon clung to her sweaty skin. It was like being in prison; a prison you carried about with you and could never escape. Even in America, where no one wore the *bui-bui*, hadn't it still been her prison? In four years she'd never stopped feeling naked when she walked to class in only a skirt and blouse, in four years she'd never managed to talk to a strange man without casting her eyes down modestly.

Halima paused in the airless stairwell between the second and third floors. Where was she going? All right, so she could not stay in the office after revealing so much of her feelings to this *mzungu* boy who was in love with his blonde compatriot. But neither could she bear to go back to that walled yard in Old Town where the old aunties sat all day gossiping and grating coconut and pounding rice. Not yet. That might be all the future she had, but this day was still hers. She was supposed to give Garrett Mpotha notice that she was leaving her job, wasn't she? Very well, she would do just that. She still had the key.

Before reaching the street, Halima flipped her face veil forward so that instead of just covering her mouth and nose, it hung down from the strings of the headcloth to cover her entire face in a length of black nylon. The fabric was fine enough for her to make out her way through it, but no one could see her face and possibly tattle in Old Town that they'd seen that wild girl of the Nasir household going into a block of apartments where she could have no business. And the black cloth helped to filter out the strong sharp smells from the harbor. There was something wrong with the water there; her cousin who owned a part share in a dhow said the fish were all floating, dead, and . . . crazy things. She didn't need to think about the strong, rusty-salty smell that filled the hot damp air. Strange things sometimes came in on the tides. They would go away again.

After she'd let herself in to Garrett's apartment it occurred to her, tardily, that he might well be out until evening on his political business. Well, she couldn't risk staying that long; if he didn't come home before the call to afternoon prayer, she would leave him a note. At least she would have a few hours in peace and quiet before going back to the overcrowded Nasir family house where there were always babies shrieking and poor relations asking if one had a headache and grannies clucking their tongues about how skinny one had become since going off to that wicked place, the University of Virginia. Halima settled herself uncomfortably on the stiff Swedish couch that Garrett was so proud of and tried to divert herself by flipping through his magazines: *Forbes*, *The Economist*, *African Business*. All imported from the West, even the one called *African Business*, and all weeks old and mutilated by the censor's black marker. What the Wazeer of Propriety and Decency had left untouched was so boring that she couldn't imagine how anybody in the Wazeer's office had stayed awake long enough to read through the whole magazine and mark out possibly offensive passages. Probably they'd just blacked out paragraphs at random to give an appearance of efficiency and productivity.

When she heard Garrett's key in the door she jumped up and spilled the magazines all over the carpet.

"Halima! What are you doing here?"

"My father has commanded me to stop working for IRHRA," she said. "He says it is not proper, now that the *mzungu* girl does not come to the office any more." She managed a shaky laugh. "He is worried about *Alan*, can you imagine?"

"Good, good," said Garrett absently, as though more than half his mind were on something else.

"How can you say good! Do you not understand? I will have no excuse to leave the house now, *none!*"

"At least he has not guessed about me. That would be a complication I do not need." Garrett rubbed his forehead, where the tribal scars were almost covered by the dark hair that he greased until it could be combed forward and down.

"But what about *me*?"

"Halima, we have to be practical. This is no time to be worrying about little personal problems. I have enough else to be worrying about," Garrett said righteously, "with all the wild rumors that are upsetting the Sheikhs. Some fools are saying that all the ships have broken to pieces in the ocean, that it is a sign from Allah that He is displeased with the independence of the Coast."

"My cousin says the sea has turned to blood."

Garrett made a sharp dismissive gesture with one hand, chopping imaginary obstacles down. "Rumors. Rumors and superstition. It is an oil spill, that is all. Perhaps one tanker has had an accident, perhaps the other ships are not calling at Mombasa because they are concerned about the political situation, but that is not exactly the end of the world! We are modern educated people, you and I. We do not listen to wild stories. The Sheikhs are a bunch of old women, and I am tired from trying to make them calm. It is good you came here, after all. A man needs some relief." He smiled at her. It was a toothy, proprietary smile, one she disliked, but at the same time she felt the old excitement rising in her. *One more time* . . . And maybe, if she was very good this time and did everything he liked, even those dirty tricks he'd learned from prostitutes in Nairobi, maybe he'd want to keep her around enough to think up some way around her family; maybe he'd insist that Kaci come back to the office . . .

Baraka

There were two marketplaces that furnished most of the needs of Old Town, one on either side of the grove of mango trees from which they took their name. At Mwembe Kuku, or Chicken-Under-the-Mango-Trees, one could find not only protesting chickens in cages, but also waist-high sacks of rice and turmeric and cloves, baskets of fresh hot peppers and onions and mangos, cooked food and strips of smoked shark. At Mwembe Tayari, or Ready-to-Wear-Under-the-Mango-Trees, vendors had stalls for anything that couldn't be eaten: used bicycles, slightly bent egg beaters that almost turned a full circle, aluminum saucepans, plastic dishes, Giriama grass mats, frayed white shirts for the snappy dresser, long white robes for the Persian dhow captains, coarse-woven *vitenge* in brilliant red and orange stripes for men to wear sarong-style and finer printed *khanga* with pink and purple flowers and traditional Swahili sayings for the women to wear in similar fashion under the enveloping black bui-bui.

Six weeks after Achana, Mwembe Tayari was half empty. Anything made in Europe or America or even Nairobi had been bought up by canny hoarders right after the Sheikhs closed the Moslem Free Coast boundaries, and more than half the dealers in local goods were either sick of the blackspit or afraid to take a bus or *matatu* into town from their village homes.

Baraka bin Hamid figured that if he had good sense he would leave the city, too. But each day when he got up, the blackspit and the Sheikhs and all the other troubles of Mombasa seemed less frightening than the prospect of being absorbed into the superstitious island life of Linganya the way his little cousin Halima was about to be sucked back into invisibility in her father's house. It might be a waste for a man who'd been to college in Nairobi to spend his days selling *khanga* and *vitenge* cloths in Mwembe Tayari, but what else was there for him? Most educated men got jobs with the government. But when Nairobi had been the government, Moslems from the Coast had been passed over in favor of loud, brash men from the up-country tribes that controlled the country. And now that Mombasa and the Coast were independent, the old irrational fear of "those witches from Linganya" would shut Baraka out.

Some day soon, he told himself, he would go back to Linganya, where at least they didn't have the blackspit yet— or not that he'd heard—and where the Sheikhs' soldiers didn't beat up anybody who said what they did not wish to hear. But not today . . . not yet. Maybe after the hot season was over. He did not remember being so troubled by the heat in earlier years; perhaps he was getting old. The sun seemed to hang low in the sky, like a fire roaring nearer and nearer. Baraka reminded himself that he was an educated man. He knew the sun was a fixed star. It did not move. Nor could the earth change its orbit and come closer and closer until they were all burnt to cinders. Newton. Physics. There were laws governing these things.

All the same, he was sweating so much that his glasses were blurred. He took out a white handkerchief and gently polished his glasses and pushed them back on as well as he could. The straightened-out frames hung awkwardly over his nose where the wire had been patched together with gray duct tape, and a star of cracks radiated from the center of one lens, so that he had a dizzying dual vision of the market; his left eye saw red dust and half-empty stalls and weeds scorched brown by the heat, his right eye saw the same thing overlaid by radiating rainbow streaks.

Right now, both eyes reported that the young *mzungu* from the Peace Corps was walking his bicycle through the market, looking for something. Baraka waved and Alan turned towards his stall.

"*Christmas* decorations?" Baraka repeated incredulously when Alan explained what he was looking for.

"You know—colored lights, tinsel, pretty stuff to hang on a tree?"

"I thought your people worshipped a cross, not a tree."

"Um. Well. It's not that much of a religious holiday any more; it's more about giving presents and having a good time and lighting everything up at the darkest, coldest part of the year." Alan grinned. "OK, so maybe it's going to look kind of funny to throw a winter solstice celebration at the height of Mombasa's hot celebration. But Kaci's real down—she doesn't even pretend to come in to the office any more—and I thought it might cheer her up. She got real excited about the idea just before Achana."

Baraka shook his head. "Yes, but . . . you will not find these things in Mwembe Tayari, Alan!"

"I was figuring on buying them at Shihabuddim Zaidi's store by the Hindu temple, but he's gone out of business."

"So have most of the waHindi." Baraka touched his broken glasses ruefully. "I could at least have had new frames from Saffwan's, but I think he was already packed to leave before Achana. In any case the prescription is a complicated one, I would need to send to London for new lenses, and you know how hard it is to get anything from outside now." Two weeks after Achana Day the Council of Sheikhs had decreed that no one was to leave the Moslem Free Coast until the present "state of emergency" was over . . . but by that time, the Indian shopkeepers who kept the retail economy of Mombasa going had mostly vanished, taking their goods with them. The few shops that were left mostly featured empty shelves and complaints about the difficulty of getting anything through from the mainland any more, never mind European goods! The big ships that used to keep the new harbor busy had stopped coming; there'd been half of a vaguely troublesome article in the latest copy of *Time* to reach Mombasa newsstands, something about problems with the great tankers and other ships breaking up in mid-ocean. There would probably be oil slicks along the coast from that, but the last half of the article had been cut out by the censors because of a swimsuit ad on the back of the page, so he hadn't been able to read what *Time* had to say about the dire consequences of these accidents to trade, the economy, and the ocean ecology.

"I thought . . . don't people who are going home, I mean back to England, sometimes sell their old stuff to traders here?"

"Yes," Baraka said, "but they too were leaving even before Achana."

"I guess it was probably the smart thing to do." The people Alan knew in Mombasa weren't hostile to *wazungu*, but he'd learned to stay out of the way of the Sheikhs' soldiers and out of crowds where no one knew them.

"You should go home too," Baraka said.

"What about you?" Alan challenged. "You don't have to stay here either, do you? Halima said you have family on Linganya. You wouldn't even need to get a pass from the Council to go to Linganya, all the offshore islands are technically inside the Free Coast boundaries."

Baraka smiled. "So . . . I am stupid."

"So am I," Alan said.

They grinned like idiots for a moment, two stupid men who stayed in Mombasa when everybody who could was getting out.

"Most of what you will find at Mwembe Tayari now is just what we on the coast can grow or make or catch for ourselves," Baraka said. "Even my stock of *khanga* is running low." The brightly printed cloths with Swahili sayings on them, used by local women as skirts, shawls, food wraps and baby carriers, were block-printed in Indonesia. Now Alan noticed that Baraka had no bright new prints hanging from the upper poles of his stall; all the *khanga* were soft from years of washing, almost gauzy where the sizing had long since washed out and the cotton threads had been scrubbed down to their bare essence. "Mwembe Kuku is better," Baraka said. "Fish . . . well,

there have been problems with the fish." Oil slicks in the
harbor, probably. "But there are still chickens and mangos
and maize. Rice is getting expensive, but Sheikh Ahmed
Asante has . . ." He glanced about the marketplace. Too
few customers, too many idle traders who might be
listening, and who knew which of them might go running
to the Sheikhs? He changed the subject abruptly. "And
then there are always the preserved foods—smoked shark,
mango pickle. On this side there is not so much to sell,
now. I suppose I will always have a stall, the women like
to change their *khangas*, and what Aisha sells to me Farida
will buy. For new stuff, we have grass mats from the
Giriama women, and pots from the clay pits on the south
coast."

He nodded towards a stall where all sizes of clay pots
were neatly arranged, from small table dishes to three-
foot jars with curved bellies and narrow mouths. Things
were going to get worse; Baraka might not want to go
home, he might refuse to take his place in the circle of
drummers, but he was mLinganya enough to read the
signs of warning. Soon politics would be the least of their
problems. Perhaps he could warn the young *mzungu*
without actually saying anything that could be construed
as treasonable. "You should get one of those," Baraka said
softly.

"My house is on the city water system. I don't need
one. . . . But I know people who do," Alan said thoughtfully.

"Alan, everyone should have a way to store clean water,"
Baraka said. That was neutral enough, it should be safe.
"You have a Coleman lamp for days when the power is
off, do you not?"

"You think the water system's going to fail too?"

Wazungu! Say anything they liked in the open
marketplace, never mind who might be listening.

"Some minor disruptions," Baraka said carefully, "are
nevitable in a change of government . . ." The kid just
vasn't getting it. Oh, to Shaitan with being cautious; he

sounded like one of those up-country political men. He would spell it out for the boy and hope nobody overheard them. He beckoned Alan to come closer, until their heads were almost touching, and dropped his voice lower. "How reliable is the city electrical power these days? How much do you want to trust any of the other services you *wazungu* set up for us? Most of your people left when the days of colonialism ended, when my father was young. The few who stayed left after Achana; the engineers they trained are mostly up-country men who have been deported back to Old Kenya, and the Sheikhs will not keep these things running."

At least all that was a rational argument that two educated men could agree on. He would not speak to Alan of the dreams in which he saw the sky cracking open, the sea boiling; or of his superstitious, mLinganya certainty that these were not dreams but portents. "Go home, my friend. Or if you must stay, get a water jar . . . No, better, buy bottled water. All you can carry."

Garrett

While Halima was dressing, Garrett flung himself down on the couch and switched on the television. The Sheikhs had forbidden residents of the Free Coast to watch East Africa Public Television, otherwise known as "the infidel rumormongers of Nairobi," but until they did something about their plans for a Mombasa-centered television station, there wasn't anything else to watch. Not that EAPTV was much better; they alternated between old taped American sitcoms and "news" broadcasts that were little more than official versions or denials of the superstitious rumors that had upset his contacts in the Council office here. He half-drowsed through a rerun of some show about a group of hulking adolescents talking back to their parents over the roar of canned "laughter."

When the Moslem Free Coast Television began, they would need trained men, educated men, and Garrett had entertained enough of the Sheikhs' officials to be assured that his up-country origins would be no barrier to advancement. The post of Director of Programming was practically his already; then he could quit wasting his time with trivial things like this useless relief agency. It might be a good idea to write another memo to the Wazeer of Propriety and Decency, detailing his plans to develop good conservative programming instead of this kind of foreign comedy that encouraged children to laugh at their parents and broke up the sacred family home . . . of course without revealing that he had just been watching the show on EAPTV . . . The artificial laughter rose to its peak during the scene where the father finds the nest of baby snakes in the toilet, then stopped abruptly enough to snap Garrett out of his daydreams.

"EAPTV Special News Update," scrolled across the screen, together with the relentlessly upbeat trumpet rendition of the Kenyan National Anthem that accompanied every such update; then the picture dissolved into jagged lines, quivered, and coalesced into a grainy image of a sweating man in a white shirt and dark tie.

"The rumors of blackspit devastating the United Kenyan Army are completely without foundation," he announced. "Any day now our loyal soldiers will cross the borders of the so-called Moslem Free Coast and liberate its unhappy citizens from the unjust and oppressive rule of the Council of Sheikhs. Meanwhile, in other parts of the world, the empire of the colonialists is breaking apart from the weight of its crimes," he began without preamble. "This last transmission from one of the American ships shows the destruction." Blurred, indistinct images filled the screen; by squinting, Garrett thought he could make out the skyline of Manhattan, but it was canted at an odd angle, as though the cameraman were drunk or ill. As he peered at the screen, the towers seemed to crumble. There was a babble of shouts and screams from off-camera, drowned out as the picture dissolved into a pattern of flashing bars and spots. Then came a wavering voice speaking in English.

"To the peoples of the civilized world: *this is not a fake*. The American continents are suffering an unprecedented wave of disastrous earthquakes and other Acts of God. Speaking from his command post at an undisclosed safe location, President Lucas has declared the entire east coast of the United States a disaster area. President Lucas ceased transmitting at 0732 hours this morning and we have been unable to raise any communications from the western half of the country. This is George K. Hester, for NBC, coming to you from the departing ship. . . ."

Crackling static drowned out the voice. Someone in the background might have been shouting something about blood. Then the sound and the dizzying pattern cut off abruptly, to be replaced again by the image of the young Nairobi broadcaster yammering something about this being the time for the erstwhile Third World to become the First World in the new order. Garrett yawned and turned the volume down. It was a hoax; it couldn't be anything else. Wasn't there some old story about the Americans being convinced by a radio play that Martians had invaded? Something of the same sort, here. No rational person would be convinced by these flickering, grainy pictures that the Western world was physically falling apart. Special effects, that was all, and not particularly good ones. He'd seen much better in *Independence Day*.

But if this hoax fooled many people, what better time for a man who kept his head to *get* ahead? Garrett found his shirt and prided himself on his forethought in hanging his clothes up neatly before enjoying Halima for one last time. The power was so unreliable these days, it might be some time before his clean shirts came back from the laundry. He stood before the bathroom mirror, knotted his tie and wiped at the sweat on his forehead. The heat was terrible. He wished the air-conditioning would come back on. Somebody would have to do something about that. Perhaps he wouldn't wait for that position as Director of Programming. The Sheikhs could use an intelligent man now, to make decisions and maintain public order. Or . . . if the army decided that it no longer needed the Sheikhs . . .

"Garrett! Is it true, what they were saying on the television?"

Why couldn't Halima just go home? "Don't interrupt me, I'm *thinking*," Garrett snapped. "And of course it's not true, it's special effects, that's all."

"But why . . ."

"Who cares? We have to be practical," Garrett said. "Crazy stories about America don't matter. What does matter is that Kenya can't invade us; too many of their soldiers have the blackspit."

"How do you know?"

"Because EAPTV denied it," Garrett explained patiently. "That is exactly what I would do if I had been threatening an invasion and couldn't bring it off. Don't you see, that means there is nobody for the Army of the Sheikhs to fight. And *that* means the balance of power here just might be about to change. The Sheikhs and Wazeers might not be so important any more." He snapped his fingers as inspiration came to him. "Time for a party, Halima."

"A *party*? Now? Are you crazy?"

"Well, it's almost time for that Christmas party. I've already bought the beer. See, we can invite my good friend Major Musali and as many other officers as he can find. I'll show them how a rational, practical man keeps his head in a time of plague and rumormongering, suggest that now would be a good time to have someone who understood the army's needs in charge of some vital post among the Wazeers and Sheikhs."

"I have to go home," Halima said. "It is almost the end of the office day; my father . . ."

"You will *not*," Garrett said sharply. "A party needs girls. You're a girl. You stay."

To think he'd almost sent her away! To make the party swing he'd need Halima, and any other girls he could find . . . Some of the "working girls" downtown would be glad to come for a free drink. He'd collect a few of them while he was getting more cold beer. But it would be good to cool off before he went out in that scorching heat. He turned the tap, admired the set of his tie in the bathroom mirror while waiting for the protesting pipes to deliver their cool water, and looked down to see that there was nothing but a rusty red trickle coming out of the faucet. It stank, too: hot and salty and sour. Ugh! A good thing he had looked before getting it on his hands. That was another thing Major Musali would understand, the need to hire some competent people to keep the city water and power going. The Coast definitely needed some practical, take-charge guys to replace those lazy Arabs the Sheikhs had put into office.

Kaci

It wasn't *fair*. She shouldn't have to stay on an island where people were getting sick and throwing up and doing even yuckier stuff right in the street. She was an American citizen; the government ought to get her out of here. But nobody did anything and nobody came for her and when Kaci finally gave up on waiting for the government and went to the airport by herself, three weeks after Achana, there were those *askaris* in the Sheikhs' uniforms, talking nonsense about the airport being closed until after the emergency.

"What do you mean, after the emergency?" Kaci screamed at one of them. "*I* don't have the blackspit! Do they expect me to stay here and *die*?"

The man she was screaming at smiled broadly and

suggested that the two of them could find something more fun than dying to do while they waited for the airport to reopen. Kaci kept her dignity while she walked back to the cab . . . all right, she *backed* to the cab; she was afraid to take her eyes off the grinning soldiers. Even the cab driver scared her. It wasn't that she was prejudiced. But they were all foreign; she didn't understand half of what they said, and she wanted to go home.

She cried herself to sleep that night, and the next day her head ached and her eyes were sore and she might have been coming down with something and it wouldn't be fair to expose the other people in the office to her flu or whatever it was. So she stayed in the air-conditioned apartment, alternately watching old sitcoms on EAPTV and meditating with one of her crystals. She had a necklace of smooth polished green jasper beads; wearing it made her feel as if she were encircling herself with the strength and stability of jasper. Tomorrow, or the next day, she would go back to the office; today she would concentrate on healing herself. Kaci visualized herself surrounded by golden healing light and green walls of protective jasper.

But the next day, she could look out from her balcony and see *askaris* all over the streets, stopping people for no reason and shouting questions at them. You'd have to be crazy to go outside alone at a time like this. Instead she sat cross-legged on the carpeted floor of the tiny living room, mentally extending her protective shield over all the IRHRA folks: Halima and Garrett and even Alan, although she did think Alan might have come to see if she were all right. They were Americans together in this. He wouldn't have left without her, would he? Of course not, she told herself, the airport was closed. She turned on the radio to catch the news and make sure the airport was still closed, but the Swahili was too fast and complex for her to follow, so she watched TV instead. Coming out of Nairobi, EAPTV wouldn't have any local news, but at least they had an English broadcast hour every afternoon, and lots of old taped programs in English during the day.

She lost count of the days; she fell into long meditative trances and sometimes didn't even notice when night came. She started sleeping more, too. What else was there to do? The power kept going off, sometimes for hours at a time, and without air conditioning the little apartment was stifling. But there were still plenty of cans of food in the kitchen, and it was too scary outside, and such a long way to the IRHRA office, and she didn't know anybody else in Mombasa. She hadn't wanted to know anybody, hadn't wanted to be here, had wanted the two years to pass in a dream. Why did all this bad stuff have to happen just when she was here? It wasn't fair. She hadn't been bothering anyone. She just wanted to be let alone.

At least there was plenty of quiet time to meditate, and she had her candles. Kaci lit just one candle at a time, to make them last. She crouched before the one burning candle and looked at the flame through her quartz crystal. If she stared at the dancing rainbows inside the crystal long enough, she could forget that she was hot and sweaty and scared; she could forget everything and enter into a sacred place where there was nothing but love and peace and happiness.

But it didn't work all the time, and it couldn't work when the pounding on her door was loud enough to break through any meditative trance. Kaci huddled in a ball, arms round her knees, and waited. If she didn't make any noise perhaps they would go away . . .

"Kaci! Kaci!"

The voice was distorted by the closed door, but she could make out her name. Alan, it had to be Alan, he'd finally come for her and now they could get out somehow. She couldn't get all the locks and chains on the door undone fast enough.

"Oh, Alan, I knew you'd come, have you thought of some way to get away from here . . ."

Green and brown uniforms, grinning black faces. Kaci

shrank into frozen stillness. That horrible man at the airport. Things *happened* to nice American girls in these Third World countries, but not to her, she hadn't been careless, she hadn't even gone outside the apartment since everything got crazy.

"*Wewe* Kaci," one of the men announced, and took her by the arm. It seemed she was coming outside now.

Alan

On the way back from Mwembe Tayari Alan saw a lot more army Land Rovers and soldiers in the Sheikhs' gray-green uniforms than there had been that morning. Three times between the bus stop and his house in the Arab quarter Alan was stopped by soldiers. The first time he had to wait on the sidewalk, standing perfectly still, for half an hour until a black Mercedes-Benz escorted by motorcycles rolled down Kilindini a block away. The next time was the same sort of thing, except this time he had to kneel with his hands clasped behind his head, and the soldier behind him kept fiddling audibly with the mechanism of his pistol. The third stop was almost a relief; all they wanted was the few shillings in his pockets.

He had left the doors and windows locked; now the door was smashed in and the thief-wiring that covered the windows had been wrenched off. Alan saw without too much surprise that his collection of secondhand glasses and plates had been smashed and his clothes and radio were gone. He wondered why they had left the bed; perhaps it was too much trouble to clear the splinters of broken glass off the mattress.

Bibi Salma next door was still alive, and she lent him a room to clean up his rooms and told him her version of the latest news while he was standing on her front step. According to her, America and Europe had fallen into the ocean, and Kenya—"the former state of Kenya," she hastily corrected herself—had sent an army to invade the Moslem Free Coast, but the blackspit had stopped the army before they reached the borders. So all the soldiers gathered in Mombasa didn't have enough to do—"except make trouble," she said in an undertone. "You stay in my house, Bwana Alan. They see you, you get more trouble."

Without the Christmas lights there didn't seem much point in going to Kaci's apartment to try and cheer her up; Alan decided to head for the IRHRA office instead, to see if he couldn't get a less garbled account of the news. Halfway there a soldier commandeered his bike, which didn't surprise him; he figured he had been lucky to get that far.

The rest of the building was deserted, but there was noise coming from the IRHRA office. A lot of noise. Alan tried to open the door and found himself pushing against heavy, squashy weights that gradually shifted and revealed themselves, as he sidled in, as two sweating officers in the Army of the Coast. At least, from the number of decorations, ribbons, and gold chains they were wearing, he assumed they were officers.

The rooms were filled with people standing toe to toe, laughing too shrilly and drinking too fast. The air was thick with the smells of smoke and spilled beer and something else, something sharp and salty that Alan couldn't put a name to. At first he thought it was the smell of fear.

"Alan, my man!"

Garrett Mpotha lurched across the room, elbowing people aside, and gave Alan a beery hug. "About time you showed up. Pretty good Christmas party, even if it i a couple of days early, hey?" He laughed, too loudly, an released Alan with a final squeeze. "Don't look so stif Next time I will send you an engraved invitation."

"There won't be any next time," said one of the arm officers. "No next times for any of us. It's the end."

His companion looked at him and muttered somethin about treason; the officer shrugged. "Run and tell th

Council, then, you fat load of donkey shit. Maybe the Sheikhs are still alive. Maybe you won't die of the blackspit before you get there, maybe this island won't fall into the sea before you get back. That invasion the Sheikhs mobilized us for isn't going to happen . . . and I'm going to have another beer."

Alan glimpsed a swathe of silver-blond hair by the window and for a moment his heart seemed to stop with sheer relief. Whatever disasters had scared these guys, at least Kaci was all right—and she was *here*. He left the officers wrangling and edged through the crowd until he reached the window ledge where Kaci stood with a paper cup in her hand. Halima was beside her, but she was already tying the strings of her bui-bui under her chin.

"Have a drink, Alan." Kaci smiled sweetly and waved her cup. An amber wave of beer sloshed over the rolled paper rim and splashed his shoes. "Halima's not drinking, because she's a good Moslem, aren't you, Halima? But you'll have a drink with me, won't you, Alan. We'll celebrate Christmas together. We don't belong here. We can go home." Her face crumpled. "Except we can't go home. It isn't there any more. This is all there is now."

"You're drunk," Alan said.

Kaci giggled. "Always did admire your fine grasp of the obvious, Alan darling. Sure I'm drunk. Alcohol does that. And it isn't safe to drink the water in Africa. Didn't anybody ever tell you that? It isn't safe to drink the water," she repeated emphatically, and downed the rest of her beer with one long swallow. "Get me some more, Alan, I'm thirsty."

"Alcohol does that too," Alan said, taking Kaci's paper cup and resolving to fill it with water. "Halima?"

She followed him to the little room that had been the office bathroom. It was piled high with cases of bottled drinks; mostly beer, but there was one crate of Fanta. Halima took one of the orange sodas and popped the cap off with a twist of her wrist. "You can give Kaci this," she said in a voice so soft Alan could barely hear her over the noise of the party, "but she will not drink it. She wishes to be drunk. They all do."

"Then they're crazy," Alan said. "Last thing anybody needs in this heat is to get dehydrated from alcohol. The rest of them can kill themselves if they want to, but I'm not letting Kaci drink any more. She'll drink water and like it."

Halima started to say something else, but Alan ignored her and moved a crate of beer aside to get at the sink. It was filthy, splashed with brownish-red splotches. Had somebody been throwing up in it? But the stuff looked more like dried blood. He felt cold in the midst of the heat and the crowd. Had somebody in these crowded rooms come down with the blackspit?

He twisted the handle of the faucet and a trickle of warm red liquid spewed into the sink, smelling of salt and iron. "Holy *shit!*" The stuff splashed on his hands. He was frozen with shock. Halima reached past him and turned the faucet off. "There is no more water," she said softly. "I tried to tell you. The water has turned to blood."

That was the hot, bitter smell that filled the office: the smell of blood. A half-forgotten memory out of childhood tugged at Alan's mind. Plague, and a sea of blood, and rivers of blood . . . When he tried to track down the elusive memory, all he saw was Miz Bartlett the Sunday school teacher, smelling of magnolias from the scented powder on her dangling double chin, sitting at the piano and singing "Jesus Loves Me."

Alan poured a bottle of beer over his sticky hands, took a Fanta to drink, and steered Halima into the hall outside the IRHRA offices. "What's going on?" he pleaded. "You seem to be the only sober person here."

Halima, when he pressed her, told much the same story as Bibi Salma. The continents were breaking apart; yet she was sure, she'd seen it on East African Public Television before the station in Nairobi abruptly quit broadcasting

"I thought the Council of Sheikhs had forbidden EAPTV," Alan said.

"Oh, yes," Halima said, "it is death or imprisonment if you are caught watching. But when the blackspit came, it did not seem to matter which killed you first, the Sheikhs or the plague, so Garrett . . . most of us started watching again. Anyway it is over now. I think Nairobi is gone."

Alan shook his head. "That doesn't make any *sense*. Continents don't just break up and drift away. Well, plate tectonics . . . but I thought that took like kazillions of years."

"It is written," Halima said. "There shall be a day when the earth and the mountains shall shake, and the hills shall be a toppled heap of sand."

"You still believe all those old stories?" Garrett Mpotha shouldered his way out into the hall. "You are making yourself miserable for nothing."

"It is ending as it is written," Halima snapped, "When the heaven is split open, when the stars are scattered, when the seas swarm over, when the tombs are overthrown, then a soul shall know its works. And these are our works!" She gestured at the office full of drunken soldiers.

"Stories," Garrett said, "stories for children. I went to the Methodist Mission for five years when I was a boy; they told stories too, they said the world would end in fire and blood and only the righteous would be saved." He hiccuped and Alan realized that he was very drunk indeed, only held upright by the wall behind him. "Wrong. The practical men will be saved. The ones who know how things work. You be nice and friendly now, Halima, and I'll take care of you." He wiped off the neck of his beer bottle and held it out to her.

"I do not drink alcohol," Halima said.

Garrett slipped sideways, partway down the wall, and grinned at her. "You keep the word of the Prophet. Good Moslem girl. But only keep the rules that suit you, hmm? Don't drink, wear the veil—that bui-bui comes in pretty handy, doesn't it, Halima? Nobody can tell it's you under the black veil when you come to my apartment. You damned hypocrite!" He raised his voice. "Look down your nose at the rest of us for having a little drink, and everybody knows about you and me!"

"Garrett, *please*. Not here!" Halima was near tears.

"Leave her alone, Garrett," Alan said. He tried to sound forceful and confident.

"Have a drink with the rest of us," Garrett insisted. "Stop acting like you're too good to join the party. Or you want me to tell everybody how good you really are, Halima? How good in—"

Alan surprised himself by hitting Garrett in the mouth. His knuckles stung and he could feel that he didn't have any weight behind the blow, stupid city boy, student, he castigated himself, don't even know how to punch somebody out. But Garrett's drunken balance was so precarious that he slid down the wall anyway, more surprised than hurt.

"Hey, Alan," he said plaintively, "what's the matter? What'd you come here for, if you don't want to be friendly?"

"Kaci," Alan said.

Garrett laughed. "She can take care of herself, that one. Got herself a Peace Corps gig instead of going to jail, didn't she?" He mimed Alan's look of astonishment. "Little Kaci doesn't tell you much, does she? You really still think she came here for love of Africa, all the bitching and whining she does? Got caught pushing drugs at home, cut a deal with the judge, nice girl from nice family, two years of public service instead of jail. Only, nice family thought it'd be too embarrassing to have her doing public service at home, so they persuaded the judge Peace Corps would count. All these bloody nice girls," Garrett mumbled, sliding a little further down towards the floor, "nice little liars. Take Halima, now—" He squinted uncertainly. "Where *is* Halima?"

Alan glanced around.

"She left," Kaci said, "and I don't blame her." She w

close to tears. "Garrett Mpotha, you are a *pig*. What did you do, get a copy of my file from one of your government friends?"

"It's true?" But Alan found he wasn't surprised, not really. Kaci had always made it perfectly clear she hated being here.

"Not like he said." Kaci blinked back tears. "We weren't doing drugs for *fun*. It was, like, a short cut, you know? I mean, meditation, it takes so long to get anywhere..."

"Instant enlightenment," Alan said. "Just add water . . ."

"And the third angel poured out his vial upon the rivers and fountains of waters, and they became blood," said a dreamy, slurred voice near their feet. Garrett was lying quite supine now, hands crossed upon his chest, still clutching an empty bottle of Pemba beer. "Tol' you," he added, "five years Methodist Mission. First angel, a noisome and grievous sore upon the men which had the mark of the beast. Thass the blackspit. Second angel poured out his vial upon the sea and it became as blood of a dead man and every living soul died in the sea."

Alan remembered Sunday school, and Miz Bartlett's powdered chins trembling, and a colored picture card for every kid who recited a Bible verse. Back then he'd thought Revelations was more fun than all the gentle-Jesus-meek-and-mild stuff; he'd taken a kid's delight in the images of a world smashed to bits like the end of a monster movie. "And the fourth angel poured out his vial upon the sun; and the power was given to him to scorch men with fire," he said wonderingly, remembering the hammer blows of heat and sun that had nearly stunned him on his way through town.

"I don't understand what you're *talking* about," Kaci wailed.

"Wanna find a Bible, check out last three angels?" Garrett proposed from the floor. "Can't remember . . . something bout darkness and madness . . ." He gave up in midsentence and emitted a long rattling snore.

"Halima," Alan said. "It's crazy out there. Kaci, we'd better go look for her." At least he could do something that made sense. Well, anyway, it beat trading Bible quotations with a drunk.

"You go if you want," Kaci said. "It's *hot* out there."

"Not any more." The windows across the room showed blue-black clouds pressing down over the streets, turning midafternoon into tropic night. The Long Rains must be starting early. "Anyway," Alan pointed out, "you're better with me than here alone with these guys. All the other girls have left, except those two." He jerked his head towards two girls with hugely frizzed hair, tribal scars on their cheeks, sturdy bodies poured into tight Western-style sequined dresses. One of them had just taken a challenge to drink down a bottle of Pemba without stopping for breath, while her friend giggled and squirmed on the lap of a man in uniform.

Kaci followed, but grumbled all the way down the stairs.

Outside it was worse than Alan had guessed from his glance through the office windows: the sky a dirty gray-green streaked with black, and winds whipping up the dust into a haze through which he could barely see anything. Kaci coughed and choked until he found a handkerchief she could tie over her nose and mouth. He felt as if his lungs were being abraded by the black grit he drew in with each breath. He pulled his shirt off and tied it by the sleeves over his own face, squinted through whirling clouds of gritty dust. The street opened before them in a black gaping hole where the roundabout at Salim Road should have been. Alan grabbed Kaci's hand, not to lose her in the crazy blackness, and went down a side street that ought to turn and meet Salim Road within half a block. Only it didn't. It twisted and spiraled in on itself until Alan was dizzy, and the office buildings on either side seemed to be leaning over to crush them.

A thicker blackness in front of him whirled, solidified into the form of a woman in a bui-bui. "Halima?" Ala called. But this woman was big enough to make three of Halima. He tried again. *"Mwanamka mjana, aliovaa buibui kama wewe . . ."* A young woman, wearing a bui-bui like you . . .

"Mwanamke moja hatoshi?" One woman isn't enough for you?

Before he could collect his wits and reply to this sally, the veiled woman spun around and dissolved into a column of black smoke that dissipated into the prevailing gloom.

"Alan, I don't *like* this," Kaci wailed. "Let's go back!"

Back where? The street they'd been walking on was all changed behind them; it looked like the main road to the ferry, and Alan knew they hadn't been anywhere near there. But ahead of him he heard a conch-shell horn sounding through the shadows. They had to be near the Hindu temple, and that meant Mwembe Tayari was somewhere to his left, and the rest of the Arab quarter was ahead and to his right. Unless he'd got turned around? No— those were the square, soft-edged yellowish-white houses of the quarter, less than a city block ahead of him, where the paved road gave way to narrow sandy pathways that curved in snail-shell patterns around whatever buildings anyone had chosen to put up.

And between him and the safety of his house in the Arab quarter was a ditch ten yards across and no telling how deep. Alan came to a juddering halt, dug his heels in and flung out one arm to stop Kaci from falling in. "Mwembe Tayari, then," he said to no one in particular, and headed to the left, along the side of the ditch that shouldn't have been there. The fabric of his shirt stuck to his mouth, he had to suck air through it. Was this what it was like for Halima all the time, wearing that floor-length black veil with its swathes of fabric to wrap around her head? No wonder she took it off the minute she got to the IRHRA office each morning.

The choking clouds of black dust seemed to fade as they got closer to Mwembe Tayari, and there were no

more sudden openings of the ground at their feet. But
the air smelt of something burning that had never been
meant to burn, like plastic or bones, and the greenish-
black cast of light made everything, even the stalls under
the mango trees, look like stage settings for a play that
had closed after a long run.

Most of the stalls were gone; the few that remained
standing were bare boards with no pots and pans and
khangas and sandals hanging for display. A few traders
squatted disconsolately under the mango trees, sitting on
bulging sacks that must hold their remaining merchandise.
And a slender girl wrapped in the black bui-bui, with slim
hennaed feet in gold sandals showing beneath the hem
of the veil, wandered aimlessly through the remnants of
the market.

"Halima!" Alan called. The shirt, damp from his breath,
stifled his voice. He unwound it and called out again.

"It could be anybody," Kaci said fretfully, "they all look
alike in those black veils."

But Alan knew those elegant feet and the frivolous gold
sandals—ridiculous, he realized later; half the Swahili girls
in Mombasa hennaed their feet and hands on occasion,
and they all wore sandals. All the same, he saw as the girl
turned her face towards them that it was Halima. She had
let her face veil drop, so that the black bui-bui framed
her from forehead to waist like a miniature painting in an
oval frame, and she seemed to glow inside the black fabric.

"It is very hot here," she said, "and Baraka has gone
north to Linganya with Melissa. I thought he would take
me, but now there is nowhere to go."

Her voice was as flat as if she were reading a Form
352-C.

One of the traders under the mango trees groaned
suddenly and bent forward, clutching his stomach. A stream
of black liquid spewed from his mouth. The other men
jumped up in alarm; all but one backed away. That one
stayed and held his friend's head.

"Blackspit!" Alan said under his breath. After these weeks of waiting, it was finally spreading through the city. That was why the market was deserted. People withdrew to their own homes in time of plague, each house shuttered and isolated. All that other stuff, the blackening sky and his crazy feeling that the city was twisting and collapsing on itself . . . Well, he didn't need to think about that now. "Halima, you can't stay here."

"I have no place to go," Halima said, still in that dead-flat voice that sent creeping chills down Alan's spine. "My father knows that I have dishonored the family."

"Tell him it's a lie?" Alan suggested. "Malicious gossip? Somebody who's jealous of your good job and wants him to keep you locked up in the house forever?"

Drops of sweat beaded Halima's forehead and ran into her thick, dark brows. "Alan, if I go home, he will not lock me up. He will kill me."

"Wait a minute," Kaci said. "Garrett can't have told your father anything. He was still at the party when we left. This doesn't make *sense*."

"He was at the party, and he will be at my father's house, and when I came to my father's house it was after Garrett had been there, and I will have been dead by then. The city is falling in upon itself. So is time. If I stay here perhaps I will wander into a time before Baraka left. But if I go home, my father will strangle me and throw my body off Ras Kisauni for the fish to eat, and I do not think it will help to tell him that he cannot have heard Garrett's story yet."

"People don't *do* things like that!"

"I think they do here," Alan said. He couldn't understand what Halima was saying about time, and it made his head hurt. But he remembered a girl who'd been found in the Old Harbor when he was training here with the rest of his Peace Corps group. "Jimmy Connor," Alan said suddenly. "He was sent away before we finished training, and nobody knew why."

"He was sent away," Halima agreed. "So was Fatima. If I return to my father's house, perhaps you will find me off Ras Kisauni tomorrow. But probably not, because my father is more intelligent than Fatima's brother. He will probably pay a dhow captain to take my body far enough offshore that the great currents will sweep me away from Mombasa forever."

The man who had vomited was rolling on the ground now, clutching his stomach. His pants were stained black to the knees. His friend tried to give him water from a tin cup, but it spilled over the contorted, blackened lips and soaked into the red dust of the marketplace. Behind him, the green leaves of the mango trees seemed to be haloed in golden light, as if a few rays of afternoon sun had somehow made it through the clouds.

Alan looked up and saw that the clouds had changed shape. They looked if anything more ominous than before; jagged lines outlined the puffy gray-green shapes and separated them like pieces of a jigsaw puzzle that didn't quite fit. And between the lines was a blackness so pure and intense that it hurt his eyes. It hurt like staring at the sun, but it felt like staring into absolute nothing.

"There should be stars," he said. "Shouldn't there be stars?"

"Alan, it's *daytime*," Kaci snapped. "It's just a little bit cloudy, that's all. I don't know what's wrong with you."

"Me neither," Alan said. Perhaps he was coming down with the blackspit. Most Americans didn't seem to get it, probably because of the related fevers that had swept the States when he was in junior high, but it was only a matter of time before the virus mutated to a form that wouldn't recognize those ten-year-old immunities. And he was certainly hallucinating, he thought. "You didn't used to be able to see the downtown office blocks from Mwembe Tayari, did you?" he asked the girls. Those tall golden towers rising behind the mango trees, shimmering through a haze of light that never reached the ground . . . well, they had to be the office buildings and hotels that clustered around Kilindini and Salim roads, there wasn't anything else near here that was that tall. Of course, even those modern office buildings weren't *that* tall; the light must be distorting them somehow.

"I wouldn't know," Kaci said. "I've never been here, and I don't like it here, and I want to go *home!*"

"How beautiful," Halima said, following Alan's gaze. "But that is not Mombasa. Where are we?"

"Mwembe Tayari."

"It doesn't . . . I feel so hot!" Halima wailed. "And . . ." Whatever she had been going to say was choked by a tide of tarry black liquid that swelled out of her mouth and spilled over the black bui-bui.

Alan caught her before she hit the ground. Kaci was already ten feet away. "Alan, put her down! You'll get sick!"

"I think I am already," Alan said. That would explain the hallucinations, the way the whole city seemed to be flickering in and out of existence. Maybe the virus had mutated into something that was unpleasant but not fatal; that would explain why he didn't feel so bad yet.

Halima, though, was as sick as anybody he'd seen. The virus *had* mutated; with the first cases people had taken one to three days to die, but Halima was already vomiting blood with the black liquid, and her body had the spongy feel of something that was beginning to decay before it died. Blood and vomit soaked Alan's shoes and the bottoms of his trousers.

And he wasn't strong enough to hold Halima up, and there was no place to lay her down except on the bare red dirt of the marketplace. Alan knelt and settled her as gently as he could, then cursed himself for an idiot. If he'd taken off her soiled bui-bui first, he could have rolled that up for a pillow.

"Alan, I want you to take me home now!" Kaci called from a distance. "Look, Alan, you have to be sensible. Nobody ever gets over the blackspit—no natives, anyway.

Halima's essentially dead now. If you stay you'll catch it. You have to take care of yourself."

Her voice sounded tinny and as if it were coming from much farther away than the twenty feet that separated them; it dissolved into a meaningless noise, a ringing in Alan's ears. He looked around the marketplace for something he could use as a pillow. Halima mumbled something and tried to clutch his hand when he stood up. "I'll be back," he promised her.

"Well, thank goodness, I thought you'd never be ready to go! Don't get too close to me, you're covered in guck," Kaci said in one breath.

Alan walked past her and approached the one trader who'd stayed with his sick friend. "*Tafadhali*," he began, and then stopped. What did he want to ask? Please, can I use one of those sacks as a pillow for my friend? Please, where did you get the water? Please tell me what to do?

"Alan," Kaci called, "I'm leaving now. I really mean it. I won't wait for you." But she folded her arms and tapped her foot instead of walking away.

"Don't wait," Alan agreed.

The trader told him he was welcome to anything he wanted to use to pillow Halima, but as for the water—what water? He handed the cup to Alan with a grin. It was neat gin.

"I can't give her that," Alan said. "There *has* to be some water somewhere." He looked around the deserted marketplace. One of the abandoned boxes had the logo of a French mineral water stenciled on its side. He barely heard the sounds of the sick man thrashing about as he dashed to what had been the site of the booth three stalls down. "Ha! What about . . ." His voice died away as he pulled the first bottle out of the box. Whatever was inside was thick, opaque, blood-red.

The trader looked up with a sympathetic shrug. "Give her the gin," he said in a soft, barely accented voice. "Here is the bottle."

"Your friend . . ."

"He does not need it now."

The man on the ground was lying quite still, limbs contorted in the final painful convulsion that had occurred while Alan was chasing after bottled water.

Alan took the bottle and the tin cup. It seemed quite a long way across the empty marketplace to where Halima lay, and it was hard to make out her black-robed figure in the gathering gloom. He should move her under the mango trees for shelter . . . But it was hard enough to make his way back to Halima; he kept having dizzy spells and the illusion that the ground was opening beneath his feet, disclosing alternately bottomless pits of blackness and gleams of golden light.

"Hallucinations," he said aloud, and walked across the gold-lit chasm. Sweat beaded his forehead, and his feet felt as if they were slogging through something as thick as blood. *Don't look down.* How could it take so long to reach Halima? He had to be catching the blackspit. Funny, no one else had mentioned the way space and time seemed to stretch and split around you in the first stages. Maybe he was lucky, maybe it was just malaria. Halima seemed as far away as when he'd begun walking.

"I'm going back to the office," Kaci said beside him. "One of us has to be sensible."

He didn't have the energy to reply, and anyway when he looked at her she wasn't there any more. And he could hardly see Halima for the illusory golden glow that rose around his feet. Walking forward got harder and harder, like leaning into an invisible wind. Alan pushed forward and said, *"Hallucinations,"* firmly. The strange light died down, and so did the sense of something holding him back. Straining against a resistance that was suddenly no longer there, he lost his balance, stumbled and fell forward on his knees right beside Halima. The tin cup went flying out of his right hand. A freakish breeze snatched it up and spun it round and round and up and up, flashing bright and dull like a miniature satellite, then dropped the cup into the thick green leaves of the mango trees.

"Djinni," Halima said in a strange thick voice. "As it is written . . ." She coughed and a lump of black bloody mucus came up. Alan felt dizzy and nauseated from the smell.

"Don't try to talk," he said. "Look, I managed to hang on to the bottle. This will make you feel better."

Forget whatever they told you in that two-week first aid course, Alan told himself. She's not going to make it. She wouldn't live even if I could find water to keep her from dehydrating so fast.

If he could get some of the gin into her, maybe she wouldn't feel the last painful convulsions of the disease. But like the trader's friend, she was too weak to swallow. The liquor ran out from the corners of her mouth. Maybe if he held her head up . . . Trying to trickle a little gin from the half-full bottle into Halima's open mouth occupied him for an unmeasured period of time. Somewhere behind the clouds, the sun moved; where there had been an eerie greenish light illuminating a haze of dust, there was now the stifling dark of the sudden tropic night. The last of the gin spilled over Halima's soaked, filthy dress.

"Ah, *fuck it*," Alan said under his breath, and shifted his weight down against the ground so that he could hold Halima's head on his lap.

When dawn came they were still there, and he didn't know exactly when Halima had died; his watch had stopped, and anyway it had been too dark to read the numbers. He had begun dozing off for seconds at a time, until the fall of his head startled him awake again. At one time Halima had still been breathing, and then he'd drifted and wakened again and she was cold under his hands and he did not know exactly when it had happened. This seemed to him more important than the fact that he himself had still not begun vomiting black blood, or that there was something seriously wrong with the sky. It was th

·ong color, and the deserted market under the mango
·ees was also wrong somehow: attenuated, fading, as if
· were an old photographic print superimposed on the
lden city that he'd seen in glimpses the day before. At
other time Alan would have been seriously interested
all this. Now he was too dazed with sleeplessness and
·nger and loss to care much about anything.

A Land Rover rolled into the marketplace. Alan looked
· dully and saw Garrett and Kaci sitting in the front
·at, next to a driver in the green and black uniform of
·e Army of the Sheikhs. Four or five more soldiers were
·nmed into the back. They all appeared to be drunk.

"There he is!" Kaci cried out. "See, Alan, I told you I'd
me back for you."

Alan had to think this over carefully. Something was
·zzing inside his brain, turning all his thoughts into
·gled fragments. "Did you?" he said at last. "Do you
·ow what time it was?"

"Huh?"

"When she died. You see," Alan explained, "if I knew
·actly when it happened, maybe I could go back and be
·re to stay awake this time. I think that's why she died,
·u see. I kept dozing off. I couldn't keep her here." Kaci
·dn't seem to get it, so Alan tried again. "See, it's like . . .
·hen my father died I was away at college. I didn't even
·ow he'd been taken to the emergency room with a heart
·tack until it was all over. If I'd been paying attention . . ."

"Alan, we're getting out now," Kaci said, "and if you
·ve any sense you'll come with us. There must be some
·fe place up the coast where we can hide until all this
·aziness is over."

Alan shook his head. "What's wrong with this place?"
·e golden towers were brighter than the morning sun
·d far more real than the dusty marketplace. What was
·e point of going anywhere else? He would just sit here
·th Halima and look at the beautiful light. She had seen
· too.

Kaci squinted against the light. "*Everything's* wrong
she said shrilly. "This whole place is collapsing."

"Alan, my man, we must be practical," Garrett said. "Th
is no time to stay in the city."

"Then what is it time for?" Alan asked. "Do you thir
it's any different someplace else?" He could see no poi
in leaving Halima, or in turning his back on those golde
towers. Music was coming from them now, a whisper o
the breeze of trumpets playing far away. He listened f
the music and never heard Garrett's reply.

The ground tilted under him, shuddered and seeme
to gather itself together into a much smaller area. Witho
too much surprise Alan saw that the marketplace, th
coastal point of Ras Kisauni and Barclay's Bank were a
now occupying the same space.

"Earthquakes," Garrett said hoarsely. "Drive on, *askar*

"Not without Alan!"

"He had his chance," Garrett said.

The soldier at the wheel of the Land Rover stampe
on the accelerator. The Land Rover's wheels spun in du
and it jerked forward. Alan wondered if Garrett had notice
that he was ordering the soldier to drive into the sol
stone façade of Barclay's Bank.

The ground tilted again. The Land Rover seemed to b
striving upward against a steep inclined plane. The fe
things left in the marketplace—boxes, empty bottles, a to
khanga cloth—tumbled down towards a blood-dark ocea
Alan felt Halima's body sliding from his grasp. So she w
going to end up floating off Ras Kisauni after all, just
she'd predicted. But it wasn't Garrett's fault or her father
fault. It was because he hadn't been able to keep awake

"Garrett, we'll never make it up this hill," Kaci whine
"Why can't we go there?" She pointed at the golden towe
overshadowing the collapsed city.

Garrett shook his head. "Mirages. We must be realisti
Kaci. Look at this map. It shows the roads on the nor
coast, across the bridge."

The Land Rover coughed and spluttered but made no progress. One of the men in the back put his hand on the side and vaulted onto the tilting ground. "Light," he said wonderingly. "*I* will go there, if you will not." Where he pointed, Alan saw a bridge of light that began in the marketplace and ended somewhere among the glimmering towers.

"Don't be ridiculous," Garrett snapped, "you can't walk fast enough to get to safety."

The *askari* ignored him and held out a hand to Alan. "You coming with me?"

Alan shook his head. He wanted to get closer to that music more than anything else, but he didn't deserve it. "I let her die, you see?"

"She is ahead of us," the soldier said. "We better catch up."

Alan looked where the man was pointing, into an infinite golden haze from which the towers rose like surging waves. The other end of the bridge was much too far away for anybody to make out faces; all the same, he saw Halima there.

"They're waiting for us," said the soldier.

Alan grasped the offered hand and pulled himself up. All his joints creaked after the night of sitting with Halima's head on his lap. Talk about ridiculous—he felt as stiff as an old man, and he was only twenty-three. But then, that was probably as old as he was ever going to get. And it didn't matter now, did it?

As he stepped onto the bridge of light, Alan realized that there were many bridges, infinitely many. On one close to him he saw the trader who'd given him the bottle of gin, waving enthusiastically at a friend on the far side of the bridge. Some distance away, Musa was prodding his arthritic grandfather along another stream of light. Beyond that, all the lines of light seemed to braid together into one ever-flowing stream going towards the towers and the music.

"Wait!" someone called below them. Alan looked back at Kaci. She was scrambling out of the Land Rover. She ran towards the golden bridge . . . and through it. Alan called to her to come back, she had missed the way, but the trumpets drowned out the sound of his voice.

"We can't leave her," Alan said.

"We cannot go back," the *askari* said. Below and behind them, the bridge had melted into a formless mist. The only way to go was forward, towards the new city.

The trumpets reached a crescendo and paused briefly, just long enough for Alan to hear Garrett and the other *askaris* arguing about which road to take, stabbing fingers at the map while the Land Rover struggled endlessly up an infinite slope of red dirt.

"Kaci! Garrett!" Alan called through cupped hands. "Come *on!*" But Kaci was already out of sight.

One of the soldiers in the Land Rover looked up, pointed over his shoulder at the city of light that now filled the whole sky. Garrett shook his head irritably. "Be realistic, my man! I can't waste time on your dreams; we have to find a road out of here." He gunned the motor again, but the music drowned out the sound. There were flutes and harps mingling with the trumpets now, and the collapsing city was sinking out of sight, so far below this bridge that Alan could no longer make out Garrett's Land Rover. There was no way to go but forward.

The walk across the bridge took either forever or no time at all. At one moment Halima was impossibly far away; with the next step she was leaning over a crystal wall, hands outstretched in greeting. And behind her Alan was not particularly surprised to see his father.

A pointed arch pierced the wall, layered with something that shone white like mother-of-pearl against the gold of the city itself. Beyond that Alan could make out another wall and another gate, and yet another . . . He couldn't count them. He didn't need to. There would be exactly twelve. Words learned in Sunday school for the wonderful sound they made in his mouth were coming back to him.

A staccato sound that was not quite part of the music drew closer and resolved into a clatter of hard plastic heels on something equally hard, nothing like the golden mist that made up Alan's bridge. "I had to find my own bridge," Kaci panted, "and it was made of crystal."

"Of course."

"Say, what is this place, anyway? I never saw anything like it. Garrett said he didn't see anything at all and I was crazy and it was my own problem if I wanted to jump out of the Land Rover and run away. But I don't think I'm crazy. I had to come. I never saw anything so beautiful in my whole life." Kaci's face was transfigured in the golden light; suddenly Alan realized that he had never seen her looking happy before. She didn't look mysterious or fragile or brooding or any of the other things he had read into her delicate, petulant pout. She just looked like somebody who'd finally, after long traveling, come home.

"A new heaven and a new earth . . ." But it didn't feel new; it felt like some place he'd lost a long time ago and had been searching for ever since.

"I know," said Kaci. "I mean, I know now. Of course it had to be like this. Look at all the crystals!" Close to, the seemingly insubstantial foundations of the walls were revealed as translucent sheets of gemstones, cut and faceted and joined to reflect the light in multicolored bursts of brilliance. "Look, it starts with jasper, that's a very stabilizing and grounding stone. Then the next level is sapphire, for purifying our energies; then . . . I don't know what this one is . . ."

"Chalcedony," Alan said. He didn't remember ever seeing the milky white stone, but words he'd heard long ago were coming back to him.

Kaci snapped her fingers. "Of course! Did you know that the Native Americans considered chalcedony a sacred stone?"

"And the foundations of the wall of the city were

garnished with all manner of precious stones," Alan said, ". . . the fourth, an emerald; the fifth, sardonyx; the sixth, sardius; the seventh, chrysolite; the eighth, beryl; the ninth, a topaz . . ."

But Kaci had seen someone she knew on the other side of the gate of pearl, and darted forward without waiting to find out what the tenth, eleventh, and twelfth foundations were. Alan passed through the arch himself and took the hands outstretched to him. Halima's brown face shone as bright as the gold of the city, and her clinging black veil was nowhere to be seen.

"Welcome home," his father said.